The Way Evil Does

THE
WAY
EVIL
DOES

The Eisenbrey Trilogy

AMARA DRASKA

Thrill Press Publications

The Way Evil Does

Thrill Press Publications

Cover design by Yocla Book Cover Designs
Edited by Read Owl Publishing

ISBN: 978-0-9906379-0-5 (Trade Paperback)
ISBN: 978-0-9906379-1-2 (eBook)

For my daughters

ONE

October 24th, 2012

I struck the match and held it up, examining the yellow-blue flame, taking in the scent of sulfur. A light breeze caused the flame to flicker. It would extinguish if I didn't do this quickly.

The paperback was already in place: face down, fanned open, and soaked in lighter fluid inside my metal firepit. I held the match under it and the pages ignited, flames engulfing the damned thing in a ball of fire. The heat felt good against my bare arms.

I put on my sunglasses and sat back in my patio chair, admiring my handiwork. The sun was still low in the eastern sky. I was tired, but couldn't go back to sleep. Lying in my bed with all of that time to think would only herald darker thoughts than the ones I had.

The chilly air didn't faze me although I'd been outside with no sweater for quite a while. Birds chirped at each other, and in the distance I heard my neighbor's car door shut and its engine start. Some people had jobs to go to. Not me. As a writer, I could claim I worked at home, but honestly, I wasn't working.

I was forty, no husband or kids, a plethora of acquaintances, but no friends I felt close to except Andrea, my agent, and Kat, whom I was avoiding. She had just landed on my shit list for giving me an overdose of unasked-for advice, which had just turned out to be poorly disguised criticism. But I couldn't blame her for the rut I was in. I had done this to myself.

Maybe Kat was right—maybe I was fucked up.

I took another sip of my Bloody Mary. At least I wasn't on anything serious. I looked at my watch—7:46 a.m., and this was my third drink. I probably should have put some food in my stomach before this mini boozathon, but it could be argued that a Bloody Mary was a good breakfast. Tomato juice has a vegetable in it, well technically a fruit, and possibly even a few vitamins. It was almost like drinking a salad.

Was this what failure felt like? My lack of friends could be directly attributed to my lifestyle. Ever since I had moved to Bellevue, Washington, I stopped socializing. I blew off functions when invited, and the invitations came less often. I never called my old friends from California, and allowed their calls to go to voicemail. I had become an island. Isla Rebecca—land of sunrises, Bloody Marys, and bullshit.

I filled my time with writing, or the attempts therein, but at that moment I felt like I lived dangerously close to watching the career I loved go swirling down the crapper, a possibility that frightened me. My first two books had done well, but my last book had been a colossal stink bomb. Everyone who had read the third book felt disappointed with it, and with me. I had taken a mediocre idea and then done a poor job of fleshing it out into a story. My agent, Andrea, hadn't liked it either, but we had pushed it out anyway.

At one point, I felt as though Andrea was trying to drive me to insanity with sleep deprivation. It wasn't her fault. I spent long, desperate hours in front of the computer, feeling like an empty vessel. My muse had abandoned me, the little fucker. I wished I could exact some penalty upon it for its faithless desertion, but that wasn't how the universe worked. In the end, I forced myself to deliver something, even though it wasn't what I had wanted. My heart hadn't been in it, and it showed. Releasing that third book had been a mistake, and God, how satisfying it was to watch the bitch burn.

I had no boyfriend, which was not something I usually dwelled on, knowing that in this day and age a woman wasn't supposed to need one, but I added it to my list of shortcomings anyway. I felt like stewing about everything that morning. I wouldn't mind getting laid, that usually took the edge off my depression. But I didn't see any sex in my immediate future. All I needed was a little violin music to see me off while I drowned in my whine.

Somewhere inside the house my cellphone started to ring. Curiosity provided just enough motivation to get me up out of my chair. The sound drifted toward me from the kitchen. I found it on the table right before it went to voicemail. "Yeah."

"Oh, you answered! Sorry to call you this early. I was just going to leave you a message." It was Andrea. She had a pleasant voice with the subtle remains of a British accent, even though she'd been living in New York most of her adult life.

"What's up?"

"Are you still having trouble coming up with an idea for your next book?"

"I think the real question is: does anyone still want another book from me? Haven't you read the reviews? I blow."

"Rebecca, you need to stop this negative thinking. I have an idea for your next book. This will be a good thing for you to work on until your muse returns."

"That's really sweet of you, but I think my muse might have offed herself." In fact, I thought my muse had gotten naked, climbed into the bathtub, took a bottle of pills, then slit her wrists and bled her way into the eternal, dark silence. This seemed like a very thorough kind of death, one there was probably no coming back from. Part of me felt like following her to the other side. "I just can't come up with anything. There might not be a fourth book in me."

"You aren't listening. If you take my assignment, you don't need to come up with any original ideas at all. You sound funny, have you been drinking?"

"Drinking? Are you kidding, this early in the morning?"

"Hmm. How did it go with the doctor yesterday?"

"Fine," I said. Bullshit. The psychiatrist I'd agreed to see confirmed the obvious: I was depressed. She'd wanted me to start taking Prozac immediately—a medication that had a warning against drinking alcohol, but abstinence was obviously out of the question. I accepted the prescription to shut her up, having no intention to fill it.

"Really?" Andrea sounded a little dubious. "What did she prescribe?"

"Oh, for Chrissake! I'm not having this conversation with you right now."

"Look, I worry, darling. It wasn't so long ago that I thought you might top yourself."

"I'm not going to kill myself," I said, and it was probably true. However, a month's worth of sleeping pills still sat on my nightstand since the evening Andrea alluded to. They belonged in the medicine cabinet. "It was just a case of the blues. I'm fine. Just settle down."

Andrea let out a heavy sigh. "Well anyway, I know this isn't the norm, but I have a project for you, something I think you'll be good at given your background with thrillers. I loved what you did with the psychopath in your first book." *Making mention of my past glory, a nice touch.* "In this case, you'd get to write about a real one instead of having to dream one into existence, far less taxing on your creative energy. How would you like to write a book about Thomas Eisenbrey, aka the Hunter?"

"Eisenbrey...the serial killer?" My voice wavered. The unwelcome, long-banished memory tried to force its way back in, but I pushed it away—an ongoing struggle my friend was blissfully unaware of. "Why do you want a book about him?" I asked.

"Because it sells. People are fascinated with psychopaths." She cleared her throat. "It was Jason's idea. You remember him — that publisher you met at Toni's apartment last fall?"

"Yeah, I remember."

"Well, he and I were talking about Eisenbrey at the party, and it turns out that he pitched the idea. He called me early this morning to tell me we have a contract, and here's what sold the idea — I have a friend that works at the prison where Eisenbrey is kept."

"So he hired *you,* and whatever writer you choose?"

"No. He wants *you* to do this. He likes *your* work. He wants someone with a background in fiction for this project — someone who understands plot, suspense, and intrigue. And lord knows it's time for you to get back to work. You haven't seemed right since your last book. I don't want you to go all peculiar on me."

That ship had sailed. Two nights ago I drank so much that I had hallucinated, seeing an ethereal presence of some kind that warned me to *beware.* That strange experience had left me shaken, unsure of my own mental stability. I'd never lost it like that before, and I vowed not to touch any more whiskey for a while. A vow forgotten the next morning, but those things were none of Andrea's business.

"I've never written a biography before," I protested. I felt that if I tried hard enough, I could come up with a real reason why I wasn't qualified for Andrea's project. The simple truth was, I just didn't feel like I could write a biography, especially not one about an inhuman bastard that thrived on destroying other people's lives.

"You can't afford to turn me down," she said. Then her tone softened. "You need to write something, anything. And then you need to write some more. Just work on this non-fiction assignment for me and I know your muse will return. You'll be creating again in no time. Go on, it'll be good for both of our bank accounts as well. That couldn't hurt."

No, that wouldn't hurt. She was spot on about that. My book sales had been steadily declining since the release of the last book. The bad reviews seemed to have put people off purchasing my first two books. "I hear that."

"Good. How much do you know about him?" she asked.

"Not much. I still lived in San Jose when he was caught."

"I've already done a little of the legwork for you. My friend's name is Ralph Barnett. He's a captain at the prison, in charge of approving visits with the prisoners. He spoke with Eisenbrey for us and got his consent to be interviewed. You'll be allowed plenty of time with him, and you won't have to use the visitation rooms. All you need to do is call, set up a time with them, and then get in your fucking car and drive out to Walla Walla."

"Walla Walla? Crap! Isn't that in Eastern Washington? I don't like long drives." I had to hand it to myself, I wasn't going to make it easy for Andrea to help me out of my current dilemma.

"And sober up before you drive out there. Yes, I can tell. Don't deny it," she said.

I hesitated for a moment, but then realized it would be just as foolish for me to refuse this assignment as it would for a starving person in the desert to refuse manna from heaven. It was a very generous offer from someone who apparently still believed in me, and she might not offer twice. "Okay. You're right. I'll do it."

"Excellent. I've sent you an email with Ralph's number, and I've attached some forms you need to fill out for the criminal background check they do prior to the visits. Ralph said he would expedite it, so get those to him today. You can get started this morning."

"Okay Andrea. I'll get on it right away. And…thank you, I appreciate the push." That wasn't true, but I figured she deserved a modicum of gratitude. Also, I had discovered over the years that saying the lines and going through the motions helped me get back on the right track.

"Anytime, my dear. We all need the occasional kick up the arse." She hesitated, then added, "Are you nervous about getting back to work?"

"Yes," I admitted. "And apparently it shows."

"Don't worry. You'll do fine. Interview him a couple times and then send me something to read—your first chapter or whatever you've got."

I sighed. "You want to check up on me."

"I want to help. I know how difficult it's been for you since *Epitaph* was released. Show me what you have after a week so I can help you get off to a good, healthy start."

"Don't be ridiculous. I won't have anything for you in a week."

"Rebecca, I know you. I know how you operate, and I've seen how fast you are when you feel enthusiastic about a project. You'll have loads to send me in a week."

"Well." She was right. "Ten days," I told her.

"You have yourself a deal, my dear. Email me if you have any questions. I'm going to be in meetings most of the day."

"Will do."

"Ta-ta," she said, and the call disconnected.

TWO

After draining the last bit of coffee from my mug, I still wasn't entirely sober, but felt a little more clearheaded. The thought of writing another book so soon, not to mention on a person I knew almost nothing about, felt daunting. And then there was the subject matter. Perhaps this wasn't wise. Perhaps I should have declined.

Why am I being such a pussy about this? It wasn't as though I had never written about a killer. Despite my past, I had been okay when I allowed my mind to go there, to create a completely warped murderer for one of my novels. In fact, I seemed to thrive on it. *So what is my problem now?* It was real. This one was made of flesh and blood; knowing we would meet in person unnerved me.

No. That's not who I am. Rebecca Reis jumps in with both feet and gets the job done. I turned on my laptop, read my email, and printed out hard copies of the information Andrea had sent me, giving it a cursory peek. I filled out the forms for the criminal background check and faxed them to Barnett. Then I went on the Internet and began to compile all of the information I could find on my subject from various news archives.

In the first article, three hunters were found in the forest near Eisenbrey's hometown — Carnation, Washington — back in 1983:

Burt Nolan, Kevin Nolan, and Stephen Wilcox. The men had all been bound and had their throats slit. There was also mention of mutilation, but no details. The article was dated December 13, 2001 — when Eisenbrey was arrested and charged — a remarkable eighteen years after the murders.

I skimmed another article dated December 14, 2001. Eisenbrey had been charged with two more murders that took place in October of 1998 — hunters found in the Idaho forest near British Columbia. Both men had been tied up and had their throats slit. He was also charged with the murder of Special Agent Peter Johannson who died in the line of duty.

I sifted through a couple dozen more articles and found five other incidents of small hunting groups found dead in the forests of Canada, Washington, and Idaho, and two other parties that went missing. The authorities acknowledged that some, or all, may have been the work of the Hunter, but could not confirm it. I found most of the articles barren of details other than the victims' names, dates, and places where they had located the bodies. I imagined the police thought it unwise to release more information to the public back when the investigations were still open, but since Eisenbrey was in prison and awaiting execution, I thought I should be able to get some additional details about the crime scenes from the detective.

So the Hunter wasn't a shooter but a slasher. This was way worse, and much more up-close and personal. Perhaps I'd assumed that he used a rifle because of the special little nickname the press had given him. One could have a certain amount of detachment with a firearm, but a knife required a colder mentality. And torture was the mark of a truly twisted mind.

Goddamn. He was a sick bastard. What the hell was I doing? Why had I said yes to this messed up, morbid project? I took in a deep breath and let it out slowly, then leaned back in my chair away from the computer. I needed more distance from the damned thing before the dead from my own past found their way back inside my thoughts. I would not let them in, not today.

I wandered into the kitchen, filled the electric kettle with tap water, and set it to boil. Tea was my aunt Susan's answer to everything except for those particularly bad situations that required home-baked cookies.

I felt a pang of regret as I realized I hadn't called her or my uncle Harry for a few months. It was a very long time for us to go without talking, and I missed them terribly. But I had been living under a black cloud, and I hadn't wanted to dump my rain all over them. They were always so good to me. It was enough that I was soaked.

After bringing the cup of tea back to the desk, I typed up what I had, then started making a list of questions for my interviews with the detective and Eisenbrey.

Ralph Barnett told me over the phone the prison didn't allow visiting Tuesday through Thursday, and weekends were busy, so mine would take place every Monday and Friday from noon to two o'clock. He scheduled my first visit that Friday. He seemed sure he could finish vetting me by then. That left me two days to kill.

Then I called Detective Scanlon of the King County Sheriff's Homicide Unit. I gave him my name and explained who I was writing about. "I've been told you're the expert on this guy. I'd like to meet with you if you have time."

"Sure. What kind of information do you need?"

"Everything I can get. I just started collecting information on Eisenbrey this morning, so I don't have much yet."

"Well, why don't you come out to my office, and I'll see what I can do to enlighten you. I've got some time around three o'clock today." He gave me his address, and I jotted it down on a notepad. Sammamish wasn't far. I could leave my house about thirty minutes before our meeting.

"That sounds great. I'll see you then."

THREE

I took a few minutes to freshen up, changing into a new pair of jeans and some ankle boots with a three-inch heel. At 5'4", a few extra inches never hurt, and made it easier to look other people in the eye. I took my long, brown hair out of the ponytail, and it fell down past my shoulders. Then I touched up my eyeliner. All in all, I cleaned up pretty well. I felt it was important to look nice when meeting someone for the first time. I grabbed my leather jacket and headed out to my car.

I plugged Scanlon's address into my GPS and allowed it to direct me, via some winding roads, through a sprawling residential area. Having been developed more recently than Bellevue, everything looked newer in Sammamish including Detective Scanlon's workplace, the Sammamish Police Department, which was a new building. It stood two stories high with flat, slanted rooftops. The outside was comprised of red brick and wood paneling. A solid line of windows ran down the length of the building on both floors.

A police officer directed me to the second floor, and I found Scanlon's space in a large room with several other desks. The openness of the work area seemed designed for better communication between the staff. He rose when he saw me and gave me a smile that illuminated his features.

I have heard that when a person looks at something they find appealing their pupils dilate to take more of it in. This was the first time I'd seen it happen, the light golden-brown of Scanlon's irises being the perfect background to emphasize the change. "Hello," he said, giving my hand a comfortable squeeze, his gaze fixed on me. "Ms. Reis."

He held my hand much longer than was customary. I would be lying if I said it wasn't flattering. "That's me."

"I know. I Googled you after we talked. The photo on your website doesn't do you justice. This must be my lucky day," he murmured.

Scanlon stood about six feet tall, was physically fit, and radiated enthusiastic energy. I could picture the guy eating a three thousand calorie meal and then running it off.

He offered me a seat in front of his desk and sat down. "So—Eisenbrey," he said. Then he picked up a stack of papers and held them out to me. "I can't give you a copy of my entire file, but I copied some of the reports and other info that I thought you would find useful."

"Thanks. I really appreciate this. Firsthand information is extremely valuable."

"That covers most of what Johannson and I found, minus any investigations that are still open."

"Oh, I was going to ask about that. There seem to be quite a few news articles about other killings in the Northwest attributed to the Hunter that Eisenbrey hasn't been convicted of."

"That's true," he said, nodding. "He was convicted of eight murders prior to his stay at Walla Walla, and then one more after his incarceration."

"Is there any way I could find out more about the scenes of those other murders, the ones with no convictions?"

"Not from me." He broke into a big grin. "I'm sorry. You're very pretty. I wish I could give you all of my information, but rules are rules, and those are still open cases. We weren't able to nail him for everything, but it was enough to get him the death penalty. That's not bad."

My face felt warmer, and I realized that Scanlon's compliment had caused me to blush. I came at him from another angle. "You don't think there's any chance that there could be a second killer out there, do you? Someone else responsible for the unsolved murders?"

"Hmm, do I get to say something off the record, Ms. Reis? Something to make you sleep better at night? I don't want it to show up as a quote from me in your book."

"Sure," I said and shrugged.

"All of those murders involving hunting parties that our local papers pinned on the Hunter were committed by Eisenbrey. There is no doubt in my mind. We just didn't have the evidence to prove it. I cannot divulge any specific details from those crimes, but I will say, off the record, that they all bore the evidence of his ritualistic behavior."

That caused me to lean forward. "Ritualistic? What do you mean?"

Scanlon slid his chair around to my side of the desk and scooped the papers out of my hand. He found what he looked for and handed several of the pages back to me. These were police reports. Then he laid a document on top entitled Serial Murder Victim List. "Here, we can talk about the triple murder near Carnation in 1983. Eisenbrey was sixteen years old; the three victims were all guys from his hometown in their mid-twenties." Scanlon leaned back in his chair and flopped his feet up on his desk. At first I wondered if he expected me to sit there and read through the stack of documents, but then I realized he was just taking a moment to collect his thoughts. As it turned out, he was able to recite all of the details of the crime without referring to any papers.

"Those murders are believed to have happened in the early hours of the morning on October 20, 1983. The men had gone into the forest for a hunting trip. They found no evidence linking these murders to Eisenbrey at the time; however, in 2001, items collected from the scene back in '83 were DNA tested and matched to Eisenbrey. The first victim on that list is Burt Nolan. His body was found in the forest near Carnation. He secured him to a tree with duct tape—Eisenbrey loved his fucking duct tape—then he tortured the poor guy prior to slitting his throat with a knife. The second victim was Burt's brother, Kevin Nolan. He was also found taped to a tree and was tortured prior to his death. In addition, Kevin's body had seventeen postmortem stab wounds to the torso, and his head had been removed and placed on the ground facing Burt. The third victim was Stephen Wilcox. His hands were duct taped behind his back, and his throat was slit. But for whatever reason, he didn't receive the same level of attention from Eisenbrey that the Nolan brothers did."

"They weren't shot?"

"No."

"I don't understand. How did he capture three armed men and secure them with duct tape without shooting them?"

"Precisely," Scanlon said with a nod. "And, oh, how I wish I had a definitive answer. He must have administered something to make them lose consciousness, like chloroform, or better yet some kind of gas that could knock them all out at once, but forensics wasn't able to find evidence of that. Each time we found one of these crime scenes, they were already a few days old. Rain, decomposition, and other factors made our investigations difficult."

"So no one knew these men had died because they were out in the wilderness?"

"Yes. They'd planned to be gone for several days, so their families didn't report them missing until after they were expected home. Steve and the Nolan brothers had probably been dead four days by the time the search even began. But that was a long time ago. Nowadays, most of these guys bring a cellphone. If we think they need assistance we can ping their phones for a location, sometimes even if they're in an area with no service. It's easier than it used to be."

"That's great," I said. When the weather was nice, I took the occasional day hike on trails in the forest, but there were always plenty of other hikers around. That gave me a sense of security. I didn't have any desire to go camping overnight somewhere isolated, away from civilization. What a risky thing to do. Anything could happen out there, and in this case, it had. "So, I was wondering, when you say these men were tortured…"

"Once they were restrained, he started tearing off fingernails, then cutting off the tips of the fingers, then the rest of the fingers, toes, hands, uh," Scanlon rubbed his chin and his eyes closed momentarily as he searched his memory for more. "Let's see, he cut off someone's ear at this site, and he gouged out one of Kevin's eyes prior to the decapitation. There were also several burn marks all over both of the Nolan brothers, probably inflicted with a lighter. When I first began familiarizing myself with this case, I wondered if the killer had been trying to force information from them.

"We questioned Eisenbrey shortly after the bodies were discovered, but we never found any reason to believe that he had a score to settle with those men. He didn't seem to know them, although they were all from Carnation, and they all liked to hunt. It's a very common hobby out there. He admitted that he recognized two of them as the Nolan brothers. He said he'd seen them around town before but they didn't talk to him, which seemed reasonable since they were ten years older. And he said the third victim looked familiar, but he didn't know his name."

"So you ruled him out as a suspect?"

"I didn't personally." Scanlon smiled. "I was in high school at the time. Eisenbrey and I were born the same year. But yes, the officers that were working the case back then ruled him out. They reported that he was a loner, and he seemed a little odd, but he said all the right things during the interview. The fact that his brother's body had been found in the forest a year earlier raised some red flags but, in the end, they had absolutely nothing to link him to the killings back in 1983."

"When did you start working on this?"

"I met Eisenbrey in 1989. I was a rookie with the sheriff's office. His mother came into the station to report that her husband hadn't come home the night before, and she was very concerned that something had happened to him. So we searched the woods around their house thoroughly. We even brought dogs out there, but we found no sign of her husband anywhere."

"I'll never forget the feeling I got when I first laid eyes on Tom Eisenbrey. I knew…" Scanlon paused and shook his head, apparently reconsidering what he would say. "That was before I'd even heard about his brother's death seven years earlier. When I questioned him about his dad, I could tell he knew I suspected him. Something about that guy just made my heart rate climb and my adrenaline surge. My senses felt sharper."

Scanlon got a faraway look on his face. "I can recall strange details, like hearing a lawnmower through the open window, and Eisenbrey smelling like Irish Spring soap and spearmint gum." He paused, and his expression became troubled. "I remember being struck by how unnaturally still he stood, and how he didn't look away from me. He could go a long time without blinking. It made him seem almost reptilian. I could tell that I had to be on high alert when I stood near that guy." His eyes returned to me. "And right after I questioned him, he disappeared. I didn't see him again until Agent Johannson and I apprehended him in 2001."

"I've heard that the police don't tend to like the FBI because they barge in and take over the investigation, but you were working on this together?"

"Well, yeah, the FBI got jurisdiction back when we realized we were dealing with a serial killer, but I didn't mind. I'm not into pissing matches."

"I read that the FBI captured him. Did it bother you that they took the credit?"

He paused to chuckle. "Okay, I can see where you're going with this, but I don't need a pat on the ass for doing my job well. The bureau has better resources and training than we do, and I just wanted to catch our killer." He shrugged. "In 2001, Johannson had just inherited the case from the previous agent in charge. There were twenty-two victims that all fit the same profile: men that were out in the forest hunting. We had suspected they were all killed by the same guy, but he was very careful not to leave evidence linking him to the crimes. There was no confirmation yet of the Hunter's identity, but by that time Eisenbrey was our prime suspect. In the end, we were only able to get Eisenbrey's DNA from two of those crime scenes: the three guys from Carnation and the double murder of the Canadian fellas in Idaho.

"He also committed two other murders that didn't fit his profile. One was a woman he was involved with named Tammie Lancaster. She was confirmed as one of his victims after we captured Eisenbrey, got a DNA sample from him, and started looking for other matches. There was also a murder he committed with another man, Roddy Jenks. They killed a club owner named Philippe Devereaux in British Columbia. We didn't get any of Eisenbrey's prints or DNA from that site, but there were eyewitnesses that saw him leaving the crime scene with Jenks. He was convicted of that one in 2002. Jenks is still wanted. To this day there are still seventeen other murder victims, and eight men missing and presumed dead that we suspect as the work of Eisenbrey.

"Anyway, Johannson and I got together a few times. I gave him all the info I had on Eisenbrey. He said he was going to speak with the mother, Sarah Eisenbrey, and I offered to go with him because I'd interviewed her several times and we had a good rapport. She wasn't home, but while we were in her front yard Eisenbrey came walking around the side of the house toward us. I couldn't believe our luck. I think it was just a crazy fluke we happened to show up at the same time he did because his mom hadn't heard from him in ages.

"We chased him. I was the first one down, Eisenbrey had grabbed a metal wheelbarrow and swung it into me, but then I managed to call for some backup while Johannson continued after him. When I caught up with them, Johannson had his gun on Eisenbrey and was about to put him in cuffs. Then Eisenbrey whipped around and attacked him. It happened so fast. I've never seen anything like it." Scanlon closed his eyes and I could have sworn I saw a shiver run through him.

"Did he take Johannson's gun?" I asked.

"No." Scanlon shook his head slowly. "He, uh, look, I don't know how close you're going to have to get to him for these interviews, but don't ever forget this—he's a biter." He pointed to the scar on his neck and pulled the collar of his shirt back to give me a clearer view. I wished he hadn't. It looked like the kind of wound you would expect to see after an attack from some wild animal. I gasped.

"How awful! That looks like it must have been life-threatening."

"Sure as hell was. I was lucky I didn't bleed out at the scene, but by some miracle he didn't manage to tear open my jugular or carotid. If he had, we wouldn't be having this conversation. Johannson wasn't so lucky."

"That's so horrible. Why would someone do such a thing?"

"To avoid getting apprehended. And in Eisenbrey's case, because he enjoyed it. The sick fuck was laughing when I took him down and cuffed him. He's a psychopath." Scanlon's jaw tensed, and I could see he was clenching his teeth as he recalled the events. "We gave him a polygraph at the station, before he was transferred to the jail."

"How did you get him to sit still for that?"

"Oh, he consented to the test. He found it amusing. It turned out to be a useless pile of shit."

"Why?"

"Because he was unnaturally calm the entire time. The psychiatrist that evaluated him told me that it isn't uncommon for people like him to ace the test. They don't experience guilt or feel a normal level of anxiety. Eisenbrey didn't show any change in heart rate, blood pressure, muscle tension, or breathing. And we knew he was definitely lying part of the time because he denied attacking me and Johannson. The only thing I got from him was that twisted, fucked up grin.

"Taking the test was just a way for him to show off for us. I even dug up the crime scene photos of his brother from 1982. I showed him a photo from when they'd found his body in the woods, and let me tell you, it was fucking sick. The guy's throat had been slit so deep that he was nearly decapitated, and the body had decomposed quite a bit during the six days he was out there." Scanlon paused and closed his eyes for a moment. "Seeing his brother in that condition should have caused... something, but the photos didn't elicit any reaction from him, and the polygraph didn't show one either. That's just wrong. I understand that it had been several years since his brother had died, so maybe he was over that loss, but shit, any normal person would have become upset from looking at that mess, even if the victim was a complete stranger."

"So you believe that his brother was one of his victims?"

"I didn't say that. His brother is not on the victim list I gave you, and neither is his father." He shook his head, obviously disgusted with the situation, then he leveled his eyes at me. "Ms. Reis, do you know what they have to do with animals once they're trained to attack and kill humans? They have to put them down. There's no way to change them. They just are what they are. And people like Eisenbrey are the same way. It isn't possible to rehabilitate someone like him. There's no way to take the desire to kill out of him. He just needs to be put down." There was no hint of malice or hatred in Scanlon's face as he spoke. He was just relaying a series of facts to me.

The phone on his desk rang and he took the call, telling the person on the line that he would be there in a minute. Scanlon looked disappointed as he said, "I'm sorry, Ms. Reis. I'm needed elsewhere."

I leaned back in my chair. "Duty calls. You know, Detective, I appreciate your candor and directness about Eisenbrey. So many people don't say what they really feel, and I prefer it when people do."

Scanlon flashed me a boyish grin. "I'm just happy to be of assistance, Ms. Reis."

"Please, call me Rebecca," I said, as I got up.

"Okay, Rebecca, if you call me Darryl," he smiled and took my hand in both of his, encasing it, caressing it with one of his thumbs. His hands felt so warm. I imagined that the rest of him was too. I thought about how nice it would be to have a guy like that wrapped around me on a cold night.

"It was nice meeting you," I added.

He took a business card from his desk drawer and scribbled something on it before handing it to me. "Here's my number. This one is my personal cell," he said as he pointed to the handwritten number on the back of the card.

Interesting. He just gave me his private number.

"Feel free to call me with more questions…anytime."

"Yes. I'm sure I'll have a long list after I read through all of this. Thank you so much." I took one last look at him as I left — the light-brown hair, the honey-colored eyes, the easy smile. I liked him. *I might even call him if I don't have any questions.*

FOUR

October 26th, 2012

I waited at a stoplight not far from the prison in Walla Walla, staring at the ass-end of the vehicle in front of me: a late model Porsche 911. At least it had a nice ass. The cars proceeded so slowly that it looked like I would have to sit through another red light, my third one at that particular intersection. I was surprised by the miniature traffic jam. I hadn't expected there to be enough cars in Walla Walla to impede the flow of traffic. As it turned out, the city wasn't quite as small as I had envisioned it.

The drive from Bellevue had taken me more than four hours. I tried to enjoy some of the scenery along the way as I drove through the Cascade Mountains and then through the high desert and farm landscape of Eastern Washington, but I spent most of the time focusing on Eisenbrey and dreaming up various scenarios on how our first interview would go. I had felt calm most of the way there, but as I neared the prison I realized that I was gripping the steering wheel so tight that my knuckles were white.

A feeling of nausea came over me. The same feeling I used to experience nearly every time I had exams in college. I was completely out of my comfort zone, having never set foot inside a prison or conversed with a convict. I was also nervous because our first meeting could make or break the success of the whole project. If he decided he didn't like me and became unwilling to cooperate, the book would lack the quality that would make it meaningful for the reader. Writing was such a delicate art form. I needed the element that would breathe life into Eisenbrey on the page.

I turned onto Thirteenth Avenue, the road leading into the prison. To the left sat the entrance to the parking lot, to the right groomed patches of earth awaited crops. According to the thermometer in my car the temperature was seventy-eight degrees, a warm day for Washington State in October. The dry, barren hills off in the distance reminded me of California. I entered the prison grounds, identified myself to the uniformed man in the small guard booth, and the barrier arm lifted allowing me access.

I had already done a little research on the Washington State Penitentiary in Walla Walla. The original facility, built in 1887, was now only a corner of the current compound, which had since been expanded to more than four times its initial size. The old stone perimeter walls had several lookout towers built into them, each tower constructed of red brick, while tall chain-link fencing topped with copious amounts of razor wire surrounded the newer sections of the penitentiary. I had been told to report in at the visitor's entrance of the newer section of the prison. I parked and glanced at my dashboard clock. Twenty minutes early. I couldn't have timed it more perfectly.

Reviewing my notes one last time I thought about Scanlon, his good looks marred by that horrible scar on his neck. I thought about how painful it must have been for him when the teeth pierced his skin and tore at his throat, how frightened he must have felt when he thought that he faced death. About to see the man who exacted the brutality, the monster, Thomas Eisenbrey, I trembled slightly.

That wouldn't do.

I felt beneath the driver's seat of my car for the stainless steel flask that I kept for times like this, when my nerves felt a bit delicate. I took a generous sip, reveling in the exquisite warmth of the Jack Daniel's as it descended down my throat. I sighed, feeling calmer already. I took one more gulp, then secured the lid and returned the flask to its hiding place. I checked my glove box for some chewing gum and was irritated not to find any. I'd just be careful not to be too breathy when I said hi.

It was time to leave the security of my car and dive into the belly of the beast. I grabbed my bag and walked with deliberate steps into the penitentiary.

FIVE

Once inside the visitor's entrance and after a thorough search of my purse and person, which included a pat down, I was met by a guard who had been assigned to escort me to death row. My meeting with Eisenbrey would take place there instead of a visiting room, a deal that Andrea had worked out with her friend, Barnett. I agreed with her that it would be good for me to see his living environment. Because of the special arrangement, they allowed me to keep my handbag where I had my items for the interview.

The guard introduced himself to me as Amos Tilly and shook my hand. I detected an accent that smacked of Oklahoma or perhaps one of the states right next to it. Officer Tilly was a good old boy. As I noted his belly, which put a lot of stress on the buttons of his dark-blue shirt and hung down over the matching pants of his guard uniform, I wondered how long it would take him to address me as Little Lady. It certainly didn't take him long to get through the pleasantries and into his opinions. At least he could walk and talk at the same time. Tilly led me through the building, and then outside to a cement walkway that crossed the grounds. As we hurried along it, the pleasant scent of freshly mown lawn hung in the dry air around us. I held my hand up to my forehead to shield my eyes from the bright sun, irritated with myself for leaving my sunglasses in the car.

"I think it's a disgraceful commentary on our society that these motherfuckers get so damned much attention. That's exactly what the bastards want. They eat it up. Why do you people keep writing books about them? No one ever writes about the officers that put their lives on the line every day to bring these peckers to justice."

"Well, several books have been written about law enforcement personnel also, but I get your point. I agree the good guys should get far more recognition than they do." We passed a water tower, and I saw several white cement buildings around the compound. I couldn't tell yet which one he was taking me to.

"If I had my way, Eisenbrey would have been executed a long time ago, and the American people would have forgotten his goddamned name. He doesn't deserve any glory. Do you know why you're going to his cell for these visits and not a visitation room?"

"Not exactly. Because I'm writing a book about him?"

"Several other writers have graced us with their presence before you, and they used the visitation rooms. You aren't being allowed to do this in the cell block because you're special. It's because of Eisenbrey. Every time we have to transport that son of a bitch anywhere outside of his cell, we run the risk of harm to one of our officers. Do not trust that man under any circumstances." Tilly glanced at me, his expression grave, as we continued walking at a steady clip. He nodded toward the building we approached and said, "This is where we keep him, the IMU North, that's short for Intensive Management Unit. We keep all of the death row inmates here." A white cement building with narrow windows stood before us. It was solid. The place looked like it could contain the Incredible Hulk if it had to.

Tilly held the door open for me and a blast of cool air hit my skin as we entered. As expected, the inside of the building had an institutional appearance: polished cement floors, sparsely furnished, a dull color scheme of off-white and tan. It was clean. Tilly led me through the lobby and down a hallway in silence. I heard the click of a lock being released as we approached the steel door at its end. Tilly held the door for me again, then paused before we entered and said, "One more thing, Miss Reis. He's a crafty son of a bitch. Don't underestimate him."

"I understand."

"No, you don't. Not yet. He is going to get inside your head, I can guarantee that. I can also guarantee that you aren't going to like it when he does. Maybe when you get to the point where you have nightmares about him every night, you'll drop this asinine project of yours."

"Uh, okay, duly noted."

The atmosphere inside the entire prison was tense, still, there was something even more palpable hanging in the air—a feeling of doom and desolation— as we entered the unit that confined the death row inmates. *It must be the fear getting to me. I'm just nervous about meeting someone like him.*

"This is the control booth," Tilly said stopping at an observation room. Three walls inside the room were comprised of windows. A computer, phone, small standing microphone, and several monitors displaying various areas inside the building sat on countertops that ran along the windowed walls. In the center of the room, a table and chairs were unoccupied. Tilly introduced me to the two men in uniforms sitting at the counter. The one named Downey appeared to be in his mid-thirties and had a relaxed air about him. The one named Lutz looked young enough to be in his teens. On his head was a mop of unruly light-brown hair, unlike the majority of the other guards that I had seen so far who wore their hair buzzed short. I wondered what the minimum age requirement was to become a guard. Both men stood, smiled, and shook my hand, and based on what I saw so far, neither seemed to have a stick up their ass like their coworker.

Tilly grabbed one of the gray, metal folding chairs from the stack against the office wall and looked at me. He asked, "Are you sure about this?"

"Yes, but I'm a little nervous. I was just wondering, will one of you be close by while I'm in his cell?" I asked.

"Are you shitting me?" Tilly yelled, causing me to flinch. "You're not going inside the cell with him. Hell, we don't even go in there anymore unless we have protective gear and other officers for backup. He's a mean motherfucker!" Tilly shook his head and muttered under his breath, "What a crazy goddamned thing to say."

Officer Lutz smiled at my faux pas and winked one of his large, hazel eyes at me as he turned and led us up a long hallway lined with steel doors on one side. Each of the doors had a narrow window made of thick glass, and in several of those windows I saw pairs of eyes watching me. He stopped in front of the one that I assumed belonged to Eisenbrey and, after looking through the window, he spoke into the radio that was attached to his shirt. "All clear."

Tilly unfolded the chair and plopped it on the cement floor facing the metal door, positioning it about four feet back and told me, "Eisenbrey's cell has a second door that the others don't have. It makes it easier for us to deal with him."

Lutz stood in front of the opening, watching the prisoner as the steel door slid along its runners and revealed yet another door constructed of steel bars. It was a very sturdy affair, and I felt more at ease knowing that I would be communicating with him through that barrier.

Lutz spoke quietly to the prisoner. "Hey Tom, your visitor is here." I didn't hear a response.

Tilly crossed his arms and wore a stern expression as he imparted some rules for me to follow. "You are not to hand anything to the prisoner or accept anything that he tries to give you. If you have something for him, you will give it to the officer on duty. The officer will inspect it and determine whether or not it can go in the cell. If the officer clears the item, he will hand it through to Eisenbrey on your behalf. Officers Lutz and Downey will keep an eye on you from the control room. Any questions?"

I couldn't think of any questions at that moment, but I figured I would as soon as they left me. Lutz had been watching my expression closely and said, "If you need anything, just wave at the camera." He pointed to where it was mounted high on one of the walls. "I'll come right over."

"Thanks," I said.

Then Tilly delivered his parting shot. "Okay, Little Lady, knock yourself out. Oh, and don't get too close to those bars otherwise that piece of shit might just do it for you." He jabbed a finger in the prisoner's direction.

Lutz gave me a nod, said, "Ma'am," and then followed Tilly back to the control booth. I stood by the chair, left alone with the murderer.

His cell was seven feet wide and eight feet deep. The cement walls and floor were furnished with a steel sink and toilet that mounted on the back wall, a mattress supported by a steel sheet attached to a side wall, and across from it another piece of metal secured to the wall served as a table. Some clothing and a towel hung from hooks on the wall, but no pictures, and no window other than the tiny one on the door. On the table sat a small TV, a newspaper that he had folded neatly, and a few books. I couldn't make out the titles. No frills. Every bit as nice as I had expected his living quarters to be, and considering the behavior that landed the guy in there, way better than he deserved.

Eisenbrey was tall and lean, this I could tell in spite of the fact that he did not get up to greet me. His long form, clothed in prison issued khaki pants and a white T-shirt, was stretched out comfortably on his bed, the back of his head resting on his hands with his pillow propping him up just enough to have a clear view of anyone approaching his cell.

In spite of the air of indifference suggested by his body language, his eyes sparked, alive and beguiling, tracking my movement, taking in every detail. He sneered and I had the disturbing sensation that he could see something beyond the physical, like he knew some dark secret about me, and apparently he found it amusing. Not exactly sure who I had expected him to be, but the man before me didn't come close to anything I had imagined.

I remained standing. "Mr. Eisenbrey? Hello, I'm Rebecca Reis. I'd like to speak with you. Is that all right?" Pushing my hair back behind my ear, I felt a slight tremble in my fingers. But why? There was no sense to it. He was secured in his cell. He couldn't touch me.

"Miss Reis, are you from the church? Are you here to witness to me?" he asked, although I knew he had been told exactly who was coming to visit him.

"No. Are you disappointed?" I asked standing tall, portraying more confidence than I felt.

"I suppose that depends on your intention for being here," he replied. He smirked and sat up, swinging his long legs over the side of his bed. "You must be the writer then." He scanned me up and down with a critical eye.

"Yes."

"I don't recognize your name. What have you written?"

"I have three published novels: *The Liar's Promise, Unto Me,* and *Epitaph.*"

"Are those true crime novels?"

"No, they're thrillers. This will be my first non-fiction work." I tried to steady my breathing, but I felt like a five year old being questioned by the teacher after I had been caught doing something naughty.

He looked nonplussed. "Oh good, you want to practice on me."

"I've sold a lot of books. My agent asked me to do this because she felt I was the best person to write about you."

As he leaned forward, the cast of the overhead light illuminated his face making an impact that caught me off guard. Everyone in Washington State, and beyond, had seen this man's likeness countless times in photos and video clips of him sitting in a courtroom or being escorted down a courthouse hallway wearing shackles and orange coveralls, flanked by guards on either side. His capture and murder trials had been prominent in the news from December of 2001 through September of 2003, albeit in the shadow of 9/11.

But the photos hadn't done justice to his striking features: the artful arch of his eyebrows over the wide-set, almond-shaped eyes, the perfectly sculpted nose, the full lips curling into a wicked grin. Everyone else I had seen that day seemed so dull and bland by comparison, almost as if we were in a black-and-white movie and he was the only character filmed in color.

Eisenbrey ran his fingers through his dark, chin-length hair as he pondered me. With his nearly-black hair, blue eyes, and somewhat fair complexion he looked like someone my grandparents would have described as "Black Irish". The good-looking killer finally said, "I'll read your books, and then I'll decide whether or not you're the best person to write about me."

I took a measured breath, trying to quell the dislike that had already started to rise in me, but it was no use. Control freaks just irritated the shit out of me. I found myself glaring at him in spite of my nervousness.

"Look, Rebecca, you seem like a nice kid, but I think they should have sent someone with a little more experience, don't you?"

The sudden increase in tension gave me the urge to throw something, but instead I let my breath out slowly. *How dare he insinuate that I am inexperienced.* I'd been a published author for seven years, and I was able to support myself on the income from my novels for the last five, a feat that the vast majority of writers would never accomplish. I didn't need to sell my qualifications to this cretin. "Right. Do you think we could go through some preliminary questions today, or should we just bag the whole interview?" I snapped.

"You're a testy little thing, aren't you?" He regarded me for a moment. "Well, sure we can talk a while. I don't have much else on my calendar anyway, and at least you're nice to look at." There was hunger in the way his deep-blue eyes inspected me, which, considering the source, felt unsettling. I saw his muscles tense, reminding me of a tightly wound coil ready to spring forward at any moment. There could be no mistaking that the man on the other side of the bars was a predator.

Sitting down on the hard metal chair, I gave him what I hoped looked like an amiable smile. "May I call you Thomas?" I inquired.

I had let my guard down somewhat and started to relax until he squelched it by saying, "No. You call me Mr. Eisenbrey."

I quickly switched gears. It looked as though I was going to have to get into the *let's just get through this* mindset. It was just as well. After all, this guy was a vicious murderer. I wasn't supposed to enjoy talking with him, but just to try to maintain a good enough rapport with him to collect the information I needed. I wondered how many meetings it would take before I had enough to cut him loose.

"All right, Mr. Eisenbrey, may I have your permission to record this interview?"

"Sure, honey."

Crap. He sounded curt and dismissive, and he then looked away. I needed to engage him somehow, get him invested in the conversation. I took a small digital recorder out of my bag, turned it on, and set it on the floor between us.

"Let's start at the beginning. Where were you born?"

"Carnation," he said in a monotone.

"Is that here in Washington?" I asked, knowing the answer already because the city of Carnation was only a few miles east of where I lived in Bellevue. I'd never been there, never had a reason to make the short trip. I'd heard the town held nothing more interesting than a few cows in a field, so there was no point for me to visit.

His eyes narrowed. "It's not far from Seattle. It was a little farming community, still is I suppose. But why haven't you heard of it? You're not from around here?"

"I moved here from California. Did your family have a farm?"

"No, my parents didn't own one, but when I was a kid I did a little work on a couple of farms for spending money."

"What are your parents' names?"

"Joseph and Sarah Eisenbrey."

"What do they do for a living?"

"Dad was in construction. Mom was a housewife."

"Do you love them?" I asked quickly.

That took him by surprise, and he seemed to contemplate my question for a moment. "I don't know. I suppose I was fond of my mother…I don't think about them much anymore."

"What about your father?"

He paused, and regarded me in a calculating manner. "We've talked enough about them. Tell me Rebecca, do you love your parents?" he fired back at me.

"Yes," I said and I held his gaze. *I loved them in a way that you'll never love anyone, and I wish like hell that they were still here. God, I miss them.* His expression changed. Something had piqued his interest. Once again I had the uneasy feeling that he could read my thoughts. I asked another question. "Do you have any brothers or sisters?"

"I had a brother," he said slowly. I felt a tingling on the back of my neck, and I didn't want to look into his eyes anymore. I studied my list, remembering the vivid description that Scanlon had given me of the condition of his brother's body when they found him in the forest.

"You said that in the past tense. What happened to him?"

"He went hunting and…well, they found his body a while later. The police suspected foul play. Someone had gotten a little carried away with a blade of some kind," he said, his voice flat and calm.

I looked up again and watched Eisenbrey closely as I asked my next question. "Do you miss him?"

"Not particularly," he said, and I believed him. The questions about loving or missing his family failed to elicit any discernible emotional response, but I should have expected this, given his diagnosis of anti-social personality disorder. Apparently, whatever I'd heard about the ability of serial killers to charm didn't apply to this one. Eisenbrey glanced away from me, but not before I caught the corner of his lip curling up in amusement.

"Was he older or younger than you?" I asked.

"He was older."

"What was his name?"

"David. We called him Davy."

"Were you with him when it happened?"

A slight stiffening in his posture as his eyes returned to me. "Hmm. Your question leaves me in a bit of a quandary, as you can probably imagine. I'm going to lay down some ground rules for you here, Rebecca. We won't discuss my actions or whereabouts in regards to any deaths except those that I have been convicted of in a court of law" — he paused and his eyes fell to the digital recording device resting on the floor between us, then he glared in my direction — "Especially with that running. I might be on death row but that could change at any moment. Do not mention any other cases that could result in a new conviction or you will find yourself on my shit-list."

"I could turn it off if that would make you feel more comfortable speaking candidly with me about your brother," I offered.

Eisenbrey wagged his finger at me. "So it can wind up in your little book? No," he said forcefully and then seemed to rein himself back in. "That is *not* going to happen. If you want to continue this interview, you will follow my rules and never write about anything other than those occasions that turned into convictions."

"All right," I said, holding my hand up solemnly. "You have my word."

"Good, now why don't you just try a different question?"

"Okay. Do you talk with your parents very often?"

"Are you kidding me?" He glowered at me like I was an idiot for going right back where he had just told me not to, but then gave a resigned sigh and answered me. "I haven't seen my father in over twenty-two years. He ran off." Eisenbrey crossed his arms and smirked. Apparently he found his father's disappearance humorous. "And my dear mother doesn't speak to me anymore. For some reason, she seems to be afraid of me," he said, shaking his head as if he assessed his mother's reaction as odd. I couldn't blame the woman.

"Do you have any idea where your father ran off to?"

He rubbed the stubble on his chin pensively. "Not exactly, but I have the feeling that none of us will ever see him again." Eisenbrey leaned back and seemed relaxed, yet my spine tingled like an electric current had jolted it. My senses screamed, *Run!*

Goddamn. So he did kill his brother and father. And it looked as though he wanted me to understand that, even though I had been forbidden from putting it in the book. If I was his mother, I would have changed my identity and moved somewhere far away from here. In fact, I felt like I wanted to get away from him now.

I ran through the rest of my list of questions for the day's session, obtaining some information on his extended family—whom he had never been close to—and his early life, but it all seemed mundane. He didn't insinuate that he had been involved in any other deaths. After a while, the guard signaled that my time had run out.

"Well, what do you think?" I asked. "Are you willing to try this again next week?"

He shrugged. "Yeah, that's all right."

"Monday?" I asked.

"If I'm in the mood." He gave a non-committal shrug, but still, it seemed like a yes.

"Okay." I stood and bent over to pick up my bag, and then I noticed my digital camera toward the top of its contents. "Do you mind if I take a snapshot of you? I find it useful to have a visual reference," I told him.

"Sure, but then I get a picture. I'd like to have a visual of you as well." The wicked grin had returned, and it creeped me out. He stood and leaned casually against the cement wall and studied me, sensing my hesitation. "It's only fair," he chided.

"Uh…" I didn't think it a good idea but I couldn't conjure up a reason to say no to him at that moment. "All right, but I didn't bring one with me."

"That's okay. You can give it to me at our next visit. How do you want me?" He stood and tugged lazily at his T-shirt, and as he smoothed it down I saw a generous amount of dark chest hair peeking out over the collar, which matched the hair on his arms. He leaned casually against the wall, bringing one of his knees up and resting his foot on his cot. Somehow he had managed to make his jail-issued gear look like something from Calvin Klein. This man could have been a model very easily. "How's this?" he asked, as if he were aware of the effect his appearance had on me. At least he seemed to be enjoying our meeting now.

I managed to keep my tone businesslike. "That's great." I took a quick shot.

"You'd better take a few," he suggested. "Just in case some of them don't turn out well. I'm not sure if the camera likes me." He was a liar. He seemed utterly confident that he would photograph well. I snapped two more shots of him like that. Then he sat down on his bed, leaning forward, his fingers entwined in front of him, and he looked up at me with a contemplative expression. "How about a couple like this?"

Yes, that was a good idea. I nodded and got three more shots of him in that position. Then he stood and came up to the bars, grasping them with his hands and leaned his head against one of them. He towered nearly a foot above me. Closer to me than before, his hypnotic, blue eyes pierced through me; their color a vibrant, unearthly shade of blue. Mesmerized, I just gazed at him for several moments until I heard him clear his throat and say, "Miss Reis, why don't you get a couple of close-ups now."

In a fog of confusion, I slowly lifted the camera up and took three more pictures of him. Then I thanked him for his time and said goodbye. His eyes followed me as I ambled up the hallway. Feeling lightheaded and giddy, I checked out of the prison and walked back to my car.

SIX

"Well, how did it go?" Andrea asked. She had called my cell before I'd even left the penitentiary parking lot.

"It didn't."

"You didn't get in?"

"I got in. I spoke with Eisenbrey, but I just don't feel like I got anywhere with him. He doesn't like me."

"So? This guy kills people for kicks. Did you expect him to be nice to you?" She had a point. "You can't count on success your first time with him. It may take a few more visits before he starts to open up."

"He was so rude and arrogant," I complained. "He's just such an asshole." I didn't mention the photo shoot to Andrea, or that I had gotten an unusual lightheaded feeling from it, or that with only a few minutes of flirtation Eisenbrey had somehow managed to make my hormone levels go apeshit. I wasn't exactly sure what had just happened, but sitting in my car and replaying the scene in my head, I felt like an idiot.

"Look, Rebecca, I want you to do a few more interviews before you try to weasel out of it. Give it a chance. You should enter into this expecting him to be a mean son of a bitch. Perhaps you'll get lucky and be pleasantly surprised."

"Yeah, you're right." She had proven herself correct about a lot of things over the years. It made sense to listen to Andrea. "I already have the next appointment set for Monday."

"Good! So he agreed to see you again. Things are looking up."

As I sped down I-90, across the vast expanse of Eastern Washington's desert landscape, I started kicking around ideas for my to-do list. I should ask Eisenbrey for names of any friends or relatives I could interview. He'd mentioned his mother, who didn't speak to him anymore, but that was all I had so far. I would also need to interview the victims' family members and some of the prison guards.

My mind conjured an image of Detective Scanlon's smiling face. I definitely needed to interview him again, soon. He was easy to chat with, easy to smile for—such a contrast from Eisenbrey. And he'd said to call him, anytime. The idea was appealing. It had only been two days since he'd extended that invitation. Was it too soon to call? I didn't want to appear too enthusiastic. But, on the other hand, this was clearly work related.

I caught motion in my peripheral vision, checked my rearview mirror, and saw someone sitting in the back seat of my car. I shrieked and jerked the steering wheel, causing my car to swerve, narrowly missing a collision with an SUV. Then I chanced another peek in the mirror as I pulled over to the side of the freeway, but saw no one this time.

Jesus! The fucker probably ducked down where I can't see him.

My car skidded to a stop and I tore the door open, jumped out, and looked into the side window to see the back seat. It was empty.

I couldn't understand. There was nothing in my back seat: no coat, no blanket, no shopping bags—absolutely nothing a person could hide under. It was completely barren. And I had definitely seen someone…hadn't I?

My heart pounded in my chest, as I paced next to my car. Less sure of myself, I tried to recall what this person had looked like. It seemed like a man, but I couldn't remember any of his features. All I had really seen was a dark shape. I looked in the car again. The day was sunny; the back seat well lit. There was absolutely no reason I wouldn't have been able to see a passenger with clarity. Had I imagined it?

My eyes rested on the lock release button by the headrest. The back seat could fold down to allow access from the cabin into the trunk. My breath came out in a gush. *Crap. I need to search the trunk.*

A thought came to me. *Was this person armed?* Could someone have climbed into my car while I was parked at the prison? If so, why had they waited so long to show themselves? My commute had started more than an hour ago.

It was a little after three o'clock. Looking around, I saw a steady stream of cars driving by. If I found trouble, someone would pull over to help. I reached in the driver's door and pulled the trunk release. Then I walked to the rear of the car and whipped the trunk open, jumping back and to the side to avoid any maniac that might jump out at me. It was empty.

I felt like an ass.

In the trunk, there was nothing but my hiking boots and a backpack with emergency supplies—far too small to secret the object of my terror—no need to open it and look for him. It seemed obvious that my mind was playing tricks on me. But that dark figure had seemed so solid, so real. Perhaps, my visit with Eisenbrey had spooked me more than I realized.

When I got home, I loaded the photos into my laptop and set them up as a slide show. Then I picked a favorite, one of the shots where he hung onto the bars of his cell and peered through at me; the last one

I had taken. A damned good-looking man, it felt difficult to draw my eyes away from his picture. I set that photo up as the wallpaper on my laptop. It gave me a guilty feeling, as if I was looking at a dirty magazine. I was almost acting like some smitten teenager. What a ridiculous thought. In fact, I distinctly remembered that I had disliked him the moment we met. This had nothing to do with fondness. My new wallpaper photo was nothing more than an aid to help me with my writing.

Eisenbrey stared from my screen with his deep-cerulean eyes, and I could feel something stirring inside of me. I was beginning to creep myself out. "Stop staring at me," I whispered, and I snapped my laptop shut.

I spent the next couple days listening to the recording I made of him over and over as I typed notes about our interview. I enjoyed the sound of his voice, deep and masculine. I looked at the pictures of him several more times as well, just to help me get into the right frame of mind to write.

I immersed myself in him so much that he should have seemed like a pest, yet when I tried to take a break and concentrate on something else, a strange craving for something I couldn't identify would nag me. I found myself in the kitchen, removing the whiskey from the cupboard and setting it on the counter, out of habit I suppose. Later, back in my living room I realized I didn't have a drink. I hadn't poured one. I didn't particularly want one.

Much to my frustration, that Saturday and Sunday night I spent an inordinate amount of time awake, unable to rid my mind of Thomas Eisenbrey.

SEVEN

October 29th, 2012

I had found him lying face down on the beige carpet — the carpet they had purchased less than one year earlier. They were particular about keeping it clean, so much so that they took their shoes off before entering the house. A large, dark-red bloodstain soaked into the rug next to his head, and the crimson saturated the beautiful, silver hair that had always looked so shiny whenever he stood out in the California sunshine. I worried that the left side of his head would never look right again. But even as that silly thought raced through my mind, I knew he lay there unconcerned. He wasn't worried about anything anymore. My eyes traveled to the wall close to him where more blood had splattered in a misshapen fan pattern. No. I needed to clean him up. I needed to fix this. I needed to make this go away.

"Jesus!" I said as my eyes jerked open. I glanced around realizing that I'd dozed off in my car after parking. I was at the prison. It was Monday. Time for my second meeting with Eisenbrey. I had arrived thirty minutes early and decided to close my eyes for a few minutes. That had been a mistake. In my defenseless moment the memory had forced its way in. The ghosts had free reign.

Familiar feelings of emptiness and despair surfaced. I took a deep breath and rubbed my temples, trying to chase away some of the remaining grogginess without ruining my make-up. Then I got up and hurried into the prison.

When I came into the control booth in Eisenbrey's section, Lutz greeted me, and then introduced me to the other man at the desk, DiMaggio. Officer DiMaggio had one of those ageless faces; he could have been anywhere between thirty and fifty years old. I felt reasonably sure that he had spent a lot of time in the military before coming to the prison, a conclusion drawn in part because of his appearance, but mostly because of his demeanor. He looked like an extremely disciplined man. DiMaggio nodded, but didn't smile. It was hard to tell if he was radiating hostility toward me, or if I was dealing with someone who was just not overly friendly.

Lutz got up to escort me to Eisenbrey's cell, but then DiMaggio said, "Hang on a second, Andy. I'll take her back. I haven't had a chance to visit my little buddy yet today." Lutz looked a little put out by this, but he stepped aside. The way the young man's eyes cast downward screamed at me that he had no intention of fucking with the other guard. I followed DiMaggio back to the cell. As the outer door slid open he said, "Hey asshole, you're girl's here to see you. Ain't that great?"

Eisenbrey casually lay on his bed, reading a section of newspaper. He did not look up or acknowledge DiMaggio, and it got under the guard's skin.

"You'd better answer me when I speak to you," he yelled as he struck the outer door causing a ricochet of sound down the hall. "Or I'll take your clothes and your sheets and you can just sit here naked in the cold and think about how you should have shown me some respect."

Eisenbrey lifted his eyes slowly to look up at the guard who glared down at him. "Relax, Ricky. I respect you just as much today as I always have." His attention returned to his newspaper.

"I told you not to call me that, Eisenbrey, and there will be a consequence." He turned to me, "So, you're doing a biography about this corpse-fucking piece of shit? I wonder just how many dead bodies he's raped. He really gets off on that sort of thing."

Eisenbrey spoke up. "Well actually, Ricky, I am not sexually attracted to dead people. They don't scream like the live ones do, and that's what really turns me on." I saw a wicked gleam in his eyes. "But, I'll bet the sight of your corpse would give me a great big hard-on."

It felt uncomfortable standing here while these two exchanged unpleasantries, but I was gaining some valuable information about what life must be like for him in prison. I couldn't understand how DiMaggio had the nerve to antagonize Eisenbrey that way. It seemed unwise to provoke a dangerous killer. He might have been secure in his cell at that moment, but surely this guard would have to deal with him face to face at some point during the course of his duties later.

DiMaggio rapped the steel bars with his baton; the sound again reverberated around the hall. "That's twice, you fucking piece of shit. Now there's gonna be two consequences." Then he gave me a mirthless smile and said, "You two have a nice visit now." He strolled back to the guard booth, grinning as if he had been triumphant in that exchange, but I couldn't tell who the winner had been. I suppose that would depend on what these mysterious consequences turned out to be.

"Holy shit, he seems like a real sweetheart," I said. "Do you think he's really going to do something bad to you?" I set the recorder on the floor between us and looked at Eisenbrey who nodded his consent. I flipped it on.

"I don't care what that puffed up little man does." He waved his hand dismissively. "Where's that photo you promised me, Sugar?"

I had hoped that he wouldn't remember, but I came prepared. "Oh, I should have given it to the officer before he left," I said, looking back in the direction DiMaggio had just gone.

"Hold it up toward the camera," he told me.

I did, and a few moments later Lutz appeared. I breathed a sigh of

relief that it wasn't the other guard again. "Got something for Tom?"
he asked.

"Yes," I said, handing Lutz the 8" x 10" sheet. In the photo I wore a
simple, black dress and a choker with a decorative jade carving in front.
It was a classy shot, not flirtatious or slutty in any way. Lutz looked
at it for quite a while. "I assume a photo like this is appropriate?"

"Oh, we don't care about that. Heck, it could even be a nudie.
I'm just supposed to check to make sure there aren't any paperclips
or staples—that sort of thing." He shrugged and then slid the paper
through the food tray slot in the cell door and stepped back.

"Thanks Andy," Tom murmured as he took the photo.

Lutz nodded and walked back to his station. The farther away
the young guard went, the more my tension increased. Paperclips or
staples? Were those things supposed to be dangerous in some way?
The idea seemed nuts, but I supposed a violent and resourceful man
could fashion weapons out of them.

I felt my heart rate increase. I was out of sorts, probably because
I hadn't consumed any alcohol before our visit. Or was it more than
that? Yes. I was bothered that Eisenbrey had an image of me. It
seemed sinister.

I sat down on the metal chair and took a spiral notebook out of
my bag. He looked at my hand and I sensed he had noticed the slight
tremble in my fingers. His eyes lingered on me for a moment. He
chuckled and nodded, but didn't otherwise acknowledge the uneasy
demeanor that I attempted to hide.

Eisenbrey returned his gaze to the photo, sizing me up on paper
the same way that he did in person. "This is very nice. Thank you."
Then he set it down carefully on the table and sat on his bed.

"You'll be pleased to know that I've read all of your novels since
our last meeting."

That surprised me. None of my books were short. It was quite a
bit to read over one weekend.

"I enjoyed the first two. However, your third effort… well, should we really call that an effort? I was left with the impression that you just didn't care anymore. What were you aiming for? Frightening? Suspenseful? Creepy? Whatever it was, you missed your mark." He shook his head, feigning disappointment. Or perhaps it was genuine. I wasn't sure. "You know, I could teach you a thing or two about creepy if you want…" he promised, his voice drifting off. He studied me for a moment and asked, "Are you sure you're up to this?"

"Pretty sure I can handle it," I said dryly.

"Literary critics can be so vicious, especially the ones who reviewed your work. Things must be difficult for you lately, with your career going up in flames the way it has. Are you under a lot of pressure now to prove that you can still write?" I hated the uncanny way he had of saying what I was thinking. "I don't have a lot of confidence in you, Rebecca. Do you?"

"Don't kid yourself, Mr. Eisenbrey. I've risen from the ashes, but this book isn't going to happen if you spend all of our limited time lobbing insults at me. At some point today we're going to need to have another chat about you." He studied me silently as I stared right back. "Do you want me to write this book or not?"

He kept silent for a little while with his eyebrows raised. "Hmm. I'm beginning to think that we might be a good fit, Rebecca. Yes, I do want you to write it." Then he leaned back on his bed and said, "All right, let's talk about me, darlin'. Fire away."

I consulted my list of questions and said, "I forgot to confirm your date of birth at our last visit. Is July 12, 1967 correct?"

"That's right," he said. "You're a very beautiful woman, Rebecca. I didn't realize just how beautiful the first time we met. It looks like you took a little more care getting ready for me this time. You spent more time on your eye makeup and you're wearing a bra that pushes up your tits. I like that."

I held my palm up to him. "Whoa, what the fuck?" The most

infuriating thing was that he was right about all of it. I had spent a great deal of time trying to look nice for him. At least his unpleasantness seemed to be taking the edge off of my jitters.

"Oh come now, Rebecca, don't complain. You know I don't have anything else to look forward to besides screwing with you. Why would you want to deny me that one small pleasure?"

I merely shook my head and forged onward. "So you're forty-five years old?" I said absentmindedly, looking over my questions to get my bearings.

"Yes, but that's something that we both already knew. How old are you?" he asked. He noted my hesitation, then he added, "Come on, it's only fair now, isn't it?"

"I'm forty," I told him.

He leapt up from his bed and came toward me with surprising speed and agility, causing me to flinch, then peered at me through the bars of his cell. "Now, that I do not believe."

"It's true. I'm past my prime. So perhaps we can dispense with your ridiculous attraction to me and get some actual work done."

"No, no, no…we can't dispense with that at all. Not at all…" He examined my face with a fervid interest that I found alarming, as if I was bacteria on a slide under the lens of a high-powered microscope. I squirmed. Part of me wanted to put a great deal of distance between myself and this nutjob as quickly as possible, but that wouldn't help me get the information I needed for my book. Instead, I took a deep breath and tried to relax while he stared at me.

"Have you been under the knife, Rebecca?" he asked. I shuddered as I had an involuntary vision of Eisenbrey slitting the throat of a hunter that was duct taped to a tree, and I felt grateful I wasn't under his knife. "If so, you're plastic surgeon is very good."

"No, I haven't."

"So you're just the product of good genetics and healthy living?"

"Yes, I suppose so."

"I'm impressed." He studied me with an intensity that made me think that he was about to hurl a significant question my way. "Tell me, Rebecca, when you're alone at night, do you touch yourself?"

What an asshole. I struggled to keep my eye contact from wavering because I didn't want him to think he got me. "Nice. So our conversations are just for your juvenile amusement."

"Au contraire, I can assure you that this topic amuses grown men as well." He waited for my answer.

I opted for a direct approach, hoping that it might shut his bullshit down. "Of course I do on occasion, everyone does." I had no intention of asking him how he passed his time alone in his cell after lights out. Allowing him to regale me with tales of spanking the monkey wasn't going to get this book written.

I needed to shift the topic back to something productive, but before I could form my next question he asked, "Do you think about me when you touch yourself? Do you look at the photos you took of me?"

Something about his eyes gave me the creepy sensation that he could see inside of my head, as if he could see all the way through me and into my innermost thoughts and desires. At some point I became aware that I must have looked like a doe staring into the headlights of an oncoming car, and with some effort I shifted my expression back to one of casual indifference, all too late of course.

Then my surprise gave way to anger as I realized he had no intention of giving me anything useful for my goddamned book. This guy just aimed to be a dick and I could see his game plan. He wanted to see just how far he could push me until I abandoned our interview. I fumed inwardly as I tried to determine what response would give me the best odds of getting our conversation back on point. "No, I do not."

His gaze pierced through me and then a smile spread slowly across his face. He leaned toward me, his body tensed like a serpent poised to strike. "That isn't true. That isn't true at all."

Suddenly, I was filled with the desire to take a baseball bat to this man's skull, repeatedly. Part of my anger stemmed from the accuracy of his statement but that didn't defuse my reaction. Even with a bat, the bars of his cell would be in the way of me getting at him, not to mention that the guards might not appreciate it if I attacked him. Not *all* of them anyway. Lutz would probably object, Tilly would probably help me, and that other guy — DiMaggio — he looked as if he might just sneak back here and execute Eisenbrey himself when no one was looking.

I would have to use my words instead of my fists to deal with the jackal. And I needed to be careful about my reactions. I felt fairly certain that any micro movement would not escape his notice.

"I'm going to ask you to do something for me, Rebecca. I want you to refrain from pleasuring yourself until our next meeting. That's four whole days; do you think you could do that for me? I want to see what you're like when your sexual tension hasn't been alleviated right before our visit."

"Asking a human being not to do themselves is like asking a monkey not to eat a banana, or worse yet, asking it not to do itself." What on earth had possessed me to say that?

Eisenbrey burst into laughter, genuine throw-your-head-back, hearty laughter, which surprised me, and I wondered if I'd found a way in. I had witnessed a portion of his evil side earlier when I watched him engage DiMaggio but, at that moment, watching him laugh, I got a glimpse of the attractive, younger man he must have been. I could see a pinpoint of light seeping out through the small crack in his exterior and, wasting no time, I swooped in with another question from my list.

"Do you have any hobbies?" It sounded ridiculous to me after I said it, like I was trying to write a dating profile for him, but still, it was territory that I needed to cover.

"Well, Rebecca, I've been known to enjoy a little hunting now and again," he said in a nonchalant manner. He sighed. "I suppose if I could have just stuck to animals I wouldn't be in this mess." He looked around his cell and rubbed his face, feeling the short beard that he had started to grow. I noted that it had filled in quite a bit since Friday. "I like camping and fishing, you know, just generally being outdoors."

"Hiking?"

"Yeah, I hike to get where I'm going." He shrugged. "Well, I used to."

"It must be harder for someone like you to have to be…indoors all of the time like this," I said.

He leaned forward and glared at me. "I spend twenty-three hours every day in this tiny, little shit-box, waiting to die. How do you think I feel?" he snapped. "Of course it's not easy." His sudden anger made me jump in my seat. He seemed to notice that I had tensed up and his expression softened, the flash of anger dissipating as fast as it had come. "Uh, I also used to love to carve. I could make all kinds of things out of a chunk of wood." He smiled.

"Do you do that in here?" I asked, and then I immediately felt like a dipshit when I saw the sympathetic expression spreading across his face.

"Let me put it this way Rebecca: if you were in charge of this place, would you let me have a knife?"

"Oh, of course not, what was I thinking?" I could feel my face flush a little.

He sighed. "I'm sure I wouldn't know what goes on in there, honey, but you didn't really drive all the way out here to discuss my hobbies, did you? So let's get down to it. What would you really like to ask me? Was I abused as a child? Did I wet the bed? Was I breast-fed or bottle-fed? Or shall we go right to the nitty-gritty? When did I first realize that I wanted to kill? When did I commit murder for the first time? How did it make me feel?" He stopped and examined my expression. "You look a little green around the gills. Tell me, Rebecca, how do you feel about me killing things?"

"I don't like it, of course."

"That's it? That's all you've got to say? You look a little more upset than someone who just doesn't like it."

"Sure, it upsets me."

"But why does it upset you so much? What happened to you?" He peered at me with a sudden intensity that I wasn't prepared for, and I had the unnerving feeling again that he already knew the answer to his question. "I'm not just being an ass," he insisted. "I genuinely want to know." Oddly, his voice had become gentle, and I felt myself relaxing a little. Part of me felt like telling him, but I couldn't speak about that. I couldn't even allow myself to think about it. He waited for my answer for several seconds and then shook his head. "Don't you think this is a funny assignment for you? How are you going to write about this subject matter if you can't even cope with hearing about it?"

"I didn't say I couldn't cope," I snarled.

"I did."

"No one would enjoy hearing about your activities."

"That's not true. Some people are excited by it. Take my psychiatrist for instance, when I used to go into details about my kills he always looked like he was going to ejaculate all over his clipboard. Your readers will want the details. Why do you think your agent wanted you to write about me? Because it's what the public wants." He leaned forward. "And, Rebecca, let's not forget the most important thing of all — the reason I'm willing to meet with you and share information with you about my infamous deeds — I enjoy it. I want to relive it all again and again, the thrill, the rush. I love to recall how it was when I felt the life leaving their bodies." He closed his eyes and breathed deeply.

As I watched him, a tingling like an electric current travelled down the length of my spine and settled between my legs. He was such an attractive man with his dark hair and sharp features, and the look of rapture on his face as he remembered killing was the same expression one would expect him to have when making love. I could see why his psychiatrist got aroused while listening to him. My mind started to wander and waver as a scene came into focus where I lay in bed with this murderer.

Suddenly his eyes snapped open, his gaze piercing, and I hastily lowered my eyes to the papers I held. I pretended to read something for a moment and then forced myself to look at him again. "Mr. Eisenbrey, I have been told that you suffer from antisocial personality disorder. Do you believe that's true?"

"Sure, sugar, but I'm not the one who suffers from my antisocial personality, it's generally those around me. And you don't have to try to be all politically correct about it. The first psychiatrist that evaluated me said that I was a psychopath. That seems like a much more apt description of me, don't you think? I mean, sure, slitting someone's throat is an antisocial thing to do, but so is peeing in public. Classifying me as antisocial just seems a little too tame." He looked bored. "Did you know a lot of psychopaths choose law enforcement as a career?"

I was dubious. "Do you really believe that?"

"Yes, I do. Take Scanlon, he does whatever he pleases and gets away with it because he's the Sheriff's little golden boy." Now I knew he was being ridiculous. There was no way that the detective I spoke with last week was a psychopath. "Scanlon…" he murmured, and then he seemed far away. "He's got the sixth sense, that's for sure. He knew what I was the first time we met, way back when my father disappeared. He was brand new. Wasn't in homicide yet. Probably hadn't even written a speeding ticket. After our little chat, I knew I had to leave. Do you know he planted evidence at my party site in Idaho?"

"You can't be serious."

"They found a comb I carved when I was a lad, a comb that I hadn't seen since I left my parent's house nine years earlier."

"Hmm," I said, as I thought to myself that this had to be bullshit.

"You don't believe me, but he sure went out of his way to help those fellas with their investigation and that was more than a little bit out of his jurisdiction." He seemed to drift away to another place for a moment, but then his mood changed quickly to what I would describe as alert agitation.

"And now here I am on death row. I've got eleven months left to live. It's scheduled for September 30th, but it could get drawn out a little longer if my attorney manages to frustrate the process some more. He's good at that. They told me that I can choose between lethal injection and hanging. I don't want any damned chemicals in my body. I'll take The Fourth Floor; I'd much rather suffocate."

"What's The Fourth Floor?"

"It's The Gallows. They drop you from The Fourth Floor but then you don't quite make it all the way to the third floor, courtesy of one of those special necklaces that the engineer makes for you."

"An engineer?" I repeated.

"Yes, they have a college graduate in charge of The Gallows. I'm glad he's an educated man. Apparently it's not as simple as you'd think to hang someone properly. It's comforting to know that I'll be in his capable hands."

This new topic of conversation made me feel sick. "What a horrible thought."

"Oh, it's more than a thought," he sniggered. "Anyway, I've watched someone go by strangulation. It didn't seem so bad."

"How did you see someone die of…" I began, then I thought *duh*.

"A girl I was dating," he explained.

"One of your girlfriends?"

"Yeah, sure." He laughed.

"What's so funny?"

"I don't know if I'd say that she was a girlfriend. I don't do relationships. Sure, I get laid, but…" he trailed off.

"But what? Don't they live long enough to be called girlfriends?"

"No, that's not it, but I can see why you might jump to that conclusion," he said and chuckled again. Apparently, the subject of death really tickled this guy's funny bone. I gave him a stony stare. "She's the only woman I've ever killed." He said that as if I was supposed to be proud of him for only murdering one.

"Why is that?"

"I don't know, I suppose I don't really feel compelled to kill women. I mean we usually get along just fine. We make each other cum, and then I go on my merry way. It's not like I spend any time talking with them." He also found this amusing.

"Why?"

"I don't have any interest in talking to women. We've got nothing in common, so what's the point?" He seemed to notice my expression and something in it registered. Perhaps it occurred to him that he was, in fact, talking with a woman at this very moment. "But it's different with you, darlin'. You're special." He topped that with a big smile that could have been genuine or sarcastic. I couldn't tell.

"Well then, what happened exactly? Why is she dead? Did you catch her with another man?"

"No. But seriously, I didn't consider her my girlfriend. We just fucked a few times." Eisenbrey shrugged, then combed his hair back from his face with his fingers, his expression thoughtful. "That one had a mouth on her. She said something that really ticked me off." He looked as though he had just tasted something bitter.

"What did she say?"

"Uh, I don't remember anymore."

"This woman said something that made you so angry that you strangled her to death, and you're telling me that you don't remember what she said?" I asked, not attempting to mask my incredulity.

"Well shit, darlin'. That was a long time ago."

"But still, it must have made an impression." He merely shrugged. I referred to the papers that Scanlon had given me. "It was March

24th, 1995. Her name was Tammie Lancaster. She was twenty-five years old," I said.

"Yes, and now it's 2012. Seventeen years is a long time, honey. I haven't thought about her in ages." He seemed to understand that I wasn't satisfied with his response. "I'm not refusing to tell you what we fought about. I just truly don't remember." He held my gaze and I had the feeling that he had spoken the truth about it. But how could a person ever know with a psychopath? Lying was their specialty.

"I know you don't like some of the things I've done. I can understand that. But on some level, you like me," he pointed out.

"What are you trying to say?"

"Nothing, I'm just stating a fact."

Yes. He was right, and it bothered me.

EIGHT

October 31st, 2012

I jolted awake, a feeling of urgency bearing down on me. It took me a moment to pinpoint what caused my unease, but then I realized — I had the feeling that someone was watching me. My bedroom was dark except for a shaft of moonlight filtering in through the open blinds. When I lifted my head to scan the room, I saw a tall, dark figure standing very still at the foot of my bed. I saw no face, although the moonlight should have been enough to illuminate it.

I watched in silence for a while, unnerved not only by his presence, but by his motionlessness. Then, slowly, I reached over to the lamp on my nightstand, not taking my eyes off of the intruder. My hand fumbled and I was unable to find the switch until I glanced, just for a split second, at the lamp to get my bearings. Suddenly, my room was filled with light. But when my eyes returned to the foot of the bed, he was gone.

Had this been some nightmare that I was still experiencing as I awoke? Or had I seen something that wasn't there — like when I was in the car? Of course there was the possibility that this person had gone from being a statue, to moving faster than Speedy Gonzalez in order to make it out of the room while I looked for the light switch. Unlikely, but I still searched the upstairs of my house. I found no one.

I checked the clock on my bedside table — 3:00 a.m. My heart still pounded, and I knew there would be no more sleep for me at this point. I didn't even want to be in my bedroom anymore.

I got dressed and went downstairs. Might as well get some work done.

11:00 a.m.

I took another sip of my coffee, noting that I had the jitters. The realization dawned that I was on my fifth cup that day, much more than my normal caffeine intake. No wonder I felt like doing one hundred jumping jacks. And speaking of Jack, I hadn't had any Jack Daniel's for a while. My last drink had been right before my first meeting with Eisenbrey five days ago. And the really odd thing — I didn't feel like I wanted any. Ever since the dismal reviews of my last book, being separated from my alcohol was the kind of thing that made me feel like lashing out at anyone or anything within reach. But somehow I had become so engrossed in my new project that I hadn't even thought about drinking. And I felt better, chipper even. Perhaps the time was ripe for Jack and I to part ways. Perhaps I didn't need him anymore; I had Eisenbrey now.

My thoughts traveled to the question that Eisenbrey had asked me during our last meeting, right after he had accused me of not being able to deal with the project. He wanted to know what had happened to me. *Why had he asked me that?* It seemed apparent to him that something from my past interfered with my ability to focus on and deal with the morbid details of his crimes. It was true, thoughts of my parents surfaced more often since I started working on this book, but how could he sense that? He seemed to look inside of me and discern things he shouldn't have been able to know. His accusation that I admired his photos while I took care of my sexual needs was correct, but it was preposterous to think he could actually see things in my mind. It had to just be a series of lucky guesses.

Frustrated that I couldn't get this man out of my head, I wanted to be free of him for a while, but at the same time I recognized that I could spin my compulsion into a good thing. The more I allowed my mind to dwell on him, the more time I would spend working on the book, and the faster I would be able to finish it. Did he think about me the way I thought about him, the way I had started to obsess about him? I wanted to know.

I looked forward to my next opportunity to see him a little too much, and more than that, I found myself actually missing him. I needed to get out of the house and find something to do that would give me a sense of connection to him, something to get my fix. I decided to drive out to the address of the house where he grew up.

I cruised along Highway 203 on my way to Carnation, enjoying the scenery as I went. In contrast to the suburban city where I lived, this rural area was peaceful and picturesque with low, forested hills all around, full of deciduous trees in all of their bright-orange and yellow autumn glory. And though fall was supposed to be the season of death and decay, when all of the leaves finally let go and move on, it was the time of year when I felt most alive. The vibrant colors and fresh, crisp air seemed to awaken something in me. I felt happier then than I had in the summer. Of course, some of my newfound happiness could be attributed to working with Eisenbrey. *No. The new project*, I told myself, *not Eisenbrey.*

I passed by several fields with old barns, some with obvious repairs made to them, others in various degrees of dilapidation, all of which had their own beauty as they blended into the country landscape. Out there, I could point a camera in almost any direction and get a photo that would be worthy of display on a postcard. I passed a strawberry farm, making a mental note to return there next summer. The speed limit dropped as I entered the city and then I found myself looking at the shops on either side of the road as I drove through the tiny downtown area of Carnation.

The grade school had just finished for the day and children got into cars or climbed onto their respective school buses, most of them wearing Halloween costumes. Until that moment, I hadn't even realized it was Halloween. I saw pirates, vampires, zombies and I even spotted a Grim Reaper, none of them frightening. Just innocent children. I wondered what costume Carnation's own real monster, Thomas Eisenbrey, had worn as a child.

I drove past a hardware store and wondered if he had ever shopped there for the items he later used to kill people.

Turning onto his street, I found the address a few blocks back from the main highway through town. The house, perhaps built in the 1940s, had a steep pitch to the roof, which was covered with a thick carpet of moss. The pale-green clapboard siding on the house also enshrouded the detached garage. I saw two old cars parked in the yard and would bet neither of them was operational based on the height of the grass around them. A quick glance at the mailbox told me that no Eisenbreys lived there. I hadn't expected any. It was the Johnsons' house now, and their priorities did not include yard work or keeping up the place.

I parked across the street and looked at the house for a while, trying to imagine Thomas Eisenbrey living there, wondering if the place had been in a better state of repair back then. Many of the houses nearby looked as though they had been built in the last twenty years, so he likely had few neighbors back then. The large wooded area on the other side of the new homes had probably extended even closer to the Eisenbreys' house.

I got out of my car and walked up the street a few hundred feet, taking several pictures of the house and yard, wishing I could get some photos of the way it looked when he was here. As I returned to my car I wondered — what the hell could have possibly gone on in that house to create the Hunter?

NINE

Sparks flared from the fire in the corner of the otherwise dark room. The flickering light from the flames danced around the left side of his body as he skulked slowly toward me. Gone were the prison clothes, the plain, white T-shirt that I had always seen him in and instead he wore blue jeans and a blue shirt that hung partially open. His hands worked quickly, undoing the rest of the buttons. The warm glow of the fire illuminated his fair skin and caused the dark hair on his chest to glisten.

He came to me, and lay down on top of me. I felt the delicious weight of his body, the pressure of his mouth pressed against mine, the warmth of his skin, and the urgency of his erection as he rubbed it against me. I wanted more. I wanted Eisenbrey.

I found myself moaning and thrashing in my sheets as I awoke.

I lay there in a state of confusion. Had I been sleeping? Getting my bearings, I frantically searched around my dark bedroom and then flipped on the lamp next to my bed. He was gone. Had Eisenbrey actually been here in my room? If so, where was he? I sat up and tried to shake off the feeling. No, he couldn't have been here, but the dream had seemed so real. My skin still felt as though his body had just been up against it.

I couldn't understand how a dream could cause such a genuine physical sensation. I trembled, but not from the cold. I pulled my covers up around me because it comforted me, and I marveled at the way my thoughts about this man could make me feel. I was in need.

TEN

November 2nd, 2012

Seeing him as his cell door opened unraveled me. My heart sped, lightheadedness caused me to sway, and I clutched the metal folding chair to steady myself. The rational part of my mind told me the vision before me was utterly impossible, and yet — Eisenbrey leaned on the edge of his table, waiting expectantly for me, wearing blue jeans, a blue, denim shirt, and a huge grin.

"How have you been, darlin'? Did you get a good night's sleep?" He sounded friendly, cheerful, casual.

I tried to feign casual indifference, but I was honestly taken aback.

He stepped forward and pressed his head against the cell bars, watching me with a knowing expression. "You had a dream about me, didn't you?" His colder tone sent a chill through me as did his penetrating, deep-cerulean eyes. He wasn't just throwing it out there, he actually knew. *But how could he know?* "Tell me, Rebecca, what did you do when you woke up?"

. I put out the fire. In fact, my fantasies about him had kept me going for about forty-five minutes before I finally knocked it off and went back to sleep. I didn't even need to look at my favorite pic of him anymore. I had every pixel of that image of him, gazing longingly at me through those bars, memorized. As I sat across from him, that image competed with the sinister smile he wore as his eyes bore into mine. My heart rate increased and adrenaline surged into my bloodstream—a panic reaction I told myself, and tried to brush it off. There was no need to get upset about this small thing. I had to remind myself it was impossible for him to see inside my head. I eyed him warily as I attempted to dismiss my train of thought. "You're not wearing your usual clothes," I said in measured tones.

"Yeah, Lutz got me some blues today. I like these clothes better. The color sets off my eyes," he remarked as he adjusted his collar.

I nodded silently in agreement.

"This is what they used to issue to the prisoners. I should be able to keep them until DiMaggio gets back. He won't let me have anything but the khaki and white. That guy can be such a bitch." Eisenbrey chuckled and shook his head. By all appearances he wasn't very concerned about DiMaggio.

"It's hot in here, don't you think?" Eisenbrey slowly unbuttoned the blue shirt and allowed it to hang open, exposing his fur-covered chest. He leaned back on his bed putting his feet up and hooked his thumbs in the belt loops of his jeans above the front pockets. The positioning of his hands drew my attention to the bulge behind his zipper.

"Goddamn," I muttered under my breath. I tried to look at my notes for the day's interview but my eyes refused to be torn from the wickedly delicious sight before me.

Eisenbrey smiled, apparently pleased by the reaction he elicited from me. "Hmm, if you don't want to talk about what you did after that dream, what would you like to talk about?"

Momentarily flustered, I couldn't remember what I had intended to ask during our visit. "Uh, I'll just start the recorder," I stammered, setting the device on the floor next to the bars and activating it. I consulted my notes and found my bearings. "Let's see, I have some questions about your education. Did you graduate from high school?"

"Yes." His smile started to disappear and I felt a foreboding.

"Class of '85?" I asked.

He nodded.

"Did you go to college or a trade school of any kind?"

"No."

"Why not?"

Eisenbrey glared at me as he enunciated each word slowly and with deliberation, "I pursued other interests."

"Okay. Have you ever had your IQ tested?"

"No." There was a hard quality to his response that set off an alarm in me, but I didn't seem to be able to stop myself from plunging forward.

"Would you be willing to take an IQ test if I could arrange it?"

His body became remarkably still, reminiscent of an ice statue, as he stared at me for several moments until I began to wonder if he had understood me. Then he said, "Look, Rebecca, I know all of my goddamned ABCs. Would you like to hear?"

"That won't be necessary," I said. I could feel my face flushing. I took the page with the sampling of test questions that I was about to ask him and slipped it under my stack of papers.

He jumped up from his bed and grabbed onto the bars of his cell, his eyes full of menace. The muscles in his chest and abdomen flexed as his fingers clutched the steel. "Of course it isn't necessary, and it isn't necessary for me to prove my intellect to you either. Where the hell do you get off asking me to do that?" he practically shouted at me.

"Okay, I'm sorry," I said, holding up my hands in a placating gesture.

"That fucking psychiatrist wanted to test me too but I told him to sit and spin. If you want to know how intelligent I am, you could just ask for a copy of my school transcripts." He paused, pondering that for a moment, and then added, "Except the only thing that would tell you is that I wasn't interested in school." He shook his head and sighed. "Are you concerned that I'm not smart enough for you?"

"No," I said quickly. "Not at all."

"Well then why did you ask me that? What were you hoping to get?"

"I'm not sure," I admitted. But I did get something, the sense that I was in peril while he was angry with me, and it exhilarated me.

"Don't do it again," he warned. "I'm not making myself available to you so you can test or study me. Bars or no bars, I'm no fucking lab rat. I have allowed you to come here so you can make a record of my life story."

As he sat back down on his bed and regarded me, my eyes wandered back to his chest. Why did the bastard have to sit there with his shirt open? Seeing this much of him unnerved and distracted me. How was I supposed to stay calm, cool, and collected during our interview while I daydreamed about pressing my face against his chest? I wondered if his hair would feel coarse or soft and what his scent was like; I was always too far away to tell.

"Take your hair out of that ponytail," he demanded in a quiet voice.

"What? Why?" I sputtered.

"Because I want to see what you look like with your hair down. It'll give me something to think about later."

So he did think about me after I left. It was nice to have that question answered. And I found that I liked his answer. "Okay." I removed the band and fluffed my hair a little.

"Hmm. Now put it back up."

Irritation swelled up in me that he felt he could order me around. The man's arrogance knew no bounds, yet a part of me enjoyed the way he took charge. I wanted him to be the alpha male. "Did it ever occur to you that your behavior might be offensive to me?" I snapped as I wrapped the band around my hair again.

"Are you here to write a book on etiquette?" He paused and glowered at me until I looked away from him. "I didn't think so."

I sighed, disgusted with myself. I had allowed him to have too much control over the interview. I needed to get something accomplished. I hadn't driven all the way out here just so he could screw with me. "Let's talk about you. Tell me, Tom, how many times have you killed?"

"Hey, I told you, it's Mr. Eisenbrey to you," he grumbled.

"Fuck you," I said. "I'm calling you Tom." Danger swirled around me as I said it and I felt an unmistakable thrill at having spoken like that to a creature so deadly, something I would never have done if not for the protection of the formidable steel barrier between us.

Eisenbrey sat up straight and gawked at me, then seemed perplexed as I managed to hold his steady gaze for several moments without flinching. He finally settled back against the wall again and answered my question. "Oh hell, I couldn't even guess how many animals I've killed."

"How many people have you killed?"

"Ah-ah-ah." He wagged his finger at me. "You promised that you would be a good girl and not ask me anything that could get me in any further dutch with the law. Remember what I said about not burning any bridges."

"Yes, but I'm supposed to be writing a book about a bad boy. I want to know just how bad you are."

Tom leaned forward, his elbows rested on his knees and he pressed steepled fingers against his chin. As he studied me I felt the tension between us ratchet up a few notches. "I don't think you really do."

Flustered, I glanced at my notes again and then said, "Tell me about the incident with the guard."

"Which one?"

"Is there more than one?"

"Okay," he relented. "I suppose there was one guard that actually got injured. The other stuff was just bullshit."

"The attack on Wilson Stills is what I want to hear about. You bit him. I want to know why. Is biting a compulsion? Do you have some kind of fantasy about being a vampire?" It was meant as a serious question, but that had no bearing on his reaction.

Eisenbrey fell back on his bed and crumpled into a fit of boisterous laughter that seemed to shake his entire body and rendered him completely unable to respond. The sound of his guffaws bounced off of the walls of the otherwise silent cement hallway, slicing through the bleak atmosphere of death row.

I cast a self-conscious glance toward the control room and found the guard standing in the window, watching me. I crossed my legs and waited patiently for Eisenbrey's fit to subside, feeling like a complete idiot. I took that moment to flip through my notes and questions for the day. Eventually he seemed to compose himself. He sat back up on the edge of his bed and sighed heavily.

"Tom," I started, but then I was interrupted by a fresh wave of raucous laughter. "I'm glad you find me so hilarious," I said tersely.

"Me too, sugar. God knows there's precious little to laugh about in this place," he said as he shook his head and then pushed his dark hair back from his face.

That was a sobering thought, and it lessened the irritation I felt at being the subject of his amusement. After several moments he finally quieted, but then another tenacious giggle escaped him and I lost my patience.

"Oh, for Chrissakes! Settle down! I have to ask you this stuff. I need to understand what motivates you."

"Fine, now you know something that motivates me to laugh my ass off. You've been reading too many of those Twilight books."

"Okay, I'll take that as a no to the vampire ideation, but what about my other question. Is it a compulsion?"

"No, I don't feel compelled to bite people. I'm just not squeamish about doing that if it serves my goal. Teeth can come in handy in the absence of other weapons, and getting bitten hurts like a motherfucker."

"Have you ever been bitten?"

"Of course I have; I had a brother and once upon a time we were children."

"Did remembering that make you want to bite the guard and the other law enforcement personnel?" A vision of the massive scar on Scanlon's neck flashed through my head, unbidden.

"Rebecca," he said, and then sighed wearily. "Do you want to hear that I had a fucked up childhood and that it molded me into who I am today? The psychiatrists have already barked up that tree. Maybe parts of it were bad, but I don't have any memory that stands out that involves biting. I didn't particularly like to bite those fellas. Like I said, it was just one of the methods at my disposal for getting what I wanted, so I did it."

"What did you want from Stills?"

"I wanted to get even with the little fucker."

"For what?"

"He insulted me about seven months earlier. It didn't set well with me. I decided that I would do something to him later. I was friendly with him for a while. I let him think that things were okay between us so he would relax around me. Then, one day when he came and put me in the handcuffs and entered my cell, I got him. In retrospect, it wasn't my brightest move to do that while I was handcuffed. I wasn't able to cover my head when they started beating me with their batons, but then I'm always restrained when one of the guards is in an enclosed area with me."

"You waited seven months? And you were angry with him that whole time?"

Eisenbrey nodded.

"Why so long? Was that your first opportunity?"

"No. He came in my cell at least a couple times a week. I was just waiting for the right time. That's important to me, to wait until it feels right to attack."

"Why is that?"

"So I will…" he paused a few seconds as he searched for the right words, "enjoy it fully."

"What do you mean? Do you get sexually aroused when you kill?"

"Sometimes, but everything isn't about sex. There's a much bigger desire that I need to satisfy. I want to conquer. I want complete control, and what's more complete than murder? The ultimate power trip. Make no mistake; there is nothing in this world that I love more than taking a human life. I *need* to kill." He shrugged. "That's who I am, and I sure as shit am not going to apologize for it."

I was surprised by his blatant admission, amazed that he had opened up to me like that.

"You know it's odd, I haven't seen Stills since then. He must not want to work with me anymore." Eisenbrey smiled fondly and he said, "Why do you look so surprised? Seven months isn't a long time; I waited ten years to get even with those hunters." His smile vanished and iciness crept into his eyes. He was feeling something different just then, something far darker than he had felt while remembering the guard. I could feel the vice-grip of tension surround me. I couldn't tell if it radiated from him or if my mind reacted to what I knew him to be, but I was grateful for the bars that separated us.

"Ten years? Which hunters are you talking about? The first group —the triple murder in 1983?" I glanced at the victim list then back at him. I saw him nod almost imperceptibly. "You were sixteen then. Do you mean they did something to you as a child? Would you like to talk about the hunters?"

"Not today," he said simply. I watched him as his mood changed. It looked as though he employed some kind of mental technique to calm himself. His breathing became controlled and steady and I could see the hatred leaving his features. He gazed at me with a placid smile, that perhaps would be better described as caressing me with his eyes. "I've never spoken this much to a woman…to anyone."

"What about your mother?" I asked.

"No. We didn't talk that much. I liked to be alone. I used to spend most of my time in the woods. I used to find things to kill… animals." He checked my reaction and then continued. "Dad used to take us hunting."

"You and your brother, David?" I interjected.

"Yeah. I remember one time Davy managed to hit a deer and it went down. When we got to it, we found that it was only wounded. The deer seemed afraid, but it was injured too badly to run. Dad said we had to finish it off and put the poor thing out of its misery. He didn't look too pleased about it. The funny thing was, I didn't mind watching it suffer. I liked it." He seemed distant for a moment, lost in his thoughts.

"Dad got out his hunting knife and tried to hand it to Davy, but the pussy wouldn't take it, so I grabbed it. Dad started up like he was going to explain what to do, but I already knew what to do. I was in a trance. I held the deer, wrapped my arms around its head and shoulders, like I was giving it a hug. Then I brought the knife around and slit its throat wide open." Tom smiled fondly. "Then it went limp. I felt the life go out of it. I realized — I did that. I took its life and I felt so intoxicated with power. Surprised the hell out of Dad and Davy. They just stood there and stared at me for the longest time. And it made such a goddamned mess. There was so much blood. It got all over me and my clothes. I was a sight." He smiled widely, still far away.

I found it interesting that his fond memories of childhood were so very different from mine, which tended to involve a vacation or a trip to the beach with my parents.

"When we got back to the house, and mother saw me, she nearly lost it. At first she thought I had been mortally wounded, but I was grinning from ear to ear. I couldn't help it. Then she became afraid. Oh, the look of relief on that woman's face when Dad and Davy walked in the door behind me…" he laughed and shook his head. "I just know she thought I'd actually done it."

"Done what?"

"Killed Dad, or Davy, or both of them." He sat silent for a while, watching me, gauging my reaction. "Then Dad showed me how to butcher the deer. We cut it up and gave the pieces to mom and she put it in the freezer. That was fun. That was the only time Dad was fun, when we were hunting or fishing. He didn't…trust me." I detected bitterness in his tone. Then he smirked. "What are you thinking about?"

I suppose I had been staring at him, enrapt as he spoke about his childhood, and it had given me that lightheaded feeling again. His unusual eye color, a deep and vibrant blue that didn't seem like it could occur in nature, made me curious. "Do you wear contacts?" I asked.

He seemed mildly perplexed. "No Rebecca, I don't. My eyesight is 20/15." He leaned toward me as he spoke, his expression so intense that it caused my pulse to quicken. "All the better to see you with." I flinched, which seemed to amuse him. "It's one of my attributes that makes me an excellent hunter. I can see a lot of things that other people don't."

"I know you do," I muttered. Then I caught his sneer out of the corner of my eye. "What was that?"

"What?" he said, wide-eyed with innocence.

"I saw you smile. What's so funny?" I asked, irritated that he enjoyed my unease.

"I didn't smile. You must be seeing things."

"I thought you wanted this book too. I don't see why you need to be so damned unpleasant to me."

"Unpleasant?" he said, feigning surprise. Then his face hardened into a cruel mask. "Are you sure you're not seeing things?"

I froze mid-breath, thinking of the dark figure in the back seat of my car, and then again at the foot of my bed. The only explanation that made sense was that my mind had caused me to see these things. And I suspected it was in response to the stress I felt when I was with this man.

Enough. He had my nerves on edge again. It seemed like a good place to end the interview. I turned off the recorder. "It's time for me to go." I picked up my bag and stood.

"Why are you leaving so soon? You're allowed another thirty minutes with me." He seemed genuinely disappointed.

"I'm sorry. I need some time to see my aunt and uncle on my way home," I said. "They're in the mountains. I'd really like to avoid driving out there in the snow when it's dark." I gave myself a mental kick for telling him something so personal.

"I see, are they your surrogate parents?" A direct hit, and my face told him so.

My mouth hung slightly ajar.

"How old were you when your parents died?" he continued.

"Who said my parents are dead?" I countered.

"I just did, and you did...with your eyes." He smiled kindly. "Initially, I thought that perhaps my age and the early loss of your father might have been the cause of your intense attraction to me, but that was when I labored under the delusion that I was twenty years your senior. Now that I've had to rule out the daddy complex theory—what is it that keeps you coming back? Why are you so drawn to me? Is it merely the *bad boy* aspect? Or is it something interesting?" He tapped his finger on the table as he awaited my response.

What was it, indeed? I squirmed, involuntarily. I had no answer for him. I certainly didn't need this motherfucker peering into the depths of my soul.

"Tell me, Rebecca, should I do something bad to turn you on? Something very, very bad? I'm sure I could think of something you'd like."

I didn't like the look on his face as he said it, hard and unyielding. I cleared my throat. "That won't be necessary."

"I have done many things over the years that weren't necessary."

"What I would like for you to do is follow the rules here and remain in good standing so your visitation privileges aren't revoked," I said, my voice level.

"You would miss me wouldn't you? Are you sure I shouldn't try something small? I really don't mind doing bad things." Then he added in a whisper, "I've even been known to enjoy it." He winked at me.

I searched his eyes, and found a darkness that stretched on ad infinitum. At first I mistook the iciness, the absence of kindness, for emptiness, but no. Something malevolent inside of him peered back at me, causing me to shiver. And whatever that dark entity was, it made Tom smile.

ELEVEN

It took a little more than three hours to drive from Walla Walla to where my aunt and uncle lived in Easton. The small town populated with less than five hundred people, sat close to Interstate 90, The Summit at Snoqualmie ski resort, and was surrounded by the Okanogan-Wenatchee National Forest. Easton saw a lot of snow during the winter so all of the buildings there had steeply pitched, metal roofs. My aunt and uncle lived in the woods about a mile out of town. It was remote. Their yard consisted mostly of forest with a small patch of lawn and a deck.

I felt the last of my stress dissipate as I drove up their long, gravel driveway that was blanketed in about eight inches of snow. The sky was dark, the moon concealed by cloud cover. The only illumination other than my headlights came from the security light attached to their log cabin styled house.

Aunt Susan showered me with kisses as I entered the house and the warmth of their wood stove took away the chill from the winter air outside. Her pale-blue eyes and silvery-white hair reminded me of my mother. My aunt seemed to look more like her every year though she was well past the age of my mother when she had died. "It's been too long," she said.

"You're right. I'm sorry," I told her.

Uncle Harry gave me a wave of acknowledgment from the living room, but kept his ass planted in his La-Z-Boy chair. He had his feet up and I knew how loathe he was to leave his comfy place once he settled into it. My aunt and I shared the couch next to Uncle Harry's chair, and I put my feet up on their coffee table, thankful that this was such an informal house, a place where I could relax completely, where I truly felt at home.

We all sat facing the 65" big screen TV, which must have been out of commission at that moment. A small table in front of it held the 19" TV that I recognized from their guest room. Did this qualify as a tragedy? I examined Uncle Harry's face, wondering how he was taking the loss.

"You poor thing," I said. "What happened to your baby?"

"She's gone. She passed away this morning at 10:34 a.m., we then observed a few minutes of silence." Harry looked more like a man who had lost a family member than an electronic device.

"It was only silent until he set up the spare. God, it was wonderful to hear myself think for a little while," Aunt Susan said wistfully.

Harry grimaced. "There's nothing more emasculating than having to watch a small screen. We'll have to go into Ellensburg tomorrow morning to replace her. I can't live this way very long."

Nor did I want this big, beer drinking, NFL watching man to have to live like this, nay exist. I loved my aunt and uncle very much. It pained me to see Uncle Harry reduced to this. Aunt Susan decided to lift the mood. "Would you like a cookie, dear?" she asked me. Then to him, she said, "I know you would."

She walked into the kitchen and he called after her. "I love your chocolate chip cookies, baby. I didn't think you were going to let me have any."

She returned in an instant with a decorative bowl full of the treats. "I had to hide them," she told me. "Otherwise he would have eaten the whole goddamned batch."

"That's true," Harry confessed. "You're a good woman, Suzie." He leaned in, grabbed two of the cookies and gave her a wink.

I took one and tasted it. "These are really good, Aunt Sue. Thanks."

"Now, let's get down to more important matters," she said, sitting herself next to me on the couch. She faced me. "Why the hell haven't we seen you in three months? What's going on?"

"Well, first it was because I was depressed and drinking too much."

"Oh-oh," Aunt Sue said under her breath.

"But lately, it's because I'm working on another book."

"You should have called me! Why were you depressed?" Aunt Susan asked.

"Well…you did read the last book, didn't you? Wouldn't you have been depressed?"

"I hear ya, pumpkin. That third one really blew chunks," Harry agreed cheerfully. Aunt Susan shot him a look, but before she could scold him, he added, "What's your new story going to be about?"

"I'm actually working on a non-fiction project, a book about a serial killer."

"No shit?" Harry said leaning forward, his interest piqued. "Which one?"

"Thomas Eisenbrey," I told them, and tried to gauge their reactions.

"The Hunter? I'll be damned," Harry said. "He's a sick one if the news people got it right. Have you met him?"

"Yes. I just did my third interview with him at the prison out in Walla Walla."

"I'll bet it makes you feel creepy to talk with him," Susan said in a knowing way as she gave my shoulder a gentle pat.

Yes, Aunt Susan, that's one of the feelings that he gives me and the other ones I probably shouldn't tell you about. I nodded in solemn agreement.

"What's his deal?" Uncle Harry asked. "Is he some kind of crazy environmentalist that hates people who kill animals or something?"

"No, I don't think so," I replied, recalling Eisenbrey's vivid description of the time he killed his first deer.

"Well, why did he keep taking out hunting parties?"

"I don't know. He hasn't been willing to talk about that yet. I'll ask him again."

"How many people did he kill?" Uncle Harry asked.

"He won't tell me that either. He's been convicted of nine murders —eight prior to his incarceration, and one inside Walla Walla. I'm positive those are only a fraction of the killings he's responsible for."

"What *has* he told you?" Aunt Susan asked.

"We've talked about his family and his childhood, and a girlfriend that he strangled to death."

"God Almighty, that poor girl! Wouldn't it be a nightmare to be *his* girlfriend?" she said. It was a real blessing she couldn't see any of the unsavory thoughts I had rolling around in my mind on that topic. "What did she do to piss him off?"

"She said something that irritated him, but he couldn't remember what."

"Maybe she said he had a small dick," Uncle Harry offered. "Us boys don't like to hear that sort of thing from a woman." He gave Aunt Susan an accusatory glare, to which she raised an eyebrow. Then she smiled and winked at him, and he smiled too. I had to hand it them, they had a bizarre way of flirting with each other, and judging by their expressions, that was definitely what it had turned into. Those two always joked around, flinging insults back and forth, but I couldn't recall ever seeing them engage in anything I would call a real fight.

"Here, you can have another cookie," she told him in a low, husky voice, handing him the bowl. I had the distinct impression that cookie had become a metaphor for something else. The mood was getting a little uncomfortable. I let my eyes settle on the TV until they finished their silent message to one another.

Uncle Harry took a bite of his cookie and said, "I think she might love me."

"You might be right, you silly, old fart." Aunt Susan stood up and bent over him, kissing the bald and shiny top of Harry's head. A contented smile settled on his features.

My aunt and uncle looked so cute together and they both seemed really happy. It made me realize just how alone I was, and how much I wouldn't mind having what they had created together. I managed to stay and visit with them for another two hours, and then drove back to Bellevue, to my big, empty house, and the mysterious presence that haunted me.

That night as I lay in bed, waiting for sleep to come, I knew it was time to clear my mind of Eisenbrey. I must go somewhere else, somewhere pleasant. I thought of that nice detective, *Scanlon…Darryl… eyes the color of honey, the warm smile, and the phone number handwritten on the back of his business card.* I sighed at the happy thought. *What if I called him?*

But the thought trailed off, replaced by another, *blue eyes peering at me through steel bars, a hand outstretched…reaching through…inviting me. Inviting me where? Inside…*

My eyes snapped open and I found myself sitting bolt upright, clutching the edge of my mattress.

I needed relief. The need was intense, but I couldn't tell what would satiate me. It was maddening, like having an itch that was impossible to reach, a craving for some unknown entity I wasn't even sure existed.

I felt a void inside me and I knew of only one way to deal with it. I went downstairs, prepared some vodka and orange juice, then brought it back to my bedroom where I downed it with a couple of sleeping pills.

TWELVE

November 3rd, 2012

As I stood in front of the kitchen sink staring out into my backyard, I didn't see lawn, or trees, or the little shed where I kept my lawnmower.

I stood beside the body on the beige carpet, and the blood, and the pieces of something I didn't want to comprehend splattered on the wall behind him. I recognized the lifeless form as my father, although it seemed to have nothing to do with him. No, it was not really him, not anymore. I tried to fathom what had happened, feeling strangely disconnected from myself. It couldn't be true, but it was. He was gone — taken from me while I wasn't there to have any say in the matter. The reality of the situation started to take hold in my mind and I put my hand over my mouth, stifling my cry. A wave of nausea threatened.

This was terrible, unspeakable, inconceivable. How would my mother take it? She would be devastated. She needed me now more than ever, but where could she be?

My head turned toward the hallway and I sensed that something dreadful lay ahead, more horror to find, more nightmare to be revealed. I moved slowly, purposefully, up the hall, and then I saw the foot. My mother's foot. Her sandal had fallen off and it lay on the floor not far from her leg. I could see her painted toenails, the pearlescent nail polish that I had put on for her the night before. I stepped forward and peeked into the bedroom to see the rest of her. More blood. Mom lay on her side, shot through the torso. Had she been running away, and shot in the back? It was possible. There was blood splattered on the wall and bookshelf she faced. Could the person who killed my parents still be here lurking in the house? That was possible too. But I didn't really care. I felt tired and dazed.

I didn't enter the room that held my mother; the hallway seemed to be the closest I could go to her. I staggered slowly back to the living room and dialed 911, and after I had told the operator that they were dead, the sobs overtook me. I laid down the phone, unaware of whatever else the woman said, and sat out on the front steps in the sunshine, weeping, until the officers arrived.

And as I stood in my kitchen, twenty-four years later, the tears overtook me again. I let out a scream of frustration, then I hurled the glass I held across the room and it smashed into the cupboards. It was shattered. Who was I kidding? I was shattered. And nothing in the world could ever fix me.

THIRTEEN

November 4th, 2012

Scanlon had picked the perfect time to set up another meeting for us. My mood had crashed, and I'd felt more than a little unfocused until he had called. I knew seeing him would cheer me up and probably help me get my head back on my work. I wasn't going to complain about having a nice dinner on the Edmonds waterfront with a handsome detective. We watched the ferryboats come and go as Scanlon and I hashed over information that I already knew about Eisenbrey. There were no new revelations on that front.

"I read your books," he said. "The first two books were amazing." He seemed sweet, with his ready smile and his honey-colored eyes so full of like for me. Being with Scanlon felt like taking a happy pill. He didn't even mention the third book; God bless him.

The waiter brought the bill, and we both reached for it at the same time. "Oh, no you don't," he said.

"Darryl, I should get it. It's been very nice of you to meet with me and share information about Eisenbrey."

"Yes, but that's not why I wanted to see you. I asked you out; I'm going to get this." He snatched the bill from me.

"Oh, was this a date?"

"Well, that's what I was shooting for. You couldn't tell, huh?" He chuckled.

"It was very subtle," I admitted.

Darryl tucked his credit card into the leather bill folder and handed it to the waiter. Then he rested his arms on the table, tapping it absentmindedly with one of his fingers. Gazing at me, he said, "Rebecca, there's something I want to tell you."

"Okay," I said.

He swallowed and said, "I'm extremely attracted to you."

His directness startled me. "Thanks, Darryl. I'm attracted to you too."

Even in the dim light of the restaurant, I could see a little more color in his face than there had been moments earlier. He seemed fidgety. "Yeah, but what I really mean to say is…it's more than that. I've never felt this attracted to anyone else."

This admission surprised me even more. And there was something odd about his expression. He didn't look happy about what he'd said. He looked worried as he studied my reaction. I wasn't sure how to respond. After a beat, I realized my mouth was hanging open, so I shut it and then I gave him what I hoped looked like a warm smile. It would be disingenuous to tell him he was the most handsome man I'd ever met. I could think of a man in Walla Walla that was better looking, although Darryl was a close second. Right about when my continued silence had caused the moment to become awkward, the waiter returned and handed Darryl the bill folder.

Darryl thanked the waiter and signed the credit card authorization. Then he smiled at me and said, "Okay. Ready to head out?"

"Yes."

Darryl came around to my side of the table where I stood. He removed my jacket from the back of my chair and held it up for me as I slipped into it. "Thanks," I murmured.

Then he donned his own jacket, and we left the restaurant.

We spent much of the drive back to my house in content silence, and after a while, I decided to bring up something that had been nagging away at me. "Darryl, Eisenbrey told me something funny during our last visit."

"Yeah, I'll bet he's a real comedian when you just give him a chance."

"He said you planted evidence in order to get him. He was sure he hadn't left anything incriminating behind when he killed those hunters in Idaho." I looked out the window. I smiled, feeling a little amused that Eisenbrey would stoop low enough to make a claim like that. I felt sure that most inmates said similar things. When I looked back at Scanlon, he wore an expression that I didn't expect to see—wary, guarded.

"I got the right guy. Eisenbrey is the one who killed those people," he said tersely.

Not quite the response I had expected. That sounded surprisingly like an admission to me, and it momentarily shut down our conversation. I wasn't sure what to do with that little jewel. Was I supposed to feel bad for Eisenbrey? Should I be incensed at the injustice of it? That seemed ridiculous. Scanlon was right; he had gotten the right man. Eisenbrey had boasted about killing them, not to mention the pride that he displayed about what he'd done to Scanlon's throat.

The murderer had gotten what he deserved. What was there to feel bad about? And yet, I found myself feeling protective of Eisenbrey and harboring some resentment toward Scanlon. I tried unsuccessfully to push those thoughts from my mind, but then I had to ask, "Are you saying that you did it?"

"What's worse—allowing him to run around killing whoever he pleases, or making sure we had a solid case? Personally, I can sleep easier because he's locked up."

I inhaled sharply, surprised that he was being so forthright with me. This man was so different from other law enforcement personnel I'd met over the years—different from most men in general. He was opening up to me.

"Look, you don't know what it was like back then. He was still loose. We didn't know if we were going to have enough evidence to convict him for the triple homicide near his hometown, and his more recent kill sites were providing even less. We were afraid that, if we did manage to capture him, we wouldn't have cause to hold him. That's one rollercoaster ride I don't ever want to be on again. And then I heard about the kill site they found in Idaho."

"So—a moment of weakness…"

"It wasn't weakness," he snapped. "That decision took strength."

"Hmm. You must have struggled all night with it." I hadn't intended it to sound as sarcastic as it had.

"No. I didn't," he said, his voice harsh. It seemed as though those might be his last words on the topic, but then he continued. "A man in my position can't get all emotional about this crap. Bottom line: less innocent people are dead. And now I know I won't be called out to some campsite in the forest to clean up after another one of his dark little parties. Judge me if you must, but I know my actions have saved a lot of lives."

"I don't want to judge you, Darryl," I said quietly, and it was true. His reasoning wasn't incomprehensible. He'd shared something important with me tonight. He'd let me in. I felt an affinity with him. "It must be difficult for you, and for the other officers, when you have to deal with a murder scene." A feeling I knew all too well.

Scanlon stole a brief glance in my direction as he drove. He appeared tentative, cautious. "Yes it is. The images always pop back in my head when I least expect it."

We remained quiet in the car for the rest of the drive. Then, after parking in my driveway, he leaned over and surprised me with a kiss on the mouth. "Have you ever woken up next to a detective?"

I thought about that for a moment and then answered honestly, "No. I had a quickie with one once, but no overnights."

"Hmm." He chuckled, raising an eyebrow. "Would you like to?" He wrapped his arms tighter around me which felt awkward because we both had to lean over the stick shift in the center panel between the seats. I had just realized this position was putting an uncomfortable strain on my back muscles when I felt his hand slip not only under my blouse but inside my bra as well. I gasped. Scanlon's fingers moved gently, and he began to caress my nipple, making it hard, and making me all too aware that it felt extremely good to be up against him.

"This seems kind of fast," I mumbled into his shoulder. But his body felt warm, he smelled of spicy cologne, and his insistent hand caused my arousal to grow. I felt my senses drifting and thought I could really enjoy this man, if only I didn't feel so confounded. If only I could stop picturing Tom Eisenbrey on top of me every time I closed my eyes. My eyes blinked open and my body jerked, though I was still pinned against the car seat.

Scanlon whispered into my hair, "It's okay."

He seemed like a nice man. There was no question that I found him attractive, and it had been far too long since I had been in bed with a man, so I couldn't believe my own words as they tumbled out of my mouth, "Darryl, I'd better not."

"Are you sure? You don't know what you're missing," he said with a wink.

"I can see you think that detectives are all the rage, but honestly, I haven't been trying to catch one." It was a lame attempt at humor, and I suppose I was trying to be gentle about having to reject him. I hadn't said or done anything about his wandering hand however. I didn't particularly want him to stop. It felt good to be desired after being lonely for such a long time. Scanlon had skills, and if he was that good with the top half it seemed reasonable that he would be good with my bottom half too.

"Forget I'm a detective then. I'm just a man, and you're a woman, and I want you," he breathed into my ear. His hand slipped out of my bra. Then, in one fluid movement, he leaned into me, pressing my back into the car seat, and moved his hand up my skirt until it rested between my thighs. "Come on, Rebecca, let me in," he said gently. I wanted to, but my emotions were conflicted. His fingers moved around on the outside of my panties slowly, exploring, then he applied some extra pressure to my clit with his forefinger. I had a sudden jolt of pleasure that caused a sharp intake of breath. Did I just cum? No, there wasn't any kind of release, the tension still continued to build. "Hmm, you liked that," he noticed.

"Darryl, please…"

"Can you say pretty please?" he said as he kissed my neck. He pushed at the lacy material and slipped his fingers inside my panties. The skin on skin contact felt amazing. I moaned. His mouth was at my ear, "Come on, let's go to your bedroom so I can do this properly. There's not enough room in the car."

"Please," I said again, not feeling sure what I wanted. He continued with the slow motion of his fingers and found my wetness. He had just begun to slide his finger inside me when a jolt of panic interrupted the moment. I felt a clear message, as if someone had spoken in my ear, but I didn't know where it came from. *You cannot allow this to happen.* "Darryl, please stop," I managed, breathlessly.

"Huh? Stop?" He sounded confused. "It feels like you want this, like you need it as much as I do," he said in a bedroom voice that softly tried to persuade me. Then he leaned back to gaze into my eyes, and his tone changed, and became more guarded. He moved his hand to a slightly safer location, my thigh. "What is it? You're not attracted to me? I put you on the spot back at the restaurant, didn't I?"

"No," I said.

"Is it my scar?" He touched his neck with his other hand as he said it. "Pretty bad, isn't it?"

"No way. Scars are sexy," I assured him. "That only makes you hotter."

"So I'm hot, am I? Does that mean you like me?" He leaned into me again and his hand slid back to the danger zone. He buried his nose in my hair and sighed. No one could accuse Scanlon of traveling too slow through an intersection after he saw what he perceived to be a green light.

"Whoa!" I said, more forcefully than I'd intended. He withdrew his hand, and I could see hurt and confusion competing in his features. I wanted to soften the blow. "I like you very much. Too much."

"What does that mean? Why is it too much?"

"I'm going through some stuff right now. I'm a mess." Was any of that true? It sounded vague and ridiculous, even to me. I suppose I had been a bit depressed lately, and had been drinking more than normal, but that had tapered off since I started working on the new project. And anyway, it didn't really escalate enough to pose any barrier to getting laid. I mean, seriously, it had been more than a year for me. But the feeling was still present—the warning.

"What kind of stuff?" he asked. He leaned back to examine my reaction, ever the detective.

"I'm under a lot of stress with the book…deadlines…"

"Yeah, the book," he repeated. "This has something to do with Eisenbrey, doesn't it? Are you attracted to him?"

"No! Why would you say that?" I asked.

"Uh-huh." He didn't seem to buy it. He was probably very good at his job. "How do you feel about people like him—murderers?"

"Well, I'm against it, of course." I sounded like a smart-ass just then, but it irritated me that he would even ask.

"What about the death penalty?"

"I'm all for it in certain cases—for people that kill repeatedly."

"And in Eisenbrey's case?" he shot at me.

"Well, I uh…" I tucked a strand of my hair behind my ear and considered Tom's upcoming execution. He was scheduled to hang on September 30th of next year, a thought which brought me no joy. In fact, it felt wrong. "Yeah, in his case, definitely." I found myself nodding to support my own statement.

Darryl's gaze didn't waver. "You know what, kiddo?" he said, tracing the back of his finger down the length of my nose in a playful manner. "You hesitated a little too long there. He's getting in your head, isn't he?"

"No, it's not that. It's just…he's not quite as unpleasant as I thought he'd be." That was all I was willing to confess, but his eyes narrowed, and his expression told me he suspected I was struggling with a lot more.

"Rebecca," Darryl said. He started caressing my hair. "I want you to be careful with that guy. I care about you. I don't want to see you get hurt."

"How could I get hurt? He's locked up in a cell. He can't touch me." I said.

"He's a smart guy, and a convincing liar. He manipulates people."

"He's not going to manipulate me. I won't let him."

"Sure," he muttered. His eyes dropped to my blouse. I realized my top button was undone. It must have happened when he slid his hand in my shirt. I could see he was still aroused. I fastened the button, and he gave a disappointed groan.

"It's time to say goodnight, Darryl. Thank you for a lovely evening."

He had to be angry, or at the very least really irritated, but he forced a smile. "All right, if you want me to go, I will. But are you positive that you want to pass up the opportunity to tap this? I am a fine piece of ass, if I do say so myself." He laughed his infectious laugh, and I giggled along with him. It made me want to kiss him again, and I did give him a quick kiss on the cheek as I got out of his car.

I stood in the driveway and waved as I watched him drive off. No longer could I hide from the reason I had said no to Scanlon. I went straight to my laptop and opened my slide show with the pictures of Eisenbrey.

FOURTEEN

November 5th, 2012

When I arrived at the guard's booth, Lutz greeted me and told me that he would walk me to Eisenbrey's cell. "Hey Andy, I'm curious about something. I was wondering if you could shed some light on it. Why does DiMaggio treat Eisenbrey so poorly? What's his deal?"

"Oh, that guy's mean to everyone, but he has taken an exceptional dislike to Eisenbrey. I don't know why. Those two are always swapping insults." The young guard had a troubled expression. He leaned toward me and lowered his volume, making sure that we were out of earshot of the other guard on duty that day, Officer Jones. "Sometimes DiMaggio goes down to Eisenbrey's cell and talks to him. I can't hear what he says, but I'm sure it's nothing good. He likes to taunt him. It must be awful to be trapped in there and have to listen to DiMaggio's shit." Lutz shook his head sadly. He had more empathy for the prisoners than anyone else in this place.

"I'll bet he was the meanest kid on the playground."

"I'll tell you something strange. Don Avery went to school with DiMaggio. They've known each other most of their lives. And he said that DiMaggio used to be a really nice guy. They were friends back then."

With great difficulty, I tried to imagine a world where DiMaggio was a pleasant human being, but I just wasn't able to make that materialize in my head. "Hmm, I wonder what drove him to the dark side."

"Maybe it was this place. People change when they start working here. It can make them ugly."

"Not you though, Andy."

"Thanks." He glanced down, and dimples formed on his cheeks as he broke into a bashful grin. "I'm glad you're here to see Tom today. He's been missing you. He really looks forward to your visits."

I was tempted to ask Lutz what made him think that Eisenbrey missed me. Had he said something about me? But the thought of asking him made me feel like I was in middle school again. Still, I smiled as Lutz told Jones all was clear and the solid steel door slid open. I felt a little more upbeat after Lutz's comment.

Eisenbrey's question caught me off guard.

"What happened?" He walked up to the bars and wrapped his long, slender fingers around one of them, peering at me with narrowed eyes.

"What do you mean?" I said. Lutz quietly set up the folding chair for me and walked away, leaving us to our conversation.

"Something's happened. You saw someone. Who was it?" he demanded.

Tired of asking myself how he knew these things, I just decided to accept it. I knew he wasn't referring to my chat with Lutz.

"I saw Scanlon yesterday."

"Really. Was it business or personal?" As I tried to sort out how to describe my time with Scanlon he fired another question at me. "Was it a date?"

"Well…I thought we were meeting about you, but then he told me that he wanted it to be a date."

Tom breathed out slowly as if trying to calm his temper. It sounded like a hiss. "Look Rebecca, I won't have you fraternizing with the man who put me in here. Do you understand me?"

"Yes. I think I have all the information I need from him, so I shouldn't have to see him anymore."

"I don't care whether or not you have the information you need. You are not to speak to that man again. I mean it. I'll know if you do, and I will not be pleased." There was a sharper edge to this statement than any of the other things he had said.

"Why?" I said. My arms hung at my side, palms out.

"I don't want anyone to interfere with the connection that we have. If you see him again these interviews will stop."

So he felt the connection too. I definitely felt it, and was flooded with relief that I wasn't alone. I wondered if he would seriously stop our interviews if I spoke to Scanlon again, but I didn't want to risk it. The thought of not seeing Eisenbrey caused an unexpected wave of anguish in me. I nodded weakly. Then we both sat down, and I started the recorder.

I studied his face. It looked like he had about two or three days of razor stubble this time. Some guys just seemed sloppy when they didn't shave, but it made Tom look sexy. He sat on his bed with both feet on the floor and leaned forward in a relaxed manner, elbows on his knees.

I started asking him the questions I had prepared, but at some point I must have started spacing out. Focused solely on his appearance and what it did to me, I lost track of what I had planned to ask.

He ran his fingers through his dark, wavy hair, pushing it away from his forehead, and leaned his back against the wall. He was like a work of art by Michelangelo, so magnificent, so unattainable. Frustration dug its pointy, little fingernails into the back of my neck and raked downward as I pined for what I could not have. My pet, my beloved pet, secure in his cage, where no other women could ever touch him, unable to run away from me. *My precious pet that I will never be allowed to pet.*

His lips parted, one side of his mouth curling into a half smile, and his eyes narrowed again. I sensed the wheels turning inside that beautiful head of his. He rubbed his jaw. I watched him and wondered, *are his whiskers rough like sandpaper?* I wanted to know. In spite of my fear, I felt the desire to touch him, to feel his skin. I couldn't help myself—I started to visualize Tom in my bedroom, lying down on my bed. He had captured me with his cerulean eyes, and I felt mesmerized. I was bewitched, and almost as if he had lassoed me with an invisible rope, he pulled me toward him. The silent, unspoken, irresistible draw of Thomas Eisenbrey.

His effect on me was so overwhelming, I worried about the power this gave him because he would only abuse it. He had already proven he was the kind of man who victimized others again and again in the most terrible ways, reveling in the joy it brought him. He wore a serious expression, and I realized he must have said something to me.

"Hmm?"

"What planet were you visiting? Am I boring you?"

"Oh, I'm sorry. I must be a little tired," I said.

"You weren't sleepy. You were daydreaming about being in bed with me."

He already knew me too well. And of course he was right, so I let that go without commenting. Then I noticed an open envelope on his table and a small photograph lying next to it. Curiosity got the better of me. "Is that a letter?"

He rested his elbow on the table and chuckled. "Yes, it's a letter from a woman, and a photo. Would you like to see?"

"Sure," I said. He stood and held the photo up close to the bars. I leaned forward to get a good look. The young woman was tall and had long, blond hair. She was wearing a cowboy hat, boots and a G-string. I resisted the temptation to roll my eyes. "She's very pretty."

"Yes, she is. Some of them are. I only answer the good-looking ones." He placed the photo on his table again and sat on his bed.

"You have women writing to you? Are these women that you knew prior to being incarcerated?"

He leaned back, hands clasped behind his head, and regarded me with mild amusement. "No. It's just fan mail, but it can be entertaining, especially when they send nude photos."

"Really?" I suppose that shouldn't have surprised me. I had heard of women becoming obsessed with other serial killers, and he was infamous. But what kind of sick woman would want to communicate with a man who she probably knew nothing about except for the fact that he loved to kill and sat on death row? Perhaps I should be asking myself that question. And why did this new information make me feel so…irritated? No, I did not like it.

"My, what an interesting expression you have on your face," he commented. "You're jealous, aren't you?" That knowing look had returned, and it infuriated me.

"Don't be ridiculous."

"You don't like me talking to other women. Do you consider me your territory that you have to defend? Hmm. I've hit a nerve. You're ticked off." He was right.

"Okay. Would you like to know how I feel? It really pisses me off that I can't interview you without having to listen to a bunch of desperate, delusional horseshit about how my panties get wet every time I come to see you. It's getting old and tired."

I must have said that louder than I had intended. Jones shouted up the hallway, "What's the matter over there? Trouble in paradise?"

My subject leaned forward in his chair, his expression cold and hardened. "All right, Rebecca, if that's how you want it, that's how you'll get it. Fire away with your next question."

And I did, but it felt as though the rest of the interview was a waste of my time. He became distant and businesslike, and I didn't get anything more of value from our time together. The real Thomas Eisenbrey had withdrawn.

FIFTEEN

When I returned to the car, my first order of business was to grope around under the driver's seat to find my flask and dump the remaining whiskey down my throat. The lightness of the container in my hand depressed me. It hadn't been nearly enough.

I checked my cellphone and saw that I had two voicemails. The first was from Kat, a simple message consisting of two words, "Call me." In fact, this was the second message from her this week. I needed to return her call. Kat was an understanding woman. She would allow me to vent, then she might tell me off for getting involved in this, but Kat would care, and that went a long way.

The next message was from Andrea. I played it. "Right. You haven't answered my emails yet so, apparently, it's time for me to proceed to the annoying message phase of our relationship. You were supposed to send me your initial chapters two days ago, yet here I sit with nothing to read. Hello! And, need I remind you, I used to be employed as an editor, so I'm going to help you with some preliminary editing. Just send me what you've got so far. I don't care if it's rough. I—look, Rebecca, I want this project to work out for us. Just call me when you get this message."

Andrea seemed a bit frazzled. I knew she worried about what my finished product might look like. The most recent sample of my writing she'd seen, book number three, had been a disaster. She also had her suspicions that I might be drinking enough to impede my progress on the book, evident in some of the comments she made in her emails to me. She was right. I'd been stalling and we were past the day I'd promised to email something to her.

My thoughts wandered back to Eisenbrey. He had gotten under my skin, turning frigid on me after my remark about his desperate, delusional horseshit. In retrospect, that had been the wrong approach to take with him. I should have flirted with the man a little, appeased him, so he would keep telling me what I needed for my book. What I had accomplished instead, with that insult, was to effectively shut him down and blow a good-bye kiss to any cooperation I would have otherwise gotten from him.

I felt overwhelmed. Perhaps I had been the wrong choice for this project. Perhaps I didn't have the right type of personality to be able to deal with Eisenbrey. How was I going to get him to warm up to me again? I felt like giving up.

And the option of giving up waved in the air in front of me, an almost palpable temptation. I needed to remind myself why I had taken the project in the first place. I reflected on that for a moment and came up with several reasons. The first was that Andrea was wonderful. Andrea had believed in me at a time when no one else did, not even me. She'd given me my start as a writer. As far as my career was concerned, I owed her everything. I didn't want to let her down. And of course, I considered her a good friend, probably my best friend. Yes, there were a lot of reasons. Good reasons. And another, much darker, reason loomed—if I quit, I would never see Tom again. Of course I had to finish this.

That night when I laid my head to rest on my puffy pillow and closed my eyes, I dreaded the thoughts that would come. This was my worst time. Loneliness enveloped me and the darkness seemed oppressive. It was the time of day when I felt so sure, and so unsure. And it was the time when I obsessed the most about Thomas Eisenbrey. He was nearly all I thought about before falling asleep, and with increasing regularity he was also in my dreams. Until that ceased to be true, I was screwed.

I knew myself well enough to know I would be up the entire night fretting about him, in spite of the three helpings of vodka and orange juice I had slammed down to help me sleep. I didn't want him to be angry with me. At my age, I was familiar with the feeling you get after you've just had a big fight with the one you care for. I'd been through the drill on many occasions. I felt anxious, twitchy, and restless.

Something had infiltrated the emotional part of my brain. I'd always been sensible; in control of my behavior, and made decisions that were in my best interest, even after several drinks. But this new feeling was unfamiliar. It was going to make me do something stupid. It was behind the wheel. It frightened me.

Part of me hated it, but another part felt awake and stimulated, and enjoyed the new sensation—of being out of control. As disturbing as it sounds, this feeling was better than anything else I had ever experienced. I wasn't prepared to let go of it yet.

SIXTEEN

November 6th, 2012

I decided to call Kat. Forget about the fact that I had not sent the promised chapters to Andrea. A visit with Katherine was long overdue. I needed some girl talk first before tackling anything else. My mental health was at stake.

She answered on my first attempt and told me to meet her at the mall after she got off work. I found her in front of Nordstrom's. For the first thirty minutes we managed to talk exclusively about her as we shopped. I kept firing questions at her to deflect attention from myself, but after a while she noticed what I was doing and called bullshit on me.

"Why haven't I heard from you for a month? You didn't return my calls. Were you avoiding me?"

"I've just been really busy. I started working on a new book."

"Oh, thank goodness! I was hoping that you would get it back." We both understood that she was referring to my underhanded, backstabbing, abandoning little muse that I depended on so heavily to maintain my sanity. She seemed chipper as she asked, "What's the storyline?"

"This one is not a fiction book; it's actually a biography." I paused, wondering how long it would take her to notice the truth of my affliction. That would surely cause her to rip into me. "My subject is the serial killer Thomas Eisenbrey."

"Eww! How awful!" Her look of displeasure about him was so opposite of the way I felt. It seemed wise to keep that to myself. "Are you going to have to meet him in person?"

"I've already met him. I've had four visits with him at the prison over in Walla Walla."

"You've seen him four times and you're only just now telling me? What took you so long to call me?" She looked very shocked and appalled by my lack of communication about such an exciting new development in my life.

"I'm sorry. I've just been really busy with this. I drive out there twice a week to interview him, I've spoken twice with the detective that led the investigation, and the rest of my time disappears reading news articles, police reports, etc., and typing up the information I collect." It was all true.

"Detective?" She quickly honed in on that tidbit. "Is he hot?"

"Well...yes he is." Another truth; although I spent much more time thinking about Eisenbrey. "We went out on a dinner date a few nights ago."

"Jeez, Rebecca, you had a date and you didn't call me about that either? There's something wrong with you." She shook her head. "How long does it take to dial a phone number?"

"A few seconds, but our conversations are never short. You know I always have to block out at least an hour if I'm going to call you."

Kat ignored my insinuation that she was long-winded, and forged on with exaggerated brevity. "Details," she demanded, making a give-me gesture with her hand. "Now."

We sat down at a table in the food court to have our drinks. "What does he look like?" she asked.

I took my cellphone from the pocket of my jeans and pulled up the photo of Eisenbrey peering through the bars, then I held it up for her to see. Even in such a small image you could easily discern the vivid, cerulean-blue of his eyes.

"Wow," Kat remarked, eyebrows raised. "I was asking about the detective. You have a picture of the killer in your phone."

For a moment there I had thought she'd say something about his smoldering good looks, but she didn't. *Here it comes,* I thought, squaring my shoulders. I slipped my phone back into my jeans pocket without mentioning that I had way more than one pic of him in there.

"So you have a thing for this guy?"

I let out a heavy breath and rolled my eyes, exasperated. I had been very careful not to include any indication that I lusted after the man, yet she had seen it. I remained silent and took a sip of my latte.

"Oh, come on, Rebecca. I know you," she said. "Don't try to deny it. I can't blame you; he's a good-looking guy." She shrugged her shoulders.

"Okay. He's easy on the eyes. Whatever."

"And there's definitely more to it than that," she persisted. "What else is it that draws you to him?"

"I don't know what it is yet." Her expression was dubious, so I added, "Honestly, I'm not sure."

"Interesting." Kat's eyes wandered over to the entrance of one of the department stores, and she stared at it without really seeing. When she spoke again her voice sounded detached and unemotional. "What's he like when he talks with you? Is he nice?"

"Well, yes I suppose, except when he's busy insulting me. We didn't hit it off very well at the beginning, but then I started to feel like I had a good rapport with him. He was starting to open up to me and share some things that were personal. Then at the end of our visit yesterday we had an argument and it all went to hell."

Kat's eyes returned to me, her gaze keen, piercing. "What did the two of you argue about?"

I hadn't originally intended to tell Kat, but I decided to let her in a little more. "He accused me of being jealous about a letter that he received from some woman."

"Were you jealous?"

"That's beside the point," I snapped.

"So you were jealous. What happened next?"

"I lost my temper with him. He accused me of being territorial. I told him he was delusional."

"But he wasn't delusional; he had just picked up on the fact that you were feeling jealous, and that made you angry."

"I guess so. I just hate it when he gets like that. He keeps telling me that I'm having dreams and fantasies about him. I feel like slapping that smug, self-satisfied expression right off of his face when he does that. It's infuriating!"

"Interesting," she said again as she sipped her coffee and mulled that over.

"Yes, it's interesting that I'm getting that same urge to smack someone right now while I'm talking with you," I said, glaring at her. "Do you think you could try to sound a little less like a headshrinker?"

"Hmm. He's got you all worked up in a tizzy. I wonder how he managed that. Do you flirt with him?"

"No. And I'm not sure what to say to him when I see him next. He's liable to still be mad at me."

She nodded, and said. "You need to reopen the dialogue now — get what you need for your book."

"No shit," I breathed.

"You might consider apologizing to him for what you said. Apologies can go a long way, and I would suspect that hearing you say you're sorry is exactly what he wants."

"He doesn't deserve an apology. I'm way nicer to him than he is to me."

"This is not about equity. Try not to let your emotions into the equation. Your goal is to get him talking to you again." She made it all sound so simple.

"You're probably right," I admitted. "I could give it a shot."

"Rebecca, there's something else—you haven't mentioned your parents at all today. I would have thought that working with someone like him would bring up all kinds of bad memories for you. How are you holding up?"

I swallowed and managed to push back the tears that threatened to show themselves. "I'm okay. That happened a long time ago. I don't really associate him with what happened to Mom and Dad."

"That's great," she said, resting her hand on my arm. "But if you need to talk about anything don't hesitate to call me. You'll remember that, won't you? I don't want you to talk yourself out of it if it happens to be two in the morning."

I nodded.

Her expression changed as though another thought had just come to her. "There isn't any chance that Eisenbrey could get released, is there? I mean, he's on death row, right?"

And then I buried my face in my hands and began to sob, and Kat wrapped her arms around me.

SEVENTEEN

November 7th, 2012

The next day I was a mess. My depression returned in full force, and even though I drank a load of caffeine, went for a long walk in the sun, and tried to dwell on everything that had gone right in my life of late, it didn't waver. By two o'clock, I broke out the liquor. Unfortunately, the item at the top of my happy list, which dwarfed everything under it, that sick bastard out in Walla Walla, had left me feeling bleak and empty about my future. It was surprising how much a little disapproval from Eisenbrey could squash me like a bug.

My phone rang several times that day, but I allowed my voicemail to deal with the calls. When I finally played back the messages, I found that they all had come from Detective Scanlon. Apparently he was suffering from the same thing I was. It was fortunate that I hadn't answered the phone since Eisenbrey had warned me not to talk to Scanlon anymore. I didn't know how to handle the situation. I felt relief to have put it off. His last message sounded a bit desperate. "Was I out of line? I was, wasn't I? I wasn't trying to upset or offend you. I'd really like to see you again, Rebecca. Please call me."

Eventually, it started to get dark outside, which happened too damned early during autumn in Washington State. It caused an ache in my heart for California. The dark and the rain weren't a good mix for me. I hadn't accomplished anything all day, and sat in my living room with the lights down low, a pleasant mixture of "Jackie D" and cola in my hand, as I listened to a group called Garbage sing "#1 Crush". It was interesting how right it felt to play their music and get bombed while staring at a picture of Eisenbrey on my laptop. I still had my wallpaper set with the sexiest pic I had of him, the one where he peered at me through the bars on his cell, the one where he looked as though he longed to be with me, if only he could get past the locked door that held him back.

The doorbell rang, yanking me out of my reverie and annoying the hell out of me simultaneously. I decided to ignore it, but it was so loud that I found it impossible. After a few moments, the steady ringing was enhanced with the addition of insistent knocking. This was not the kind of person who was going to go away easily. I needed to deal with it.

I opened the door to Scanlon's smiling face. He held up a bottle of wine and then handed it to me. I read the label. "St. Michelle's… good stuff," I said with a smile of approval. He had been right to bring alcohol instead of flowers. "That was thoughtful."

As Scanlon leaned forward to peer inside my house I caught the scent of his cologne. The musky fragrance stirred my senses, a different scent than the one he wore the night of our date. Damn, he smelled good. "Are you having some kind of party?" he asked over the music.

"It's just a party of one," I told him. "Come on in." I then realized what I had left open on my computer screen. I rushed ahead of him into my living room and snapped my laptop shut, but I could tell by his expression that I hadn't been quick enough. And why did it have to be that particular picture? I walked over to my stereo and turned down the volume to a more reasonable level.

"Hmm." He narrowed his eyes at my computer, but then smiled when his eyes returned to me. "I'm sorry to just drop-in on you like this, but I'm worried. Are you upset with me? Did I screw everything up? I'm really sorry if I came on too strong the other night."

"No, Darryl, I'm not upset," I assured him.

"When you didn't call me back, I just got…well, I needed to see you."

"I understand." That was very true. I knew exactly what he felt, it was miserable. "I think you're a very nice man. It's just that I can't start anything with you right now."

"We don't have to be in a relationship or anything. We could just be friends. I'd really like to see more of you."

A part of me wanted to see more of him too, but it was dwarfed by the part of me that already belonged to Eisenbrey. I desired the serial killer. Obviously the wrong thing to desire. I was headed down a twisted helix of depravation with no will to stop my descent. How does one get out of a pit when they don't want to be rescued? It wasn't fair to take Scanlon down with me.

He seemed to be a nice guy. I needed to cut him loose. I struggled against myself, fighting to comprehend the sinister poison that ran rampant within me, afraid of what I was turning into.

"Darryl, I think that if you and I spend any more time together we will wind up being more than just friends. I'm just not in a place in my life where that makes sense right now."

"What's going on, Rebecca? Does this have to do with Eisenbrey?" I saw realization dawning, his golden-brown eyes locking on mine. "Oh no, tell me you don't have feelings for that asshole."

How could I tell him that? I stayed silent, staring back.

He continued talking, "That guy is crafty. He screws with everyone's head. Don't let him get to you, Rebecca."

"I'm not letting him get to me," I said. "I just feel frustrated about my book. I think I'm getting writer's block or something. You wouldn't understand."

"I'm trying to understand," he said. He put his hand on my arm.

I felt warmth where he touched but the rest of my body felt cold. My messed up thoughts about the damned murderer kept me from pursuing Scanlon, who I recognized might otherwise be perfect for me.

"I wish there was some way for me to fix whatever's hurting you," he said.

I balked at that. To say that I hurt took it a bit far, although the more I considered it, the more accurate it sounded. Maybe he was right. "I'm okay," I told him. "Really, I just need some sleep, and I need to get this book finished."

"All right," he said. His eyes scanned the room, his expression perplexed. "Are you sure no one else is in the house? It feels like someone's here."

"No one but us," I told him.

"Okay. I'll go home," he said, taking my hand. We walked back to my front door. "I know it's hard to tell sometimes, but I really am a gentleman."

"It's easy to tell," I said. And, though I knew what would happen next, I chose to keep my feet planted firmly in place, and made no attempt to block him.

Darryl scooped me up into an affectionate embrace and kissed me fully on the lips, exploring my mouth with his tongue. The warm hand that rubbed my back was gentle but insistent, and as he pressed his body up against mine I could feel his erection. The slight buzz I had from the alcohol felt good, so did being wrapped up in Scanlon's arms. I wanted to remain in this happy place, but I knew if I didn't act soon, my willpower would dissolve.

I pulled back gently and he reluctantly let go. "Wow," I said, the only word that came to mind.

He'd kissed me. Had he not heard the part where I told him that I couldn't start anything with him? *They hear what they want to hear.* And I was just as guilty, standing there like an idiot, waiting for it to happen. True, Scanlon had interesting boundaries, but I found it difficult to complain since I had been craving his touch. Perhaps he'd sensed that I was on both sides of the fence.

"Goodnight Rebecca," he whispered close to my ear.

"Goodnight," I repeated. I shut the door slowly as I watched him turn and head toward his car.

Yes, that behavior would cause some to say that he was not a gentleman. Some might also argue that a gentleman wouldn't have planted evidence. I had mixed feelings about that situation, especially since I had acknowledged my feelings for Eisenbrey. But I understood what had motivated him. He was looking at the big picture. His goal had been to protect the public. Scanlon was a good man.

I shook my head at the duality of my own behavior and returned to the pictures of Eisenbrey on my laptop, feeling conflicted.

My cell phone chimed, letting me know I had just received a text message. Jeez, had Scanlon texted me already? Had he even had time to climb in his car? I knew I shouldn't ignore it; he'd just knock on the door again if I didn't respond. I glanced at the screen and found a text from Andrea: "This is your agent/editor. Why haven't you sent me anything to EDIT!!!"

The question didn't even have a question mark at the end of it. She must be in a state, although I considered that very tame behavior for her while trying to spur me into action. I should appreciate her restraint. I checked the time on my cell phone, it was ten thirty at night. I wondered why she was texting me at this hour. In New York it was one thirty the next morning. I texted one word in return: "Soon." That would appease her for a little while, but I needed to get back to work and make good on my promise.

I had two chapters for her. Granted, they weren't polished, and I hadn't been entirely sober when I'd written them. But it was a nice start. I just needed to read through them again once my buzz wore off. I knew they'd be good enough to restore Andrea's confidence that I could still do this.

The woman understood me well. I worked better under pressure. But my best work was fueled by obsession, and I had no shortage of that.

I took a sip of my drink. Three days until my next visit with Eisenbrey, and I worried about how it would go. I didn't know if he would accept my apology or how long he planned to stay mad at me. I needed something productive to do that would take my mind off of our spat. Then it came to me. It was time for me to pay Tom's mother a visit.

EIGHTEEN

November 8th, 2012

My windshield wipers made a steady smacking sound as they moved back and forth across my field of vision, something that could lull me to sleep under other circumstances, but I was excited that morning as I drove to Mrs. Eisenbrey's address. This was not the typical drizzle that the greater Seattle area was famous for, but the kind of downpour that caused traffic to slow down to a crawl, and it didn't help my impatience or my worry over how she would respond to my visit.

I could have called ahead and asked permission, but what if she said no to me? It seemed far easier to refuse people over the phone than in person. I had weighed my options and decided the best way for me to approach Mrs. Eisenbrey was to surprise her by showing up on her doorstep — the stealth method.

She lived in a small house in a quiet neighborhood in Mountlake Terrace, not far from Seattle. I parallel parked on the street in front of her home instead of pulling into her driveway. It just seemed less pushy. I had to chuckle at myself. What did it matter where I parked my car? It didn't get much pushier than dropping in on her with no warning so I could ask her a bunch of personal questions about someone she probably hoped to forget.

I double-checked the tote bag I had packed to make sure I hadn't forgotten anything. I didn't expect a warm welcome from her so once I gained entry to the house I should stay put, no running back to the car to get a forgotten item, lest she change her mind about speaking with me.

I pulled the hood of my raincoat up around my head, grabbed my bag, and made a break for her house, trying not to get drenched. I didn't hear any sound when I pressed the doorbell button, and I wondered if it was broken. Her front doorstep was slightly enclosed, so I lowered my hood and smoothed my hair as I waited for her, trying to make myself presentable. I was just about to knock when the door opened.

There was no question that the woman who answered was Tom's mother. The family resemblance was striking. By all appearances she was in her late sixties. Her long, silver hair was pulled back from her face, which showed no evidence of make-up, yet she was beautiful. She wore jeans, comfortable shoes, and a deep-purple flannel shirt. My attention was drawn to her eyes of that strange and wonderfully vibrant shade of blue I knew so well, minus the icy and distant affect.

"Mrs. Eisenbrey?" I asked.

"Yes," she replied with a smile.

"My name is Rebecca Reis. I'm a writer, and I'm currently working on a book about your son, Thomas. May I speak with you for a few minutes?"

Mrs. Eisenbrey's surprise was evident, but she recovered quickly and started to shut the door. I slipped my foot in the jam just in time to experience the thud, and I felt thankful for my sturdy shoes.

"Please," I said through the small opening that my foot had provided.

"What makes you think I'm his mother?"

"He told me your name, Sarah Eisenbrey, and you look just like him. I know I've got the right woman." I saw her hesitation and I added, "I'm not here to try to upset you ma'am."

She looked down at my foot irritably and snapped, "Well, if you're not trying to upset me then what the hell did you sneak up on me for? You should have called first."

"I was afraid you wouldn't want to see me," I admitted.

"You're right. I don't want to see you," she agreed.

"I'm sorry. It's just that it would really help me out with my project if you would share some of your memories of him with me."

"Why on earth do you want to dredge up all of that old shit again?"

"For the book. I'm trying to understand him, and to try to comprehend why he did what he did."

She let out a long sigh. "Well…" she said tentatively. "No, I don't want to be in a book about him."

"You won't be in the book. At least, I won't mention your first name or include a picture of you. And I don't need to specify what information came from you."

That seemed to provide her with some level of relief. She contemplated the matter some more, but then shook her head wearily, still unsure.

"Please," I repeated. "I want to show all sides of him. It would help me so much to learn more about his early years."

"Oh, all right," she relented, but she didn't look happy about it. She opened the door for me. "Come inside then. You can sit on the couch." She motioned toward her sitting room near the entry. "Would you like some coffee?"

"Sure," I said. When she went to the kitchen I took the opportunity to examine the room. It was very neat and clean; I couldn't even detect any dust on the end tables or shelves. There were no books on her bookshelves, just the kind of knickknacks one would expect in a country home, however I spied a Bible sitting on one of the end tables. The furniture seemed new and comfortable. The TV, an older model, was small and without a cable box. I surmised that she didn't spend a lot of time watching the tube.

Tom's mother returned with two coffee mugs and asked, "How do you like it? Sugar? Milk?" She was tall and thin, close to 5'10", with the same long, spidery arms and legs that Tom had. I imagined that the two of them must have looked even more alike before her hair turned gray. But unlike Tom, she seemed uncomfortable, jittery, and her eyes darted around the room.

"Plain is fine. Thank you."

She set the drinks on her coffee table and we sat next to one another on her couch. She turned toward me. "Miss Reis, I don't want people to find out that I live here. You don't understand how awful it was for me after they discovered that Tom was the Hunter. It was so humiliating to live in a small town like Carnation where everyone knew our family. People were unkind to me after that. Some folks even had the balls to claim that my poor parenting had caused him to turn out like that. I finally had to move away from there."

I wasn't sure what to say to her, but I felt the desire to console her. "I'm so sorry."

"My new neighbors don't know that Tom is my son. I told them that I'm not related to those Eisenbrey's. Please don't speak with any of my neighbors about this."

"Yes, of course, I have no intention to do that. I'm more than happy to do everything I can to protect your privacy."

"Thank you." Mrs. Eisenbrey cleared her throat and sat up straighter, placing her hands on her knees. "Tommy was always a solitary young man," she said quietly. I had a hard time picturing a world where Tom Eisenbrey had ever been little, and innocent, and been called Tommy. It seemed unlikely for someone who duct taped people to trees and slit their throats to go by such a cute name, but I set that aside for the moment and gave his mother my full attention. I could let my brain struggle with that concept later.

She looked a little lost and then she told me, "I don't really know where to start. What do you want to know?"

"I have an idea. Do you have any family photographs you'd be willing to show me? That might help get the conversation going." And I had another motive besides wanting to see the pictures; I wanted her to have a place to look, a place to focus her attention, other than on me. I hoped that it would allow her to feel more comfortable about the whole interview. I worried that she might shut down on me.

"Sure," she said. She left the room to find her pictures. I scanned the walls and found no family pictures at all, just a few paintings of mountains and lake scenes. And then I saw it. On one of the end tables sat a wooden box, the same size and shape as your average shoebox, adorned with intricate carvings. The perimeter of the design was cut to look like a braided rope, inside of its borders I saw a series of geometric shapes, and in the center a three dimensional flower—a rose that sat higher than the rest of the pattern. The level of detail boggled my mind. I had never had a talent for art myself, so I found it hard to imagine how the artisan had accomplished the carving. Mrs. Eisenbrey returned and noticed me admiring the box. "It's beautiful," I told her.

"Yes, it is. Tom made that for me."

"Really? You kept it?" That surprised me, given that she hadn't communicated with her son since he had been transferred to Walla Walla nine years ago. I recalled Tom telling me that he enjoyed carving, but I had no idea he could be that good at it.

"Tom gave it to me for Mother's Day, and it's a good box," she said simply.

"It's an amazing piece of art. I only asked because I've been told that you don't visit him or write to him, and I don't see any pictures of him or the rest of your family on the walls."

"I don't have a family anymore." I wasn't able to discern how she felt about that. She seemed emotionally detached, but any fool could guess that she must be devastated.

"I wondered if you might be trying to get rid of things that remind you of him."

She nodded slowly. "I can understand why you would wonder that. It's complicated. I love my son. I don't love what he did." Looking back at the box, she said, "He was a very talented artist." She stared at it for a moment and then, pulling herself out of the memories, looked down at the old photo album she held in her arms. "Why don't we sit at the kitchen table with this; I think it will be more comfortable." I carried our mugs of coffee to the table and sat in the chair that she indicated. She sat next to me, opened the book in front of us so we could both see it easily, and began to gently turn the pages.

"Would you be willing to allow me to scan some of these photos into my computer?" I asked. She gave her consent and I took my laptop and portable scanner out of my bag, setting them up next to us on the table.

"What is that thing?" she asked, pointing at the long, wand-like gadget that I had set next to us.

"That's the scanner."

"Really? Well, I'll be. Mine's like a little photocopier. It's amazing how small they can make things nowadays, isn't it?"

I reached back in my bag for another item. "Speaking of small gadgets, would it be all right with you if I record us? I don't want to forget part of our conversation."

"Sure." She shrugged.

I laid my digital recorder next to us on the table and turned it on. "I understand Tom had a brother, David?"

"Yes," she said, resting a finger on one of the pages. "These are some pictures of the two of them when they were playing in the yard."

I studied the series of color snapshots that she indicated. They came from the early years of color film and were getting a bit yellow with age. Tom was easy to identify in the pictures—the younger of the two and he had much darker hair than his brother's. The boys didn't look much alike.

A sudden glimpse of Tom's face in my peripheral vision jolted me out of my reverie and I snapped my head up to look at him. Staring back at me were Mrs. Eisenbrey's eyes—Tom's eyes—icy, cruel, and malign. A chill ran through me as I beheld the familiar countenance I'd seen glaring at me through the bars of his cell. Then, in an instant, it was gone.

Mrs. Eisenbrey seemed perplexed, giving me a kind smile. "What is it, dear?"

Had something strange just happened? Or was it my imagination? This woman wasn't evil, in fact she seemed quite normal. *Just my mind playing tricks on me.* Letting out a shaky breath, I placed a hand over my racing heart. "I'm sorry. For a moment, I thought I saw him. The two of you just look so much alike."

"Well, we are mother and son."

"Right," I murmured. My gaze returned to the photos. The boys were both smiling in each of the shots. "They look happy. Did they get along well?"

Mrs. Eisenbrey's eyebrow raised. "Well, I suppose they did at times, but they had some terrible rows too. You know how brothers can be," she commented dismissively.

"It looks like David was older. Did he ever pick on Tom?"

"No, I wouldn't say that. Tom was the one who did the picking. The few times that Davy was ever foolish enough to start a fight with his little brother, Tom finished it. I don't recall that boy ever being afraid of anyone, except his father, of course. He never tried to bully his father."

I should hope not. What kind of kid would be able to bully their parent? Then I thought about the countless times that I had witnessed children having tantrums in stores because they wanted a toy or some candy, and it occurred to me that it wasn't that rare at all.

She lifted the clear plastic sheet that covered the photos of the brothers, gently removed them and handed them to me. I then started feeding them through the scanner one by one. The machine hummed quietly as we continued to chat.

"Do you have a photo of the whole family together?" I asked.

"Yes." She flipped through some more pages. "Here's one that we had taken at a studio." It was a pleasant photo. Everyone was dressed nicely and smiled for the camera, even Tom—his smile showing a conspicuous gap where he was missing a tooth in front. The boys both looked as though their mother had run a comb through their hair just seconds before the picture was taken. I could see that David resembled their father, with the lighter hair, and he wasn't as tall and gangly as his little brother. "I think Davy was about twelve years old in this one, and Tom would have been ten."

"Did Tom and his father get along well?" Other than the time he probably killed him, I thought to myself.

Mrs. Eisenbrey looked shaken, and I wondered if the same thing had just crossed her mind. "Well..." She looked like she was trying to remember. "When Tommy was a little boy he used to try to follow Joe everywhere, but Joe didn't have much time for the boys, especially Tommy. He spent more time with Davy because he was older. And then when Tommy got into his teens, he and Joe started to argue."

"What did they argue about?"

"Oh, everything. Tommy didn't want to do what he was told at all. He wouldn't go to school. He'd stay out all night and refuse to tell us where he had been. We didn't know what he was up to. Joe thought he might have been on drugs, but I don't know. And I would find blood on his clothes sometimes. He was very evasive when we questioned him. He said it was none of our damned business." She looked scandalized that a teen would say something like that to his parents.

"Then one day, after Joe had to beat the tar out of him, Tommy admitted that he had been hunting. But what on earth could he have been hunting for in the middle of the night? He never brought any animals home afterward. We weren't sure what to believe about that."

As she brought her fingers up to her temple and rubbed it, I noticed the wedding ring, a single diamond on a gold band. Was this the ring from her marriage to Tom's father? He had disappeared back in 1989. Surely, no one would still be wearing a ring from someone who had disappeared that long ago, but her last name was still Eisenbrey, so I didn't think that she had remarried. I scribbled a note to myself to clarify that later.

"You say he had to beat him. Did your husband discipline Tom often?"

"Oh, yes. With a boy like Tommy, so willful, always defying us the way he did, he needed a lot of thrashings. And still, he never seemed to learn from it. He got quite a bit taller than Joe in the end. It was a lucky thing that Joe was such a strong man. Otherwise it could have been much harder to keep Tommy in line."

"What about Davy?"

"Oh, Davy was a sweet boy by comparison. Joe didn't have to fuss much about him. There just wasn't much to correct." Suddenly she put her hand up to her mouth and her eyes started to water. "Oh hell," she muttered. She got up and stepped quickly into the kitchen, returning with a box of Kleenex. "Miss Reis, you know what happened, don't you?" She searched my eyes for a moment. "My Davy was murdered."

"Yes, Tom told me about that," I said. "I'm so sorry."

"He did?" That seemed to light a fire in her. "Did he tell you who did it?"

"No." It wouldn't help Mrs. Eisenbrey if I told her that he had insinuated heavily that he had done it, so I left that unsaid. Besides, I was more interested to hear her theory. "Do you know the identity of the killer?"

"Of course I do. It was Tommy. We all know that now, even though the police were never able to find any evidence to prove it," she spat bitterly. "But you have to understand that, back when Davy died, we didn't know for sure. Joe and I had our suspicions, but the thought of him doing that to his own brother was just too awful to believe. And Tommy was still…living in our house." Her discomfort over the memory was obvious.

"And then, nearly a year later, those three hunters were found dead out in the forest, and we were worried all over again that Tommy might have been involved, but he just acted like nothing was wrong. He didn't look guilty. A lot of people in town told us that they thought Tommy was behind it, and the police came and took him to the station for questioning two different times, but they didn't get whatever they were looking for. I recall having a conversation with Joe at some point and I told him I was afraid of Tommy. We talked about sending him away, but there was nowhere to send him."

She seemed to pull herself out of the bad thoughts and she smiled, pointing to another picture. "Here's a picture of Tommy when he couldn't have been more than a month old. He was such a cute baby." At least she had one family photo that made her happy, a picture of her youngest son before he had done anything unpardonable. Those were the days she could hold onto. "I missed out on some of the time when he was a baby. I regret that, but I got real depressed after Tommy was born. It was terrible. I just couldn't bring myself to look at him or his brother and I even went to stay with my mother for a while. Joe had to take care of the boys for a few months until I was myself again. But Tommy was too young to remember that. I don't even think that Davy remembered it and he was two years old."

I returned the first group of pictures she'd given me and she handed me a few more. She didn't offer the photograph of the entire family together and I didn't ask for it.

Mrs. Eisenbrey rested her finger on another photo. "In this one he and Davy were building a table together." Then a troubled expression crossed her face. "This was taken right before Tommy broke Davy's hand. Davy told us that his brother had hit him really hard with the hammer. It was awful, he broke several bones and it was a long time before Davy had the full use of his hand again. Tommy told us he did it because Davy's hand was in his way and he didn't move it when he was told to. Tommy didn't seem to think he was in the wrong at all; he just felt like he had a right to do it because Davy had irritated him. I have to say, that attitude was somewhat typical for Tommy."

"Mrs. Eisenbrey, was there ever an incident of some kind that could have been traumatic for Tom when he was a child?"

She contemplated that for a moment as she fiddled with a corner of one of the pages in her photo album. "Yes, there was, although I have to say…I still don't know exactly what happened. One day he didn't come home for supper. We called his name and walked around the yard to look for him, and then we searched the woods where he'd play. It took us quite a while and it got dark. We were close to calling the police for help, but we finally found him in the forest quite a distance from any houses. He was such a little thing, just six years old at the time. He'd curled up in a ball in the leaves, shivering. It was cold and wet that day. He was a mess—someone had beaten him pretty bad. He had bruises all over his body, his nose was bleeding, he had a black eye, and I remember he had what looked like a rope burn on one of his wrists. There was a scratch on his neck that Joe reckoned could have been done with a knife."

"Tommy refused to tell us who had done that to him. He didn't talk at all that day. He just looked so distant and empty. I was really worried and I told Joe I thought we should take him to a psychiatrist, but Joe said shrinks were for sissies, and no son of his was going to have his head worked on. He wouldn't even allow me to take him to our general practitioner to see if he had a concussion. I don't know if I did the right thing. He probably needed a doctor. But Tommy didn't want to go to the doctor anyway. I thought maybe he was trying to be brave for his father. The next day he was up and around, and he spoke to us, but not about the incident of course. Other than all of his physical injuries, he looked fine. He seemed like he was back to normal. So we never talked about it again."

"I couldn't help but notice your ring," I said. "Did you remarry?"

"No, heavens no, I'd never get married again. This is the ring Joe gave me. As far as I'm concerned, we're still married, even though…" She looked like she might cry. She took a fresh tissue from the box and held it up to her face.

"Even though he disappeared," I finished for her.

"Oh hell, he didn't disappear. He was murdered. They just haven't found his body yet. And I think we both know who's to blame for that. You know, Miss Reis, Joe was a good man. He didn't deserve that kind of end, and neither did my Davy." Her lower lip trembled. "It must have been my fault; I'm his mother after all. I feel like I should say something in my defense, but nothing could excuse this."

"No, Mrs. Eisenbrey, I'm not judging you at all. How could any of this be your fault? Children grow up and then they go their own way. You can't control them."

"I don't understand how he could turn into the kind of person that would want to do those things. I just feel so terrible about it. I must have done something wrong."

"Like what? Didn't you try to raise him to be a good person?"

"Yes, I tried," she said in a feeble whisper.

"Look, none of us are perfect. I'm sure you did your best. You can't force another person to be good. They make their own choices. Don't torment yourself with those thoughts anymore. If there was anything you could have done to prevent him from committing the murders, you would have done it. Right?"

She nodded weakly. I hoped for her sake that what I said rang true. If not, the guilt would surely torment this woman for the rest of her life.

NINETEEN

November 9th, 2012

When I parked at the prison, I immediately fished my flask out from under my car seat, thankful that I'd remembered to refill it before the trip. It only held six ounces, enough to take the edge off of my frazzled nerves. Most likely, Tom would still be angry with me. He was the kind of man who kept a firm grip on a grudge. I drank deeply, feeling the satisfying burn as the whiskey slipped down. I hoped he wouldn't do something crazy like refuse to see me, a possibility that had only just occurred to me.

I polished off the contents of the flask, popped a stick of minty gum in my mouth, and gathered my bag. On my way to the building, I felt the earth shift briefly under my feet, but then I realized it was just the alcohol hitting me. I wasn't drunk, no, but perhaps tipsy. I probably shouldn't have done that on an empty stomach, but it was too late to do anything about it. It wasn't like I could un-drink it. I just needed to be careful not to be obvious since any level of intoxication would be grounds for them to cancel my visit.

As I was screened and scanned, one of the guards kept a steady gaze upon me for several seconds before finally looking back at his newspaper. I caught my shoe on the edge of a small area rug just inside the metal detector and momentarily lost my balance. Then his annoying little eyes were back on me. It seemed like more scrutiny than I normally received, but it was probably my imagination. After all, I was a virtuoso at looking normal after copious quantities of alcohol. Sure, no one could tell.

But Eisenbrey knew. He had seen it as he conducted his critical examination of my motor skills with those sly, cerulean eyes. He watched me in silence as I placed the metal chair in front of his cell and sat down. I felt the controlled fire burning under his surface as he stared me down. Apparently, a friendly visit would be out of the question.

"Thomas," I began.

"Mr. Eisenbrey to you," he corrected. "There's a matter we need to discuss." His speech was cold and clipped.

It looked as though I would be able to get my apology over with right out of the gate, a good thing since I was feeling very nervous about his potential reaction. I opened my mouth to speak but then he fired an accusation at me.

"You saw him again."

"I uh, what?" I stammered. Certainly not a good way to begin our visit, but he had caught me off guard. "Who?"

Tom glared at me in a way that said, *you must think I'm an idiot,* and raised his long, slender finger at me. "I'll give you one guess, and if you don't answer right you can go piss off."

I studied his face and tried to wrap my brain around this unexpected development, uncomfortable about being in the spotlight of his scrutiny. Did he know Darryl had been to my house? But that was crazy. How could he? The obvious answer—he couldn't. He must have asked to test my reaction.

I knew I looked surprised, so there was no point in pretending otherwise. Regardless, I wasn't sure which response he would consider correct. If I admitted I'd seen Darryl, Tom would be angry, which didn't seem fair. It wasn't as if I had invited him over. At the time, I'd had no intention of betraying Tom. It hadn't occurred to me I was doing something he'd warned me against. Conversely, if I claimed I hadn't seen Darryl at all, Tom would probably rip into me for lying, and rightfully so. I thought it safest to answer him with a question. "Do you mean Scanlon?"

He crossed his arms slowly. "Is that your answer?"

"Uh, yes?"

"Rebecca, what did I tell you about seeing that man?"

"You said not to." I looked down, duly chastised.

"That's right. So why did you do it when you knew it was against my wishes?"

"Well, he just came to my house unannounced. He was worried because I hadn't returned any of his phone calls," I stammered.

"Have you made it clear to him that he's not welcomed?"

Oh-oh. "Well, I thought I had. I mean, I told him that I couldn't have a relationship with him."

Tom raised an eyebrow and cocked his head to the side. "Did you tell him that you don't want any contact with him?"

"No, I haven't."

"You will," he stated with authority. I swallowed, though it was difficult; my mouth felt dry. I nodded in agreement with him. He remained silent, apparently finished with that subject.

"I was wondering if we could go back to the way things were before I...complained about your behavior. I don't like this tension," I said. I closed my eyes briefly in an effort to dispel some of the wooziness. The alcohol was beginning to hit me harder.

"That's because it's not sexual tension anymore. It's just tension. I understand. Our talks used to be friendlier and more relaxed. But what if I don't feel like flirting with a bitch who doesn't know how to appreciate me?"

"Well, I'm sorry that I, uh, wasn't nice the last time we talked."

"You were a bitch," he said flatly. "Tell me you're sorry that you were such a bitch the last time you were here."

The smart thing would probably have been to tell him to fuck off and just finish the book without any further input from him. At least I would have been able to salvage some of my dignity. But I couldn't cope with that anymore. I had just spent the last four days unable to eat, or sleep, or laugh about a goddamned thing because we'd had an argument. During every minute of those four days I had wished I could get back in his good graces. And why? Because it felt good to be there.

I wanted to scream. I wanted to kick something. Instead, I took a deep breath and said, "Okay. I'm sorry I was such a bitch our last time."

He closed his eyes and a beatific smile spread slowly across his face. "Ah, music to my ears. Now was that so hard?"

I shook my head, and I marveled at how I could feel so afraid of this man and yet so drawn to him at the same time.

"Do you know what I find most touching about what you just said to me?"

I shook my head again.

"You said 'our last time'." He sighed. "You make it sound so intimate. And sometimes it is, isn't it? I'll tell you what, Rebecca, things are going to get even more intimate today. I'm glad to see you're wearing a skirt because you're going to do something for me in a little bit."

He grinned, no, it was more of a sneer, and yet it looked so fucking attractive on him. I started to fantasize about having him on top of me, inside of me. I wanted to know what his face would look like when it was contorted in ecstasy. He leaned forward slightly with a questioning look in his eyes. He'd just sensed something, but what was it? I had the uncomfortable yet familiar sensation that he knew what I was thinking. I had to dismiss that idea. It would drive me crazy if I allowed my mind to go there.

"We can talk for a while first. What questions do you have for me?" He leaned back on his bed, his hands tucked behind his head, looking all too satisfied with himself.

I gave my head a small shake to clear it and consulted my list of questions for the day. "Okay, let's talk about your life between 1989 and 2001, after you left Carnation."

"What do you want to know?" he asked lazily.

"Where did you go? Where did you live? What did you do for work?"

He fired a couple of questions back at me. "What do you already know? What did Scanlon tell you?"

"Apparently your whereabouts and activities were unknown except for the two murders they were able to link to you: Tammie Lancaster in 1995, and Philippe Devereaux in 2000. What else did you do during that twelve-year stretch?"

"Hmm," he said. He rubbed his chin as he pondered my question. "No, I don't think we're going to talk about that right now. It's too personal. But I have a question for you." He paused, taking a moment to run his tongue along his teeth, his eyes not leaving mine. "When we get together and have these little chats, does it make you want me? Does it make you wet?"

The papers I held dropped into my lap. "Seriously? Come on, I have a deadline. We need to get through another page of questions or I'm not going to have anything to give my agent." Why had he even said I could ask him my questions? He obviously had no intention of answering anything. He was just screwing with me, and it was so frustrating.

"That's not my problem, dear. I thought we agreed to put the sex back in our tension? Now look, I can't do everything all by myself. This has to be a two-way street. Right?"

"Okay," I said, a sense of foreboding creeping up my spine.

"Now I want to talk about your pussy. Is it wet right now?"

I opened my mouth, but couldn't speak, a nervous knot forming in my stomach. I nodded. His eyes were burning into mine and it was hard to hold his gaze. I looked down.

"Are you embarrassed?" he asked. "You shouldn't be. There's nothing to be ashamed about; you're just pleasing your man. Right, honey?"

"Uh-huh," I managed, although it sounded a bit strangled. What could he have meant by that? Surely, whatever he was going to demand would be out of my comfort zone. I could feel myself blushing. I don't think being embarrassed even began to describe what I was experiencing. My hands gripped the sides of my chair as they would the ledge of a cliff that I had to hold onto for dear life, and my muscles went rigid as I waited to hear what he would require of me. The guards weren't far away, perhaps thirty feet. I was confident that they couldn't hear us talking as long as our voices were low, but still, Tom's sinister expression caused my heart to pound. I watched him and I tried to will him not to go where I feared he planned to take me.

"Now I want you to reach between your legs and rub your panties into your pussy." My entire body stiffened even more, and I gasped.

"But the cameras…I can't."

"Oh, are there cameras, really? Do you think the boys in the control booth can see?" he asked innocently. Then the mask fell, his features warped with malice, and I knew that I looked upon his true face. "That's not my problem, is it? Do you think I'd tell you to do this if it didn't bother you? This is paybacks for the way you spoke to me Monday." He leaned toward me and his voice became even angrier. "Do it!"

I flinched. With great difficulty I loosened the vice-like grip that I had on my chair. I glanced toward the two guards who seemed to be wrapped up in conversation with each other, and then slowly did as he commanded. Tom moaned quietly and leaned back on his bed. "Yeah, that's right, baby. Make sure they're nice and wet. I want those panties to smell like cunt. Now take them off and give them to me."

I didn't like the way he talked to me. It made me feel like punching him in the face. That urge competed with the desire to grab him and kiss him, to hell with the cell door that stood in our way. But, no, I had to stay four feet back from him at all times. He couldn't be trusted, and he had quite a reach with those long arms.

I'm not sure why I actually went through with it, maybe it was the whiskey, or perhaps something much darker was driving me. I started to pull my panties down and then glanced at the guards again. I saw Jones standing just outside the doorway to the guard's booth looking my way as my panties were at mid-thigh. Damn, I hated getting caught. He said something to the guard that sat inside the control booth and then I saw Avery appear as he rolled out of the doorway on his office chair. They both stared as I pulled them the rest of the way off. My face flushed with humiliation as I tossed the flimsy fabric to Eisenbrey through the bars. They watched me for several more seconds, probably to see if I planned to shed any more of my clothing, and then resumed their conversation. Neither of them busted me for breaking the rule about having a guard pass any items through to the prisoner.

I felt glad that I wore something nice and lacy that day. The lavender panties came as part of a matching set with my bra, and I was sorry to see them go, but I told myself that they went for a good cause.

Tom tugged his T-shirt up, exposing his abdomen, covered with dark hair. My eyes traveled down as he unzipped his pants, then reached in and started stroking himself. "Goddamn…" he said quietly. He put the panties up to his face and breathed deeply. "You smell so good just like I knew you would the first day you came to me. Show me your tits."

"Holy shit! Stop it. This area is not even remotely private," I hissed. My raised voice brought the attention of the two guards and they both watched me again.

His eyes flickered in their direction and then returned to me. "They don't care. Come on, honey, give me some fuel." He pulled his shirt up higher, baring most of his chest. I leaned forward to get a better view of his cock — so thick and long. I wanted to be the one rubbing it instead of him. More than that, I wanted to ride him.

"Oh my God! I can't do that!" I whispered, not wanting to be heard by the guards or watched by them. I had never understood people that were exhibitionists. How did a person get the nerve to undress in front of an audience? I was far too shy for that sort of thing.

"Don't be like that. I know you're not wearing panties anymore. Spread your legs apart for me," he demanded. My hesitation made him angry. "That was not a suggestion!" he barked. I stared at him, my disbelief melting into lust. Seeing Tom do this to himself made me so hot I couldn't help myself anymore. As I watched him my knees came apart and my skirt slid up a few inches.

"Fuck!" he said as he stared between my legs. He liked that word and he repeated it a few more times, stroking himself harder and faster. Then his head fell back and he moaned. He arched his back, grabbing hold of his bed sheets with his unoccupied hand, and he moaned louder. I felt panic and exhilaration coursing through me, shocked at the amount of noise he made. He really didn't care who could hear him or who might see him, which was good because Jones started to make his way toward us. Tom ejaculated all over his chest, and then his body relaxed and his head fell back onto his pillow. He wore a happy, contented grin, such a beautiful sight.

"Eisenbrey! Put your dick back in your goddamned pants!" Jones yelled. Then under his breath he said, "Fucking pervert." Eisenbrey was right, they really didn't care what he was up to. Jones had already turned around and was headed back to the control booth.

"Yes officer," Tom said congenially. "Thanks for waiting until I was finished before ordering me to do that. That was very decent of you." Then his attention fixed back on me. "That was real nice, sugar."

"Whatever possessed you to do that?" I gasped, my heart still racing.

"I believe that it's customary for couples to have sex after they've been dating for a while. Given my incarceration, that's the best I could manage. Was it good for you?" He didn't seem to notice my lack of response. He muttered, "Where's a cigarette when you want one?" He grabbed a small towel and wiped his chest off with it.

"Uh, did you just say we were a couple?"

"Wouldn't you?" He looked taken aback. He fastened his pants and put his T-shirt right. "If not, then I think you should spend a little more time pondering the nature of our relationship."

The truth was that I spent all too much time pondering that quagmire and I still couldn't clearly define it. Perhaps he was right. I smoothed my skirt back down and tried to look like nothing out of the ordinary had just happened, though I felt completely excited. We were quiet for several moments and Tom's breathing slowed down to its normal rate.

"Oh, the things that you'd do for me if I wasn't locked up in this cell," he said dreamily. At the time it didn't even occur to me just how backward that was. "So how's the book coming along, sugar?"

"Pretty well. I've got a couple of chapters written. Once I have it all written, there'll be editing and reworking."

"How long's all that gonna take?"

"I'm not sure…perhaps a few more months."

"Hmm. I want to see what you've written so far. Bring some of it with you next time."

"Sure. Yes, I'll do that." I nodded. He appeared happy and relaxed, so it seemed like a good time to mention the other interview I had done since I last saw him.

"I saw your mother yesterday," I blurted out.

"What?" Tom suddenly sat upright, alarmed. "Why the hell did you do that? Why would you want to bother her?"

I felt a jolt inside as I witnessed his angry outburst. "It's important for me to get information from multiple sources."

"Not without my permission, it isn't." Tom leaned back on his bed, taking a couple deep breaths to calm himself. After a few moments he looked relaxed again, as though nothing had alarmed him in the first place, a true acrobat. "What did she have to say about me?" he asked in a cool, detached voice.

I relayed our conversation to him honestly, and he didn't become surprised or irritated about anything she had said about him. After he'd heard all of it he visibly relaxed. Oddly enough, he turned out to be very understanding about his mother's fear, and he was content to respect her need for distance from him.

There wasn't any more game playing from Tom that day. Perhaps the gift of orgasm was a good way to manage his behavior. He was kind to me for the rest of the interview. The downside came when I walked past the control booth on my way out; I had to endure Jones staring me down with that great, big, jackass grin on his face.

TWENTY

Later, as I dwelled on the stupidity of what I had done and worried about who might find out, the realization hit me: It didn't really matter if I responded in kind to his flirtation, and I could classify that last episode as mere flirting since we hadn't actually touched. Who had to know what we said or did during our visits? I was the one to decide what went into the book, the only one to report what happened. I could slant it any way I wanted, and there was no reason to come out looking like a villain in something that I wrote. The public didn't need to be apprised of my foolish behavior.

But as for what I knew, I had no illusions. A war raged inside of me and I was going to be the casualty. I missed mom and dad. It hurt to remember them, or to be more specific, it hurt to wonder what they must have felt right at the end. How much had they suffered? Was it quick, or had Death taken its sweet time? How much terror must they have felt?

I was angry. Angry at Eisenbrey. But why exactly? He hadn't killed my parents. What about all of the people he had killed? The count was most certainly higher than the nine he'd been convicted of. What about their families? Surely, those people had suffered like I had, like I still suffered. None of us had deserved to lose the people we loved before their time, especially in such a depraved way.

Tom was the enemy. Why had I allowed myself to have feelings for this man? And I was sure I cared for him, although I didn't know if I could say I had allowed it. It just seemed to have happened in spite of my efforts to stop it.

My loathing for the evil side of him that I hated, feared and felt repulsed by wasn't strong enough to beat back the feelings of affection I harbored for his attractive and compelling side. But what had attracted me? His looks, certainly, and his charm. At times he was dominating and controlling, and other times I thought I could see the hurt little boy inside of him. I had even seen glimpses of kindness during our visits. In all, I'd witnessed a mixture of contradictions that was alluring. Those two personas — the good and the evil — seemed like two completely different men. I wasn't able to reconcile the two into one individual, and it was really fucking with my head.

I worked on the book for several hours that evening, quitting close to midnight, and felt satisfied with the amount of work I'd completed. I stood and stretched, feeling sleepy. Bedtime.

In my peripheral vision I caught a dark shape moving toward me from the hallway and whipped my head around to look at him full on. The hall was empty. I took quick steps toward the place where I had just seen him and then peeked inside the open doorway of my home office — the one location where I never seemed to write. This was the only room close enough for someone to duck into that quickly.

Flipping on the light, I surveyed the room. No intruder. I let out the breath I'd been holding. There was no other place he could have disappeared to. But it was still smart to be thorough, so I turned on all the lights and searched every room on the ground floor of the house. I found no one.

It was vodka time. I went to the kitchen, poured some vodka and a little orange juice in a glass, and gave it a stir. Then my drink and I went upstairs to my bedroom, where I curled up with a book, hoping to become sleepy again.

TWENTY-ONE

November 12th, 2012

When I arrived at the guard's booth I saw Jones leaning back in his chair with his feet up on the desk, twirling a familiar lacy pair of lavender colored panties around on his finger. "I wonder what color it'll be today." He spoke to the other guard, but looked me up and down without actually turning his face to me.

"Five dollars on black," the other one mumbled, not glancing up from his magazine. I didn't know him yet, and it didn't look as though Jones intended to introduce us. Jones stood and sauntered past me. I followed him back to the cells without acknowledging their bullshit. The other guard had actually guessed the color correctly, so if Eisenbrey managed to get another pair of panties off of me, Jones would be out five bucks. That warmed my heart a little.

As we approached Tom's cell, Jones decided to converse with me after all. "So Miss Reis, how are your visits going?" He smiled at me, which I returned reflexively, but then his smile morphed into an intimidating glower. Jones leaned in close. Though his tone was intense his volume was barely above a whisper. "Are you having fun talking with the monster? It can be a bit tricky. He doesn't like most people."

"He's fine with me. He seems to like me," I said.

"He likes you when you take your panties off. Don't become complacent and don't allow yourself to believe that it's okay to wander within his reach. You may feel like you're getting along great, but you still need to stay back from the bars. He can do some real damage when he chooses to, and he's fast. Do you know about the guard he attacked?"

"Wilson Stills?"

"Yes. And have you read his description of Eisenbrey's demeanor immediately prior to the attack?"

"No, I haven't."

"He stated that Eisenbrey was calm that morning. He seemed to be in a good mood. He joked around with Stills while being hand-cuffed and they both laughed. In fact, Stills thought he was really good with Eisenbrey. He used to volunteer to be the one to transport him whenever he had to go outside of his cell." Jones paused, his face filled with anger and resentment. "He said he didn't understand how or why it happened. One second everything was hunky dory, just two fellas having a pleasant chat, and then Eisenbrey struck like a viper. He sunk his teeth into Still's throat and tore him open, severing the carotid artery in the process. Stills lost a great deal of blood within a few seconds. He's very lucky that one of his coworkers used to be an Army medic; he clamped the artery. There happened to be a visiting physician on site who helped stabilize Stills until the medics arrived. The fact that he survived is nothing short of a miracle. My point is, he never saw it coming, and paid dearly for that. He never should have relaxed around Eisenbrey."

"I'm very sorry to hear that."

"Don't think for a second that he wouldn't do the same to you. You just need to make sure that you aren't within striking distance."

He reminded me of a kid telling a scary story by the fire during a camping trip. I could tell it gave him a perverse thrill to try to frighten me. Jones glanced through the narrow sliver of a window on Eisenbrey's cell door, then said, "clear" into his radio. The heavy, steel door began to slide ever so slowly to the side, revealing Tom's dismal enclosure.

Jones watched me as I pulled from my bag the pages I'd prepared for Tom. He set them in the tray slot, and I sat down on my folding chair. As Tom got up and took the stack of papers Jones decided that it looked safe to leave us to it. He headed back to the control booth. I had given Tom just enough to show him how the book was going, and I watched him as he read for several minutes in silence. Finally he spoke.

"I wonder if this book is really about me. Half of what you've written seems to be about how I make you feel. Hmm, the intensity of my gaze and the cadence of my speech are having a hypnotic effect on you…are they?" One side of his mouth curled into a grin, then he chose a small portion to read out loud, "And yet I don't know how to reconcile this charming and amiable man who sits before me with the murderer that I know him to be." He was correct. Everything I had written so far almost went so far as to glamorize and glorify him and, try as I might, I hadn't been able to lose that tone. My accounts of our interviews were heavily laden with observations about his appearance, his mannerisms, and how spending time with him affected me. "Since when have I ever been charming and amiable?" he asked with a chuckle.

"Artistic license," I said, shrugging my shoulders.

"So accuracy doesn't concern you?" he chided.

"Look, if you want we can strike the words 'charming and amiable man,' and replace that with 'hot motherfucker'…in the interest of accuracy."

That raised some laughter from both of us. Tom leaned back and crossed his arms. "This is so revealing. I like this very much. I think it's a good angle, a good way to approach the book. It's bold. I enjoy knowing how you feel about me, watching you bare your soul. And it's going to make our visits much more enjoyable now that I know you're in love with me."

"Hold on a minute, I never said—"

"Maybe not in those words," he interrupted. "But you did say it. And another thing—if this book comes out before my execution, and it better, then you might be able to stir up some kind of public outcry. If they make enough noise the governor might be obliged to come to my aid." He placed his hands behind his head and reclined on his bed. "You just might prove to be good for something other than giving me a hard-on."

"There's that charm I was talking about. Fuck you, Eisenbrey, and fuck your hard-on." I snapped.

He sat up on the edge of his bed. "Hey sugar, what are you getting so pissy about?"

"Maybe I didn't like being talked to that way. Did you ever consider that? Maybe it hurt me." I watched him process that. First he looked speculative, then confused and then worried. It was fascinating to watch him struggle with a concept probably entirely unfamiliar to him—empathy.

He leaned toward me and said, "I'm sorry." I rolled my eyes at that, and he added, "I really mean it. I am sorry. You wanna know something? You could hurt me too," he said. "You could hurt me so easily. Do you know that?" Tom had a pained expression like nothing I'd ever seen on him before. He looked so vulnerable. He looked like someone else.

"How?" I asked, and I really wanted to know. Everything I had seen so far suggested that he had a hard shell around his heart, and any vulnerable place that might exist seemed even more untouchable than the rest of him.

"If I tell you, you have to promise me that you'll never, ever do it."

"I promise."

He leaned closer and started to whisper. "If you ever decide that you want to destroy me, all you have to do is stop coming to see me." His voice broke. Was he crying? Oh shit, he was. I could see tears in his eyes.

I stared at him, mesmerized. This couldn't be real, could it? He was so hardened, so devoid of any tender feeling. He had to be faking this, but he looked so sincere. I marveled at what an incredible actor he must be. "If I couldn't see you anymore, I just wouldn't be able to take that."

"That's not going to happen, Tom, because I feel the same way," I said quietly. I told him the truth. I knew then he'd been right when he said I was in love with him, and I might as well stop pretending it was something else.

My reassurance brought a smile to his face, and we sat there in silence, gazing at each other through the bars for a long while. Then Tom said, "Aren't you going to ask me any more questions today? Are you tired of hearing about me?"

"Don't be silly, I'll never get tired of hearing about you." I checked the list I brought to remind me what I had planned to cover. "Your mom said that when you were a child you used to sneak out of your house at night. Where did you go?"

"I used to sit in the woods and listen to the sounds the night makes. I'd look for animals to stalk and kill. I loved to hunt, especially when it was dark. And I loved to look at the moon. I wish I could see it again." He closed his eyes like he was trying to remember what it looked like. "I just felt like I was one with the night, like that's where I belonged, the predator stalking his prey. It made me feel alive."

"How long has it been since you've seen the moon?"

Tom looked up at me and answered. "I haven't seen it since I was transferred here in 2003. It's been more than nine years," he said dismissively. "Would you like to know what else makes me feel alive?"

"Yes."

"You do," he spoke softly. "You make my heart beat faster, darlin'."

Hearing that caused a flood of euphoria to wash over me and as we gazed at each other I could feel myself being drawn in. Present now, the mesmerizing quality I'd mentioned in the pages I'd given him. He caressed my face with those unnatural, deep-cerulean eyes of his, and I leaned toward him involuntarily. Tom studied me intently.

He said, "Sometimes you make me wish I could take back every bad deed I've ever committed. I wish I would have met you instead. We could have gotten married and lived in a nice neighborhood and had two-point-three children."

"And how would we get the point-three?"

"Uh…" he pondered that with a dreamy expression. "Well, let's say we started off with three but one of them annoyed me." He chuckled.

"Thomas Eisenbrey, you awful thing," I whispered.

"Yeah, but I'm your awful thing," he whispered back playfully. Tom didn't need a knife to kill; he could take down his prey with flirtation. And those eyes.

I let out a sigh as his words melted me. I felt happy to have images floating around in my head of the two of us living together as a family. Regardless of how wrong it was, I ached to be with this man. If only there was a way. But instead of trying to verbalize all of that, I just said, "That's a nice thought, Tom." And regret wrapped its unfriendly fingers around my heart, giving an oppressive squeeze, as I remembered that a thought was all it could ever be.

The sound of footsteps approaching caused me to look up. Jones let us know that our visit was over. As I got up to leave I rubbed my temple, trying to chase away some of the grogginess. I had the odd sensation that I had just awakened from a dream. "Is Lutz there?" Tom asked me, nodding in the direction of the guard's booth.

I glanced up the hallway. "Yes, I see him."

"Good. There's something that he's going to show you."

"What's that?"

"Aw shit, I don't wanna talk about it." I looked at him questioningly, but he shook his head and told me, "It's for the book. Just let him give you a tour on your way out."

I said goodbye to Tom and then went to where Lutz was waiting for me at the control booth.

"Hi, Rebecca. Follow me," he said and I fell into step next to him, or tried to at least. The skinny young man moved as if we were in a speed-walking competition. I followed him up the hallway that led outside of the IMU building. "We'll have to be quick. I only have twenty minutes before I need to get back to the control booth."

"Where are we going?"

Lutz looked surprised at my question, but continued along at a fast clip. "The Gallows. Tom said you wanted to see where he's going to die."

That halted me and Lutz spun around to look at me. "Oh no, are you serious?" I said. I didn't want to see The Gallows. Not then. I wasn't even ready to think about that place. Why had Tom arranged it?

Lutz seemed disappointed by my reaction. "Well, yeah, Tom said you needed to see what it's like, so I got clearance to take you back there, and I made time before my shift starts to show it to you."

"Oh. That's really nice of you, Andy. Thank you. I'm sorry, I was just taken by surprise. Tom didn't tell me about this."

"He didn't?" Lutz looked deflated. "Well…do you want to see it?"

"Yes, I suppose I should, especially since you've made all the arrangements."

We went outside and Lutz led me across the grounds to the old stone wall that encompassed the original prison, unlocked a metal door in the wall and held it open for me. We hurried down a cement walkway that ran along the inside of the perimeter wall to a far corner of the penitentiary where a tall brick building loomed in front of us. We entered through an unmarked, metal door with weathered, blue paint.

This seemingly unused part of the prison was a neglected and desolate place, silent except for the echoes of our own footfalls. Paint flaked off of the walls, and the entry was decorated with copious amounts of dust and spider webs.

"It looks like the cleaning lady hasn't been," I said in an attempt to dispel the heavy blanket of depression that settled down upon me, threatening to smother.

"I don't suppose there's any reason to clean it. People hardly ever come here. We don't have many executions."

"What a creepy place," I said. The Gallows unsettled me in a way that a Halloween haunted house never could. Lives had actually been taken here. In those halls I could feel the distinct absence of joy.

"It's probably haunted," Lutz opined.

"Why do you say that? Do people see things in here?"

"No, I haven't heard of any ghost sightings, but people have died here. I expect some souls choose to remain where they die."

"Perhaps," I said absently, my eyes scanning my surroundings with trepidation. "You won't come back to haunt me after you die, will you Andy?"

Lutz chewed on that for a moment, then said, "Ma'am, given our respective ages, yours being quite a bit senior to mine, it seems more likely that you would be the first to go. So...*you* won't come back to haunt *me* after you die, will you?"

"I will now you little smart-ass!" I was grateful for our laughter as it ricocheted off of the walls around us. The brief moment of levity helped me cope with the task at hand, but my sadness returned. Lutz recognized my expression. In silence, he took me gently by the arm and led me up the three flights of stairs, like an undertaker in a funeral home, to the room that I needed to see.

"This is the viewing arena," he said flatly. We stood in a room furnished with heavy wooden benches that all faced the same direction, toward the spot where the main event would take place. A sheet that probably used to be white, but was coated in a layer of the same grime that covered everything else, hung in the spot where the recently executed would normally be.

"What's with the sheet?" I asked.

"They put it there so the witnesses won't actually see the prisoner. They turn on these lights back here," he gestured to some floodlights on the back wall aimed toward the viewing area. "The only thing they will see is his shadow." Lutz had his hands clasped in front of him and wore the appropriate somber expression. He was such a clean-cut, handsome young man, a real sweet kid. He didn't belong in this dark place.

"Oh, right, I guess it wouldn't really be appropriate for them to see the prisoner's face when it happens."

Lutz perked up. "I don't know about that, but there is an interesting story behind it. One time when they hung one of these guys they screwed-up and his head nearly came off. His blood squirted all over the place; it even got on the people sitting here in the viewing area. It must have been like something out of a horror movie." His eyes opened wide with excitement, the somber expression gone, and he shook his head with wonder. "Can you imagine that?"

"No," I said quietly, when in reality it was quite easy. Lutz's story had conjured all kinds of death images in my head, unfortunately all of them involving Tom in particular.

"They hung the sheet up to protect the spectators from any squirting blood in case it happens again."

"Super," I said. I pressed the back of my hand to my mouth in an effort to quell the nausea that had come upon me, then fished my camera out of my bag and snapped a few pictures of our surroundings. Looking up at the platform above us, I noted two trap doors in the floor. That's where Tom would be taken to be killed.

"Why are there two trap doors, Andy?"

"In case they do two executions in one night, or if one of the doors malfunctions."

"Have they ever done two at one time?"

"Yeah, I think one time there were some brothers that they did together."

So that room was the last place Tom would ever see. I knew I wasn't supposed to feel bad about it. If anyone had earned a place on death row it was Tom. But seeing the place overwhelmed me. I looked back toward the stairwell, trying to hide the unbidden tears that had found their way into my eyes, knowing that I shouldn't feel what I felt. I didn't want Tom to die in this horrible place. I didn't want Tom to die at all.

"You're really fond of him, aren't you?" Lutz asked quietly.

I nodded.

"Are you in love with him?"

I hesitated for a moment, pondering whether I should allow him in, but as I studied Lutz's face I saw kindness. "Yes, I suppose I am," I said. "You must think I'm incredibly stupid."

"No. I just feel sorry...for you, for both of you. I like him too. As inmates go, Eisenbrey isn't so bad. I mean, I know what he's done, but he's always been nice to me."

I nodded, not trusting myself to speak, and then I did what I'd been working very hard not to do—I started sobbing. Lutz didn't say anything, he just put his arms around me and we stayed like that for a few minutes until I finished.

"Would you like me to walk you to your car?" he asked.

"No, I'll be all right. You need to get back to the control booth, don't you?"

"That's okay. I can be a little late. I think you need someone to walk out with you."

"Thanks, Andy."

TWENTY-TWO

November 16th, 2012

I came back to the prison for what would be my seventh meeting with Tom. As I neared the guard's station I thought about how far my relationship with Tom had progressed in such a short time. It didn't seem possible, but I had only known Tom for three weeks. If anyone had told me four weeks ago that I would be feeling this way about a convicted serial killer I would have laughed my ass off, and possibly even taken a swing at them. It alarmed me to realize how quickly I'd become emotionally attached to him, and how quickly I was becoming someone I didn't recognize anymore. Officer DiMaggio stood when he saw me approach, not to be polite, but to block my path. He placed himself too close to me, his face in my face. His narrowed eyes held some emotion indiscernible to me, not quite anger, but perhaps one of its close cousins. Yes, his attempt to intimidate me had worked out very nicely. "I heard Lutz took you on a tour Monday. How did you like to see where we're going to kill your boyfriend?"

I struggled to hold my ground and maintain eye contact with DiMaggio. "What do you want from me, Ricky?"

If there hadn't been hatred in his expression earlier, there was now. I wondered if I was going to receive the same lecture about consequences that Tom had. "I feel bad that Lutz is the only one who's been able to show you around. I've got something to show you also." His hand gripped my upper arm so tight it hurt. He intended to take me somewhere, and I intended to refuse.

"No thanks," I said curtly, trying to tug my arm free of his grasp without success.

"Oh, come on, you don't even know where we're going yet."

"We aren't going anywhere together. Whatever it is that you want to show me, I don't want to see it."

"So you're one of those bitches that says she doesn't want it, huh?"

"I don't want it. Stay away from me," I said clearly.

"Your mouth says no, but I'll bet I could find another part of you that's saying yes." He shoved me backward into the wall and I felt pain in my shoulder blade where it collided with a metal pipe that ran along the wall. He had me pinned. Before I could respond he slid his hand up my skirt and along my inner thigh until he rested it between my legs, the only thing between me and his fingers, a flimsy layer of fabric. "Aw, darn, you got panties on. I thought you quit wearing those so you could show Eisenbrey your snatch."

"Let go of me!" I hissed, knocking his hand away from my crotch. His other hand still held me against the wall.

"DiMaggio!" a stern, male voice shouted. Relief came over me as I spotted one of the nicer guards, Don Avery, in my peripheral vision. He approached us, and planted himself just as close to DiMaggio as DiMaggio was to me, the three of us in a close huddle, making me aware that both men towered over me by several inches. I thought about Lutz's comment that these two used to be friends when they were kids, and that DiMaggio hadn't been a bad guy then, but I couldn't believe that DiMaggio had every been anything but a bully.

Avery's proximity didn't seem to faze DiMaggio. He kept his attention on me. "I don't think you fully appreciate the situation you're in.

I'm not one of the guys locked up in here. I have days off. And your home address really wouldn't be that hard for me to get."

"Jesus, DiMaggio! She could report you to the warden, and you know she's a personal friend of Barnett," Avery warned him. Hearing the misconception amongst the guards alleviated some of my stress. Captain Barnett and I were not chums, but I certainly didn't feel compelled to correct him.

DiMaggio transferred his stony stare from me to Avery as he pondered his words, then glared at me once more, finally letting go of me. Avery rested his hand on the small of my back and led me away from the guard's office, then dropped it as we neared Tom's quarters.

"You okay?" he asked as we walked.

"Yeah. No worries," I assured him. It would be counterproductive to turn DiMaggio's tantrum into the next world war. And I had no interest in wasting the precious time I was allotted inside the prison —two hours, twice per week.

Avery looked me up and down, chewing his lip, his brows furrowed. "You wanna file a complaint against that asshole?"

"No. I'd rather not. It'll just eat into my visitation time. I didn't drive all the way out here to sit in Barnett's office."

"Okay," he said. Avery had already set up a chair for me by the cell. He peeked through the window at Tom. "Oh, shit, he's meditating," he told me in a whisper.

"Really? Is that something he does regularly?" I asked.

"Yeah, pretty often. Sometimes he does it for hours. Doesn't move at all. It's fucking creepy." Avery pressed the button on his radio and said, "Clear." He turned to me, his expression somber. "You know, I'm awful sorry about what happened back there." He spoke quietly as the outer door to Tom's cell began to open, his voice barely audible over the hum of the electric motor. He shook his head. "DiMaggio's a prick. Just let me know if you change your mind."

"Thanks Don," I said.

Tom had been sitting on his bed when the door to his cell opened, but he uncrossed his legs and rose to his feet as he saw me. "Uh-oh, what happened?" he asked.

It took a nanosecond for me to consider whether or not to tell him about the rude welcoming I had received. I decided it would be nicer not to trouble him with that information. It would only make him angry, and I didn't see how that would help either of us. "Why do you think something happened?"

"You look different," he remarked.

"I'm just feeling low. It was the visit to The Gallows. I didn't want to go there," I said as I sat down. Tom remained standing and leaned against the bars, tapping the metal softly with one of his knuckles.

"Well, shit, I can assure you that I don't want to go there either."

Giving myself a mental kick for my lack of sympathy, I said, "Of course. I'm sorry. I don't know why I'm down. You're in a terrible situation, Tom. I don't really have anything to complain about."

"Sure, unless you might be upset about someone you care for being executed in a little while."

I nodded silently and swallowed. His capacity for understanding how it made me feel surprised me. "Why didn't you give me any warning? I could have used some time to prepare myself."

"If I hadn't sprung that on you, you would've just thought up reasons to put it off and you wouldn't have done it. You needed to see that place." That too was a little more insight than I had expected from him. During the course of my research, I'd read that psychopaths didn't have the ability to comprehend other people's emotions since they lacked any real emotions themselves. Perhaps in his case that wasn't true.

I sighed. "You're probably right."

He stepped back from the bars and crossed his arms, staring down at me. "What else happened?"

He knew something had taken place. I figured I couldn't hide it from him anymore and I rationalized that he wasn't the kind of man who needed to be sheltered anyway. "DiMaggio," I said. Then I relayed the entire incident to him.

"That motherfucker," Tom hissed, his countenance full of loathing. "He's going to pay for that."

"Tom, how do you intend to make one of the officers pay when you're locked up in this cell?"

"I'm sure I'll come up with something. I sure as hell ain't gonna let that slide." Tom started pacing back and forth, not easy in such a confined space. He looked as though the slightest thing might throw him into a rage. I could see I needed to be careful not to set him off. I shouldn't have told him about DiMaggio.

I ran through the questions I had prepared for our session that day, but he seemed preoccupied while he answered. No doubt his thoughts kept returning to that horrible guard. The more his mind drifted from our conversation, the more I stared at him, and finally I just had to say it. "Thomas Donovan Eisenbrey, why couldn't you be ugly?" I looked up into his eyes and a dizzy feeling that was mixed with exhilaration overtook me. I was swooning. I couldn't help it.

He laughed, "I am ugly on the inside, darlin'. What do you want me to do—stop shaving? Get a beer belly? I can't help it if I was born with a pretty cover, but I'm not sorry at all if that's what brings you here." He wrapped his fingers around one of the bars and caressed it absentmindedly. "I'm so glad that you keep coming to see me, baby. You make me so happy."

The literature on the issue of rehabilitating someone like him painted a bleak picture. Being honest with myself, I couldn't even say I knew for sure that the words he spoke came with sincerity. I wanted to fix him, to heal him, to make him into someone I could justify loving. I couldn't see any way to do that, but there had to be a way. There had to, because I needed it.

We had both become quiet as we watched each other through the bars. A guard finally broke the silence. "Time's up." I looked up, thankful to see Avery and not DiMaggio.

"Tom, I want more than two hours with you."

"I know," he whispered. "Me too."

"It's not enough."

"I know," he said. He looked afraid of something, but what could the Hunter be afraid of? He was the scariest thing I had ever known. I stood up and reached toward him, wanting to be closer, wanting to touch him, knowing it was unwise.

"No touching," Avery reminded me.

I dropped my hand.

I began the long drive back to Bellevue, feeling hopeless. It wasn't until I got to the west side of the mountain pass that I realized just how much all of the Eastern Washington sunshine had been improving my mood. As I entered the dark drizzle under the thick cover of clouds, so common to Western Washington, my feelings of hopelessness joined with doom and despair. Now they could all have a party with each other, but not one that I wished to attend.

Spending time with Tom made me feel crazy. I wanted to touch him, to be near him. The drive home after a visit was always depressing, and even more so when I acknowledged the fact that the man I had fallen in love with had a date with a hangman's noose in less than one year. It wasn't fair. Why couldn't I be this sexually attracted to a man that hadn't killed several people? I had to ask myself— *what the hell am I doing?*

TWENTY-THREE

"The chapters you sent me are…a bit unusual," said the voice on my cell phone. Andrea's verdict hung in the air for several moments while I tried to form a response. God bless the British for their subtlety, although Andrea wasn't likely to understate her feelings for long. The people I had chosen as friends weren't what I'd classify as "yes people". Andrea would have no qualms about ripping me a new one if she felt it was warranted. She hadn't actually said she disliked it but, let's face it, if she had liked it that would be the first thing she'd mention. I felt the need to defend what I had written.

"I know, but I keep returning to this particular voice, this way of describing him that's intertwined with my feelings."

"Feelings? Whoa," Andrea said. "Are you beginning to actually like this guy?"

"Well…"

"What you've written isn't well rounded at all. It feels like you're trying to paint him as something other than the monster that he is. You need to interview the relatives of one of his victims. I think it would give you a more healthy perspective if you spoke to someone who's actually lost one of their loved ones to a murderer."

"I have…in a way. My parents were murdered when I was in high school. I was the one who found them," I confessed.

"Rebecca…" Andrea started. Then I heard her exhale slowly, followed by a long stretch of silence. I waited. Finally she said, "I thought we knew each other well. Why haven't you ever told me this before?"

"It's not something I like to talk about. I didn't see any reason to bring it up."

"You should have mentioned your parents when I asked you to write about this man. If I would have known, I wouldn't have asked you to do this."

"You wouldn't have? Really?"

"Well, all right, maybe I would have. I suppose having that in your past gives you a unique perspective another writer might not have." She sighed heavily into the phone. "The point is—we should have talked about this before I sent you out to Walla Walla. This must really be messing with your head."

"Andrea, this guy would mess with anyone's head, even someone whose background was…clean." *Even someone who hadn't come home one day after school to find half of her father's head blown away.* I struggled to suppress that mental picture.

"I don't suppose it helps that he's so bloody handsome," she remarked.

"You could have sent a man out there who was one hundred per cent heterosexual; he wouldn't have been safe either."

"Yes, wonderful, I can see that you're deeply affected by his charms, but seriously Rebecca, you need to put those thoughts to rest. Your infatuation with him has got to stop. I need to get some pages from you that deal with the horrendous murders this man has committed, and the impact it's had on the lives of his victim's families."

Andrea was right. It had to stop. I couldn't keep flirting with the devil. Sure, I could leave my bullshit out of the book. Sure, the world didn't need to know I was falling in love with the incarnate of evil. The trouble was that I knew, and I couldn't hide what I had allowed myself to become *from* myself.

TWENTY-FOUR

November 19th, 2012

I selected one of the phone numbers for the prison from my speed-dial and hit send as I barreled down I-82, doing as the prison officials suggested and confirming by phone an hour prior to my scheduled visitation time with Tom. Close to the city of Richland, about sixty miles from the penitentiary, I slowed the car, pulled over to park in a wide graveled area beside the freeway and hit the steering wheel with my balled fist. "Goddamn it! Shit! Fuck! Shit-fuck!"

The man on the other end of the line had just told me our visit had been cancelled due to the prisoner's bad behavior. I'd already driven over two hundred miles. That was more than three hours of my life wasted, not to mention all of the time I'd spent anticipating my chance to see Tom again. How could they let me drive all that way before telling me? When I'd asked the prison employee why someone hadn't called to tell me before I'd been in the car three hours, he told me that it wasn't the prison's policy to call people that were scheduled for visits to notify them of cancellations. It was the responsibility of the visiting party to call the prison for the status.

It could have been worse, I told myself. At least I'd saved myself the last sixty miles by doing the one hour check. That did little to console me. Extremely curious about what kind of bad behavior

Tom had been guilty of, I decided to call Andrea's friend, the Prison Captain, Ralph Barnett.

I dialed his number and then watched the other cars as they sped by me, every one of the drivers exceeding the speed limit, rushing to whatever places they had to be. I'd bet their meetings hadn't been cancelled.

After explaining who I was to Barnett's secretary she patched me through to his phone. "Hello Miss Reis," he said with curt efficiency. I got the impression that calling him Ralph would be a bad move for me.

"Hi Mr. Barnett. I'm calling because I was just told my visit with Eisenbrey has been cancelled. Do you know anything about that?"

"Yes, I do. This may come as a surprise to you, but some of the inmates that we house here have been known to misbehave. Eisenbrey is no exception."

"Do you know what he did that caused the cancellation?"

"I know plenty Miss Reis. For instance, I know one of my guards found some lacy panties when they inspected his cell ten days ago. Do you know anything about that?"

"Uh, oh crap," I muttered. "Yes, I gave those to him."

"And that's not all you did according to the guards that were on duty. Tell me, did you at any time reach through the bars of his cell?"

"No sir. I wouldn't do that."

"I sincerely hope not, but I'm not sure what you would or wouldn't do anymore. You aren't exactly the person I expected from Andrea's description. You were told to stay back four feet from the opening to his cell at all times. How did you get the panties to him?"

"I tossed them through the bars."

"Well don't do it again," he said, his voice harsh. "The prisoners here get away with a lot of shit — kinky love letters to their girlfriends, phone sex, making out during their visits. Hell, some of them even figure out creative ways to have sex in the visitation area while they're surrounded by visitors, some of which are children. I don't approve of that sort of behavior around the kids, but most of the other stuff doesn't bother me. It helps with morale and that makes it easier for us to manage these men. But Eisenbrey is a different story. That motherfucker is on death row for several good reasons. I don't mind you doing your little interviews, but I don't feel that his remaining time here needs to be a party. I expect you to conduct yourself in a more professional manner when you visit him or your visits will be terminated."

"I understand, and I'm very sorry about that Mr. Barnett. Is there any way you could allow me to see him today? I was almost to the prison when I found out the visit was cancelled. This is a very long drive for me."

"No way. It's too bad about your long drive, but he assaulted a guard. I don't have any intention of rewarding him with a visit from a nice looking woman after that."

"Oh no. Which guard did he assault?"

"It was Officer DiMaggio," he answered. I breathed a sigh of relief. I didn't care if something bad happened to that particular guard. In fact, I had fantasized about assaulting the man myself. "That reminds me, I need to ask if Eisenbrey has ever made any statements to you that seemed threatening or insinuated that he intended to harm any of the staff here."

"Uh, no, I don't recall any," I lied. I remembered Tom telling me that he was going to get even with DiMaggio, but I couldn't disclose that to Barnett. Tom might shut down during our interviews if he thought I reported what he said to prison officials. Besides, I wasn't feeling a warm and fuzzy alliance with Captain Barnett.

"Well, I want you to let me know immediately if he ever makes any statements to you that lead you to believe he's going to harm someone. That goes for my staff, the other prisoners, and you. Don't ever allow yourself to believe that he wouldn't physically harm you if he could reach you. That four foot rule is an important one. Got that?"

"Yes. I don't have any problem with staying back from his cell. I agree that it's a necessary safety precaution."

"Whether or not you agree is irrelevant. Just see to it that you comply. It would give me no pleasure to have to terminate your visitation. I wanted to do this favor for Andrea."

"When will I be able to see him again?"

"I'll let you see him this Friday provided he doesn't break anymore rules. As assaults go, this one wasn't too bad. DiMaggio didn't sustain any injuries, so I'm not going to bust Eisenbrey down to level one… yet." I cringed at the mention of level one. That meant complete isolation, no visitors whatsoever. The possibility was something that I dreaded to hear. It would put a serious damper on my book.

There was a pause and when Barnett spoke again he sounded a lot less like a drill sergeant. "And, Miss Reis, I uh, didn't actually realize that you hadn't received a phone call from one of our staff when the visit was cancelled. If it looks like this Friday isn't going to happen, I'll give you a call before you make the trip."

"Thank you, I appreciate that," I said. My rapport with Barnett had taken a beating, but it looked as though I hadn't completely demolished it.

I hung up and, after taking a few deep breaths, I had calmed down enough to safely pull back into traffic. There was nothing else for me to do east of the mountains so I turned around at the next freeway exit and headed back home to Bellevue feeling irritated with Tom for causing our visit to get cancelled.

I had assumed he would be on his best behavior with the guards because I thought our time together was important to him too. Was that too much to ask of him? Based on the exchange I'd witnessed between him and DiMaggio, he seemed to be allowed to say whatever the hell he wanted to the guards, so it appeared that the only thing he had to do to keep his visitation privileges was refrain from assaulting anyone. And, Jesus, how hard could that be?

But how much of this was Tom's fault? DiMaggio loved to pick a fight anytime an opportunity presented itself. And perhaps I shouldn't have told Tom what DiMaggio had done to me; it had only inflamed him. Tom had made it clear he knew something had taken place, but he wasn't all knowing, he'd needed me to fill him in on the details. I wondered if a little restraint on my part could have halted his rage. I feared that my last visit had been a set-up for the perfect storm.

I felt like screaming and/or kicking something. No, I felt like yelling at him. I wanted to spew my displeasure while it still boiled over. God forbid, I might be composed by Friday, my next potential opportunity to see him. I wondered what he would have to say for himself, and I had no choice but to wait until after Thanksgiving to hear it. I hated this.

November 20th, 2012

At 9:17 a.m., my cell phone rang, pulling me out of a comfortable slumber. I answered on the third ring, trying to disguise my grogginess. "Hello."

"Is this Rebecca?" a young and perky female voice inquired.

"It is."

"Good morning. This is Theresa from Dr. Shelby's office, I hope I haven't called you too early."

"No problem. What do you need?"

"I was wondering if we could reschedule your six o'clock today." Dr. Shelby? I searched my memory banks to place the name and realized she was referring to the psychiatrist I'd seen once nearly a month ago at Andrea's behest.

"I didn't realize I'd set another appointment with her," I said.

"Really? We always set the next one as you leave. I gave you a card with the date on it."

"Oh…you probably did. I just misplaced it."

"Lucky I called then," she said, cheerfully. Lucky for whom? I wasn't sure. I hadn't had any intention of seeing Dr. Shelby a second time, but having pondered the situation, I realized I had some questions that a psychiatrist might be well equipped to answer. "We had a cancellation at three o'clock today. I was wondering if it would work for you to come in a little earlier."

"Sure. Three sounds fine."

"Great! I'm sure the doctor will appreciate not having to stay so late. Thanks. We'll see you at three."

"Okay. Thanks Theresa."

I arrived fifteen minutes early, as usual. The psychiatrist's office was a two story structure, originally a house built around the 1920s, that she shared with two other mental health professionals. The conversion to office space was done tastefully, preserving much of the old-world charm. Even the small parking lot was designed in a way that seemed to fit with the landscaping.

Dr. Elizabeth Shelby was a short stout woman with chin-length orange hair and very fair skin. She flashed me a warm smile that set me on edge and motioned me to sit on the overstuffed armchair opposite hers. She opened a file folder, glancing at the paper attached to the inside. "Well Rebecca. It's good to see you. How have you been since I saw you in October?"

"Fine," I said, somewhat curtly.

She paused, watching me for a few moments, and then said, "How's the Prozac working out?"

"I'm not taking it," I said. Hearing the subtle air of defiance in my voice, I decided it would behoove me to drop the attitude and be pleasant to the woman for the duration of the appointment. I tried to make my tone a little friendlier. "I don't actually need it," I explained.

"You're not depressed anymore?"

"No. The depression's gone."

"That's wonderful," she commented, eyeing me dubiously. "What changed?"

"Well, I started working on a new book. That usually pulls me out of whatever funk I happen to be in."

"So, you're immersed in your work."

"Yes, but that's not a bad thing." And I was willing to argue the issue at length with her if she wanted to have a go.

She shrugged and set the file folder in her lap. "So, you're feeling better without the use of medication. I'm all for that. Is there something else you'd like to deal with in this session?"

Her question caught me off guard. Although I'd had most of the day to consider it, I hadn't yet formulated what I wanted to say. I winged it. "Well, this might be a little odd, but I'd like to talk about the project I'm working on."

"That's fine. Tell me about it."

I hesitated, trying to determine where to begin. "I've been having some difficulties with the subject of my book."

She nodded, and said, "The Hunter, Thomas Eisenbrey." This surprised me because I hadn't told her who I was writing about. I hadn't even known I was going to start this new venture until the day after I'd met this woman for the first time. I recalled our first session, it had been tricky. She was so nosy, so prying. And, God, how she'd yakked on and on about my depression.

Dr. Shelby continued, "There's something I should disclose—I received a call from your friend, Andrea Doyle. I didn't have a *discussion* with her. The things you and I talk about here are strictly confidential. However, she did pass along some information she felt was very important."

So the little bitches were teaming up against me. That couldn't be good. "Really? And what did Andrea have to say?"

"She told me that, in her opinion, you're infatuated with Mr. Eisenbrey. She also said you recently told her your parents were murdered, a fact she hadn't known when she asked you to write about him. She was very concerned about you."

"Swell."

"Would you like to talk about those things?"

I was momentarily speechless, but then I managed to get out, "Well…"

"When were your parents murdered?" she said softly.

"In 1988. I was a junior in high school. One day, when I came home from school, I found them dead. The sight of their bodies…" A shiver and a sharp intake of breath gave away far more than my words on the subject. That was enough for her to have from me. I had no intention of allowing her inside anywhere real. "But, you know what; I don't want to rehash all that. It was a long time ago. I need to move on."

"Who killed them?" she persisted.

"The police weren't able to figure it out. They said it looked like a home invasion robbery gone wrong."

"Do you agree?"

"Yeah, I think so. Some things were missing from the house."

"What happened after that? Who did you live with?"

"I moved in with my aunt and uncle."

"Your mom's or dad's side of the family?"

"Uh, my aunt is my mom's sister." I felt my irritation rising again. I tried to push it down, but this woman reminded me of the psychiatrist I'd been asked to see back then, not in the way she looked, the way she spoke. None of the therapy I'd gone through seemed to help me deal with my feelings about their murder. I was still incensed by the injustice of it, sad about the loss of the two people who had loved me more than anyone. I adored them. I missed them. Those feelings remained. No amount of therapy could take away the pain I felt, or help me to understand why it had happened. Therapy couldn't fix me.

Oddly enough, the only thing that had ever aided me to cope with the ticking time-bomb of feelings I had on that aching subject was creating a psychopath villain in one of my thrillers. So that was exactly how I'd dealt with it over the years. "Look, Dr. Shelby, I don't want to go on about that right now."

"That's fine. What would you like to address?"

"Well…I want to talk about Eisenbrey. I've noticed some strange things since I met him that I don't understand."

She leaned forward. "What things?"

"I — I've had some dreams about him." I shifted in my chair, crossing my legs.

"What happens in the dreams? Does he try to kill you?"

"No," I said quickly. "Actually, we usually sleep together in the dreams."

She nodded, and said, "Do you enjoy the idea of sleeping with him or does it upset you?"

"Both."

"The events we dream while we're asleep are involuntary."

"Yeah…well, the thing is…I'm awake for some of these dreams."

"So, daydreams, fantasies? Those are voluntary."

"I suppose so, but I don't feel like I can help it. It seems to happen even when I try to make it stop."

"Hmm. When you interview him, does he talk with you about his murders?"

"Yes."

"In detail?"

"Vivid."

"How do you feel when he talks about it?"

"Upset. Frightened. Creeped out."

"What else?"

"Isn't that enough?" I snapped. I didn't know what the hell she was searching for, but the way she leaned forward in her chair told me she clearly wanted something more. "What?"

"Do you feel anything for his victims?"

"Yes. I feel sad. I don't want anyone to be hurt."

Her eyes narrowed and she gave me another hmm. Then she said, "So, you feel upset, frightened, creeped out and sad. Is that all you feel when he tells you about the killings?"

"What are you driving at? What else would I feel?"

"Aroused."

"Piss off!" I said, volume raised. If anyone was in the waiting room, they'd heard me. My hands grasped the arms of my chair.

"You said you've been having dreams and fantasies about sleeping with this man," she countered.

"Not when he talks about the murders, for crying out loud. That's sick. I just have those thoughts when we're talking about other things, or…if I'm thinking about his appearance."

"You find him attractive?"

"Yes. He's extremely good-looking." This felt like a confession.

"How do you rationalize it? Do you forget who he really is? You pretend that he's someone else?"

"No. He's always Tom Eisenbrey."

"The murderer," she stated flatly. "Do you feel this is wrong at all?"

"Yes. I think it's terrible, but I'm not able to get him out of my head."

"Rebecca, you're not sexually attracted to him *in spite of* the fact that he's a serial killer; you're sexually attracted to him *because* he's a serial killer. This disorder is called hybristophilia—or Bonny and Clyde Syndrome. I think you may be suffering from some level of passive hybristophilia."

"Disorder? Hybristophilia?" I repeated. So it had a name. How precious. But that didn't give me the ability to tuck it away in a box and snap the lid shut. I wasn't closer to gaining some control over myself.

"Yes."

"I've never heard of it before. It sounds horrible."

"It is. This is not normal, or healthy for that matter. Although from a biological perspective it makes sense. A female's choice of a strong and aggressive male to mate with could ensure protection and a better chance of survival for their offspring. We may not be cavemen anymore, but our primitive instincts still surface from time to time."

"There's more going on than that. Sometimes I have the sensation he's reading my thoughts. He's right so often about what I'm thinking. Can people do that?"

"I don't believe so. He's probably a very good con artist. He manipulates you into believing that he's more powerful than he really is. Look, I don't want you to ignore this. Psychotherapy or group therapy can be very effective at treating your problem. I know a good group that deals with this issue. I'd like you to try it out. I think it will do you some good."

"Group therapy? What the fuck?"

"It's a twelve-step program, similar to AA, but for sex addicts."

"I haven't been laid in over a year. How does that make me a sex addict?"

"Rebecca, try not to take offense. I don't think you're addicted to sex, per se, but you seem to be addicted to Thomas Eisenbrey. It's not healthy to have feelings for someone who's destructive. What exactly do you see in him? Do you think you can fix him?"

"Crap," I said under my breath, rubbing my forehead. I disliked being under anyone's scrutiny, especially a shrink's. I wanted to be somewhere else.

"Let me guess—he probably takes a personal interest in you, he makes you feel special? Sure, he's hurt other people, several in fact, but he wouldn't hurt you because he cares about you. Has he told you that he loves you?"

I opened my mouth, then closed it, as she studied my reaction to this. By this point, I felt like I was just taking abuse from this woman, so why provide her with one more projectile to hurl in my face? She leaned back in her chair, and answered for me, "He has."

"I'm not a freak."

"I'm not suggesting you are, but I can't help wondering if there are things from your past that have caused you to be more susceptible to his charms than most women. How was your relationship with your father? Was he ever abusive?"

"Stop right there," I said holding up my hand. "That's enough."

"It's your choice whether or not to do something about your situation. But regardless of what you choose to do about therapy, I feel strongly that you should stop seeing this man immediately."

"I can't do that. I'm writing a book about him. I need to interview him."

"I don't buy that, Rebecca. Many people have written books about people they've never met."

"Not when they're able to interview their subject. In my opinion, that would be irresponsible. I have the opportunity to get the story directly from him."

"And what a story it is," she said, waving her hand with a flourish. "Murder, mayhem…torture." She paused, watching me, while my dislike for her simmered, and then she asked the loaded question. "What's more important to you, Rebecca, writing this book or your mental health?"

I had tried to have an open mind when I came to the session, to see if I could learn something of value from her, to see if she could suggest anything that would help me with my dilemma. I didn't want to be in love with him. I knew it was wrong. I didn't want to become his groupie or whatever the hell I was becoming. But I also didn't want to stop seeing him. I recognized it was too late for me. I was already lost.

"The book," I answered. And with that I got up and stormed out of her office.

TWENTY-FIVE

November 22nd, 2012

As usual I wound up with Aunt Susan and Uncle Harry on Thanksgiving. I couldn't have asked for a better place to spend the day and night preceding my next visit with Tom. I felt a little worried about whether or not Friday's visit would be cancelled too and it gave me the jitters, but visiting my aunt and uncle always had a calming effect on me.

Aunt Susan answered the door and took my green bean casserole into the kitchen. I followed her so I could grab a can of soda from the fridge. Then I wandered toward their family room, but Uncle Harry caught me in the hallway. He swung his arms around me and gave me a hearty squeeze. "Howdy Beck!"

I kissed his cheek and he released me. "How's it going?" I asked.

Uncle Harry pointed at a television so large it dominated the room and blocked any view out of the window behind it. "I've got a new baby!" he exclaimed, and I heard Aunt Sue mutter something about a jackass from the kitchen.

"She's a beauty," I told him. "But you can't see out your window anymore."

"I don't care. I already know what the backyard looks like. I'd rather watch Jennifer Aniston. She's got a new movie out on DVD. You wanna watch that? I'm sure you girls would love it."

"I'm sick of her. I want Daniel Craig!" my aunt shouted from the kitchen.

"Oh. I second that. Have you got one of the James Bond movies?" I knew that a good movie would probably take my mind off of things.

"Yeah, but Jennifer's not in that one," he said, pouting.

"Sorry old man. You're outnumbered here. We want Daniel," I said as I patted his shoulder. "Buck up. I'm sure you'll bounce back from this."

"Don't let him hide the TV controls!" Sue called from the kitchen.

"Okay," I told her, and I snatched the remote from the coffee table for safe keeping.

Uncle Harry eyed me with indignation and sighed, accepting his defeat like a gentleman. He sat down on his recliner that seemed to mold to his form, encasing him. His body sunk into it so far it made me wonder if he ever had the sensation that the chair would swallow him whole. I supposed if Aunt Susan ever called me to complain she couldn't find him, I could suggest a good place for her to look. I sat down on the couch next to him.

"How's your book going, honey?" Uncle Harry understood that if I was happy with my current writing project, I was probably happy about my life in general. I tended to get completely intertwined with my work.

"It's coming along. I had a minor setback—Eisenbrey caused our Monday meeting to be cancelled."

"What did he do?"

"He assaulted one of the guards."

"Holy shit," Harry said, pronouncing the latter word with two syllables. His face creased with a level of concern I wasn't able to muster up, given that the guard in question had been DiMaggio. Perhaps

Uncle Harry wouldn't care either if he knew what a bully that guy was. "Is the guard okay?"

"Yeah, he wasn't injured."

"Well, I guess it's not a big stretch for someone like him to behave that way. The guard's lucky."

Too right. That guard was lucky I hadn't kicked him in the nutsack when he reached his hand up my skirt. I felt bad about not seeing Tom, but maybe he'd gotten some paybacks for me. The thought gave me a happy feeling.

Aunt Susan emerged from the kitchen with some potato chips and sat next to me on the couch. I updated both of them on my interviews with Eisenbrey, leaving out the bits about my attraction to him and our pseudo-sexual encounter. Then I told them about my visit with Tom's mother.

"That poor woman," Aunt Susan lamented. "I don't think I'd be able to take it if I had a child that turned out like him."

"We don't have to worry about that. Ours is perfect," my uncle said, winking at me. They had no children of their own; ever since my parents had been gone they'd considered me theirs. His expression became serious, "Do you think she had anything to do with him becoming a murderer? Was she an odd lady?"

"I'm no expert, but I didn't get that impression from talking with her. She just seemed very sad. There was quite a resemblance between the two of them."

"What does that fella look like?" Uncle Harry asked. "Does he look like a killer?"

"Hang on, I've got a picture of him in my laptop," I told him. Then I opened my computer and showed one of the snapshots to my uncle and aunt. I didn't let on that I'd taken more than a dozen of him that day. They'd think it odd if they saw my entire collection.

"Does he give you the creeps?" Harry asked.

"Well…he did at first." I didn't know what else to say on that topic. I couldn't really share the confusing mixture of emotions I felt for Tom with those two. I steered us in another direction. "I saw the room where he's going to be executed."

"What do they do nowadays — lethal injection or the electric chair?" Harry asked.

"They allowed him a choice between lethal injection and hanging. He chose The Gallows." I tried to hide the sudden wave of sadness that inundated me. I shouldn't have brought this up.

Aunt Susan, sensing my grief, put her hand on my shoulder. "You shouldn't feel bad about that, Rebecca. He's earned it. Killing him is the right thing for the State of Washington to do."

I nodded slowly. "I know you're right, but it still bothers me. I can't help it."

"You're a good kid, Beck. Maybe too good to be writing a book about him," Harry said.

While I appreciated Uncle Harry's faith in my irreproachability, I didn't believe it was true. The thoughts I'd entertained about Eisenbrey, the dreams I'd had about him, and my willingness to participate in his sexual gratification at the prison proved otherwise. I was a bad girl. Even while chatting with my aunt and uncle, my thoughts kept returning to my desire to see him.

Aunt Susan looked at the clock and said, "I think everything's cooked. Beck, why don't you come with me and help me put the food on the table."

Uncle Harry got up as well and said, "Well, I guess it's time for me to go make room for dinner. I'll see you girls in a little while." He picked up a magazine on his way out of the living room and wandered off in the direction of the bathroom.

My eyes went wide at Harry's disclosure. I hadn't expected him to be quite so frank with us right before a holiday meal. "Oh, that's just wrong," I mumbled.

Aunt Susan closed her eyes and grimaced. "You know, if I was a lesbian I wouldn't have to listen to that kind of talk. Only a man would say something that crude."

"I think you might have a valid point," I agreed. Then I pushed Uncle Harry from my thoughts and pictured Tom on his bed, T-shirt pushed halfway up his chest, the zipper of his pants open and his hand sliding slowly, seductively down his stomach. No chance I would become a lesbian as long as he was around. If our visit got cancelled tomorrow, I would surely die.

I followed my aunt into the kitchen, watching as she donned oven mitts and took casserole dishes out of the oven, setting them on top of the stove. The turkey had been taken out earlier and sat on the island counter. She took a serving platter from the cupboard, telling me, "I guess I'll slice some white and dark; then we can just bring the platter to the table."

"Won't Harry fuss if he doesn't get to carve the turkey? He bought that macho, electric carving tool last year. He really seemed to love it."

"Yes, and he broke it last year too. That man's rough on his toys." Sue chuckled, shaking her head. "Trust me; it'll be easier this way."

I picked up two of her potholders that sported a charming country design involving chickens, smirked, and said, "These are very, uh…" I didn't quite know how to finish it off. We had such different taste in kitchen décor.

She returned my gaze, eyes crinkling at the corners, so full of love and concern, and asked, "Are you sweet on that Eisenbrey fella?" I knew I looked surprised, and the grin fell away from my face. I didn't answer her. "It's just us girls talking, dear. There's no need to be embarrassed. He's a handsome man. Sometimes people can't help having those kinds of thoughts. Just so long as you remember what he really is, and you don't act on it." She smiled kindly.

I nodded, still tongue-tied. Then she held one of the baked dishes toward me. "Here, Beck, take the sweet potatoes out to the table."

TWENTY-SIX

November 23rd, 2012

Time had moved slowly the rest of Thanksgiving Day, but the dreaded phone call never came so I got up early on Friday morning and started my ridiculous commute. Some fresh snow on the mountain pass slowed me a little, but I still arrived in Walla Walla well before the appointed time. I tried to read the paper while I sat waiting in my car in the prison parking lot, but I wasn't able to concentrate. When I finally got inside I was bursting with nervous energy.

Peeking inside the guard's office, I saw that the place on the wall was bare where they usually kept the stack of folding, metal chairs. "Hi guys. What happened to the chairs?" I asked.

Jones said, "Sorry, we're fresh out. I guess you'll have to stand, or you can sit on the floor." I was surprised that he chose to be such an ass. I didn't recall ever being rude to Jones, but perhaps he was close to DiMaggio. There were two empty office chairs beside the ones the two guards were seated in.

I looked to the other guard on duty, Downey, who glanced up from what he was reading and gave me a nod of acknowledgement. "Seriously?" I asked him. "No chairs?"

"Sorry," he said, shrugging, and he returned to his magazine.

Jones escorted me back to Eisenbrey's quarters in silence. He peeked through the narrow window in Tom's outer door and then gave Downey the okay to unlock it.

"What happened last weekend?" I demanded as soon as the solid metal door to his cell slid open. Tom was lying back on his bed, so I hovered near the bars for a moment and took a good look at him. There was a nasty looking dark, blue/black bruise under his left eye. He seemed irritable.

"They want me to behave like a goddamned Boy Scout in order to see you," he explained. He swung his long legs over the side of the bed and sat up, looking curiously at me and Jones.

I turned to face Jones and asked, "What?"

"You need to stay back four feet," he grumbled.

I stepped back the specified distance from Tom's cell and stood there, glaring at him defiantly. "How's this?"

Jones nodded, then he sauntered down the hallway back to the control booth.

Tom stood, grabbing onto the bars, and looked as though he was about to shout something at Jones, but I shook my head no. He sighed and asked, "Why won't he let you have a chair?"

"I'm not sure. He seems mad at me, but I didn't give him any reason to be. Whatever." I shrugged and looked at the floor. It wasn't clean, but I decided to sit down on it anyway, the most comfortable position seemed to be sitting cross-legged. I wore jeans that day, but the cement felt cold through the denim material. Still, it seemed like a better option than standing for two hours. "You've got quite a shiner."

"That's not all I've got," Tom muttered. He slipped his T-shirt over his head, exposing a large ugly patch of bruising covering the left side of his torso. He turned around and I saw some bruising on his shoulders and upper back as well, so dark in contrast to his pale skin. It occurred to me that this skin probably hadn't seen any sun in several years, since most of his time outside of the tiny box was spent walking around the open area just outside his cell; they allowed him an hour a day to do that, and there were no windows to the outside world.

I wanted to go to him, reach through the bars, comfort him, run my fingers through the dark hair on his chest. But after the warning I'd received from Captain Barnett I could be reasonably sure that a stunt like that would cost me my visitation privileges, and Jones seemed to be keeping a close eye on me. Besides I had to admit that my attraction to Tom hadn't eased my trepidation. I was still afraid to touch him. Just being in his presence felt dangerous and exhilarating, even though he looked too messed up to fight anyone at that moment. It was sweet that he'd been prepared to stand up to the guard on my behalf. "Are you okay?"

"Yeah, I suppose." Tom slipped his shirt back on and pulled it down over his torso. I felt a flash of irritation, as if he'd just snatched some treasured thing away from me. I hadn't wanted him to cover himself up.

"What happened?" I asked.

"Four of them came to escort me to the shower: Jones, Avery, Sepulveda, and DiMaggio." Tom rolled his eyes as he said the last name, and then he sat cross-legged on the floor facing me, peering through the bars.

"Four of them?" I asked in disbelief.

"Yeah, that's the standard protocol with me ever since that thing with Stills."

"That thing" being the time he tore open a guard's throat with his teeth. I'd already questioned him about that incident so I didn't revisit it. I had a sick feeling in my gut as my mind involuntarily created an image of the guard being bitten by Eisenbrey, but I pushed it aside. "Who's Sepulveda? I don't think I've met him."

"He usually works IMU South, but Downey called in sick," he explained. "Anyway, they were all wearing riot gear—suits with padding, gloves, helmets—which is also standard any time they let me out. I turned around with my back to them and Jones cuffed my hands behind me before they opened the second door, then the whole posse took me over to the shower room."

I'd seen the shower room on the death row wing. It was a slightly smaller room than the inmate's cells—cement walls and floor covered with some old, black-and-white tiles, one shower head protruding from the wall and a drain in the center of the floor. It was open to the hallway except for a door constructed of bars and crossbars like the ones on the inmate's cells, designed so the guards could secure the inmate in the shower and then supervise him from just outside.

He let a breath out slowly and pushed his hair back from his eyes. "It seemed odd that there wasn't any of the usual banter from DiMaggio as we walked. I knew that wasn't a good sign; he was stewing about something. Then, when we reached the shower room, he shoved me down on the floor and raised his baton to hit me, so I grabbed him by the throat and started choking him."

"Wait…how did you do that? Weren't your hands cuffed behind your back?"

"Yeah, but I can get them in front of me real quick." Tom could see that I didn't understand how he could do that so he elaborated. "He had me on the floor. I curled up in a ball and swung my hands underneath me to the front. Then I uncurled my legs, rolled over, and got up on my knees. He was coming down at me so I was able to reach his neck real easy from my kneeling position."

"But how could you choke him with your hands cuffed together?"

Tom moved his hands out in front of him and put his wrists together to demonstrate what it would look like if he was in handcuffs. Then he rotated his hands outward and extended his fingers. With his big hands and long fingers he had an impressive reach. "See that? It's no problem for me to wrap my fingers around a neck, and I don't have to encircle it completely to cut off the air supply, you do that toward the front with your thumbs."

"Oh," I gasped, and I instinctively raised my hand to my throat to protect it. Tom grinned at that. "I thought he was wearing protective gear."

"He was, but it was no problem for me to reach up under his helmet and get at his throat. The other guys pulled me off of him. Then he started beating the crap out of me with his baton. He kicked me in the ribs several times too. The other three just watched." Tom looked perplexed. "DiMaggio never did tell me what that was for."

"So you did assault him, but it was after he pushed you and raised his baton to hit you?"

"Yes, that's about the size of it."

"They lied?"

"If they didn't mention the part where he started it, then yes. Look, it didn't matter that I choked him; he was going to beat the crap out of me either way. I'm just glad I got the chance to frighten him a little." Tom paused and gave me a brief smile. "Why do you look surprised? You know DiMaggio's a little shit-weasel."

This was all so unsettling for me to hear. "I just didn't think they would do something that extreme here."

"Uh-huh." He looked around his cell with a bored expression. "This isn't the first time in the history of the world that an inmate has been smacked around by a guard, but I am ticked off that it happened to me again."

"Again?" I blurted.

Tom smiled when he heard the panic in my voice. "Yeah, they've worked me over with their batons on several occasions, especially DiMaggio. It's his favorite pastime. He loves it more than Super Bowl Sunday."

"Tom, I'm so sorry. Is there anything I can do? Should I report this to Captain Barnett or the warden?"

"No, they already know, and believe me they don't care." He tilted his head to the side as if something new had just occurred to him. "I want you to mention this in your book though. It might make your readers feel sympathetic toward me, and that sure wouldn't hurt."

"All right. I will."

"So…what do you want to ask me about today?" Having unloaded about the incident, he seemed resigned to whatever my agenda might be, so I decided to jump into some of the more difficult questions.

"Okay," I consulted my list, though I already knew what I wanted to ask. "Let's talk about the first group of killings that you were convicted of back in '83 — those hunters from Carnation: Burt Nolan, Kevin Nolan, and Stephen Wilcox. Why did you bind them with duct tape and torture them?"

"You wanna know why, sugarplum?" He sighed and shook his head. For a moment I thought he was going to refuse to tell me as he had the first time I broached the subject, but then he continued. "When I was a squirt, those three assholes found me in the woods. Burt was the one who pinned me down while Kevin tied my hands and feet. Kevin was also the one who told me that I was never going to see my family again and he made like he was going to slit my throat. He actually did draw some blood," he said all this in a casual manner as he rubbed the side of his neck.

"How did you feel?" I asked.

His only response was an almost imperceptible shake of his head. No.

I remembered something. "You told me earlier that you waited ten years to get even with some hunters. Are these the men you referred to?"

"Yes." His voice sounded hollow.

"Why did you cut off Kevin's head?"

Tom seemed unnaturally still, and when he spoke his eyes were an icy void. "Oh…that was because he wouldn't follow my instructions. I told him to watch me while I did his brother but he kept looking away." I felt myself shiver and I pulled my sweater around me. Tom related the events in a matter of fact way, showing no emotional response at all.

"Tom, that's very disturbing. Why would you do that? What do you get from it?"

He contemplated my question, looking past me, or more likely through me, his eyes half-closed and not focused on anything around him. "Pleasure," he said simply. "That was the happiest day of my life."

There had been many times when I wondered if he was honest with me during the interviews, but if everything else he had said had been a lie, I would always know that one admission was true.

"I also got an apology out of all three of them, and Burtie wasn't the kind to apologize." Tom smiled and leaned back comfortably with his hands clasped behind his head. He seemed completely relaxed, not poised to strike, and yet something was odd. My fight or flight instinct had just caused adrenaline to surge into my bloodstream. The metal bars did little to allay my fear.

Whatever I'd previously dreamed the two of us had in common slipped through my fingers like water. I stared dumbly at the foreign entity before me, wondering how I had ever convinced myself that we were both human.

My voice wavered as I said, "I don't understand. Ten years had gone by, but you were still angry with them—angry enough to kill them?"

"Sure. My hatred for them didn't dissipate over the years. If anything it grew. I would have my revenge eventually. It was simply a matter of waiting for the right time, and then when I heard they were going hunting that weekend, I knew it was meant to be."

"But why did you need revenge?"

"That's one of my rules: No wrong goes unpunished, not with me. I'm not the kind of man to let something go. You best remember that, Rebecca."

I had the urge to jump up from the floor, but I merely squirmed in my cross-legged position and asked him, "What about the third guy?"

"Steve, yeah I just made his painless and I even gave him a few moments to make peace with his maker first."

"Really? Why were you nicer to Steve?"

"It was the fair thing to do. There was no reason to make him suffer. He didn't take any part in abusing me with the Nolan boys. But he still had to die. He should have gotten me out of the damned mess I was in, yet he did nothing to defend me. So he's just as guilty of making me what I am." He stopped suddenly.

"Tom? What is it?"

"Well shit, I've just said…" he paused with a perplexed look on his face. "Huh. I didn't realize that before. I guess those fellas had an awful lot to do with me becoming the loveable guy that I am today." With that he broke into a wide grin.

"How old were you, exactly?"

"I was six. It was right after I started the first grade."

"How old were they?"

Tom rubbed his chin as he thought about that. "Well, let's see…I think Burt and Stephen were sixteen, and the older Nolan boy, Kevin, would have been about eighteen."

"Oh Tom, you were so little compared to them. That must have been terrifying for you. What do you recall feeling when it happened?"

Tom was silent for several moments, possibly irritated with me for revisiting this question, but I wanted my answer. I allowed him to formulate his response without interruption. The cold, hardened expression returned, and I had the impression that he was withdrawing into himself. His voice was steady and hollow as his eyes met mine. "Do you know what it feels like to be chased down and hunted?"

"No, I can't say that it's ever happened to me."

"Do you have nightmares? When the bogeyman comes, what happens? You don't just stand there, do you? You run from him."

"Uh, I guess so." I squirmed, feeling pierced by his steady stare.

"Rebecca, do you ever feel like you're trying to escape from a room but then you find someone has greased the doorknob, and try as you might you just can't get away?" He grinned unpleasantly. "If not… maybe you should."

I should have been prepared for that, but I wasn't. I'd let my guard down, pushing aside the fact that he was a predator, and the implication of what I must be to him. Unbidden memories of my mother and father came flooding back in. My eyes began to water and I choked back a sob. "Are you trying to frighten me?" I asked him. "Is that what you want me to feel when I see you?" I shifted my legs and started to get up.

"No!" He looked alarmed. His posture straightened abruptly, then he climbed to his knees and came to the bars, leaning against them. "I didn't mean that, darlin'. I'm sorry. I want you to feel happy when you see me. You make me…feel things." He looked down and swallowed. When he looked back up his eyes were filled with sincerity. That was enough to make me settle back down on the cold, filthy floor.

He studied my face for a moment, and then said, "Rebecca, what happened to your parents? How did they die?" His eyes narrowed and he seemed suspicious. How had he known to ask me that right then? He couldn't know what I'd nearly cried about. But his question was far too specific to be a wild guess.

"How do you do that?" I demanded. "How the fuck do you always know what I'm thinking?"

"They were murdered," he stated in a flat tone. He sighed. "Look, I didn't mean to bring back something that you were trying to forget, but now that they're in your head again, do you want to talk about it?"

"I don't know," I whispered, feeling so vulnerable. I wanted to trust him, but that was insane. Underneath it all, he was unfeeling, a game-player, and a murderer. If I shared something so personal with him it would surely come back to bite me on the ass. On the other hand, what did it matter? He was on death row. What could he really do with the information? At worst, he could taunt me about it in future interviews, and if he decided to treat me that poorly, I could always tell him to fuck off and terminate the visit. He was watching me, waiting for me to continue. I decided to confide in him.

"It happened when I was in high school. I came home one day and...found them. Dad was in the living room—he'd been shot through the head. Mom was in their bedroom—shot in the back. Some items were taken. The police said it looked like a home invasion robbery gone wrong. After that, I moved in with my aunt and uncle. I stayed with them through college."

"Not a sorority girl?"

"No, I preferred living with them. They're lots of fun. And besides, I didn't want to move out. I wanted to be with my family."

"You didn't want to lose them too," he said. Ouch. That was too insightful. I felt as though he was prying somewhere that he shouldn't. It made me nervous. "You'd already lost so much. It must have been a difficult time for you. I can see you loved your parents a great deal. You were close."

I started to answer him but found myself getting choked up. I swallowed instead and remained silent, not trusting myself to speak.

"Shh. You don't have to tell me how that made you feel, darlin'. I know how you feel." Tears slid silently down my face as I listened to his sympathetic patter. "I'm so sorry about what happened to your parents, darlin'. So very sorry."

"You didn't kill them," I mumbled.

"I know, but I'm still sorry. I wish it had never happened to you, or to them. If there was any way I could bring them back, I would."

How interesting to picture Tom reanimating dead people instead of killing live ones. "Thanks," I said, sniffling.

"You know, if I was free, I would never hurt you or your loved ones—your aunt and uncle. I'd shelter you. You'd be safe with me."

Perhaps that was true, but I had no doubt the rest of society would be in danger. I tried to focus on the fact that he would ultimately hurt someone again if ever given the chance, and to ignore the love that emanated from him as he gazed at me with his deep cerulean-blue eyes, but it overtook me. I couldn't help feeling comfort and warmth from his assertion that he'd protect me.

I thought about my uncomfortable session with the psychiatrist — her inference that I was delusional to think I was special — that he wouldn't hurt me, and I had to ask him, "Why is that, Tom? Why wouldn't you hurt me? Why would you protect me? What makes me different from everyone else?"

He shrugged, and appeared to give it some thought before answering. "I've never met a woman like you before. I really enjoy talking with you. I look forward to our visits. We connect on a deeper level than I ever have with another human being." His expression turned sad. "I've never had this before."

We sat in silence for a long while, looking into each other's eyes. Then he cleared his throat and looked to the corner of his cell. "I'm sure you have better places to be than this shithole."

"No," I said simply. "There's no other place in the world I would rather be right now than sitting on this cement floor with you." It was true. It felt so damned good to be with him, but at the same time it also felt sick and wrong, and much like the contrary mixture of sweet and sour in Chinese food, it was delicious as hell. God help me.

"Rebecca, you don't know how I miss you when you're away," he said in a low voice. He looked tortured, lost. He still knelt, holding onto the bars with both of his hands. "This is killing me."

"I miss you too."

"I want to do something about this, so I can see you more often."

"Like what?" I asked.

"I don't know yet, but I'm in love with you," he said, his face serious. *Lies*, a voice in the back of my mind hissed. But Tom was like a dark empty vacuum in space, a place devoid of matter, and I felt helpless to stop myself from being drawn into him. "If I had the power to will something into existence, I'd create a future for us."

I got back up on my knees again and rested on my heels. "That's a beautiful thought, Tom. I love you too." I moved my hand toward the bars, and then jerked it back suddenly as I caught a glimpse of Jones's disapproving glare. I felt a thrill at having almost touched Tom. Jones raised his hand and tapped on his watch. Our time was over.

Tom leaned closer to the bars. "Show me your tits," he whispered, a dangerous gleam in his eyes.

"What? You fucking asshole!" That made me get to my feet in a hurry, the spell broken. "I thought you were being sincere."

"I am being sincere. I really do wanna see your tits." He looked up at me with the face of a little boy asking when Santa was going to arrive.

"You're nothing but a damned animal. Do you know that? Oh… what the hell," I said as I grasped the bottom of my shirt and bra with both hands and flipped the fabric upward, freeing my breasts. I could hear the man in the cell next to Tom whistle, and I saw part of his face through the narrow window. I didn't have a clue who he was since the other prisoner's outer doors were always closed during my visits with Tom.

"Goddamn!" Tom grabbed the bars and scrambled to his feet. "I really do love you, darlin! And that's honest."

As I got my shirt and bra back in place, Jones said, "Visit's over now." I looked back at Tom. He clung to the bars and grinned like an idiot. I grinned too as I walked out of there, and I hoped I wouldn't have to explain myself to Captain Barnett later.

TWENTY-SEVEN

November 24th, 2012

Around one thirty I stood just inside the entrance to the café near my house, too nervous to sit down, checking out each of the men that entered. I hadn't had the good sense to ask the man I was meeting what he looked like when I'd received his call that morning, so I could only make an educated guess about which one he could be. He would look professional. He would probably be wearing a suit. I blew out a shaky breath between my teeth. I felt like I was waiting for a blind date to arrive.

I wondered what he would think of me when we met in person. I wondered what he'd heard about me. Had someone at the prison told him my behavior with Eisenbrey had been inappropriate? It was certainly true. Even if he hadn't yet decided I was a nutcase, telling him what I wanted from the exchange would seal it. But no, I didn't think I'd tell him. It was better to be vague. And anyway, I had yet to hear what he wanted from me…and from Tom.

There was a tap on my shoulder and I whipped around to find a handsome, clean-cut, silver-haired man of about fifty years who wore a black suit. He gave me a cold, detached smile and said, "Ms. Reis?" I nodded. He stuck his hand out and I shook it, his grip stiff and tight. "I'm Agent Farrar, FBI." He took his ID out of the breast pocket of his blazer and showed it to me. I glanced at it, realizing that I didn't know if it was real or fake, but I felt sure he was the real deal. He knew Scanlon and had spoken with Barnett over at the prison.

"Nice to meet you," I said.

He told me it was nice to meet me too. Then he got us a table and we sat down. Farrar studied my face, but I wasn't able to guess what he thought. His manner suggested that he wasn't passing judgment one way or the other. That was nice, because I really felt like an idiot for giving Eisenbrey a pair of my panties earlier. Although it had been hot at the time, afterwards it just seemed like a colossal error in judgment on my part, and it would only make me look bad in the eyes of someone like Farrar.

He ordered some coffee for us, and then he started to explain why we were there. "So, Ms. Reis, I've been told that you're working on a book about Thomas Eisenbrey."

"Yes, that's right."

"I'll cut right to the chase. I need some information from him and I want you to help me get it."

"What kind of information?" I asked, watching the waitress flip our cups and pour us coffee. He waited until she left before continuing.

"I'm trying to locate a serial killer by the name of Roddy Jenks. He's operating around British Columbia. Eisenbrey knows him. In fact, they committed a murder together back in 2000. Have you heard about that?"

"Yes, I was told he did it, but that's all I know. I haven't discussed the incident with Eisenbrey yet."

Farrar emptied two packets of sugar into his coffee and stirred. "Okay. Here's a rundown of the crime: The victim was Philippe Devereaux, the manager of the nightclub where Roddy worked. The club was having a huge New Year's Eve party for the new millennium. Mr. Devereaux was supposed to come out on the stage at 11:59 p.m., say a few words, and then do a countdown to midnight. But when the curtains opened the audience saw the victim duct taped to scaffolding with a slit throat. Several witnesses identified Jenks and Eisenbrey as the men they saw walking leisurely away from the scene, but they were not apprehended. The date of death was listed as January 1, 2000 because witnesses reported that they still saw Mr. Devereaux choking and thrashing around until after the stroke of midnight. It doesn't take long to die from the kind of wound that Mr. Devereaux sustained, a person bleeds out pretty fast from it. That means that Jenks and Eisenbrey must have waited to slash his throat until right when the curtains were opening. The odd thing is that this guy wasn't the type of victim that either of them usually chose."

It was such a terrible thing to do. And it was extremely ballsy for them to wait for the curtains. But for some reason, I couldn't really feel the horror of the act. Was I becoming desensitized hearing about Tom's gruesome crimes on a daily basis? Or was it just Agent Farrar's deadpan and emotionless way of delivering the details of the killing? I didn't get the sense he was outraged by it at all.

"Anywho, here's my problem: Roddy's still running around, living large, and little blonde women that fit his victim profile keep disappearing. I'd like it to stop, but I don't have a clue where to find him. I think Eisenbrey knows some things that might help us out, but when we asked for his assistance a few years ago he was uncooperative, and that's putting it nicely. When I heard about you, I thought this might be worth another try. I'm hoping that you can convince him to do the right thing and give us everything he knows about Jenks."

I decided to be direct and to the point with him too, and I tried to appear confident even though I didn't know if I could convince Tom to do anything. "Yes, I can get him to tell you what he knows, but we want something in return." He looked questioningly at me, waiting for me to continue. "I can't say exactly what it is that we want yet, because I need to discuss it with Tom."

"Okay, then let me tell you a few things that I cannot offer: I can't get him released. I can't ask the prison to lighten security measures with him, as you know the extra security is there for a good reason. I am not able to stop his execution, I can't even delay it. I am, in essence, limited to getting him things for his comfort or entertainment." He spread his hands out and shrugged in a placating gesture.

"That's roughly what I expected. I wasn't going to ask for any of those things. But I want your word that we will be granted what we ask for, as long as it's not on your can't do list."

Then Farrar said something that surprised me. "Ms. Reis, I'm pretty sure I know what you're going to ask for. And yes, I can get that for you." He sneered, the judgment I wasn't able to discern earlier was fully evident.

I believed him. "Okay. It's a deal. I'll speak with Eisenbrey about it on Monday. That's our next scheduled visit."

"That's two days away. I'd like to do it sooner. Would you be willing to come with me to Walla Walla now?" He checked his watch. "We could be there by six o'clock."

"Sure, but I'm only allowed two visits per week, that was Barnett's agreement with my agent."

"Not a problem. I can get you some extra time with him. It's for a good cause." Extra time with Tom sounded like a great deal to me, and if he was offering to drive me that was just icing on the cake. I relished the thought of not having to do all of that driving for once. "Would you like to grab a few things from your house? I assume you'll want to stay in Walla Walla overnight, but if you prefer I can arrange a ride home for you when we finish up tonight."

"Yes, I should grab my overnight bag. I won't feel like another four hours in the car that late. Would you like to follow me back to my house? It'll only take me a few minutes. Or would you like directions?" I offered.

"That won't be necessary, Ms. Reis. I know exactly where you live."

TWENTY-EIGHT

As the solid steel door of Tom's cell slid open I saw that he stood, waiting for me. A smile spread lazily across his face when he gazed through the bars at me. His black eye was still a prominent feature. I'd expected it to be a little better by then, but if anything it looked larger, like it had spread farther down his cheek, still that deep shade of blue/black. I was glad I had what I considered some exciting news to impart. I sat myself down on the cold, hard metal folding chair, grateful that it wasn't the floor again. Tom remained standing.

"Hey, you scored a chair," he remarked.

"Courtesy of Lutz. He's a nice young man."

"Yeah, I agree. I wish there were a few more like him around here. So how did I get lucky enough to see my girl on a Saturday night?"

"I was contacted by a man from the FBI today, Agent Farrar. He got me the extra visit so I could ask you to help him. He wants some information from you."

"What about?"

"Roddy Jenks. He's your friend, isn't he?"

Eisenbrey paused, his expression a peculiar mix of amusement and skepticism. "Friend? You think that Roddy and I have some sort of warm, fuzzy feelings toward each other?"

"You committed a murder together, didn't you?" I asked. "Isn't that considered male bonding in your world?"

Eisenbrey just shrugged.

"You don't like Roddy?" I said.

"I don't dislike him, but I don't know if that equals like. We understand each other." He leaned comfortably into the bars and laced one of his arms through, hugging them, his eyes full of flirtation. He enjoyed having my full attention.

"What do you understand about Roddy?"

"I understand his urges and what makes him want to kill. But more importantly, I know where he takes them," he said.

I was stunned. If his claim was for real, it was too good to be true.

"I'm sure that young ladies up in British Columbia keep disappearing."

"Yes, that's what Agent Farrar told me, and several from Washington State. Do you mean you could tell the police where to find him?"

"Sure I could, if I wanted to." Tom walked away from me and sat down on his bed.

"You have to," I said urgently.

"And why the hell would I want to do that? They've got me locked up in a cell that's smaller than a goddamned dog kennel. Why should I help those fuckheads?"

"You could stop him from killing more people," I said simply.

"I don't give a shit who he kills. That's not my problem."

Although that wasn't the kind of statement that should have surprised me, it still took me a moment to find my breath again. His way of thinking was just so foreign to mine. "How can you not care about other human beings?"

The chuckle my comment elicited held no hint of mirth. "Did you think that through before you said it, or did that just fly out of your mouth?" He held up his hand. "Don't tell me, I think I know the answer. I still don't see any reason why I should assist that mother-fucking FBI Agent."

"Because it would be a great bargaining chip, but…I should warn you, Farrar said that he doesn't have the authority to do anything about your execution. That's still up to the governor or the Supreme Court. I'm sorry about that, Tom."

"I can see those wheels a-turnin', sweetheart. Just what would you suggest I bargain for?" I knew I had his interest, because he leaned forward and laid his cerulean gaze upon me in full force.

TWENTY-NINE

That evening, I helped facilitate the meeting between Tom and Agent Farrar. Tom got Farrar's word that his request would be honored, provided that the information he gave them led to the actual capture of Roddy Jenks, and Tom told the FBI Agent what he needed to know —the location of Roddy's hideout. I felt as though we'd accomplished something important. After that I was taken to the motel room Agent Farrar had arranged for me and, much to my surprise, I managed to sleep most of the night.

November 25th, 2012
I was allowed to see Tom again in the morning, and we talked while we waited for the news on Jenks. We had several hours together since it wasn't a normal visitation day. Sometime in the early afternoon the agents told us they'd captured Jenks. We both cheered and I even jumped up and down, barely able to contain my elation.

It seemed too good to be true—the willingness of the FBI to grant this request, then the rapid report that Jenks was in custody—and it was. Agent Farrar and I were asked to see the warden.

✝✝✝

Warden Hale's office was in a boxy white cement building in the original section of the prison. The barren and unimaginative style of the architecture told me it was constructed around 1960. It seemed incongruent alongside the red brick buildings from the 1880s. Inside his office, the majority of the furniture was somewhat new and comfortable. We found him sitting behind his desk, an enormous wooden bureau that, although well taken care of, looked very old. I wondered if it had belonged to the very first warden at Walla Walla. He stood to greet us.

"Good to see you again, Tim," he said to Farrar. Then he turned his attention to me. The warden seemed a few years older than Agent Farrar, probably approaching sixty. His short gray hair was parted neatly at the side. He wore taupe slacks, a beige shirt and absolutely reeked of cigarettes. "So you're Ms. Reis. I've heard so much about you," he said, taking my hand in a firm, leisurely embrace. He leered as he looked me over. I shook his hand quickly and then pulled away. The man gave me the creeps. "Please have a seat." He motioned us toward two padded chairs in front of his desk and we sat.

"I'll get straight to the point—I can't allow this insanity," he said with an air of finality. "A conjugal visit is out of the question. It's just far too dangerous for you to be in an enclosed area alone with that man. Have you forgotten the four foot rule? And why on earth is the FBI on board with this request?"

Agent Farrar spoke next, "We needed something to bargain with. Please, Leo, it really won't be dangerous. He's going to be in full restraints during their visit."

"Eisenbrey won't like that. He'll whine to that pain-in-the-ass attorney of his," Hale snapped irritably.

"Eisenbrey's no dummy, he's already agreed to the restraints. I'm sure he understands the visit can't go forward without them."

"Still… no, I can't allow this."

"Come on, Leo, we need you to honor the deal. He gave us Jenks. That's huge."

"That's nothing to do with me," the warden said with a dismissive wave of his hand.

"Sure it is. You'll be getting a new resident out of this as soon as he's convicted."

Hale rolled his eyes. "I don't care. You should have cleared this with me before you made any promises. If it was any other inmate…"

"I know, I know. I'm well acquainted with his history, and so is Ms. Reis."

The warden looked to me. "Indeed. And just why do you want to do this, young lady?"

"I, uh…" I could feel my face flushing. I hadn't wanted to have to explain myself, but it looked as though I needed to. "I have… feelings for him."

"That's extremely fucked up," the warden pronounced, shaking his head as he scrutinized me.

"Not important, Leo. The main thing is we got another one of the bastards in custody. So let's give Eisenbrey his treat. He did a good thing for once. And you never know, we might need more information from him in the future."

"Hmm…" The warden rubbed his chin as he mulled the request over. "Even if the situation with the restraints is taken care of, and I suppose I could trust Officer Avery with that, the problem still stands—you and Mr. Eisenbrey are not married. These kinds of visits exist for the purpose of keeping families intact, so the wives of these men don't commit adultery, so these men still have families to return to when they get released. I'm a Baptist, young lady. In God's eyes, if you're not married, the two of you are not a family."

"For crying out loud, Leo. That is so…" Farrar started.

I couldn't see any value in drawing out the dialogue with Leo, especially after I thought I just heard him cave on the issue. I interrupted to clarify. "So you would allow it if we were married?"

"Uh, well, yes, I suppose so," the warden said with a startled expression.

So that's all that was needed — a piece of paper, a quick little ceremony? This didn't seem like much of an obstacle to me. If Tom and I were married, I would still live in Bellevue, he would still live here in his little cell, and I'd only see him when I chose to visit. The certificate would be filed in this little town, far from where I lived. No one outside of the prison would ever have to know. Nothing in my life would change at all except I would finally be able to sleep with the man that I couldn't get out of my head. It seemed worth it to do the paperwork in order to get what I wanted, and I imagined Tom would agree.

"I think that can be taken care of," I said.

"Really?" said Farrar, leaning forward. I saw a flash of alarm flit across his face before the mask of indiscernibility returned. He relaxed his shoulders.

I nodded.

"Okay," Farrar said. "Let's go talk to Eisenbrey." We stood up, and he added, "Thanks, Leo." Then we stepped out of the office leaving a bewildered warden in our wake.

When I relayed our conversation with the warden to Tom, he broke into a big grin. And then he got down on one knee and proposed to me.

November 26th, 2012

I had to stay in the motel room another night. On Monday morning, I went to the county office and got the application for a marriage license. Then I brought it to the prison for Tom's notarized signature. The notary went to Tom's cell so they didn't allow me to visit him that day, but it didn't dampen my mood. I was elated as I returned to the county office with the signed form.

After that, I drove home. For the next three days, I saw no one, spoke to no one, remaining isolated in my house. I didn't want the annoying little voice of reason to try to talk me out of what I was about to do.

THIRTY

November 29th, 2012

On the morning of the 29th, I went to the prison in a white dress. Not a traditional wedding dress, it was more the kind of thing that one would wear to go to a dance club. It was form fitting, with shoulder straps that extended down and crisscrossed over an open back. Draped over my shoulders I wore a large sheer white scarf with an intricate floral pattern embroidered with gold thread. I must have chosen well, because Tom expressed several times in many different colorful ways that he thought I looked hot in the dress.

I stood outside Tom's cell with Officer Avery and held up the ring I'd purchased for him so he could see, a gold band with a Celtic pattern on it. I'd assumed he wouldn't be able to shop for a ring for me, so I wasn't expecting one from him. He surprised me.

"Lutz was kind enough to take some money from my account and go to the jewelry store for me. I think he did a good job. He got exactly what I asked for." Tom opened the jewelry box and showed me the contents. There were two rings inside, almost identical, except one had a diamond and the other a dark black stone. "Before we do this, I want to be sure you understand me and that you agree."

"I've already agreed to marry you. Why are there two rings?"

"You may find this hard to believe, darlin', but I have a good side.

That's what the diamond ring represents. But as you know, I have a dark side too. I can't help that. That's why one of the rings is black; it's made out of onyx. I want you to accept all of me and marry all of me. If you really love me, you'll wear both rings."

"Tom, that's amazing." And sick and twisted, my brain added, which the look on Avery's face confirmed. But this had become my path. I didn't have any doubts. My heart raced as I said, "Yes, of course I will."

Tom placed the ring box in the food tray slot. Avery took it, removed the rings, and handed them to me. Then he removed the ring from the box I held and set it in the tray slot for Tom. Avery kept both of the boxes. Tom turned the ring over in his fingers admiring it.

"Do you like it?" I asked, nervously.

"This is perfect, darlin'," Tom said with a grin.

Then the reverend and Lutz arrived. The wedding was performed with Tom inside his cell, and the rest of us in the wedding party standing back the required four feet. The two officers, Avery and Lutz, stood as witnesses of the ceremony, and Lutz also served as the best man. They both smiled as we were pronounced husband and wife.

I put the diamond ring on my left hand, and it fit perfectly. Then I tried to put the black ring on the same finger but it felt awkward. Tom was peering at me between the bars. "That's okay, darlin'. You can put the black one on the other hand." So I did. Tom beamed with joy. I'd never seen him so happy.

Tom wrapped his fingers around two of his cell bars, resting his forehead against them. The light glinted on the gold band he wore as he stared at me. "You're mine now," he told me with a dangerous gleam in his eyes.

An hour later, I paced in the hallway outside of the room that was going to be used for my private visit with Tom, all jacked up on adrenaline. There were four chairs lined up against the wall, but I was too nervous to sit down. I fiddled with my wedding rings some more — the white and the black, the light and the dark, the good and the evil.

A door opened, and a man stepped into the hall wearing a black riot suit with protective padding strapped around his knees, thighs, elbows, arms and he wore what seemed to be a bulletproof vest over his torso. As he approached me his gloved hands removed his helmet and I saw that the man was Don Avery. He smiled, then his expression turned quizzical. "Are you really going through with this?"

"Yeah," I said, although I wasn't sure if I was going to do a runner at the last second. I stepped back examining his outfit with a critical eye. "All this for Tom?"

"That's right. We have to suit up when we transport him. No exceptions." Avery's breath hissed through his teeth as he slowly let it out, his eyes fixed on me. "I gotta put restraints on him before you come in the room. We'll put his hands and ankles in cuffs, but he's wriggled out of those before." His brows creased with worry as he noted the significant tremors running through me. "Well, at least you have enough sense to be scared shitless, but I still think this is completely insane. I wanted him in a straitjacket and a Hannibal Lecter mask, but his attorney got shitty with us, so he won't be wearing any of that."

"Oh, I didn't realize Tom had been in contact with his attorney," I said.

"Do you understand how bad this guy is?" Don's voice was gentle. "You're writing a book about him, so you know the kinds of things he's done to his victims. What if this goes all wrong?"

"I understand, and I appreciate your concern. I don't think he'll hurt me." Part of me believed Tom's assurances, but I also recalled the times when I saw the darkness in him, and I had to acknowledge to myself that I never knew when he was telling the truth. I knew I was taking a risk, but I wanted to do it regardless. I needed to.

Don shrugged. "Okay, but like I said, I don't trust the cuffs. I'm going to put him in leather restraints too, so he'll be double cuffed at the wrists and ankles. And in addition to that I'll restrain him at the chest, waist, and thighs. I think it'll be sufficient. You never know, he might even appreciate seeing you enough to behave himself. I'll be back in a few minutes," he told me. Then he nodded at another guard, also in riot gear, and they both went through a door leaving me alone in the hallway.

When they returned Don said, "Right through here." He put his hand on my back, guiding me through the door from which he had just emerged, into a small windowless office. There were three guards sitting in front of a monitor on a desk: Lutz, Downey, and Jones, the latter of which was leaning back with his fingers laced behind his head. There were a few empty chairs as well. And there was another door in the wall to the side of the desk, presumably where they had placed Tom.

"Hey, Rebecca," Lutz said in his good-natured manner.

"Hey yourself, Andy," I said, smiling back at him. At that moment, it was nice to see another friendly face. I wasn't sure about the other guards, but at least I had Don and Andy.

Then the door that I had just been ushered through opened again and a short, stalky man entered. He was bald and wore a business suit that seemed at least one size too big for him. I wondered if perhaps he had lost some weight recently. "Hi folks."

"Hey, Jim," Avery greeted him.

The man turned to me and said, "Hello there young lady. I'm James Pawlowski, the attorney for the prison. You must be Mrs. Eisenbrey." He grabbed my hand and shook it vigorously.

I was momentarily confused about who he meant, but the fog cleared quickly and I realized there hadn't been a discussion yet about which last name I would use. "Oh, it's Reis. I wasn't planning to change my last name."

Avery made a sound that I would liken to a cough that had been snuffed out before it's time. "Uh, you know what Rebecca, I don't think you'll want to tell that to your new husband."

"Really?" I asked. There was a murmur of agreement between the others in the room.

"It's too late for that. I'm gonna tell him," Jones said before he took a swig from a can of cola and belched. He put his feet up on the desk.

"Well, you don't have to figure that out right now," Jim said. "I need you to sign this waiver before you can see him though. Here and here," Jim said pointing to the appropriate spots. He laid the papers on a table and handed me a pen. "Just sign twice, once as Rebecca Reis and once as Rebecca Eisenbrey. That should cover our bases."

"Okay, but what's this for?"

Jones answered before the attorney had a chance to and his voice had a nasty edge. "In case he gets loose."

I looked at Jim to see if that was indeed what he meant. "Yep, that's about the size of it," he agreed.

I didn't read the damned waiver, I just signed where I was told and Jim collected the document. "Looks like we're all set. Congratulations, dear." He patted me on the shoulder, and I thanked him as he left.

"Okay, your hour has started. We'll be right over here observing in case he tries anything," Avery explained.

"Observing?" I sputtered.

"Of course. There's a camera in the room and we will be right out here watching the monitor."

I startled and tried to wrap my brain around that new development. I had never had sex in front of any kind of audience before, but I supposed if I had to have guards witness this then Lutz, Downey, Jones and Avery were all right. It could be worse, I thought. DiMaggio could be here.

The door to the hallway swung open again and DiMaggio walked in carrying a large bowl of popcorn. "I didn't miss anything, did I?"

he asked, cheerfully. He plopped himself down in one of the chairs and put his feet up on the table, smiling at me with an air of smug satisfaction, clearly waiting for the show to begin.

Avery noted the look on my face with some amusement. "You didn't think we were going to allow him to be alone with you un-supervised, now did you?"

"Oh, that makes sense...I guess I just hadn't thought about it." I took an embarrassed glance around the room. "Swell."

"Sorry," Avery said. "We have to be ready in case something happens. Just try to forget we're here."

"Okay. Thanks," I muttered. I hesitated, taking a deep breath, and then I twisted the door handle and entered the room where they had Tom.

He was lying on his back on a double bed. His hands and feet were drawn to the corners of the bed, and hung over the mattress. His arms were bent at the elbow since he was too tall to have them fully extended. His metal handcuffs and leather wrist and ankle restraints were secured to the metal frame. In addition, the guards had placed three leather straps around his chest, waist, and thighs, which were secured under the bed. He was clad in a white T-shirt and loose-fitting, gray sweatpants. I was happy to see someone had thought through the logistics and given him some pants that weren't as formfitting and potentially hard to slide down as the pants he usually wore, which had a zipper fly.

His expression was indiscernible as he looked up at me, his face bruised, his hair tousled, but none of that detracted at all from his good looks. Once again, I found myself trapped in his magnetic gaze.

"Are you okay? Is that uncomfortable?" I asked. Seeing him like that, in restraints, frightened me. And the reality of what I was about to do started to hit home. This man was so dangerous he had to be tied down for me to make love to him.

He squirmed impatiently. "I want you. Best get on with this. We only have an hour and you've still got all your clothes on." Then he took a longer look at my face. "Why are you so nervous?"

"Some of the guards are in the other room watching us."

"Don't you worry about that, sugar. There's always someone watching in this place. Let's give 'em a show." He chuckled, but then stopped abruptly when he realized that I wasn't amused along with him. I scanned the room and saw the camera mounted on a bracket high on the wall in the corner of the room. It was aimed so I'd be facing it. I could feel my eyes welling up with heated tears. "Hey now, don't you give that any thought," Tom said in a soothing voice. "Look at me now, darlin'. I'm the only thing that you should be thinking about. Forget about everyone and everything else."

I did as he said, and focused my attention on him. They seemed to have him secured well, especially his hands. He tried to move, but the straps and cuffs held him tight. And yet, they hadn't put anything over his mouth at all, which frightened me. Tom had bitten four of his victims. The guards wouldn't go inside any enclosure with him without their gear, which included helmets that protected their throat, but they were allowing us to be as close as two people could get with his mouth completely free. I didn't believe that Tom wanted to hurt me, but he did at times have the desire to attack, to kill. Once he had even told me that he needed to kill. I wasn't sure he had complete control over his own behavior in this regard.

I hesitated, my terror making it impossible to take the next step toward him. "I'm afraid," I said in a small voice.

"Oh, hell no. Don't get like this now. I've been looking forward to this. Come on over here," he coaxed, but I couldn't move any more than he could. "Holy shit, look at you tremble. You're terrified of me." He looked amazed, then reflective, and then something else — I had the impression that he enjoyed my fear, that he felt a certain amount of pride for being the cause of it. "I guess this is a lot different than when you have those nice little bars between us." He gave a hollow laugh. "What the hell are you afraid of? I'm all tied up. I'm entirely helpless."

"I'm afraid you'll bite me," I said in a smaller voice. I could run, and if I did there would be nothing that he could do about it. He couldn't chase me. I should run.

He gave me an appraising look and nodded slowly. "Okay, I understand. Take that scarf of yours and gag me with it, then I won't be able to do that."

I knew that gagging him with a scarf was ridiculous, especially the sheer silk one that I wore. It offered no real protection from someone like him, but it did comfort me on a psychological level, and it was enough to keep me there. "Okay," I said.

I noticed the pleasant scent of soap and shampoo as I got close to him. My hands were shaking as I brought the scarf up to his face, but he held completely still while I secured it, tying a firm knot behind his head. I touched his temple, running my fingers down the side of his face and then his neck. I closed my eyes for a moment, drinking in the heady feeling of his warm skin under my fingers. I was touching him — actually touching him — the forbidden one. My senses swam.

I studied Tom's features. His eyes were calm, placid, and the blue in them seemed to stretch on forever like the evening sky. He nodded, watching me. And even though he was gagged, the part of his mouth that was still visible showed a smile. *He was grinning the way evil does when it knows it has you.*

The hesitation left me then. The nervousness I felt morphed into exhilaration, and I didn't care anymore who was watching or what this would cost me. This moment was worth any amount of fallout I would have to endure.

I tore my clothes off and climbed on top of him, sitting on his thighs while I tugged at the elastic waistband of his sweatpants, easing them down far enough to free his cock. Tom was well endowed.

I realized that I hadn't been able to see all of him the day he jerked off during our visit.

As my fingers found his erection and began stroking, I reveled in the sound of his bliss. The only thing more heavenly than closing my eyes and listening to his rich, enchanting intonation was keeping them open so I could take in the look of pleasure on his beautiful, bruised face.

My insides roiled with need and desire. I straddled him, guided his cock to the place where he belonged, and as I rested my weight down on him I felt him slide up inside of me, filling me beyond what I thought I could take. I threw my head back and groaned, the sensations of pain and pleasure from Tom's phallus being just a little too big comingling.

The gag did nothing to quiet Tom's moaning, but it did render whatever he was trying to say unintelligible. His face, wet with sweat, was a depiction of unbridled lust. I wondered if this was the way he looked when he did the sick things that he seemed to need, the acts that he said he loved more than anything else in the world, the thing that he might very well do to me if he wasn't in restraints. Those thoughts only excited me further. It was so easy for me to envision my man in the underworld with flames all around him.

I knew what I was doing was sick and wrong, but I didn't care. I wanted the evil inside of me. I needed him. I lost myself in the ecstasy, the rapture, the overwhelming feeling of victory. His eyes burned into mine as I moved, and I sensed something foreign creeping into my psyche, cementing us together, connecting us on a much deeper level than before. Then finally, I felt the sweet, magical release of endorphins flooding my bloodstream, overtaking my senses. A second later, Tom's sounds of bliss joined mine and we both reveled in a euphoria that seemed to go on forever and end too soon.

After we both came, I thought about loosening the gag so he'd be able to talk. He didn't look dangerous now that he was spent. He seemed too content and relaxed to do any harm. And he had to be affected by the intensity of the love that had just coursed through us. I hoped that was true.

I lowered my face to his slowly, carefully, and kissed his forehead as I reached behind his head and untied the knot in the scarf. I removed it, still too afraid to kiss his mouth. Then I slid downward and cuddled up to him. I pushed his T-shirt up to expose his chest and I rested the side of my head on him, rubbing my cheek and then my mouth against his thick, soft hair. I breathed deeply, enjoying the musky smell of his skin and his sweat. For the next few minutes we were silent except for the sound of our breathing.

"I feel like everything else in my life up to this point has been meaningless, just something I had to go through in order to get here with you now," I confessed.

"It was. We were meant for each other." He sighed, and I flinched as I felt his breath tickle my scalp through my hair. I hadn't realized that his mouth was so close to the top of my head. "Rebecca," he said quietly. "I know you're afraid, but I want you to kiss me."

I buried my face in his chest and replied, "I don't know…"

"I'm not going to hurt you, sweetheart. Think about it. I'd have to be insane to do that. What the hell else have I got? You're the only nice thing I have to look forward to in this world. I won't ruin that. I promise."

But was that true? He ruined a lot of things. He ruined people. He ruined lives. And for all I knew he might be insane. I felt as though I had been getting to know him pretty well during these interviews. Tom seemed to have opened up to me, but ultimately he shared what he chose to share. I couldn't know exactly what went on in his head. I still didn't feel like I could trust him entirely.

"Wrap your arms around me, darlin'. I wish I could hold you. God, I wish I could hold you." I heard a sob catch in his throat. I slid up his body slowly until my eyes were level with his, and I saw that his eyes were full of tears. "I'm in love with you, Rebecca. You know that, don't you? You believe me." He looked sincere, but why had he asked if I believed him? My suspicion rose; I wasn't sure what to believe. I hadn't realized that this visit would be laced with so much pain.

I could only nod in reply. Tears ran down his face but he held my gaze. "My wife," he whispered with an intensity that was electric.

"My husband," I answered.

"I love you forever. Even after I'm gone, Beck, even after I'm gone…"

"Don't," I said, and before I knew it my fingers were on his lips. I had taken the leap of faith without even realizing I was jumping. Then with an air of heedlessness I brought my face down and pressed my lips against his. I felt a fresh fire ignite in me. My hands were in his hair, clutching his head, holding his face against mine as his tongue explored my mouth, sending a tingling sensation through my entire body. The pressure of his flesh against mine was rapturous, the way his tongue and lips felt as he kissed me, enthralling. He filled a longing in me that I thought could never be satisfied, all the while making me hungry for more.

I could feel his erection against my thigh, prodding, insisting. I needed him. He moved his hips, pushing his cock against me and threw his head back, groaning loudly as he slid inside. This man could take what he wanted even while restrained, yet he begged, "Please baby, please baby…" He kept repeating it breathlessly until I gave him his orgasm. And when he came he yelled and thrashed against his restraints; he looked like a crazed animal that was trying to break free. One last show for the men watching the monitor.

Afterwards, I sat in my car for a long while, astounded and dazed, re-playing each second of the exquisite madness in my head. It seemed crazy that I was about to do something as mundane as drive my car after what I had just experienced, but it was time for me to go home.

I went straight to Bellevue with the exception of one stop to fill the gas tank and get a hamburger. As I drove past the exit I would have taken to visit my aunt and uncle, I felt a twinge of guilt. I hadn't spoken to them since Thanksgiving. They had expected to see a lot more of me since they knew my travels brought me so close to their house.

My aunt had mentioned that a weekly visit would be nice, but I'd probably put it off until Christmas. I couldn't see them right then, and I certainly couldn't tell them what I'd been up to lately. In fact, I felt my face flush with the humiliation I'd feel if they ever found out about my marriage to Tom and our special visit. Until then, I had never envisioned getting married without my aunt and uncle's blessing and their presence at the ceremony, but this situation was different. It wasn't a real marriage.

THIRTY-ONE

November 30th, 2012

The next day I spent most of the morning on automatic pilot, dwelling on Tom and the time we'd spent together. I stood in my driveway, just about to get into my car, when Scanlon pulled up in front of my house. He parked with the same reckless abandon that he drove, ending up well into my flower bed before he finally came to a full stop. Jumping out of his car, he slammed his door shut with such force I thought his windows might shatter. He looked far too upset to drive. It was no small miracle he hadn't killed someone or piled his car up on his way here.

"Is it true?" he yelled. "Or is this some sick practical joke the assholes at the prison are playing on me? One of the guys I know out there called me and—did you really marry that sick motherfucker? I didn't believe them, but it's just that…the marriage certificate is in the county records. I don't see how they could fake that. Can you tell me what the fuck is happening? Is this real?"

I couldn't answer him, and I couldn't look him in the eye either. Scanlon seemed ready to explode with furious energy. He began pacing back and forth in front of me as he continued to shout. "Holy shit! It's true? It's true, isn't it! Goddamn it! Is it also true that you fucked him? Of course it is! Motherfucker! I can't believe this is happening! Am I having a fucking nightmare? Oh God, it's real isn't it! Jesus!"

When he grabbed me by the shoulders I could feel his hands tremble. He shouted in my face, "Why? Can you at least answer that? Why would you do this?"

I didn't have an explanation that made any sense. The real answer was simply that I was lost. "I don't know."

He seemed to take some encouragement from my confused demeanor and changed tactics. "Look, this can't go on anymore. It can't happen again. What you need to do is start the divorce proceedings immediately, and you've got to stay away from that prison. You can't see him again. Do you think you could get an annulment? I think that would be quicker than a divorce. You could just tell the judge that you were out of your fucking mind when you did this, because honestly, I can't see any other way that this could have gone down."

"Darryl, I can't do that," my voice felt so small.

"What? My ears can't be working right. Did I just hear you say…" he stopped, stunned and speechless, and then he exploded again. "No! Oh my God! No fucking way! There is no fucking way that this is happening! You're going to fix this!"

"I can't. I'm sorry. I can't divorce him."

"Don't you understand who he is? Can you not comprehend it? You just married a murderer! Not just any murderer, but the same sick motherfucker that tore my neck open with his goddamned teeth! It's a miracle that I'm even alive. I almost bled to death at the scene. I don't know how the fuck the surgeon managed to put me back together in time to save me. That man doesn't have any regard for other human beings. We're just things for him to hunt and play with. How the fuck did you get so warped that you actually married him? Jesus, it just doesn't get any fucking sicker than that!"

Darryl leaned forward, hands on his knees, and took a few ragged breaths. I was afraid that he was going to have a coronary, and I didn't want him to keel over on my front lawn, especially as a few of my neighbors had come out of their houses to watch the festivities. At that moment, I couldn't think of anything more humiliating than the drama that played out before me.

"Darryl," I said, placing my hand on his back. I wanted to make him feel better, but was unsure what to do or say. I rubbed his back, put my other hand on his shoulder and drew him toward me. "Come on inside." He stood up and took one more deep breath. I could see that he tried to calm himself, although he was still so upset that his entire body trembled.

As I guided him to the house, I said, "You don't have a jacket. Are you cold?"

"Huh?" He seemed confused by my question, and shook his head dismissively. He followed me through my front door and into the kitchen in silence.

"Do you want a beer?" I offered.

"Haven't you got anything stronger?"

"Sure do. How about some whiskey?" I took a bottle of Jack Daniel's from a cupboard and set it on the kitchen countertop.

"Yes, that sounds really good right now." He looked tired, wiped out actually, almost like someone who was going into shock. I held up an ice tray and a can of cola with a questioning look and he shook his head no, so I poured straight whiskey into a shot glass and set it on the counter in front of him. It took only a fraction of a second for him to snatch it and swig it down.

"Wow. You're a thirsty one. Let's go sit down." He looked at the alcohol as though he worried that we might leave it behind. "I'll bring the whiskey with us. Come on, big fella."

I led him to the couch and he plopped himself down. Then he looked around my living room, scanning for whatever clues he could glean, ever the detective. His eyes settled on a picture of Tom that I had printed out and put in a nice frame. It was the only picture that I had of him on display. With regret I realized that there weren't any photos of Tom and I together, not even from the wedding. Since we had all been required to stay back at least four feet from his cell, Tom and I weren't able to stand next to each other for a decent shot.

Scanlon looked away from the picture then put his head in his hands and muttered, "Aw shit." I filled his shot glass again and set it on the coffee table in front of him. He downed this one a little slower than the first. Maybe that was progress. We sat in silence for a little while. Scanlon seemed to be trying to calm himself down. Finally he said, "I don't get it. Why do you love him? He's a monster and I'm a nice guy. Why don't you love me?"

"Who says I don't?" I shot back. His expression told me I shouldn't have said that to him, although I felt there was some truth in it. I had very intense feelings for Darryl Scanlon that definitely included friendship and attraction. To be honest, I felt something much stronger than mere friendship. Every time I'd seen him or even spoken to him on the phone I'd felt as though a great deal more could be on the horizon. I saw potential.

Darryl was a good man. He was kind, and he seemed to want to look after me, albeit in a somewhat aggressive, bullheaded manner. But now I saw a look of hopefulness in his eyes that didn't belong there. I didn't want to treat him like a yo-yo, making him think he had a chance and then dashing his hopes. He needed a clear message that he shouldn't wait around for me. He needed a clean break.

"Do you mean there's a chance for us?"

"No, that's not what I meant at all. I'm sorry."

"How do you feel about me, Rebecca?"

The eyes that looked into mine were wounded, broken. He deserved better. As I thought about him and pondered what to say, I was filled with warmth and happiness. I felt myself smile as I answered.

"I think you're a wonderful man. You're kind, handsome, intelligent, affectionate, you've got a great sense of humor, and you're so persistent; you just never give up. I'm not surprised that you finally caught Tom. You're truly amazing."

Had I really just said that? I made it sound as though Tom's capture was a good thing. But it was, or at least it should've been—only, it meant I was separated from my husband. I felt confused again.

"You like me," he said with an expression of wonder.

"Well, yeah, but—"

"I wish you could have seen the look on your face just now when you rattled off all the things you like about me. You were glowing, Rebecca. And you don't want me to give up."

"What? Oh no, I didn't mean to say that, Darryl."

"Well, what did you mean? Do you have feelings for me or not?"

"I can't. I'm married."

"You can, and you do. We both know your marriage is a farce." He touched my arm lightly, caressing my skin. "It's not for real. You don't even have a—" His expression became curious as he felt the third finger on my left hand. He looked down and saw the diamond wedding ring. "You have a ring? How? Did you buy it?"

"No, Tom did. He had one of the guards go to the jewelry store for him. Actually, he got me two rings." I showed Scanlon my right hand, and the other ring, identical except for the color of the stone.

"What's with the other ring? Why is it black?"

"Oh, well…" Indeed. How was I supposed to explain that without sounding bizarre? "It's meant to be a reflection of Tom."

"You mean as in good and evil?" Apparently Scanlon didn't need anything explained. I nodded. "That's sick. You understand that, right?"

"Look, I know the rings are a little unconventional, but I like them. They symbolize something beautiful—two people accepting all of each other." I could hear my voice talking, but even I was surprised, and even alarmed, by what I had just said.

"Yes, and that's just great as long as one of the people in the marriage isn't Thomas Eisenbrey. Think about what you're accepting. This guy didn't lose fifty bucks playing poker, or sneak a cigarette when you weren't looking, or leave the toilet seat up. He murders people! He cuts off fingers, toes, hands, heads—he tortures his victims. Oh, and let's not forget the biting." Scanlon pulled the collar of his shirt back to give me a better view of the horrible scar on his neck. "I know I sure as hell won't ever forget it."

"Darryl…"

"When you say that you're accepting all of him, just what does that entail? Does it mean you approve of what he does? Are you okay with what he did to me?"

"No. I'm not okay with what he did to you," I said, as I placed my hand on his neck, wishing I could do something to heal him of everything he'd suffered. "I'm so sorry for everything you went through. And, no, of course I wouldn't approve of him harming other people either. It's just that…I understand those things are part of his history. They're things he did in the past, but he doesn't do it anymore so there's no need to use the present tense."

"Why the hell not?"

"He's locked up."

"So what? Do you think that's going to stop him from doing it again? He's killed one prisoner and attempted to kill a guard during his stay in Walla Walla so far. Do you honestly think he wouldn't kill again if he found an opportunity? As long as he's alive, the people he has access to aren't safe."

"Okay, but he has changed a little. He helped the FBI locate a murderer he was acquainted with—Roddy Jenks. He told them where to find his cabin and they got him. He's made some progress in the right direction."

"Yeah, I heard about that." Scanlon gave a derisive snort. "Jenks swears he's going to get revenge, says he wants to be sent to the same prison so he can kill Eisenbrey. God, if they'd make those two room-mates, I think that would restore my faith in a higher power."

That information bothered me. I didn't like the idea of someone like Jenks wanting to do harm to Tom, but knew better than to voice that concern. It could send Scanlon into another tirade.

"And you do realize he didn't give his little buddy up to be a nice guy. It was just part of the deal to get what he wanted, which was apparently…" he looked sideways at me, "Jesus, did Farrar and Hale really agree to a conjugal visit for that?"

I sighed wearily. "Look, I'm sorry, Darryl. I guess I don't really have a logical explanation for my feelings or my actions."

"I do. You fell in love with a sick bastard and now you're blinded to what he really is. It's causing you to behave in an insane and ir-rational manner."

I actually felt that Scanlon had summed up my situation to a T, but that didn't take the sting out of it. "Darryl, I get that you don't ap-prove of who I married, but maybe you could try to be happy for me."

"Happy? Happy that you're ruining your life? No way. Look, you made a terrible mistake, but it doesn't have to be forever. You can still get out of this. You need to get a divorce."

"No."

"I mean it, Rebecca. File for it this week."

"No!"

"That's not an appropriate response!"

He was becoming aggressive again, so I dealt with it the only way I knew how. "Darryl, it's time for you to go home now."

"Why, because you don't want to hear the truth? Is it too much for you?"

"Yes, this is too much for me right now. I need to be alone. I need you to leave." That wasn't exactly true. I didn't want him gone so much as I wanted him quiet. I was finding the bitch session overwhelming.

He froze and stared at me. "But, Rebecca, every time we're together

I feel magic. I know we haven't known each other long, but there's such a strong connection. Don't you feel it too?"

He was right. I felt it too, and if I hadn't met Tom, who knows what would have happened. My feelings for Scanlon were like a bonfire, but what I felt for Tom was like a five alarm blaze consuming an apartment building. "Darryl, please..." *Please stop trying to wear me down.* "I can't deal with this right now."

"I just can't believe it. You want to keep him, and you want to get rid of me?" He wore an expression of incredulity, but underneath that I could see he was devastated.

I didn't want him to hurt. I certainly didn't want to be the one inflicting the pain. But I had to do what was right. I could feel my heart breaking as I said it. "Yes."

After Scanlon left I went back to the couch and poured myself a shot, using his glass since I hadn't bothered to get one for myself. Normally, I would never drink from a glass that another person had just used, not being fond of germs. Placing my mouth where someone else's had just been seemed almost as off-putting to me as sharing a toothbrush. But I didn't mind because it was Scanlon. We had kissed before, more than once, so I could hardly complain about getting his germs. I thought about that first kiss—when we were in his car at the end of our date. It had been nice.

I looked down at my hands and admired my rings. They were beautiful, but more than that, the very sight of them got my mind back on Tom, my husband. He would know somehow that Darryl had come to my house again. And he would be angry. Granted, I hadn't invited Darryl over, and I'd eventually asked him to leave. But he was here a long time, and I had feelings for him. I felt guilty and worried about how Tom would react. Thank God, he was behind bars.

It was still hard to believe that we were married. It had all happened so fast. I'd met Tom less than five weeks ago, and during that time we'd spent two hours together, twice each week. That was almost nothing, and yet I felt as though I'd known him for years.

I recognized that marrying Tom had been an irresponsible decision on my part, especially so soon, but I couldn't have stopped myself if I'd tried. And I hadn't really tried. Instead I'd been obsessed with finding a way to make him mine, and then elated when I was finally able to have him—the man who had driven me crazy.

It seemed as though, no matter where I was, or what I occupied myself with, my mind was never very far from Tom. He haunted me day and night. He was with me always.

THIRTY-TWO

December 3rd, 2012

When I arrived at the prison, I noticed a difference in the way the employees behaved. They were wary, curious, some of them were even hostile — their eyes followed me as I walked by. Tilly made a special appearance to escort me back to Tom's cell so he could give me his professional opinion of all the things that were wrong with me mentally to have agreed to marry, and sleep with, Tom — edification I could have done without.

Tom seemed different too. He was quiet and very still. His black eye was finally starting to look better; there was only the purplish remnant of a bruise in its place. His stare was unwavering as we both sat, facing each other, on opposite sides of the bars. "How did Scanlon take the news of our wedding? Did he give us his blessing or did he give you his condolences?"

"Crap," I said, feeling exasperated. "I didn't invite him over. He just showed up at my house when he found out."

Tom chuckled. He seemed unconcerned about Scanlon's visit.

Perhaps he could tell I was worried about the news I was about to deliver, news that would no doubt only add to his stress level. I couldn't think of a way to ease into the topic so I just said it.

"Tom… Jenks knows you were the one who gave away his location."

Tom's shoulders relaxed. "Well, sure he did. I was the only one who knew about that place except him," he said, with the kind of sympathetic expression one might use toward someone who wasn't very bright.

I took a deep breath. "He says he's going to kill you."

"Whatever." Tom looked bored. The anxiety I'd imagined the news would bring was nothing more than a projection of my own feelings on the matter, more proof that I didn't understand him.

"I was told he'll most likely be brought to Walla Walla after he's convicted. Why aren't you worried—because you're protected? You feel safe here?"

"Safe?" He sniggered. "People die in prisons all the time, but Jenks is just blowing hot air. I'm not afraid of him. He's afraid of me, just like all the other assholes in this place."

"Because you've killed people?" I asked. "Aren't a lot of these guys here for the same thing?"

Tom shifted position, resting his elbows on his thighs, his long fingers intertwined. "Sure, but there are different levels of bad, darlin'. In here you have to prove yourself, show them you're worse than they are, otherwise they'll fuck with you every chance they get. Besides, the guards know better than to allow me to mingle with any of the other prisoners anymore, so the point is moot."

"Which reminds me about the incident we haven't talked about yet, the altercation you had with one of the other inmates, the one that died."

Tom simply nodded.

"What happened?" I asked.

He ran his tongue along his teeth and thought for a moment, then said, "Well, the first day I was here, a group of Spics came up to me when we were out in the yard. I think they figured they were going to circle around and kick the shit out of me."

"Why?"

"Oh, that's just standard protocol when a new guy arrives."

Hearing about it made me feel bad for him. I didn't like the idea of him being ganged up on, and wished there was something I could have done to protect him. "I'm so sorry. How bad were you injured?"

Tom stared at me, dumbfounded. "You're serious? I wasn't injured. I grabbed the biggest fella, gouged out one of his eyes and bit off his ear. The other idiots scattered. Then I went for his neck and he bled out before the guards could do anything for him, which was nothing short of amazing in my humble opinion since there were several guards just standing around watching the festivities. They didn't come running until it was too late for him.

"And of course there wasn't any gibberish about self-defense in the guard's report. They just decided it was apparent I wasn't going to play nice with the other boys so they put me in segregation. I'm not unhappy about that. I prefer my own company to any of these jackasses."

"What was his name?" I asked, wondering if that incident had been on the list that Scanlon gave me. I checked; it wasn't. The last incident in Scanlon's information was prior to Tom's incarceration, although I recalled him telling me that Tom killed another inmate. He even mentioned it a second time when he came to my house to spew his displeasure about my marriage.

"Uh, I think his name was Garza, I'm not sure, anyway it was some kind of Hispanic name."

"Don't you know the names of all of the people you've killed?"

"Well, I know the names of everyone I was *convicted* of killing… except that guy."

There was that word again: convicted. It left the looming inference that there were other murders that hadn't been linked to him in addition to his brother and father. I wondered if he would ever tell me about the things he had warned me were off limits.

"Tell me, what would you do if you were out?"

That brought a smile and a dreamy look to his face. "Hmm, let's see, the first thing I'd do would be to make love to you for about twenty-four hours straight, and believe me, I've got the energy to do it. Then I'd go after Scanlon."

My muscles tensed at that revelation. "Why?"

"Lots of reasons, but the main two are: that piece of shit put me in prison, and he tried to hump my woman."

"Yeah, but that was before we got married," I said. A startled expression flashed across Tom's face that made me think he must have been expecting me to deny Scanlon had gone so far. "Tom, isn't there a chance that if you got out of prison you could live the rest of your life without harming anyone else?"

Tom became still, his gaze intensified. He took in a long breath and slowly let it out. "Sure, sugar. There's more than just a chance. I think being with you is…healing me," he said, his eyes not leaving mine. He seemed to be nodding slightly. I felt lightheaded as I nodded in return.

I wanted to heal him, to fix him. I wanted to kiss him also, but that was off limits to me. I still wasn't allowed to get that near his cell, regardless of the fact that we were husband and wife.

"Do you know it's only been four days since we made love? It feels like an eternity to me," he whispered. I leaned forward to hear him better. "What if we could have that every night? Is that what you'd want?"

"Yes," I whispered back.

"You're sure? That's what you'd really want—every night with me for the rest of your life?" His eyes held mine as his quiet, rhythmic chant continued. And I nodded again.

"Yes."

"How sure are you? What price would you be willing to pay?"

"I have no doubt," I said, which was only true in part. I was positive about what my heart wanted, conflicted about what I could actually deal with in real life. But it didn't matter because this was not real life. Those were just words. It didn't matter what I promised. My answer to his last question: "Anything."

His next words, a slow, menacing rustle, "Oh, Rebecca, would you really choose the same price I'm willing to pay if you knew what it was?"

I found myself standing. The bars between us, both a comfort and a hindrance. I desired closeness. I knew I wasn't supposed to touch him but…something deep inside told me I needed to. As I watched his eyes, I had the familiar feeling that I was in a trancelike state. I stepped forward. Tom rose and came to me, smiling.

I hadn't realized he was angry until it was too late. His right arm shot between the bars and encircled my neck, pulling me to him. I hit the bars hard, but managed to turn my head to the side and look toward the guards who were already out of their chairs and running our way. I closed my eyes. His mouth was at my ear. I could feel the warmth of his breath against my face. I thought of the terrible scars on Scanlon's neck and him telling me, "Don't ever forget, he's a biter." I hadn't forgotten, nor was I ever going to. My hands trembled as I tugged at Tom's arm, desperately trying to free myself. "How do you like this? Huh? Now you know what it feels like to be restrained!"

"But you agreed to it!" I managed to get out.

"Handcuffs, not all those fucking leather straps! I was completely immobilized. You're gonna pay for that!" Tom brought his left hand up and his fingers curled around my neck, crushing me. His right arm still held my body against the bars.

I tried to answer, to tell him the additional restraints hadn't been my idea, but I couldn't speak. His grip was too tight around my throat. He was hurting me. He was cutting off my air supply.

I heard a loud thud and realized that a guard must have hit him. I turned my head and saw Jones holding up a riot baton, ready to bring it down again. At first Tom hung onto me tighter, but then he was hit again and Avery managed to pry his arm off of me, which was no small feat. I was jerked back away from the cell by a third guard, and I spun around to see Lutz, his eyes wide, his complexion pallid. The young man held me in a crushing embrace. Then an expression of surprise darted across his features, and he shoved me behind him, extending both arms outward in a protective gesture.

DiMaggio tasered Tom causing him to fall to the cement floor and convulse as the electric current coursed through his body. I looked down at him, grateful that he had landed face down and was unable to look back at me. I didn't want to see the anger in his eyes.

"Get back to the control booth!" Jones ordered. I was happy to oblige and I nearly ran over to the guard's small office. There was some commotion and an argument between the guards. I heard Avery shout, "That's enough DiMaggio! You're gonna kill him!" Whatever DiMaggio had been doing stopped and the rest of their conversation was too quiet for me to discern.

I took a few deep breaths in an effort to calm myself, trying to comprehend what had just happened. Then I burst into tears. Why would Tom do something like that? Was it calculated to serve some purpose? Nearly everything he did seemed to be. Or was there a chance that his violent outburst had been an impulse he couldn't help? I hoped he hadn't done it because he hated me. It just didn't make sense. I hadn't had any indication he was unhappy with me until the attack.

Jones returned to the control room and said, "You were lucky as hell." I looked back toward Tom and saw DiMaggio and Avery pulling him out of his cell and dragging his limp body in our direction. Tom was facedown and each of the officers had a firm grip on one of his arms. Jones shouted, "Hey, what the fuck? You aren't suited up to handle him!"

DiMaggio replied, "We don't need it. Look at him; he's in no condition to fight." Tom appeared to be unconscious, and I saw blood in his hair on the side of his head as it flopped downward, his face nearly touching the floor. As they got close, I could see the terrible sneer on DiMaggio's face.

"Where are you taking him?" Jones asked.

"I think our boy here just needs to chill out. A cold shower should do the trick," DiMaggio said.

"The showers are the other way," Jones pointed out.

"Naw, I think we'll let him have a little fresh air. I'm gonna take him outside and hose him down. If he's good I'll even let him spend the night out there. It'll be a treat."

"Hose him down? This is December! He'll freeze to death!" I screeched. The stress on my aching throat caused me to bring my fingers up to my neck protectively. Then DiMaggio chuckled and I snapped.

I closed the distance between us, taking a swing at him with my right fist, which he deflected effortlessly. "Fucker!" I screamed in exasperation. Then he slapped me hard across the face. Suddenly, I felt a set of powerful arms wrap around me from behind, and my body was yanked back away from DiMaggio. I swung my head around to see who had grabbed me and was greeted with Jones's fiery glare.

"Jesus, Rick, not again!" Avery snapped. "You didn't need to hit her."

I turned back to DiMaggio and shouted, "What have you done to Tom? Why is he bleeding?"

DiMaggio stared me down, noting that my face was wet with tears, his voice even. "You're welcome for me saving your life, you ungrateful bitch. And just for the record, it's pathetic to see you snivel about this piece of shit." He shook his head, his contempt evident.

"Don't hurt him," I pled.

DiMaggio broke into a grin. He and Avery drug Tom's insentient body up the hallway and around a corner. Once they were out of our sight Jones let go of me.

I turned to Lutz. My voice trembled as I asked him, "What's going on? Where are they taking him?"

Lutz put his hand on my shoulder and I took some comfort in his attempt to quell my panic. "Hold still. Let me have a look," he said, his voice still shaky. He moved my hair back and inspected my neck, resting his hands on my shoulders. "Are you okay?"

"I'm fine. Christ, Andy, what about Tom?"

"They're taking him to a secure enclosure outside."

"Are they going to hurt him?" I asked. I knew Lutz could see the anxiety in me.

I saw several different expressions flit across his face as he pondered this. He finally settled on what I believe was the honest answer. "Yeah, they are." Lutz shrugged apologetically. "It's clear, so he should be able to see some stars tonight. Tom's always telling me how much he misses being able to gaze at the stars."

"Jeez, if there's any bright side, you're the guy that can find it," I said with obvious sarcasm. "DiMaggio isn't really going to leave him out there all night in wet clothes, is he?"

"No. I'm pretty sure they're going to take his clothes," he told me. I cringed. I didn't know what would be worse, being outside at night with wet clothes or no clothes at all. Either of those scenarios was untenable during the winter. Lutz saw my discomfort and added, "Don't worry, Rebecca. Tom's a lot tougher than you think. It's going to be all right." I didn't think that was true. I covered my mouth, stifling a moan.

Jones said. "I'm surprised you feel so bad for him, considering that he just tried to snuff you out."

"He wasn't trying to kill me!" I said.

"What the hell do you call that, foreplay?" Jones retorted.

"Rebecca…" Lutz started and then shook his head.

"Look, I don't know what he meant to do," I admitted. I was frightened for Tom, and angry with him, and I missed him already. "We need to stop this. Who can I report this to?"

"No way," Jones snapped. "Lady, there's not a soul in this place that would intervene on his behalf right now."

"Why?" I demanded.

"Because Eisenbrey deserves it," Jones said.

"That's not fair," I said.

Jones's eyes narrowed into slits. "I agree. If the world was fair we would have tortured the son of a bitch and slit his throat the day he arrived."

"This is bullshit. I'm going to talk with Barnett."

"I'd rethink that if I were you. Barnett isn't going to help you. In fact, who do you think he's likely to blame for this incident? Eisenbrey probably wouldn't have flipped out if you weren't here stirring him up."

"I wasn't stirring him up."

"I don't imagine that Barnett or Warden Hale will see it that way. Andy, you should walk her out to her car before Barnett hears about this. We don't need him to get hold of her for an interview. That's not in anyone's best interest."

I looked at Lutz who seemed uncertain, but he said, "He might be right, Rebecca."

"Of course I'm right. You don't want to have to explain yourself to Barnett when he's breathing fire. You want to wait until he's had some time to calm down. He's a hundred times more likely to terminate your visits permanently if you see him now. Give him a couple of days to mull this over and he'll probably just put Eisenbrey on level one for a few weeks. Then everything can go back to the way it was before."

Jones was suggesting that I run away and I didn't like it. I also didn't believe his assessment that things would be back to normal in a few weeks. I checked Lutz's expression again. "What do you think?" I asked him.

He seemed more sure of himself. "Jones is right. Let's get you out of here."

Lutz and I left the IMU immediately and crossed the grounds on one of the paved walkways. "Do you really think Barnett is going to blame me?" I asked him.

"Yes, I do. I have a bad feeling about how Jones and DiMaggio are going to spin this. I'll do my best to help out, but I've only worked here six months and those two have several years under their belts. Barnett's likely to listen to them."

We continued to the parking lot. When we reached my car Lutz asked, "How does your neck feel now?"

I ran my fingers over the area. "Sore," I admitted. "How do I look?"

He shook his head. "It looks like some bruises are starting to form. I feel like I shouldn't send you off without having medical staff examine you. Look, I know you might not want the nurse here to see your injury…"

"Yes. That's precisely what I don't want," I interrupted. "Tom's in enough trouble. If we can play that whole incident down a little, make it sound like it wasn't too bad, then I'll have a better chance of seeing him again." My eyes started to water.

"Hmm." Lutz's gaze was sympathetic. It seemed as though he was going to say something, but then he stopped himself. He rubbed my shoulder.

"Ow, that's sore too," I complained.

"Are you okay to drive?" he asked.

"Yeah, I'm fine. I'm just being a baby. It doesn't hurt much."

"I think you should have your doctor check you out when you get home. Will you do that?"

"Sure."

He seemed wary. "Promise?"

"Yeah, I will. But, listen, don't mention that to anyone here, okay? I don't want them to know there might be a medical record out there somewhere. All they need to know is that I'm fine."

"I want you to call me if you have any trouble on your way home. Put my number in your cellphone."

"That's a good idea," I said. I added Lutz as a contact in my directory and handed him my phone. He punched his number in. Then he gave me a hug. Lutz was such a sweet kid—far too sweet to work at the prison.

"Take care," he said as he released me.

"Thanks, Andy. You too." Then I got in my car and he watched as I drove away. Those were the last words we would ever speak to each other.

THIRTY-THREE

About two hours into my drive home I saw Captain Barnett's number appear on my cellphone's caller ID. I scrambled to get my headset in place as I continued down the freeway. "Hello?"

"Mrs. Eisenbrey?"

"Oh, hello Captain Barnett. Actually, I didn't change my name to Eisenbrey. I still go by Reis."

I heard a snort on the other end of the line. "I've been told there was a very serious incident this morning with your husband. What the hell happened? And why did you leave the facility without coming to see me?" he barked. Not a happy captain.

"What do you mean? He just got a little agitated with me so I ended the visit."

"That's bullshit and we both know it. I saw the security footage. He was well beyond agitated. He attacked you."

"Yeah, he reached through the bars and grabbed me, but I got loose."

"Don't play cute with me. My officers got you loose. They had to taser the motherfucker to get him off of you. Do you have any injuries?"

"No, I'm fine."

"Now why don't I believe that either? You should have allowed the nurse here at the prison to examine you before you left. You also should have reported to my office. I have a shitload of paperwork to do over this and I was supposed to interview you immediately after the incident."

"I didn't know that."

"That's crap too. Jones said he made it very clear you were not to leave the facility without first seeing me, but you left anyway."

"Did he?" I shouldn't have been surprised about Jones's underhanded backstabbery, but it made me feel disappointed and uncomfortable because I didn't understand why he'd done it. Was there something unsavory brewing in his caldron?

"I'll tell you what, Ms. Reis. This looks suspicious as hell. Why were you in such a hurry to leave? What are you hiding?"

"I'm not hiding anything."

"Then I'm sure you won't mind returning to the prison."

"When?"

"Now."

"Actually, I would mind that very much."

"Why?" he shot back at me.

"Because I'm almost to Ellensburg. I'm not driving all the way back to Walla Walla right now. That's ridiculous."

"Hmm. Very interesting. You managed to put a lot of distance between yourself and this facility in two hours. Are you sure you're not running away from something?"

"Oh, for crying out loud! Why are you trying to turn this into something it's not? Jones didn't tell me to stay, he told me to leave." I cringed at the way it sounded after I said it out loud.

"Now I don't believe that for a second. Why would one of my officers tell you to do something so blatantly against protocol? What possible motivation could he have?"

"I…well, I sure wish I knew." I let my breath out slowly and considered what would be the best way to end this conversation. "Look, apparently Officer Jones and I had a misunderstanding. I didn't realize there would be a problem if I left. I'm feeling upset about what happened and I'm really tired. I just want to go home."

There was silence over the line for several moments. I was tempted to ask Barnett if he was still there, but I held fast and he finally spoke. "Very well. You don't have to cooperate. I think I have enough information from the others involved to write my report. Oh, and just in case there was any question in your mind, Ms. Reis — Eisenbrey's visitation privileges are terminated."

When I got to my house I went straight for the Jack Daniel's.

I already missed Tom so much I felt an actual physical pain in my chest. I wanted to scream. I had to remind myself, he's probably not feeling the way I feel. He's a psychopath. They don't feel love, or at least not what I would quantify as love. It just simply wasn't possible. I doubted that he even felt sorry about what he'd done to me. He probably wouldn't lose any sleep at all over us being apart, except that my visits alleviated some of the boredom he was prone to suffer.

And yet, I was going out of my mind. It wasn't nice to be the one with the feelings. It seemed cruel and unfair to have in my mind that blurred image, never quite in focus, of what I wanted for my perfect life and to know it was absolutely unattainable: Tom, lying next to me in bed, watching me as his head rested on a pillow, a content smile on his features; Tom, cradling an infant on his chest; Tom, rolling around on the lawn with our future sons, wrestling and laughing; Tom, not choking me. My heart shouldn't be with him, but it was. And what was I left with? Confusion and anguish.

I opened the whiskey and filled a water glass half full with it, then filled the balance with cola — a lot of alcohol, but I didn't give a shit. I needed to kill the staggering pain. I drank a third of it down in one gulp.

How long would it be before Tom's visitation privileges were restored? The incident had been very serious. Would visits be allowed at all before his execution? Was it possible I would never be allowed to see him again? Common sense told me the answer was yes.

Suddenly, I felt my whole world come crashing in. The realization hit me—even the short amount of time Tom had left to live had been stolen from me because of his inability to behave like a decent human being during our last visit. I buried my face in my hands and wept.

THIRTY-FOUR

A few hours later, I worked fervently, weeding one of the flowerbeds in my front yard. It was cold, the ground wet, and the sky grew dark. Not the right time of year for this sort of task, but I'd needed a project to dive into, something I could work on furiously for a few hours. My yard had been neglected for so long it provided the perfect place to burn up some of the pissed-off energy I had pent up inside of me.

I grabbed each of the unwanted pests down low by the roots, squeezing as if choking the life out of the little bastards, and wrestling them from the soil. This was angry work. It felt good.

Another plus, the work didn't require standing. I'd consumed enough alcohol to give me a substantial buzz. Not to mention that my head still reeled from the shock of Tom attacking me and the realization that I probably wouldn't be allowed to see him again.

I took a deep breath of the fresh Pacific Northwest air, which was infused with oxygen after a recent rain, and wondered if it might clear my head. No matter. If it did, I'd just make myself another drink when I went back inside.

I heard a car pull into my driveway and I turned around to see who had arrived, still on my knees in the grass. I saw Darryl Scanlon walking toward me.

"I'm back," he said with a bashful expression.

"Really?" I said, not trying to mask my exasperation. I stood and tried to brush the dirt from my pants, but they were a muddy mess, including big, dark-brown blotches on my knees. "After the display you put on for me, not to mention all of my neighbors, the last time you were here?"

"I'm sorry about the way I behaved. I didn't mean to lose it like that."

I shrugged and decided to let it go. "That's okay, Darryl, I understand."

"And I heard about what happened at the prison, that he attacked you. I'm not here to gloat," he added. "I'm sorry about that too."

"You didn't do it," I pointed out. "You would never treat me that way."

"True, but I feel bad when things don't go right for you. Are you okay?" he asked.

"Yes, all things considered, I'm fine." I glanced away from him, feeling sure he would see the lie.

"I want you to be happy." There was nothing guarded about his expression as his eyes searched for my reaction. He was being genuine, and I was getting the vibe that if I wasn't careful he would take me in his arms and try to make me happy right there on my front lawn.

"Thanks, Darryl. I want you to be happy too," I said quietly.

"My family and friends…and coworkers have told me I should just walk away. You're a grown woman. You've made your choice. But I can't do that, Rebecca." His eyes looked sad. "I care about you. I think you're all mixed up right now and I don't want to see you like this. It hurts."

I knew it was unwise, but I wanted a hug from him. I wanted to be wrapped up tight in his strong, protecting arms and feel the warmth of his body against mine, so I took a step toward him and recognizing my intention he quickly closed the rest of the distance between us.

I allowed myself to feel the sheer happiness that flooded into me, although at the same time I found it confusing. I still loved Tom, but being in Scanlon's arms just melted my pain away. I leaned on him, and he held me steady, making me feel like there was a light at the end of this tunnel.

I stayed there, wrapped up in him for several minutes. When I finally pulled free of his hug, I noticed the woman that lived across the street from me watching us from her mailbox. Realizing she'd been caught staring, she turned away and headed back to her house.

Then I explained to Darryl, in the nicest and most gentle way that I could think of, that I thought it would be best if we didn't see each other anymore.

THIRTY-FIVE

December 4th, 2012

I shot an angry glance at the clock on my nightstand, noting it was 1:33 a.m. I thought about hitting it, hard, but my grudge wasn't with the clock, it was with whoever was outside ringing my doorbell repeatedly. The racket had jarred me out of a much needed session of deep sleep.

The events of that morning, technically yesterday morning at that point, flashed through my head again as I rolled over and felt the throbbing pain in my neck and shoulders. I pushed myself up into a sitting position. "Motherfucker," I said softly.

I was strangled by Tom — my husband. I still didn't want to believe it. I thought about our conjugal visit after the wedding, and his assurances: *I'm not going to hurt you…I'd have to be insane to do that…You're the only nice thing I have to look forward to in this world. I won't ruin that. I promise.* What did that mean — was he insane, or a liar, or possibly both?

Strange. I felt no anger toward him at that moment, just sadness. The pain in my heart was far worse than what the rest of my body had to contend with.

The noise continued until I reached the bottom of the stairs. Clothed in a purple robe and slippers, I opened the door and was not surprised to find my late night visitor was Scanlon. I'd told him less than nine hours ago we shouldn't see each other anymore. Why did I waste my breath? It was clear he would do whatever he wanted to regardless of what I told him I wanted. And to be honest, I did want to see him; it was just that I knew I shouldn't. Tom wouldn't like it.

I was somewhat surprised he didn't smell like alcohol or appear to be drunk, because I couldn't think of any other reason he'd just show up on my doorstep unannounced at this hour. Then I noticed the other two men behind him. All three were wearing slacks and dress shirts under their coats; one of them even had on a tie. They looked like they had just come from the office.

"He's escaped!" Scanlon blurted. Before I processed those words, my heart rate accelerated and body broke out into a cold sweat. "He's out, Rebecca, and one of the guards is gone also."

"Holy shit," I gasped, feeling lightheaded.

Scanlon searched my eyes, studying my reaction, and then he breathed a sigh of relief as my expression of dumbfounded shock confirmed what he had hoped it would — that I hadn't already known. His scrutiny veered a few inches down from my face and I realized, suddenly feeling naked, I'd been wearing a sweater and scarf when he spoke to me in the front yard the previous afternoon. This was his first opportunity to see the damage. "Jesus, your throat," he whispered, pushing my hair back behind my shoulder and giving my neck a thorough examination. "You're all bruised. Are you okay?" he asked, his concern unconcealed.

"Sort of…I don't know." I shrugged and then winced as I felt a sharp pain in my shoulder. His hand dropped down from my hair and he placed his palm on my back, rubbing gently.

"Listen, Rebecca, may we search your premises?"

"What? Why?"

"Oh, it's not like that. I'm not accusing you of harboring him," he said quickly, accurate about what had alarmed me. "I don't have a search warrant. This is entirely up to you. I'm just thinking about your safety."

"Oh, okay. Yes, by all means. Come on in." I stepped back and held the door open for the three men to enter. "Feel free to search the entire house."

"I should introduce you. Rebecca, this is Steve Pollock and Dan Finlay." The two men smiled and nodded, Finlay said it was nice to meet me, and they went to work, each hurrying off in a different direction to start their search. Then it was Scanlon's turn to lead me to the couch in my living room. He saw the empty glass and whiskey bottle on the coffee table. "Oh dear, you had yourself quite an evening, didn't you?"

"Yeah, I'm out of whiskey but do you want a beer or a cooler?"

"No, and you shouldn't either. You need a clear head right now."

"Fair enough," I said, but I didn't have to like it. We sat on my couch and I turned to him, pulling my bathrobe tighter around myself. "How did he escape?"

"They have security footage of two guys in guard uniforms leaving together. One of them was wearing a baseball-cap to block his face from the cameras—that was Eisenbrey."

"So he had an accomplice?"

"It looks that way. The officer that was with him didn't appear to be in any distress. They just looked like two employees having a friendly conversation as they walked."

Out of everyone I'd met at the prison, there was only one guard that seemed to like Tom, one that might have been young and naïve enough to do something reckless. "Was it Lutz?" I asked with some trepidation.

"No, Lutz is the guy they found dead in a storage area near the control room. Sliced from ear to ear," Darryl said, shaking his head.

"Andy's dead?" For some reason hearing that news frightened me even more than the news Tom had escaped. My mind whirled.

"Yes."

"Oh God, no. I can't believe this is happening. Not Andy. He was such a nice young man." While my head still reeled from the news about Lutz, Scanlon told me something that absolutely blindsided me.

"Eisenbrey left with a guard by the name of Richard DiMaggio."

"Are you shitting me? Rick DiMaggio and Tom hated each other. DiMaggio's done some very abusive things to Tom. That makes no sense."

"Yes, on the surface that's how it looks, but maybe it makes perfect sense. Their differences must have been a ruse, because no one who's seen the security footage believes that he was taken against his will. They even said goodnight to a guy on their way out. DiMaggio must have brought Eisenbrey a guard's uniform to change into and then helped him with the escape. That's the only way it could have gone down."

"Jeez! And Lutz…" Suddenly, the reality hit me. Lutz, that sweet young man who had watched out for me, who had walked me to my car on two occasions, out of kindness and concern, was dead.

The tears came. I reached an unsteady hand toward a box of Kleenex, took a few tissues, put my head in my hands, and then let it all out. Scanlon placed a warm hand on my shoulder and rubbed as the sobs shook my body, giving me several moments to compose myself. When I was finally able to speak, I told him, "Tom liked that guy. They were friends. I liked him. Oh God, do you think Tom killed him?"

Scanlon sighed. "Probably. But on the other hand, if DiMaggio helped Eisenbrey escape, we don't know what's going on in his head or what he's capable of. We have to assume he might also be willing to kill." Scanlon's fingers moved to the back of my neck as he continued the soothing motion. "Rebecca, people like Eisenbrey don't have friends. They don't care for people. I know you think he cares about you but…"

"Oh, shit, don't go there right now," I moaned, wondering if Scanlon was right.

"Look, I know you said you didn't want to see me anymore, but that's not going to work for me tonight," he said softly. "It's possible he might come here. I mean, he'd have to be crazy to think he could do it without being apprehended, but I'd rather be extra careful. I think you should spend the rest of the night at my place."

"Darryl, I can't do that." And I really couldn't. What if I did spend the night at Scanlon's house and what if Tom found out? I didn't want to think about the possible repercussions.

Finlay and Pollock came back and reported that the house was clear. Scanlon thanked them and returned his attention to me.

"Then I'll stay here. And these two will be in an unmarked car across the street. We're going to have officers watching your house tonight, just in case. Tomorrow we need to move you somewhere else."

"I don't need a babysitter," I objected.

"Yes, you fucking do, and I won't take no for an answer. I'm not willing to gamble with your life. I can't even begin to describe how I'd feel if something bad happened to you." He looked away quickly, but not before I noticed his eyes starting to water. His hand trembled as he raised it to his forehead, rubbing his temple. It looked as though Finlay saw it too.

"Yeah, we'll just be out in the car," said Finlay.

Pollock said, "Later," and the two of them made a hasty exit, closing the door quietly on their way out.

"Darryl, I think that's a bad idea too. You're not safe here."

"For crying out loud, woman. Don't be ridiculous. I'm a trained officer and I have a gun. Do you honestly feel I'm not equipped to protect both of us?" He raised his finger in warning. "If you say yes to that I'll consider it a personal insult."

He had a point. He was one of the people the public depended on for protection, but I still felt afraid for him. Tom had demonstrated, time and time again, his talent for knowing information he shouldn't have had access to. And he had told me specifically not to see Scanlon.

"Tom would be so angry if he knew you were here," I said.

"So what? Tom's an angry guy. We need to assume we're all on his hit list." His golden-brown eyes flared, defiantly. "Look, Rebecca, you've got three options: I stay in the house with you and the two FBI boys stay in the car—yes, they're with the bureau. Or the other two options are: I stay in the car and one of them stays inside with you, or, if you really want to be difficult, you can make all three of us stay in the car. But I should warn you, I'm not above bringing you down to the station for questioning if that's the only way I can keep you safe."

"Are you serious?"

"Yes."

"Fine," I relented. "I'd like you to stay inside with me, not one of the agents."

He gave me a satisfied smile. "Good."

"What time did he escape?"

"A little after midnight."

I looked at my watch; it was nearly 2:00 a.m. So it happened about two hours ago. "Were you expecting to find him here? Is that why your buddies did the search? Walla Walla is a four-hour drive."

"For all I know he could have access to a plane or a helicopter but, no, I didn't believe he was here, at least not after I arrived. I think I would have been able to tell if he was here."

"Why?"

"Well, this is going to sound a little weird, but whenever I've been near Eisenbrey in the past I've had this…feeling. I'm not sure how to describe it, but it's as if there's some kind of tension in the air around him. Whatever the hell it is, it sets off all my alarms and puts me on high alert. It's spooky."

"I know what you mean," I muttered.

"You do? Well then why the hell would you…" I saw the proverbial light bulb above his head ignite. He said, "Oh…how is it that I didn't see this before? That's what you like about him, isn't it? You like that scary feeling."

I frowned, but didn't answer, which frustrated him.

"Come on, Rebecca, we're both adults here. I'm not going to chew you out. I'm just trying to understand. You can tell me."

That was close to the truth. Scanlon was exactly the kind of man that I could tell everything to; my hopes, dreams, and my fears—well, almost everything; but I didn't want to discuss the things about Tom that turned me on. That would be a cruel conversation.

His expression seemed friendly and open on the surface, but something else stirred underneath—anger possibly? Or perhaps just pain. I remembered something, and used it to evade his question. "Darryl, I asked Tom once what he'd do if he ever got released. He said he'd come after you. I didn't tell you at the time because I thought it didn't matter. I'm sorry. I just didn't think he'd ever have the opportunity."

"That's okay," Darryl said. He didn't look phased. "I expected that. I know he hates me. He blamed me for his incarceration." He added, "Don't you worry about me. I mean that." Then he gave me one of those smiles that made me feel like, somehow, everything would to turn out okay. Scanlon was my sentinel.

Darryl took the high road and didn't fuss me when I offered him my guest bedroom. He just kissed my forehead and wished me good night. As I lay in my bed, staring up at the little imperfections in my ceiling, I considered my situation. It looked grim.

My alcohol buzz had worn off, and my head was clearing up. I thought about my last visit with Tom. The attack had come out of nowhere. What had caused him to turn on me? I racked my brain, trying to remember our conversation, wishing I could play back the recording I'd made but, in all the confusion, I'd left my recorder at the prison. I didn't know what had become of it. I recalled what I could from memory.

I'd asked him what he would do if he got out. He said he'd go after Scanlon, a threat I'd dismissed at the time, but at this point a bona fide concern. He told me that he wanted to make love to me, which I'd felt happy about right up until he put me in a chokehold through the bars of his cell. I recalled Tom asking me, "What if we could have that every night? Is that what you'd want?" And after that, "What price would you be willing to pay?" I shivered underneath the thick comforter on my bed.

I had told him, "Anything"—a word I knew would haunt me.

What was the mysterious price he had alluded to? Perhaps I'd already paid it by being choked, but that seemed too easy. Tom wasn't the type of man to make things easy. He'd complained about being restrained during our wedding visit, but that had been out of my control. He understood the restraints were a necessary part of the deal, given his history of violence. I suspected his irritation about that wasn't really what had caused him to strike. But, if not, what could his purpose have been?

And then it dawned on me—the attack had caused Tom to be moved from his cell to a different part of the prison with DiMaggio. And if DiMaggio was the officer who had assisted him in his escape—those two things must be connected. If this was true, what did it mean for me? Was it possible he wasn't angry with me at all, that he had only hurt me in order to escape? The incident had been terrifying and my neck was covered with bruises. But, worst of all, I was left with no way of knowing how Tom really felt about me.

Since meeting Tom, I had gone from wondering how soon I could get my life over with to wishing it would never end. And the irony of it all was that the odds of me dying before my time had probably increased a great deal now that Tom was in my life.

The sick things that had fed my irresistible attraction to Tom: his lust, his fury, his complete lack of moral code, his desire for domination and ultimate power, had excited my mind and my senses when they were safely contained. But the seduction of the danger only worked for me if I had the option to walk away from him. I needed that control. Without it, I felt like I was drowning.

I'd allowed myself to fall in love with him because he was unobtainable. I thought it didn't matter if I let my guard down, if I did something brain-dead and perilous. I didn't have to be strong enough to listen to myself think *This is utterly insane; you can't be with a man who might kill you one day because it's something he enjoys doing.* The penal system had done that for me. They had decided Eisenbrey should never again have the opportunity to be alone with other humans unsupervised and unrestrained. And they had been right.

No. I would never have started the relationship if I thought escape was a possibility. What had I done? The last several weeks had been one unwise choice after another, each one progressively worse than the one before, until I had finally gotten to the point where I'd lost my mind and married him, a fact that still seemed unreal to me. But, technically, I'd done nothing criminal. I had nothing to do with the Hunter's escape. So why couldn't I shake the feeling that I had just unleashed the devil?

THIRTY-SIX

Six hours ago, I'd wondered why Darryl hadn't objected to the guest room. It had seemed easy. Too easy. When I woke up, I found out why.

My bedroom door was ajar. I pushed it open to find Darryl sitting on a padded chair he'd borrowed from my kitchen for his post as sentry in my hallway. His head drooped downward, his firearm rested on his thigh and the palm of his hand on his firearm. My presence must have roused him from his restful state. His face, as he turned it up to me, held an expression of exhausted love, the likes of which I had never seen. And for a moment, I wished I'd offered him the other side of my bed the night before.

Darryl sat up straight and stretched his arms out from his sides. "Good morning. Did you sleep well?"

"Not really. I was too worried. Did you sleep at all?"

"Nah… I just closed my eyes for a moment, but I've been awake."

"Want some coffee?" I offered.

"That sounds great," he said, rubbing his eyes. He stood and brushed my hair gently back from my face as he looked down at me. "You're just a wee thing without your heels."

"No. I'm average height," I said, putting on a mock air of defensiveness.

"Sure you are," he replied. He chuckled, and put his arms around me, resting his chin on top of my head. He breathed in, and said in a dreamy voice, "Your hair smells nice." As he embraced me, I felt part of the gun he still held pressing against my lower back. I'd forgotten it was in his hand. The seriousness of my situation returned to the forefront.

"What do we do now?" I asked.

"I'll go talk to Finlay and Pollock. We'll give the house and yard another quick search. And you should start packing up whatever you want to have with you for the next few weeks. Do you have some family to stay with?"

"My aunt and uncle."

"Does your uncle have a gun?"

"Yes. I know he has a rifle; he might have a handgun also."

"Good. I'm going to have one of our officers take you to their house. I wish I could do it myself, but I'm meeting with the task force this morning and I'll have my hands full until Eisenbrey's back in custody. Where do they live?"

"Easton. I don't want an officer to drive me. I need my car."

"I'll have him follow you then. I want him to make sure you arrive safely, and he should search the house. I'll ask him to address any security issues he sees, make sure your uncle's weapons are in working order and that he has ammunition."

"Jeez."

"I'm not playing around, Rebecca. I need to know your uncle can protect you while I'm searching for Eisenbrey. I'm afraid to have you out of my sight."

After Scanlon left, I called my aunt. I told her about the escape and about my need to stay with them. I promised to fill her in on the rest when I arrived. Then I called Captain Barnett's office, and was immediately patched through to him.

"Hi, it's Rebecca Reis. I want you to know how very sorry I am about Andy Lutz. He was such a kind and wonderful young man. I just…" I could feel tears beginning to form in my eyes again, and my throat constricted in anticipation of the crying I was about to do. I swallowed. "I just thought the world of him."

"Me too," Barnett said curtly.

"I was wondering if you could tell me where and when Andy's funeral will be."

"Why? You don't intend to show up there, do you?"

"Well, yes."

"Don't you think that's a bad idea?"

"Why? Andy and I were friends."

"You're married to the guy that murdered him. How do you think his family would feel about seeing you there? I don't think you should make this any more difficult than it already is for them."

"Oh." I tried not to sound as taken aback as I was. "Okay, I guess I can see your point."

"Not to mention that most of his coworkers will be in attendance. And I have to say, you are not popular with any of the staff here anymore."

"Really?" I asked, wondering if that was actually true or if Barnett was just passing his personal opinion off as the general consensus. I didn't think it mattered though. The only guard I would have wanted to keep in touch with was Lutz. "All right. I won't go."

"Good," Barnett said, and then he hung up.

I stared at the phone in my hand for a moment, feeling bewildered. That hadn't gone as I'd expected at all. So I couldn't go to Lutz's funeral. But I also couldn't just do nothing. It wouldn't be right.

I looked up funeral homes in Walla Walla and found two listings. The first one I called happened to be the one that was handling his funeral and they told me it would take place in three days. Then I called a florist and ordered some flowers and a card to be delivered to the church on the morning of the funeral. That made me feel a little better; Barnett hadn't specifically asked me not to send flowers. The card inscription I had asked the florist to write was:

In loving memory of Andrew Lutz, cherished friend.

My thoughts and prayers to his family, and to all those who knew and loved him.

After that, I packed, loaded my suitcases and bags into my car, and made some more coffee while I awaited my escort.

THIRTY-SEVEN

It wasn't long before impatience got the better of me, and I decided to search my closet once more to confirm there was nothing in it I couldn't live without. Then I heard my cellphone, catching it on the first ring. "Hello."

"Is this Rebecca?" an unfamiliar female voice asked. I immediately tensed, and kicked myself for answering when I hadn't checked the caller ID. My thoughts had been elsewhere. There were few people I wanted to talk to at that moment. I hoped this wasn't some reporter that had managed to get hold of my private cell number.

"Yes," I said tentatively.

"This is Sarah Eisenbrey, your mother-in-law if what I hear is true." I realized it was indeed the truth, a fact that startled me. With all of the turmoil I'd gone through prior to the marriage, I hadn't considered his family would become my family. I recalled feeling an affinity with Tom's mother the day she'd shared pictures and tales of her family with me. I'd wanted to comfort her, but I hadn't known what to say. Since she'd acknowledged our legal relationship, my feelings of kinship toward her returned, stronger than before.

"Oh, Mrs. Eisenbrey! I was just going to call you," I lied. I'd been so busy with packing and planning my getaway, the thought hadn't yet occurred to me.

"I heard about the escape. How are you holding up?"

"I'm all right," I said. Another lie. "How about you?"

"I'm okay, I suppose. Detective Scanlon asked me to find someplace else to stay for a while, until Tom is captured."

"Same here," I said. I wondered if she had someone to stay with. I didn't know if she had many friends or relatives that she was close to. She'd seemed so alone the day we met. I supposed, on some level, my aunt and uncle were Tom's family too, although I felt sure they'd argue that point once I worked up the courage to tell them about it. I didn't look forward to that conversation.

I knew my aunt and uncle were the kind of rock solid people who could cope with the crazy things life threw at them. They would still love me after I told them what I'd done, even if they were disappointed. I also knew they were the kind of folks who wouldn't want this woman to be alone. "I was just packing some things. I'm going to my aunt's house. Would you like to stay with us?"

"That's kind of you, dear. But no, I'll stay put. If Tom comes after me, then so be it."

"Look, for what it's worth, I don't believe Tom has any intention of harming you. He spoke very highly of you."

"Really? Was he upset about any of the things I told you?" she asked. "Was he angry that I stopped speaking to him?"

"No, not at all. He said he understood you needed space. He was okay with that."

"If that's true, good. But I heard that he attacked you in the prison. Did you expect him to do that?"

"Well…no," I admitted.

"Tommy's full of surprises, but I guess you are also. Tell me, why on earth did you agree to marry him?"

I stammered for a moment as I searched for an adequate answer. "I fell in love with him," I said simply. "Maybe that sounds crazy."

"It's crazy all right, but I can't judge you for it. I love him too. I can see why it happened. Tommy has plenty of good qualities." There was a pause, and Mrs. Eisenbrey cleared her throat. "But, given that he turned out to be the Hunter, I'm not sure any of the good he shows us is genuine."

Once again, I felt my emotions rising to the surface. I'd done more than my share of crying over the last two days. I swallowed, trying to keep the tears at bay. "I'm, uh, sure you're right," I mumbled.

"I imagine you're feeling a little confused right now," she said.

"That's sure the truth," I agreed, relieved that she at least understood that much.

"I've been there myself." She went quiet for a few moments. The silence stretched on just long enough to make me feel awkward, but for the life of me I couldn't pull anything else out of my head to say to her. Finally, she spoke again. "You've still got my number?"

"Yes, and I'm glad you kept mine."

"Well, it looks like we're in this together, kiddo, so don't be a stranger. You call me anytime you want. All right, dear?"

"Thank you, Mrs. Eisenbrey. I will, and the same goes for you… anytime. I'm glad you called."

The next few days were filled with various degrees of tension. My aunt and uncle, though shocked by the news of my marriage to Tom, reacted much the way I had expected. They were kind and supportive, disappointed with my choice, and their love for me was unmistakable. I felt grateful to have them.

Scanlon called to check on me at regular intervals, and he'd arranged for two police officers to be stationed at my aunt and uncle's house at all times. Initially, the officers had spent most of their time in the squad car or walking around the perimeter of the house and the yard, which consisted of an acre of forest with a small, cleared area around the building. The location was remote; none of the neighboring houses were visible. It was freezing outside and, gradually, they began accepting our invitations to remain indoors. They even gave in to my aunt's offers of hot drinks and cookies.

Their presence, though it annoyed me at times, was a comfort. It was difficult for me to go from living alone to having no privacy. Between my aunt and uncle, and the officers, I almost always had another human being in the room with me. My only reprieve was going in my bedroom to read. But it beat being alone and terrified, so I wasn't about to complain.

Every news report we saw spoke of Tom's escape. Unfortunately, I was on television along with him since our marriage was common knowledge, and it upset me more than I'd expected. Being the Hunter's wife wasn't what I wanted to be known for. When I'd made the decision to go through with it, I'd allowed myself the delusion of secrecy, pushing from my mind any threat of publicity. Yes, it had been stupid, but it had allowed me to go forward. Now both of our faces were on TV sets around the country. It had just been sheer luck no one called any reporters until after his escape. I'd been spared the limelight for those five days.

When the news stations gave law enforcement their sound bite, I didn't see Scanlon. But I did see an interview with Special Agent Steven Pollock of the FBI, one of the men who had searched my house immediately after the escape. He didn't mention me, and that I appreciated. He was all about Tom. Pollock did well in front of the camera, inspiring confidence in me that the FBI would catch the Hunter soon. If my only information on the case was what I had gleaned from that news report, I might have believed all was under control. But I knew that wasn't really the case. Scanlon had told me they didn't have any leads. So far, there hadn't been a single sighting of Tom anywhere.

THIRTY-EIGHT

December 8th, 2012

I awoke that morning with Andy Lutz in my thoughts, and an overwhelming feeling of loss and depression. It was Friday, a day I would normally go to the prison. I missed Lutz, but I missed Tom a thousand times harder. I didn't know if Tom had killed Lutz, and this feeling in my heart terrified me because even if he had I still wanted Tom; I wanted to be with him more than anything else.

Grabbing the box of Kleenex I kept on my night table, I withdrew multiple tissues and spent several minutes crying it out, knowing I would never be able to see him again, and allowing myself to feel the pain. His funeral had taken place the day before and, on Barnett's advice, I hadn't attended. I wished I could have gone to the ceremony, not just to pay my respects, but to get some closure.

The police officers were still present with us at my aunt's house, though the tension had dissipated a great deal. Four days had elapsed since the escape, and there had been no sign of any trouble. Officer Walters, a pleasant man in his early fifties was working the morning shift and seemed relaxed about the situation. He told me outright he thought his department had gone overboard in agreeing with Scanlon's request for around-the-clock protective surveillance. He felt this was the last place on Earth that Tom would go. I was inclined to agree.

By late morning, the stir-craziness got to me. I felt as though I couldn't stay indoors any longer. I decided to put on a hat and sunglasses, and go for a drive back to my house in Bellevue.

Everywhere I looked along my excursion there were reminders of the approaching holiday—Christmas lights on many of the storefronts and houses. Though the holiday was overshadowed by Tom's escape, and the stress it put on all of us, I felt a little normalcy would help my frame of mind, so I decided to go to a department store to try to figure out what to do about gifts for my aunt and uncle. And should I get something for Scanlon? We were becoming close. Also, as insane as it seemed, I wondered if I should get something for Tom just in case he made an appearance. I wanted to make him happy if I ever saw him again, even though that possibility frightened me. I had no clue what his intentions would be toward me—would he kiss me or try to kill me? Either way, it might behoove me to have something ready to give him as proof that I still had warm thoughts toward him.

As I pulled into my driveway I noticed a red Honda Accord parallel parked across the street. I couldn't see the person sitting in the driver's seat very well, but I dismissed them as someone I probably didn't know.

I went into my house and grabbed a couple of reference books I wanted on the pathology of serial killers. I planned to try working on my book about Tom when I returned to Easton. Then I went around my house, giving each room a cursory glance, finding a sweater I wanted to have with me. It hadn't really been necessary for me to return to the house for these items but I wanted to see that everything was secure. I set the house alarm and locked the door. Then I got back in my car and headed to a mall that was close by.

As I neared the shopping center, I realized that a red Honda Accord was directly behind me. In fact, it looked like the one that had been parked in front of my house. I could see the driver was a woman, but I wasn't sure if it was the same person.

To my surprise she followed me into the parking lot, and pulled into a stall close to mine. When I got out of my car, she got out of hers as well and approached me. The woman was shorter than I, with brown hair just beginning to succumb to gray. Her expression seemed odd, and as she got close I noted something familiar about her hazel eyes.

"You filthy whore!" she screeched.

"What?" I asked. The woman had me stunned. I had no idea why a complete stranger would approach me and shout an accusation like that.

"Your husband murdered my son!" Realization dawned. I began to make sense of the unprovoked aggression. She was Andy's mother.

"Mrs. Lutz?" I asked.

"What the hell is wrong with you? Andy told me about how you were coming to visit that animal every week for that cursed book of yours." Actually it had been twice a week, a point that seemed ill-advised to correct. "And that's some nerve you've got sending flowers to Andy's funeral, as if you cared about him, as if you gave a shit!" She drew a ragged breath and the continued. "We didn't want your damned flowers or the card or anything else from you to remind us that the son of a bitch who murdered my son is running around free right now! And I'll bet you're just pleased as punch about that, aren't you! What's the plan? Are you going to meet up with him somewhere? Hell, I'll bet you helped him escape!"

"No! No ma'am, I didn't…"

"You lying bitch! People like you don't deserve to walk this earth! But my Andy did. He was a decent young man, and he's gone now because of that monster! I wish God would strike the two of you down!"

I stood motionless and dumbstruck as I stared at Mrs. Lutz. As shocked as I was by the intensity of the hatred spewing from her, I understood her anguish about the loss of her son. I couldn't think of anything to say to the poor woman to make the situation any better, and I was painfully aware that people were watching us. In fact, a crowd was gathering in the parking lot.

All too late, I saw the folly of leaving my aunt's house, believing that sunglasses and a hat could disguise me. Mrs. Lutz looked around at the spectators with a smug expression and shouted, "That's right. This woman is married to that serial killer, Thomas Eisenbrey! You've seen her on the news. She married him so she could fuck him at the prison! Take a good look at her, all of you!"

That shocked me into action. "Holy shit! Quiet down lady!" I said in hushed yet desperate tones, but it was no use. She continued to shout.

"Andy told me about your wedding. He said he was the best man. And this is the thanks he gets? Eisenbrey slit his throat on his way out of the prison! My son said you were a nice woman. He said the two of you were friends." Her lower lip trembled and she looked as though she was going to burst into tears at any moment. Her shoulders slumped.

"We were. I was very fond of Andy. He was a wonderful young man. I'm so sorry for your loss."

But my positive appraisal of her son only gave the woman a second wind. "How can you live with yourself, being married to that murdering piece of shit? Why won't you tell the police where he's hiding? Why won't you turn him in?"

That made me angry and I snapped. "How dare you! I don't know where he is!" I glanced around at some of the people who had gathered to watch the festivities and realized my mistake. Shouting back at this woman wasn't going to win me any popularity contests. I needed to rein in my temper and be respectful.

I didn't use to be one of those writers people recognized when I walked down the street, but I'd sold enough books that my name sounded familiar to many. Even after my picture had been aired on the news, I'd felt confident that I could make it in and out of a store without drawing any attention to myself—until this. She'd made my connection to Tom clear to these witnesses. They would remember me. Anything I said or did would be retold and criticized later, and I was too flustered to figure out the right way to deal with this situation.

"You're a lying little tramp! You need to do the right thing! You need to turn in the man who murdered my son, that serial killer, Thomas Eisenbrey!"

I could see there would be no placating Mrs. Lutz. Her main goal seemed to be my public embarrassment, and she had succeeded. I also understood why she hadn't done this in front of my house — I didn't have enough neighbors. The audience in the mall parking lot was much larger. I estimated at least forty people observing.

I recognized my defeat. I told her once more that I was sorry about her son. Then I got back in my car and started the engine, my hand trembling so badly that my keys jingled. I drove straight to the entrance of eastbound I-90 and headed back toward Easton.

The exchange had left me extremely shaken. I hoped Mrs. Lutz had gotten it out of her system and that would be the only public display I would have to endure. I was no longer in any condition to shop, and when or if I ever did feel ready to give it another try, I wouldn't return to that store.

THIRTY-NINE

When I was halfway back to Easton, my cellphone rang. I looked at the display and sighed. I'd better not hide from this woman's calls any longer. "Hi Kat," I said.

"There you are! God, Rebecca, I've been so worried! Where have you been? I've called at least a dozen times. Why haven't you answered?"

"Sorry. My phone was turned off for a while."

"I want to see you right away. Where are you?"

"I'm on the mountain pass, on my way back to Easton," I said. "I need to stay with my aunt for a while."

"They said on the news that you got married to that guy. What the fuck? Is that really true?"

I let a breath out slowly between my teeth, telling myself that her pissyness was justified, no matter that it irritated me. "Yeah, I did."

A long silence as I let her process that. Finally, she asked, "Why?"

"Look, it's complicated."

"I could tell you were getting feelings for him, but Jesus…"

"Yes, I know." I took a deep breath. "I fell in love with him. There. Are you happy?"

"No, I'm not. How the hell did this happen? You've always been so normal, you know, even on the verge of boring. And now…talk about going to the dark side."

"I know it wasn't a smart thing to do, but I just don't want a lecture right now."

"Has he tried to contact you?"

"No. I don't know that he will. There was an incident the last time I saw him. We didn't part on the best of terms."

"What kind of incident?"

"He tried to choke me," I told her.

"How did that happen? I thought he wasn't allowed to touch anyone."

"He wasn't. I was supposed to stay back four feet from the bars, but I didn't."

"Were you injured?"

"No," I lied. It had been five days since I last saw Tom, five days since I'd felt his fingers wrapped around my throat. Though not entirely gone, the bruises had faded quite a bit. My neck still felt sore, but I wasn't sure if it was a legitimate physical pain anymore, or just some psychosomatic sensation brought on by the stress of my situation.

"Are you afraid he'll come after you now that he's out?"

"Well, yeah, but we have police officers at the house around the clock."

"Thank goodness. For how long?"

"I don't know. I'm not even sure we'd have any protection if Darryl hadn't insisted."

"Darryl? Is that the gorgeous detective? You saw him again?"

"Yes. He's one of the people trying to find Tom. And also, we've become kind of close. He calls me every day. Actually, twice per day. He likes to check up on me."

"Good. He sounds like a nice guy. I'd much rather see you with him."

"He is a nice guy. He's wonderful, but...let's just leave it at that. Something happened right before you called—when I tried to go shopping. I'm still rattled." I filled her in on the details of the verbal onslaught from Mrs. Lutz.

"Oh no, Beck. That's scary. Do you think she'll do it again?"

"I don't know. I hope she's done, but who knows what the future holds."

"That's true. You need to be careful. She might not be the only one out there who wants to hold you responsible for his actions."

"For the moment, I'm going back to my aunt's house to hide, and I hope to God no one finds me. Don't tell anyone where I'm at, okay?"

"Yes, of course. I won't tell," she said quickly. "Oh, Rebecca, you must be so stressed out."

"I am."

"Why didn't you call me before you got married to that guy? For crying out loud, I would have talked you out of it."

"I know you would have tried, and that's precisely why I didn't call you. Once I'd decided that I needed to be with him, I didn't want to be talked out of it. I was in a very strange frame of mind."

"I guess so. Are you saying you've snapped out of it now? You're back to normal?"

"I'm not sure, Kat. I just…it's hard to explain."

"Try," she demanded.

"It's like the longer I go without seeing him, the more I feel like my old self. Does that make sense?"

"Sounds like voodoo," she remarked.

"Super. Thanks for that," I shot, in no mood for a smart-assed comment.

"Sorry. I just mean it's weird. It almost sounds like your saying that he had you under some kind of spell."

"Hmm." It seemed ridiculous, but there were times when I had wondered if he was doing something along the lines of hypnosis. I recalled a few occasions where I'd felt lulled and sleepy, and I didn't recall walking from his cell to my car. That, combined with his penchant for telling me what was in my head, had been downright creepy. "I don't believe in that crap, but I can't deny something out of the ordinary happened." I paused. Kat had gone quiet on me again. "Are you still there?" I asked.

"Of course I am. You think I'm going to hang up during this conversation? This is fucking fascinating."

"I know," I said miserably.

"Listen, I know what you're going through is huge, and I'm not trying to downplay it at all, but…this too shall pass."

"Oh brother," I said under my breath, while rolling my eyes even though she wasn't present to see it.

"I mean it. This may seem like the end of the world right now but, someday, you'll have your life back."

Reflecting on what she had just said, I recognized some level of truth. I didn't have my life at that moment. Too frightened to be out in public, I intended to hide from the world. This was mere survival. "I hope you're right. Listen, I'm almost there. I should get off the phone."

"All right, but call me again soon. Don't you dare hide from me. I want you to keep me in the loop from now on."

"I will," I promised.

Later that evening, I had a very similar phone conversation with Andrea, except she was even less pleased to hear about my marriage. She'd also been filled in about the conjugal visit by her buddy, Captain Barnett, a detail I'd been too embarrassed to tell Kat. Andrea chewed me out for it. It had been a short rant. Then Andrea said some things that surprised me.

"Look, Beck, I've had a go with you about all this. You know how I feel. I'm done with it. That was me speaking as your friend, but now I'm going to switch gears and speak as your agent. You've already done the dodgy deal; we can't change that, so let's see if we can make this situation work in your favor."

Miffed as I was that she had described either my marriage or my lovemaking with Tom as a *dodgy deal*, I heard her out.

"I don't have the numbers yet, but your book sales have picked up quite a bit. It's wonderful that you've been on the news every day."

"No, it isn't. It's a fucking nightmare. I can't leave the house."

"Well, I understand why you don't like the publicity. It hasn't been very flattering, but it might not last long. We've got to try to keep it alive. That bit with the woman in the parking lot was brilliant, by the way, I just saw it on the news."

"You *saw* it?"

"Yes, someone recorded it on their cellphone. Stroke of luck that was."

"Luck! Son of a bitch! How mortifying…"

"Rebecca, it's imperative that we seize the opportunity while this topic is still hot. How much progress have you made on the book?"

I took in a deep breath to quell my nerves and let it out as I tried to calculate where I was in the project. "I've collected enough information and most of it is written. I suppose it's just a matter of getting organized and doing a final rewrite."

"Excellent. Finish it by Christmas, and I'll have your publisher get it on shelves as fast as they can print and distribute."

"Whoa, that's a little fast. Aren't we going to do any advertising before the release?"

"Are you mental? Every news station in the land has already given us far more than any publicist could have. All we need to do is take advantage of it before the public gets tired of hearing about Mr. and Mrs. Eisenbrey."

FORTY

December 24th, 2012

It was the night before Christmas, and I'd spent the last twelve days immersed in my project—as it turned out, it had been good therapy. Except short periods spent on a quick meal or sleep, I spent all of my time writing. I'd finished the book and sent it to Andrea that morning, feeling very relieved, and pleased with the finished product. I awaited the long to-do list from my editor.

Twenty-one days had gone by since Tom's escape, and I hadn't heard from him. I wondered if I ever would. I thought about him constantly, and worried about what he was doing. I hoped he wasn't hurting anyone on Christmas Eve. Working on the book had made me feel connected to him. Part of me still wished I could see him, even though a bigger part of me was scared witless of that possibility.

Tom and I were still on the news every day. More than that, they kept showing a photo of me from the jacket of my books. I worried that I would never again enjoy the anonymity I used to have when I had gone to the grocery store or out to dinner.

Aunt Susan had the excellent idea of having her hairdresser come out to the house to work on me. The hairdresser cut my long, brown hair much shorter then gave it plenty of blonde highlights. With my new hairstyle, and a change in the way I applied my makeup, my appearance had changed considerably from that photo. Still, I felt I should wait a little longer before I tested my new look out in public. I wouldn't know what to do if someone recognized me. I couldn't bear to go through another scene like the one with Lutz's mother.

On the plus side, the sales were still climbing on my first three books, and Andrea was gearing up to release my new work as soon as possible. She expected the sales on the new book to be phenomenal. Great, because I would need all the extra money I could get to buy my own private island where I could just get away from everyone.

Kat had been checking on my house in Bellevue for me. So far, no vandals or break-ins. But, according to her, she'd spotted the media and various looky-loos lurking around. I'd seen my place on television too—sometimes reporters stood out front, using it as a backdrop, while they told the twisted tale of my marriage to Tom. Lately, I'd started kicking around the idea of selling, since it didn't look like I would ever be able to live there again, but that was too much for me to handle at that moment.

The police protection had stopped after one week, which came as no surprise. It was very costly. I'd been lucky to have it as long as I had. Scanlon was happy I had Uncle Harry and his rifle for protection, but I knew he didn't think it was enough. He'd told me as much. He wanted to be here to protect me, and that was impossible with the long hours he worked trying to locate Tom.

I thought about how fortunate it was that Aunt Susan was my mother's sister. They'd both given up their maiden names when they married. Susan and Harry's last name was Miller, and the friends and neighbors who knew I was their niece had been kind enough not to let that information slip to any reporters. So far, no one seemed to know where I was, which was probably my best armor. I had a quiet place to stay while I tried to figure out what to do next.

The mess I lived in was of my own creation. If only I had conducted myself appropriately during those interviews. I could have written the book without all of the madness, the marriage, the sex. Then I wouldn't be on the news with Tom at all.

How had he seduced me in the first place? I feared the only reasonable explanation had to be that there was something wrong with me, something deep and fundamental. I had consciously chosen the path to self-destruction. Why would I do that to myself? Why would I fall in love with someone I knew to be evil?

Tom was arrogant, condescending, and cruel to me. Even if I set aside the choking incident, which I had a possible explanation for, his mere absence was sadistic. He had made no attempt to contact me since his liberation. None. That was not the conduct of someone who cared. So why was he still so impossible to resist, even in absentia? Scanlon was a good man, deserving of my affection, but not Tom, and I had ignored the white and khaki, prison-issued wrapper that proved it.

As for my aunt and uncle, I loved the heck out of them, but I was getting very tired of the knowing looks that would pass between the two of them whenever their eyes met, the silent communications about me that only they understood. They were worried, not just about what Tom might do to me, but also about what *I* might do. Something lurked inside of me that they couldn't comprehend. Even I couldn't come to terms with my recent actions, which were so out of character for me.

On the other hand, it had been good of them not to read me the riot act about the dipshit mess I was in. They had stayed positive and were trying to help me come up with some reasonable plans for the near future.

My head was mired in confusion during the holiday, but there was one thing of which I was certain—I didn't feel like celebrating.

That evening, I sat on the front porch with some hot cocoa, breathing in the crisp, fresh air and enjoying the night sky. Being a city girl, it always amazed me how much brighter the stars were out here in the boonies. I meant to appreciate the view during my time here. Actually, I needed to appreciate everything I had, including my aunt and uncle, who were in the living room with the TV blaring. A few more minutes with my stars, and then I should go in and spend some time with those precious remnants of the family I once had.

I saw a light through the trees, then two, and I heard tires on gravel. A UPS van pulled up in front of the house and a man in a brown uniform walked toward me holding a box. "Evening, Miss. I have a delivery for Rebecca Reis."

"That's me," I said, hoping this delivery man either wouldn't recognize me or wouldn't feel the need to share the news of my location with reporters. I smiled and accepted the package. It had to be from Kat, Andrea, or Darryl, since they were the only three people who knew my current address; I examined the label, but there was no indication who it was from. It had been sent from a UPS Store in Bend, Oregon from an address I didn't recognize. An odd feeling came over me as I held it.

He had me sign for it and then said, "Merry Christmas."

"Thanks. You too," I mumbled, but I was already slipping back inside the house. I took the package straight to my bedroom, without saying a word to my aunt and uncle, and carefully sliced through the strapping tape with a scissor blade. Inside the shipping box, there was another package, gift-wrapped in shiny, blue-and-white wrapping paper with a snowflake design. The ribbon and bow were white. I felt a chill when I saw it. I knew it was from Tom.

I removed the wrapping paper slowly, sensing that whatever it contained would be precious to me. Inside I found an exquisitely carved wooden box, much like the one Tom's mother had, except this one was adorned with a series of intricate paisley shapes and in the center was the symbol for yin and yang. I gasped when I saw it.

Paisley was my favorite design, a fact I'd never mentioned to Tom. A happy coincidence he'd chosen it as a theme? And the yin-yang symbol seemed very appropriate for us. It spoke to me, conjuring contrasting images of light and dark, fire and water, life and death. I felt a thrill. It was beautiful. I opened the box and found nestled in some red tissue paper another wood carving—a small, smooth, heart-shaped piece that fit comfortably in the palm of my hand. There was a pleasant scent of spice and musk.

I looked through the tissue for a note and searched both of the carved pieces for an inscription, anything, but there was no message at all except for the box itself and the heart. I gave a quiet groan of frustration. A small disappointment, but at least I knew he hadn't forgotten me, and for the time being that would have to do.

I wondered where he was—probably not Bend, Oregon. Surely, he wouldn't have stayed near the place where he mailed the package. But curiosity hounded me like the subtle itch of poison ivy. I wanted to find out any bit of information I could. Had he delivered this package to the store in person? Would I be able to find someone on the phone who could recall him? How did he seem? Was he well? I went to my laptop, looked up the phone number of the UPS store in question, and noted their open hours. They were closed. I would have to call them after Christmas.

Then I held the smooth, polished wooden heart in my palm again, enclosing it in my fingers, feeling like I was holding onto part of Tom. For the first time in a long while I felt really happy, almost like I was with him. And I felt as though he loved me. I wrapped the precious heart in the tissue and placed it back in the carved box. Then I held the box in my lap, wrapped my arms around it, and a sob escaped. I ached for him.

Later that evening, I awoke to the ring of my cellphone. I looked around, startled, and realized I'd fallen asleep fully dressed, on top of my bed sheets, with the treasured wooden box wrapped protectively in my arms like a teddy bear. A twinge of guilt ran through me as I saw Darryl's phone number on my cellphone display. "Hey you," I said, a little groggily. "How's it going?"

"I'm great. Did I wake you?" he asked.

"Yeah, I must have dozed off."

"Already? It's only eleven. I pegged you for the type of kid that would stay awake to try to see Santa."

Unbeknownst to him, Santa had already been, and he'd delivered the mother lode. The relief I'd felt after that limited communication from Tom had left me exhausted. "No need. I'm sure I made the naughty list this year."

His laugh was warm and good-natured. "You just might have, young lady. How are you?" he asked.

"I'm good." Then we both managed to say Merry Christmas in unison, and he chuckled again.

"You sound happy," he said.

"Sure, I've had a nice day with my aunt and uncle. How are your parents?" I asked.

"They're pissed as hell I'm not in Florida with them, but I had a long chat with mom on the phone just now. She just doesn't get it." Darryl had promised his parents months ago he would come to see them in person this Christmas, but the escape had changed everything for him. He considered it his personal responsibility to find Tom.

"Yeah, well, you had tickets and everything. You probably should have gone."

"No way. I'm not taking any time off until Eisenbrey's back in custody. Nothing is more important than this."

"Any leads?"

"Not one. He's doing a great job staying under the radar so far, but he'll slip up."

I was silent at that, unsure how to respond. Had Tom already slipped up? Did the wooden box or the package it came in hold some clue as to his whereabouts? This made my heart race. I felt confused and torn, but I decided not to tell Scanlon about it.

"I don't like you not having police protection anymore. Is your uncle still with you at all times?"

"Yes, he is."

"You shouldn't go out to any stores without him. In fact, if you need anything your aunt should get it."

"Uh, okay, should I be worried? Did something happen?"

"I didn't mean it like that. I don't want you to be scared, just careful," he told me in a reassuring tone.

"Thanks, Darryl." I pondered our situation for a moment, and decided there was something else I needed to say. "You know what—I really appreciate you." Darryl had been kind, supportive, and he always did his best to cheer me up. Now that I thought about it, he was becoming a very good friend. If only he weren't the sworn enemy of the man I loved most.

The connection went silent for a few moments. Then he said, "I care about you, Rebecca. I feel like I should be there right now, but I've got to work."

"I understand."

"I'll come out to see you soon though, I promise."

"Good. I'd like that," I told him, and we said our goodnights.

FORTY-ONE

December 25th, 2012

In the wee hours of that morning, as I stirred, I felt the distinct and pleasant pressure of a human form up against my back: comforting me, molding into me, spooning. The scent of musk and spice reminded me of the intricately carved box on my bedside table — crafted with a sharp blade, and a great deal of love.

Then a sigh — a light, sweet, unearthly sound in my ear — coaxing me into wakefulness. I longed for something, yes, more than anything I longed for its source. "Tom," I heard myself say as I became conscious.

I reached my arm behind my body to the other side of my bed, filled with anticipation, perplexed as my hand fell on a bedspread that was flat to the mattress. The pressure was gone, had he gotten out of bed? I rolled over to face him, expecting to see his standing form, smiling down at me, but the room was empty. I was alone.

Not again. Not this cruel half-presence I'd suffered when I dreamed of him wearing the blue clothing, with the fire next to us. There was no fire this time, but the bed felt warm, as if someone had been lying there recently.

I felt salty water well up in my eyes. So it had only been a dream — a pitiless, beautiful dream of Tom. His face was in my mind, his smile, even his smell. I looked at the wooden box again, the only thing I had, and I felt close to him. Then I closed my eyes, imagining he was here with me, wanting to remain in this bliss forever.

Eventually, I pried myself from bed, went to the kitchen, and brewed a pot of coffee. Perhaps the smell would wake Sue and Harry. It was still early. I poured myself a cup, added milk, stirred, and then decided to take it outside, hoping to catch the Christmas morning sunrise.

I opened the front door and promptly dropped my coffee. The mug shattered and the hot, dark liquid splashed onto the wood slats of the porch, freezing almost instantly. The surrounding forest was oddly silent, and I heard nothing except for the sharp intake of my breath. There it was in all of its gory glory — a severed head mounted on a metal stake, and it was a head I recognized.

Skin, the pale white of the no-longer-living, shimmered with a light dusting of frost. Dark, curly hair, parts of which were matted with blood, covered the head. And the lifeless eyes of Richard DiMaggio stared blankly at me.

For several moments, I held perfectly still, unable to fully process what my eyes saw. Then, I slowly shook my head no. I looked away quickly, surveying my surroundings. Was he here? Was he watching? Gloating? He shouldn't be. No. Tom was no fool. He'd understand the police would be here soon, and they'd bring dogs.

How could he do this to me on Christmas morning? And why did I get the feeling this was my real Christmas present — DiMaggio's head, on a stake, facing the front door of the house. I thought about what it meant. Was he trying to hurt me? Taunt me? Was it a cruel reminder of my parents' murder? It didn't feel similar to that tragedy at all. No, this wasn't about my parents.

A phrase came to me, something I'd been thinking that morning as

I passed through the bewildering realm between sleep and wake — *crafted with a sharp blade, and a great deal of love*. I didn't know where it came from, but I felt the truth of it then like a blow to the gut.

I thought about the other thing Tom had given me — the thing that would be nobody's business but my own. That gift had to have taken him several hours to make, a loving gesture, no question. And I realized that, from Tom's perspective, DiMaggio's death may very well have been given with love also. In his own twisted way, he might consider my enemies head on a stake something I would feel happy to receive.

This was not the case; I felt nothing warm and fuzzy, just fear, revulsion, and sadness. I groaned as I turned away from the aberration, stumbling back inside the house. I saw my aunt standing in the hall, close to the kitchen, readjusting the collar of the robe she wore over her pajamas, her smile vanishing as she caught my expression. And then I found the hardwood floor of the entryway rising up to meet my face at an alarming speed.

When I came to, my body was stretched out on the couch. My face hurt, especially my mouth. Touching my fingers to my lip, I felt what I thought might be a scab forming. My aunt said, "You split your lip when you hit the floor, sweetie." She put her hand on my head. I wasn't sure how long I'd been unconscious, but the Kittitas County police were here and, as soon as they discovered I was awake, one of them came to speak with me.

"Hi, Ms. Reis, how are you feeling?" an officer asked. He was a tall man, about my age. He looked familiar.

Slowly, tentatively, I moved myself into a sitting position. "I'm okay, I guess."

"My name is Officer Coulter," he extended a hand toward me with a cordial smile. I reached up to him, still feeling dazed, and he gave my fingers a brief squeeze. "I pulled a shift out here once when we were providing protection, but you stayed in your room most of the time. We didn't get a chance to get acquainted."

"Oh, yes, I remember seeing you." I gave a weak smile.

Officer Coulter reached in his breast pocket, retrieving a notepad and pen, ready for action. "Well, it looks as though Mr. Eisenbrey did make an appearance after all. We've been combing the woods, but we haven't found anyone. I called Detective Scanlon; the Eisenbrey task force is en route."

I nodded, grateful to hear Darryl was on his way. The reality of the situation started to sink in. Darryl was on his way because Tom had murdered again, and he'd left the decapitated head here. *How could he do this to me? And on Christmas of all days.* One minute he had sent me that box to tell me he loves me, and the next…he committed an act that made our relationship even more impossible than it already was. There was no future for us together. I had already known it, even though I continued to suppress reality. Ever since his escape, some dark corner of my mind had hoped he would come and take me away with him — that we could both live as fugitives together. But I knew that was a life I could never abide. Tom had ruined everything.

"Are you able to confirm the identity of the victim?" Officer Coulter asked.

"Yes. It looks like Richard DiMaggio — the guard that helped Tom escape."

"That's what we thought," he said nodding slowly. I thought I detected a twinge of suspicion in his gaze. "Did you see Mr. Eisenbrey, or anyone else, in the yard this morning?"

"No."

"Did you see or hear anyone last night? Witness anything out of the ordinary?"

"No. I'm sorry. I had no idea…I just wasn't expecting this at all."

My volume trailed off. The officer seemed like a nice enough man, but I felt exhausted and beat up.

"You're sure?" He studied me with a neutral expression.

"Yes, I'm sure. I didn't know anyone was here."

"Okay," he said, the slow nod had returned. I wondered if he believed me. "There's just one other thing I want to ask you about, Ms. Reis—the note."

"There was a note?" My heart sank. Had Tom left another communication? Was it something I was meant to find and then secret from the police? I hoped not. I hadn't seen any paper lying around but, in all honesty, I was unable to look at the scene very closely. I'd felt sick, and needed to get away from it. "Where was it?" I asked.

"It was on the first porch step, directly in front of the stake. You didn't see it?"

"Well, no. I didn't actually...I mean, I wasn't able to look at... that thing. I just...I think I might have been in shock." I spluttered, wondering if I was in shock even now.

"Hmm. It was a short note. It's in an evidence bag at the moment, but I copied it down. This is exactly what it said"—His eyes dropped to his notepad—"With love and kisses, your pet." Then he raised his eyes and searched me with a quizzical expression.

"I don't understand," I said, but the déjà vu felt like a harsh slap across the face, erasing my exhaustion, and setting my heart in fast motion.

"What does it mean—*your pet*? Was that a nickname? A private joke between the two of you?"

No. It was a private joke between one of us. It was merely something I'd thought but never said out loud to him. Tom couldn't have known what I had entertained in my head that day—*my pet that I would never be allowed to pet.*

Up to that point, the things he surmised could have been written off as a series of lucky guesses, a well-honed intuition, or an exceptional ability to read people, even coincidence. But referring to himself as my pet begged me to believe something impossible. It had me worried. What else had he heard me think?

FORTY-TWO

Two hours later, Scanlon arrived, parking his dark-blue sedan next to one of the silver Kittitas County police cars. Relief flooded through me as soon as I caught sight of him. The difference like night and day: Tom made me feel frightened and out of control, Darryl's presence made me feel calm and centered. I needed that.

Darryl was dressed for success in a dark-brown suit, light-beige shirt, and a tie with a busy pattern that was predominantly dark purple and navy blue, colors that seemed to be the perfect combination on him. Another man arrived with him. He wore a black suit, but I barely noticed him; my eyes were stuck on Darryl.

Darryl stepped carefully around the nightmare scene on our front doorstep, his eyes taking in as much as possible as he moved. Then he turned around and strode inside the open door. His eyes widened when he caught sight of me. "Could you excuse us for a moment?" he said to the officers, and he led me off to the far corner of the large living room about twenty feet from the others. He studied me, his hands on the sides of my head as he asked, "Are you okay, Rebecca? What happened to your lip?"

"It's nothing. I just hit my face when I fainted. I'm fine."

"Oh God, you fainted? This must have been such a shock for you.

Are you sure you're okay? Maybe you should lie down." The pained look on his face seemed almost comical to me.

I didn't want Darryl to fuss over me anymore, so I employed the art of deflection. "Damn! You look sharp!" I said under my breath, feeling his lapel, and looking him up and down like a piece of meat. His concerned expression twisted into a boyish grin at my inappropriateness, and he quickly turned his face away from his coworkers until he got the smile under control.

"What else did you do to yourself, besides your lip?" he asked. "You seem so different."

"My aunt's hairdresser came out and gave me an overhaul. It seemed like a good idea to try not to look so much like myself."

He took a step back, examining me with a more critical eye. "Yeah, this is good. Most people probably wouldn't recognize you. Just add sunglasses and…yeah," he repeated, nodding slowly, his expression serious. Then he whispered, "You're so beautiful."

The man in the black suit glared at us. True, it wasn't fitting for me to take a flirtatious tone with Darryl given what was on my front doorstep, but we were speaking quietly and I didn't think the others could actually hear our conversation. Mr. Blacksuit was probably the type of man who disapproved more often than not.

I felt terrible that a human life had been taken, though it was better DiMaggio than someone pleasant—that last thought I would keep to myself. But for the moment, my fear was gone. I was safe and secure, surrounded by officers. I didn't understand what Tom's intentions were, but I doubted he would try to harm me physically.

We returned to the others, and Darryl introduced his coworker as Special Agent Parrish from the FBI. The dark-haired man projected a chilly but professional demeanor. He forced his face to smile and flashed his identification at me. The men from the sheriff's department stepped back outside.

When I introduced Scanlon to my aunt and uncle, and explained who he was, I saw an excited gleam flash in my aunt's eyes, though she tried to hide it. My uncle shook Darryl's hand. Aunt Susan offered coffee, but Darryl said, "No thank you, Mrs. Miller. There's no time. I'm sorry, but we need to move the three of you to another location immediately."

My aunt and uncle looked surprised. Harry seemed not to have understood. He looked around his living room, then asked, "What do you mean?"

Darryl smiled, and in a gentle voice, said, "We need to relocate you while we investigate this crime scene and hunt for Eisenbrey. The sheriffs may have to evacuate some of your neighbors too, but for now, my concern is getting the three of you to a safer location. Mr. and Mrs. Miller, I need you to go pack your clothes and whatever else you'd like to have with you for the next few days."

"Yes," Aunt Susan said. "We'll go do that now. Come on Harry." She led him off toward their bedroom. Harry still seemed bewildered, or perhaps it was just reluctance. It occurred to me that they might not have ever spent the night at another location since purchasing this house.

Darryl and Agent Parrish exchanged a look, then Darryl said, "Come on, I'll help you pack. Where's your room?"

"Follow me," I said, and he did.

After crossing the threshold into my room, Darryl eased the door shut and sighed. "Have I really, truly, finally made it into Rebecca Reis's bedroom? Pinch me."

"Don't get too worked up. We're just here to pack some clothes," I said, looking back at him over my shoulder.

Darryl caught me and turned me around to face him. "Hey, Rebecca." He searched my eyes, the air of playfulness gone. "How are you really? You must be scared."

I decided to give him a full dose of honesty. "This morning when I found that, uh, DiMaggio's head, I was fucking terrified. I didn't know what the hell to do. And I don't know, I just lost it, I passed out." I wondered if he even realized he was caressing my back as I spoke. His attention was entirely focused on my face. "But now that you're here, I know you'll protect me. I feel completely safe."

The corners of his mouth crept up slowly into a smile. "Good. That's exactly how you should feel when you're with me." His posture stiffened and he shoved his hands in his pockets — my cue to get on with the packing. I walked over to my closet. "You know what," he said. "Your aunt loves me."

"What are you on about?" I asked, while getting one of my suitcases, setting it on top of my bed, and flipping it open.

He sauntered toward me with a smug air. "She does. She loves me. She knows I'm good for you."

"Well…that's probably true, but right now I need to decide what I'm bringing with me."

"We're going to get along great," he said. "Your uncle and I will be fishing buddies and…" His eyes scanned the rest of the room, stopping at the carved wooden box on my bedside table. He froze and stared at it for several seconds, his smile slowly disappearing. Then he turned his face away from me. "Oh God, no," he said, rubbing his forehead. His eyes returned to mine. "Was he in here with you?"

"No!" I said quickly. "I haven't seen him or heard anything from him. It arrived by UPS last night. Then this morning I found the damned head and…jeez, I forgot all about the box. There was no note with it, so I don't really know anything else."

He gave me a dangerous glare, clearly not buying it. "Where's the shipping box it came in?"

I reached under my bed, retrieving the box, and handed it to him. He examined the label. "Have you called the UPS store yet?"

"No. I looked up their store hours on the Internet. They were closed."

"Good. Don't. Your calls are being monitored."

"Oh, right…" I said. Of course they were. "The landline or my cellphone?"

"Both."

"What about the Internet?"

"Yes, that too," he answered. Scanlon walked over to the wooden box and picked it up, examining it from all angles. He lifted the lid and slowly, methodically searched all of the tissue paper, the carved wooden heart, and the inside of the box. Then he put it all back together and laid it back on my night table. Staring at his hands, he mumbled, "Odd."

"What's odd?" I asked, but he merely shook his head.

"Do your aunt and uncle know about this?"

"No, I took it in here to open it. I didn't tell them."

He pondered the situation for a moment. "Okay," he said. "I'm not going to say anything to Parrish about this, in part because I don't like that guy, but mostly because he *really* doesn't like you. I don't want him to think you lied to us."

"Lied?"

"Yes, when you were asked if Eisenbrey had made contact with you, you said no. Apparently that wasn't true. You should have disclosed this when you were questioned, but as it stands now…shit, this is messed up." Darryl rubbed his temples as he considered the circumstances. "Do you think you could just try from here on out *not* to make my job any harder than it needs to be?"

"I'm sorry."

"You don't realize the seriousness of the situation you're in. We need to hide the box. Do you have another suitcase?"

"Yes," I said, retrieving a second one from my closet.

Scanlon placed the wooden box inside the cardboard shipping box and tucked them in my case, closing the latches. He patted the suitcase lid. "This one's going to stay with me."

"Oh," I said, unable to mask my disappointment entirely.

"If this gets discovered in your custody, it could change the game completely. This is for your protection. I'm on your side, Rebecca. Do you understand that?" His voice was gentle.

"Yeah, I do," I said, looking up at him.

"Is there anything else you can think of that you should have told the authorities, but didn't?"

"No. I don't think so."

"Okay," he said after considering me for a few moments. "Just make damn sure you always tell me everything — and I mean absolutely everything — regarding Eisenbrey. I'll filter it and decide whether or not to tell Parrish. All right?"

"Yes, I will. I promise."

"Okay," he said, with a curt head bob. His expression was kind, though I detected sadness in his eyes. "So…what are we going to pack?"

FORTY-THREE

Fifteen minutes later, I was glancing back at my aunt's house through the rear window of Uncle Harry's SUV as we followed Darryl to the hotel he'd chosen in Ellensburg, forty miles away. Agent Parrish trailed behind us in his car.

I secured my seatbelt and let my head rest on the back of the car seat, turning to stare out the side window. The repetition of the trees flashing by and the steady crunch of gravel under our tires had a calming effect, which I needed. Soon, I noticed the hum of pavement as we hit the main road. Other than the sounds of our driving, silence enveloped me; the three of us were too stunned to carry on a conversation. Uncle Harry stared hard at the road before him, occasionally shooting a quick glance at me via his rearview mirror, or at Sue next to him, until we arrived at the hotel.

As I got out of the vehicle, the wind whipped my hair into a mess. One of my least favorite things about Ellensburg: the air never seemed to be still. The playful grin that flitted across Darryl's features told me my hair had not opted for a sexy windswept model on the beach look, but something much more comical. It wasn't fair. He looked handsome with his short, light-brown hair in disarray. It only added to his appeal.

We walked behind Darryl into the hotel. "It's not fancy, but they had a vacancy," he told us. He was right. The building was a large, white stucco affair, three stories tall, plain and uninteresting. Fine by me. Having a clean, safe place to sleep tonight was enough to make me happy.

"It looks great," I said.

Once inside, Darryl went to the front desk and checked us in. Then he helped us bring our luggage to our rooms, minus the extra suitcase that remained in the trunk of his car. I wondered if he was still irritated about that. His normal exuberance seemed subdued.

My aunt and uncle would stay next door in an adjoining hotel room. I hadn't expected us to have separate rooms, and I felt grateful to have my own space. I wondered if this was Scanlon's way of creating an opportunity for us to be alone together at some point.

The five of us assembled in my room. I sat on the sofa with Sue and Harry, Darryl sat on my bed, and Parrish remained standing, though he was right next to a nice, comfortable-looking, padded chair. His arms were folded. He looked like a dick.

Darryl said, "I know you're under a lot of stress." Then he looked pointedly at Parrish, who remained unmoved. "I arranged for rooms on the third floor so we won't have to worry about him getting in from the outside, and we'll keep an officer in the hallway."

"We really appreciate this, Detective Scanlon," Aunt Sue said, and Harry murmured his agreement. They had both been quiet since I'd discovered the head that morning.

"I'm Darryl to you," he told my aunt. Scanlon leaned forward, placing his hand on Aunt Sue's shoulder and giving a gentle squeeze. "Don't worry, ma'am. We're going to find him and, in the meantime, we'll keep the three of you protected." He removed his hand, clearing his throat. "We received some new information while we were en route: They found the rest of DiMaggio's body dumped down a ravine in a wooded area, not far from Kachess Lake."

"Oh shit," Uncle Harry said, clearly shaken.

"Three-point-seven miles from your house," Agent Parrish told us.

Odd that the discovery of DiMaggio's body should upset me, yet it did. We'd already known he was dead, and the rest of him had to have been out there somewhere. But knowing they'd found it made the reality of what had happened sink farther in. My aunt and I exchanged nervous glances. I knew she was as relieved as I that we'd been relocated.

"I don't understand. Why was he killed?" I asked. "Did DiMaggio help Tom escape? Or do you think he was taken against his will?"

"No one believes that DiMaggio wasn't in on this," Scanlon said. "He brought Eisenbrey a guard's uniform and then led him out of the prison. That's not the behavior of someone who's under duress. He must have also arranged for a vehicle, since DiMaggio's car was left in the employee parking area."

"Of course, it's possible he could have been afraid someone on the outside would harm him, or his relatives, if he didn't cooperate," Parrish said, his eyes narrowed into slits.

Scanlon met Parrish's glare and held it. Obviously, there was some kind of disagreement between the two men that I couldn't discern. I hoped Scanlon would fill me in on it later. He turned to me and asked, "Did Eisenbrey ever talk about anyone he knew on the outside?"

"No. He didn't even mention that other serial killer, Roddy Jenks, until I asked about him. I don't know who his friends might be."

Scanlon exchanged another look with Parrish and then sighed. He seemed annoyed. "Did he ever ask you to say or do anything to threaten DiMaggio?" Darryl asked.

"Really?" I said. It was my turn to be annoyed. "You can't be serious. I've never threatened DiMaggio; it was the other way around."

Parrish spoke next. "One of the other guards, Don Avery, reported an incident where DiMaggio became very aggressive with you. He pushed you into the wall."

"Yes, and he also told me it wouldn't be very hard for him to find out my home address. His behavior was creepy."

"Did you report it to anyone?" Parrish asked.

"No."

"Why not?" he asked, his stare unwavering. His expression told me he thought this was a poor judgment call on my part.

"Well…I didn't want any trouble."

"Really," he said, continuing to watch me. "Could it have been because you were planning to settle the score with him outside of the prison?"

"No! Jesus, do you honestly think I'd do something to harm him?"

"No, we do not," Scanlon said stiffly, shooting Parrish a look that could almost have caused the man to burst into flames.

Parrish shrugged. "It's *my* list of possibilities." He paused to let that sink in, giving me a harsh stare. "Have you heard anything from your husband since his escape?"

"No, and I've already answered that several times today."

"You're sure about that?" One of his eyebrows went up in a way that might have seemed comical if I wasn't so nervous.

"Yes…" Thoughts raced through my head. Something about Parrish's demeanor made me feel like spilling my guts. His excessive eye contact bothered me. I had paused too long to not look guilty of something. He clearly expected more information from me, but I quickly dismissed any temptation to tell him about the box. "Well…there was the note, but I didn't know about that until an officer told me."

"Yes. The note: *With love and kisses, Your Pet.*" He paused, allowing my nerves to get even more amped up before he continued. "That was very telling. It's obvious your husband was giving you something that you wanted—perhaps something you'd even asked him to do."

"I didn't want DiMaggio to be hurt."

"You didn't like him," he shot back.

"That's correct. But I didn't want him hurt or killed."

My uncle spoke next. "I don't like your tone, Mr. Parrish. Rebecca's not the kind of woman that would hurt anyone. She had nothing to do with this."

Parrish ignored my uncle, and fired another question at me. "Where were you during the last twenty-four hours?"

"Beck's been with us ever since the escape," Uncle Harry snapped. "She only left the house once to go shopping, and that was more than two weeks ago."

"So she hasn't been out of your sight?" Parrish asked.

"That's right," Uncle Harry said.

"And do you watch her sleep?" Parrish said, his tone full of ice.

"No." Harry answered quietly. "But maybe we should. It looks like Eisenbrey isn't the only one she needs protection from. Tell me, Special Agent Parrish, do we need to make sure she has an alibi twenty-four hours a day from now on?"

"That might not be a bad idea, Mr. Miller," Parrish replied. "I don't have any other questions at this time. I'll be in touch." He turned to Scanlon, and said, "I'm heading back to the scene."

Darryl said, "Sounds good, but I'm going to stay here a little while longer." I could see Scanlon trying to communicate something silently to Parrish, and the other man apparently got the picture. He shook his head, not attempting to mask that he thought Scanlon was doing something that he didn't agree with.

I followed the two men to the door to see Parrish out. Then, to my utter relief, he walked down the long hallway and disappeared around the corner leading to the stairwell.

Darryl tugged my arm gently, pulled me into the hall with him, and closed the door to my room. I looked up at him, unable to mask my fear, and asked, "What the fuck?"

Darryl swallowed. "He had to ask that stuff."

"Yeah, but did he have to be so cunty about it? Jesus H…"

"That quick little interview was nothing compared to what it could have been. He wanted to use an interrogation room at the sheriff's office, but I convinced him that he'd get more out of you if you were somewhere you felt comfortable."

"Hmm," I tossed that thought around in my head for a moment. "I'm not sure what he would have gotten out of me in an interrogation room, but I'm glad we didn't find out. Thanks."

"You were honest with him, right?" he asked with wary concern.

"Yes, I was…except for the box."

"Good. Parrish isn't someone we want to mess with. You've only seen his nice side. The sooner I can get you off of his radar, the better."

Darryl opened the door and, as we were stepping back inside, a young man in a county sheriff's uniform arrived. He introduced himself to Scanlon as Dan Newell, and Scanlon introduced him to Sue, Harry and me.

After a brief chat, Darryl and Officer Newell checked the balconies in each room. Then Newell moved a chair from my room out to the hallway, setting up his post, and shut the door. Sue and Harry decided to give us kids some space. Darryl and I were alone.

We sat side by side on my bed. Darryl glanced at my trembling hands, clasped in my lap, and said, "You need a drink. Room service has beer and wine, but you look like you could use something stronger than that. The next time I drop by, I'll bring whiskey."

"You can read me like a book."

"Sometimes."

"Darryl, there's something that I've been thinking about. It's really bothering me, and…" I breathed in deeply. "I need to ask."

"What is it?" he said, pushing some of my hair back from my cheek and tucking it behind my ear.

"How was DiMaggio killed?" I asked him. "Was there any of the ritualistic stuff you mentioned before?"

"Yes, there was," he said. "His wrists and ankles had been duct taped together. We think he was secured to a tree during the torture and murder and then moved to the ravine by the lake."

"That poor man," I said. I didn't have to be a fan of DiMaggio's to feel terrible about his suffering.

"Yeah, well that *poor man* helped a serial killer escape from prison. As far as I'm concerned, anyone who aligns himself with Eisenbrey has it coming," Darryl said, in a voice full of bitterness and hate uncharacteristic of him. He stopped talking abruptly, with a stricken expression. "Oh, Rebecca, I'm so sorry. I didn't mean you."

"That's okay. You're right."

"I'm not comparing you to DiMaggio at all. You didn't turn Eisenbrey loose. DiMaggio, on the other hand, bears just as much responsibility for the death of Eisenbrey's future victims as Eisenbrey does. I'm glad he turned out to be one of the victims himself. Serves him right."

I wasn't angry, or even irritated about what he had said. I could see his point, and I didn't disagree.

He continued, "What could Eisenbrey have promised DiMaggio to get his help breaking out of prison?"

"I have no idea," I said.

"Regardless of what he offered, I don't understand why DiMaggio believed him." Darryl shook his head in wonder, then after a brief hesitation he added, "He must have been very persuasive."

Though it wasn't posed as a question, I sensed he wanted me to weigh in on this. "Tom could be very persuasive. I still don't understand how he drew me in. When I started interviewing him, I noticed right away that he didn't dish out compliments readily. I had to earn each nice thing he said to me. For some reason, that made me want to earn his approval even more. When he finally warmed up to me it seemed genuine, but…I was never really sure." It bothered me to admit that about the man I had married.

Scanlon rested his hand on my shoulder and gave it a squeeze. "Rebecca, I'm so worried about you. I wish you weren't going through this." I worried too, but Darryl's pained expression told me that his level of concern for me was off the charts. He leaned toward me and, in an instant, his mouth was on mine. I felt myself wrapped up in his sturdy embrace, warmed by his body up against me. It felt so good, so affirming, to be loved and comforted like this. At that moment, I knew without a doubt that, if Tom didn't exist, I would be in a relationship with this man.

Tom.

"Stop," I said in a breathless whisper. He didn't seem to hear me. "Darryl, please. We need to stop." My words registered that time, and he drew back, letting out a defeated sigh.

"I'm sorry," he said. "I know I shouldn't do that but, when I look in your eyes — the way you look back at me — it just seems right."

"Yeah, I understand," I told him. And I did. I was well aware I'd been gazing at Darryl with admiration, although Tom's face was now in the forefront of my thoughts.

"I'd better go back to your aunt's house before I get myself in any more trouble," he said with a grin. "I'll be back to check on you in a few hours." He stroked the underside of my chin with his forefinger, planting a quick kiss on my forehead as he left.

I knocked on the door that adjoined the two hotel rooms. Aunt Sue opened it. "Come on in, sweetie," she said. Uncle Harry was leaning back into the couch with his feet propped up on the coffee table, watching the television. He had it on a news channel.

"Darryl gone?" Harry asked without looking from the TV.

"Yes, but he'll be back later."

"Good. He's a nice young man. I like him," Sue said.

I heard a man's voice mention new developments in Easton. Harry pulled his feet off the coffee table and sat up, looking alert. I walked over to stand next to him and faced the television.

The screen cut to a pretty Hispanic woman, speaking into a

microphone. The funky, little Easton Post Office building, with its steep-pitched, metal roof and A-frame enclosure over the entrance, stood behind her in the shot.

"Early this Christmas morning, the quiet mountain town of Easton, Washington, was rocked by a gruesome discovery. A severed head was found at the residence of Harold and Susan Miller. Hours later, police located the body of the victim, identified as Richard DiMaggio, in a wooded area near Kachess Lake. Sources say Ms. Miller is the aunt of author, Rebecca Reis, the wife of convicted serial killer, Thomas Eisenbrey. And Ms. Reis had been staying with her aunt since her husband's escape from the Washington State Penitentiary in Walla Wall twenty-two days ago.

"During that time, there were no confirmed sightings of Eisenbrey and, until this morning, police believed he had fled the state. However, given that Mr. DiMaggio was the prison employee who disappeared the night of Eisenbrey's escape, and the fact that his wife's residence was targeted, police admit there's little doubt Eisenbrey is behind this murder.

"Earlier today, police commenced a full-scale search for Eisenbrey with K-9 units, road blocks, vehicle searches, and helicopters — though these measures have done little to allay the fears that Easton residents have for their safety this evening.

"Eisenbrey, also known as the Hunter, has been convicted of nine murders and is considered extremely dangerous. Law enforcement cautions: if you see Eisenbrey, do not approach him and call 911 immediately. They also ask those in the area to report anything that seems out of the ordinary — such as signs of a break in — any missing items such as: food, water, clothing, blankets, or anything else Eisenbrey could utilize while he's at large. And to take care, until Eisenbrey is once again behind bars."

I looked away from the television and sat on their bed. Uncle Harry muted the volume. "Great," I said. "Now everyone knows you're related to me. Sorry about that."

"Don't be silly," Sue said. "That's the least of my concerns. I just want the three of us to stay safe until he's captured." She gave me a pat on the shoulder.

"That's right, sweetie," Harry said. Then he cleared his throat. "Listen…I know we're all upset, but I have to bring up the subject of dinner. We haven't eaten anything all day. I don't know about you girls, but I'm starving. I'm calling for room service."

"I'm right there with you, Harry," Sue said. "It's been a long day. How about you, Beck?"

"No, thanks. I'm not hungry," I told them. It was true. The thought of eating seemed strange and foreign to me at a time when my future was in peril. More important—food would screw with the buzz I intended to have very soon.

"You really should eat something, dear," Sue fussed.

"Don't worry about me. I can order something later if I change my mind. I think I'll go lay down for a while. I'm wiped."

"That's a good idea," Sue conceded. "Just let me know if you need anything, all right?"

"Sure thing. See you in a little while," I said, and I closed the door between our rooms. Then I called room service and ordered a bottle of wine.

FORTY-FOUR

I stretched out on my bed, but didn't sleep. Instead, I fretted about Tom, wondering where he was at this moment. Had the dogs tracked him down? Were the police closing in on him? Or had he managed to get clear of the area before the road blocks and search teams were in place?

That was the most likely theory. He had to have a vehicle. DiMaggio's body was nearly four miles from Aunt Sue's house. Even if he'd managed to move his body from the kill site to the ravine without a car, he would have needed transportation to carry the head to us. Well, perhaps that wasn't true, but the main point was—Tom didn't strike me as a sloppy idiot. I didn't believe he would have set up such a macabre Christmas display without having a reliable car and a full tank of gas. He must be long gone.

I wondered how I got to this place—where I worried about a murderer's safety and didn't want him to get caught. I'd walked into that first meeting with Tom, not just with a chink in my armor; I'd gone in with no armor at all. I had been emotionally beaten down, weak, depressed. My self-esteem was as low as it could possibly be after my third book—*Epitaph*. I thought about how my own epitaph should read: here lies that lunatic, binge-drinking writer, who sunk to the furthest depths of depravation, pledging herself to a monster.

I wanted someone to talk to, someone who I could confide in, someone who would tell me this would turn out all right. Not Sue or Harry. I thought about calling Andrea, but it was nearly 11:00 p.m. here, 2:00 a.m. on the East Coast. She would be asleep. Then I thought of calling Kat. I plucked my cell phone from the night table and entered my unlock code. I had voicemails from both of them. I decided to call Kat. Hearing her voice would be a comfort, even if it came with a lecture. My contact list opened at the beginning of the alphabet. The first name: Andy.

I never made the call to Kat, but instead spent the next several minutes crying into my pillow. I recalled the young guard's smile, those hazel eyes peeking from under the mop of unruly light brown hair, and the way he had been so polite and kind to me. Guilt and pain weighed down on me as though I had been the one to kill Lutz because I still harbored love for the man who had most likely been responsible.

Eventually, I sat up and took another sip from my wine glass. In need of fresh air, I opened the sliding glass door leading to the balcony. The sky had turned dark long ago. As I looked down into the well-lit parking lot, I spotted Scanlon's car pulling into a space. I went to the vanity, brushed my teeth and gave my make-up a quick retouch. Then I waited for him to come up but, after several minutes, I lost my patience and poked my head outside my room. Officer Newell was gone.

I heard Parrish's harsh tones drifting from around the corner of the hallway. "You're too close to the situation. You've lost all objectivity. What makes you so sure she's not involved? It sounds as though you view this woman as some kind of saint."

"A saint?" Darryl's disembodied voice gave a hollow laugh. "No, she's no saint. But she's also not a killer."

"You don't know what she is. She had to be out of her mind to marry this guy. She knows exactly what he is, and she's in love with him. That makes her dangerous."

"No she's not…"

"She's on his side. If she hasn't helped him already…she will."

There was a brief silence, then I heard Darryl's voice again. "I disagree."

"You need to step back a few paces from these people and get your head straight, Scanlon. If you don't, I swear I'll kick your ass off the task force."

"No, you won't," Darryl hissed. "You need me." Another silence as I strained to hear more. Their volume had dropped. "I'm in a unique position with this family. I have an 'in' with them. They trust me. I can get things from them that no one else can — information, cooperation. They'll do whatever I advise them to — especially Rebecca. And she's the key to capturing Eisenbrey. He's going to return to her."

Scanlon's face suddenly appeared around the corner, presumably as he glanced around to see if anyone could hear him. I was caught. Our eyes locked briefly, his expression unreadable. Then he disappeared and resumed his conversation. "Just give me some time with them and let me do my thing."

I heard a few expletives from Parrish, followed by the word maniac.

"Maybe you think I'm a dick, but I've been a cop for twenty-three years, and I've spent more time on Eisenbrey's case than anyone else on the task force. Trust me," Darryl said. "I know what I'm doing."

I stepped back inside my hotel room feeling as though I would never trust Darryl again, unable to understand how I could have so colossally misjudged him. Sure, he wasn't perfect. He'd admitted planting evidence at one of the crime scenes. That was dishonest. I should have recognized it as a warning. But instead I'd coasted along believing everything he told me.

I stood just inside my room, trying to calm my breathing as I waited. After a few minutes, I heard soft footfalls out in the hallway. I whipped the door open, startling Darryl, as he had his hand poised to knock. "Rebecca…" he started.

"What the hell was that?" I demanded.

"How much did you hear?"

"Enough for two fucking lifetimes."

Darryl gave the hallway a quick glance, stepped inside my room, and closed the door. He was holding a paper bag with a decorative holiday pattern. I knew what it held; I could see the top of the bottle. He smiled sheepishly and tried to hand it to me, "Uh, Merry Christmas?"

"And what's that for, to make me pliant so I'll do whatever you advise me to do?" For a moment, I considered grabbing the bottle by the neck and swinging it into the wall — hard. But then the practical side of me took charge. "Put it on the table," I said. "I may get depressed enough to drink it later."

He set it down where I suggested, giving me his best impression of contrition. "I didn't mean it."

"Then why did you say it?"

"I had to say those things to Parrish. He needed reassurance about my abilities."

"What's that supposed to mean?"

Darryl's energy seemed to overflow. He wasn't able to hold still, so he paced a short distance away from me and then returned. "Look, Rebecca, here's the thing — I'm not supposed to be in love with you." His eyes searched mine with a desperate plea. "I can't let him know about my feelings. I need time with you. I need to protect you, and there's no other way to justify being here with you right now, when you need me most."

I stared at him for a long time, trying to discern whether he was sincere, but found no answer. Finally, I said, "Okay."

Scanlon let out the breath he'd been holding. "I'm sorry. I know it must have sounded really bad, but I just can't think of any other way to deal with Parrish."

I nodded, but I still hadn't decided whether or not to buy his story. "Where's Officer Newell?" I asked.

"I told him he could go. Law enforcement personnel are all spread a little thin at the moment with the manhunt. I volunteered to stay here and, after a lot of cajoling, Parrish authorized it."

"The night shift, huh?" Why didn't that surprise me? "And where do you intend to sleep? In my room?"

"I'm here to stand guard, not sleep. If you want me in the hallway, I'll go out there. But I'd rather leave the door open that adjoins these rooms and set up a chair for myself by the opening. Then I'll know if anything happens in either room."

I had to agree this seemed like the best vantage point for him. And I didn't expect Sue or Harry to complain about the arrangement. They were all for police protection after this morning's scare. "Yeah, that sounds good," I said, although I lacked enthusiasm.

"I should check in on them," he said. He knocked on the door between our rooms. Sue opened it, and Darryl went in their room for several minutes before returning. Then he went out on my balcony, looked around, and came back inside, locking the sliding door.

"Are you ready to turn in?" he asked. "Harry and Sue said they'd turn off the TV whenever you're ready. I'll keep the door shut until then."

Still stinging from Scanlon's earlier betrayal, my thoughts turned to Tom. I remembered the gift he'd made for me and, though I knew it would only heighten the tension between us, I couldn't stop myself from asking. "Darryl, I was just wondering—can I see it again?"

Darryl froze, eyes fixed on me, his expression guarded. If the mood in the room hadn't been suspicion and distrust before, it was then. "See what?" he asked, carefully. He knew exactly what I wanted, so why play this game with me? Masked anger rose up in me that he was withholding it. It wasn't his to withhold. It was mine.

I wanted to run the tips of my fingers over the carved patterns of its surface, hold the smooth wooden heart in the palm of my hand, wrap all of it up in my embrace once again.

"The box," I replied, my voice flat. "Is it still in your car?"

"Yes."

"What will you do with it?"

His gaze was wary, his mouth slightly ajar, but he didn't answer.

"You won't destroy it, will you?" A pang of fear shot through me at the thought.

"No. I was just going to hide it."

"I need to see it again," I told him.

He shook his head slowly, and said, "I don't think that's a good idea."

I disagreed. I thought it was a great idea. I hadn't had enough time with the box yet. I felt like I was starting to forget. Soon, the details of its design would be lost to me, and that would be a tragedy. "You don't understand. I *need* to see it," I explained.

"I know," he said. "And that scares the shit out of me. There's something strange about that box, Rebecca. When I look at it… especially when I touch it…I can feel him. It's almost like he's there."

"I know."

Darryl swallowed. "You can't see it again. Cold turkey. It's the only way to break your addiction to this guy."

As if I wanted to break my addiction to Tom. Another flash of anger, but I kept my voice calm. "At least let me take a picture of it," I said. Then I could see it whenever I wanted; I would have it forever.

"That's an even worse idea."

"Why?"

"What will you use—your cellphone? The one that's being monitored? You could shoot a photo of it in my trunk. Hell, with a little luck, you might even be able to catch my license plate in the shot. Wouldn't that be swell?" His voice had been steadily rising, but he stopped himself and took a deep breath before continuing. "Even if you use a different camera, it's too dangerous. I don't know who else, besides me, would recognize it as something Eisenbrey carved. Several people know about the one he made for his mother."

He lowered his volume, his tone infused with gentleness. "We need to make sure no one finds out about it. This is really important.

You told them you hadn't heard from Eisenbrey. If Parrish finds out you did, it will change the course of this investigation. You could become a suspect, not only in helping him escape, but helping with DiMaggio's murder."

I felt lightheaded. During the interrogation, I'd thought Parrish was just trying to intimidate me. But, after hearing the two men talk in the hallway, I knew Darryl was being straight with me. "Do you think that will happen?"

Darryl looked sad. "Parrish is a dangerous guy. He doesn't trust you, and he really doesn't care that I trust you. He's searching everything at your aunt's house. I hope to God he doesn't find anything that he could use against you. Will he?"

I paused for a moment, my mind racing, trying to recall the items in my room, but I could think of nothing that they would find incriminating. The only dangerous thing I'd had was the box. How convenient for Darryl that he had it now. Could I trust him not to use it against me? But I didn't seem to have another option. "No. I don't have anything that should make me look bad."

"Good."

"And, fine, I won't take a picture of the box. But I'd still like to see it again."

Darryl wrapped his arms around me and whispered into my hair, "No, baby. You can't see it. I can't let you see it again. I'm sorry."

Darryl didn't understand. *He really shouldn't keep the box from me.* But he could have it his way for now. I had an idea about how to deal with that. "Okay," I said into his shoulder.

He stroked my hair and then pulled away far enough to look into my face. "Rebecca, you understand that you can't see him anymore, right? He clarified any question you could have had about that with what he left on your front doorstep. His message couldn't be any clearer — that was a threat."

"That's just it, I don't think it was. I think he meant it as a gift."

"Jesus…" Scanlon's posture stiffened and he stared at me in disbelief. "What are you trying to say? How could that be a gift? Did you actually want Eisenbrey to kill that man?"

"No, not at all, but I wonder if Tom might have thought I did."

"Why? Because of the incident you had with DiMaggio?"

"Yes. I didn't want him harmed. Well…maybe punched in the face a few times, but…not what he got. That wasn't right."

"I think I understand what you mean: In Eisenbrey's mind, since DiMaggio assaulted you, he did you a favor by taking him out."

"Yes."

"Rebecca, I want you to be very careful what you say on that topic to everyone—except me, of course."

"Yeah, you're right," I said. I looked up into his concerned face, offering a tentative smile. Who was this guy? Did he really care or was he just playing me? My fingers slithered down his arm and I took his hand in mine. "Go sit on the couch. I'll get the whiskey."

FORTY-FIVE

I lay still, listening, waiting, until Scanlon's breathing slowed to a steady rhythm. I had to strain to hear him. He'd set up his post eight feet from my bed, by the open door adjoining my room with Sue and Harry's. His head lolled backward as he sat, slumped, in the chair. An uncomfortable position, I surmised. His neck would be sore when he awoke in several hours. Not my problem.

Honestly, I was surprised he'd made it all the way to the chair after downing the cocktail of whiskey, cola, and sleeping pills I'd given him—my own creation. A moment of brilliance after he'd blocked my access to what I wanted.

I climbed out of bed and quietly slipped on my jeans, sweater, sneakers and coat. Then I felt inside the pocket of his blazer, which hung over the back of his chair, and found his keys. They jingled softly as I took them. I closed my fingers quickly to silence the sound, and froze, as Scanlon twitched and stopped breathing. I held my breath with him. A moment later, his breathing resumed, and he relaxed again. *You think you can betray me? Well, right back at you, honey.*

Peeking through the open doorway to the other room, I could see Harry and Sue were both asleep. Then I slipped silently from my room.

The hallway was deserted, so was the hotel lobby. Zipping my coat shut, I stepped into the frigid winter air, dark and still. No signs of life in the parking lot either. The pavement was free of snow, for the most part, but a few inches remained in areas with no foot or car traffic. As I made a beeline to Scanlon's sedan, I could see each breath I took unfurling under the illumination of the lights.

I pressed the trunk release button on Scanlon's key fob, and pushed up the lid. There was my suitcase. I glanced back over my shoulder. No, he hadn't followed me. I scanned the third floor windows of the hotel, but I couldn't tell if anyone looked out at me. Unfortunate that the windows of our rooms faced the parking lot, but Scanlon had probably asked for that specifically.

I opened the case, then the shipping box, and removed the object of my desire. Odd—how much I wanted to see it. Scanlon was right, I really felt almost as if Tom was here. I ran my fingers over the carved patterns with a light touch, savoring it as much as I could with such limited time. Then I opened it and removed the wooden heart, cupping my hands around it, holding it to my face and breathing in the scent of spice and musk. I felt so relieved—as if I had just returned home.

A deep voice emanated from the shadows. "There you are, darlin'. I wasn't sure you'd make it out here to see me with that watchdog at your heel."

Tom stepped out from behind a navy blue SUV parked two spaces from Scanlon's car. His hair was dark and tousled, much like the last time I'd seen him. He had a little more facial hair, but not what I'd call a beard; he just looked like he hadn't shaved for several days. He wore jeans, boots, and an olive colored field coat, unbuttoned, revealing a maroon and black flannel shirt. All in all, he didn't seem to be wearing any kind of disguise. He looked like himself—like a hunter.

"Just out of curiosity, how did you manage to make it past him?" Tom asked.

"Sleeping pills…in his drink," I said.

He grinned. "Good girl."

Words began to rush out of me. "Tom, what are you doing here? You're not safe. The police are searching for you."

"Relax. They won't find me."

"How can you believe that? Anyone who sees you would recognize you. How have you made it this long without being discovered?"

He shrugged. "I have my ways."

"Why are you here?"

"I had to come back for my *wife*, didn't I?"

"What do you mean?"

"You're coming with me. That's why you snuck out here, isn't it? You're going to run away with me."

"Well…no," I said. And it was true. My only intention had been to see the box so I could feel close to Tom. As wonderful as it was to see him in the flesh, I felt alarm growing inside me now he was actually here. "I can't do that, Tom. My aunt and uncle…they need me."

"Your aunt and uncle have each other," he said. "And you and I have each other, right?"

"Yes, but…"

"What's the matter, darlin'? It seems pretty simple to me—unless there's something or *someone* else in the way. Is there?"

"No," I said quickly, taking a step back from him. I felt a shiver run through me.

Tom's eyes narrowed. He moved toward me as he spoke. "Really? It seems awful friendly for Scanlon to be spending the night here. Is he in your room?"

"Yes, but he's in a chair across the room from me, and the door to my aunt's room is open. It's not like…" I let out a sigh of frustration, no longer sure how to describe the situation. I'd allowed Darryl to get too close. He'd even kissed me again. And I had wanted it.

"Hmm," Tom said, staring evenly at me. "I don't have time to deal with the Scanlon situation tonight, but you can rest assured I *will* deal with it."

"It's police protection. For crying out loud. You left part of a dead guy on my doorstep," I said in exasperation. "How could you do that? Why did you kill again?"

"Because I *can*." Tom stepped forward, towering over me. "I'm not going to chat about this right now. We need to hit the road."

"No. I told you, I can't."

"I'm not gonna say this twice, Rebecca. Get your ass in the car!"

"No!" I darted back quickly, and Tom lunged forward grasping my arm hard enough to cause bruises.

He shook me as he shouted in my face, "Don't you talk back to me!"

I tried to pull myself free, but his vice-grip tightened. Then I leaned back and tugged, hoping my body weight would help free me, but that maneuver only caused me to lose my footing as he jerked me toward him. My knees hit the pavement, and I dropped the car keys and the wooden heart. I would have landed on all fours except Tom still had hold of my arm.

"You stupid bitch!" Tom yelled. "I know what's good for you, even if you don't. You're coming with me." He started dragging me along the ground, the jagged pebbles in the pavement scraping my knees through my jeans. Surprised by the pain, I screamed.

Tom's hand came down hard on the side of my face and I screamed again. "Shut the fuck up!" But I couldn't. He was pulling me toward the SUV, and I knew that would spell disaster. I couldn't allow him to get me in the vehicle. I screamed louder, hoping someone would hear me and call 911.

Tom bent down, wrapping his arm around my waist, and hoisted me up as he opened the driver's door. Then he tossed me inside as if he was loading something as light as a bag of potatoes. He had a surprising amount of strength for such a slender man. "Climb through to the passenger seat," he barked. "And don't even think about touching that door handle."

I crawled over the center console as he'd demanded, and then I felt for the handle while he pushed the ignition button. He saw me and leaned over, grabbing my hand, and glaring dangerously.

I looked up, feeling a sharp intake of breath, and a surge of hopefulness as I saw Darryl burst through the door of the hotel lobby, running toward us.

"Fuck!" Tom screeched. He threw the SUV into gear and tore out of the parking lot, turning onto Canyon Road in the opposite direction than I'd anticipated, heading away from Interstate 90. "What the hell is he doing out here?" Tom yelled as he floored the accelerator. "I thought you gave him sleeping pills!"

"I did," I told Tom, feeling happier than I've ever felt to see Scanlon.

"Well, you sure fucked that up!" Tom drove down the road with abandon, ignoring road surface markings and traffic lights. I had to grab onto the oh-shit handle to stop myself from being thrown around the cabin. "I don't get it. He shouldn't be awake right now. I didn't hear him at all back at the hotel."

"Hear him? What are you talking about?" I asked, breathless.

"I would have known if he was looking for me. I always know," Tom muttered. He angled onto Main Street at nearly sixty miles per hour. But just as we were leaving Canyon Road, I checked the back window and saw headlights. A car took the corner onto Canyon Road so fast it skidded sideways before straightening out and rocketing toward us. A moment later, red and blue lights began to flash from the window and I heard the siren. It was Darryl's car.

Tom eased on the brakes, preparing to make a sharp turn, as he checked for Scanlon's location in his rearview mirror. We were far enough up Main Street that Darryl's car was temporarily out of our line of vision. Tom was distracted. I saw my opportunity.

As the vehicle slowed, I opened the passenger door and jumped out, airborne for several feet before landing. My right shoulder and side lit up with pain as I collided with the paved sidewalk, and I rolled several times before coming to rest in some snow-covered lawn. A jolt of fear registered as I saw Tom's SUV come to a skidding stop sideways, my escape hatch swinging shut with the vehicle's momentum. Tom had to reach across to open the passenger door again. "Rebecca!" he shouted.

I lifted my head to see him glance from me to Scanlon's approaching car and back to me. "Goddamn it!" he yelled, striking the dashboard with his closed fist. Then he pulled the door shut and tore off, his tires burning rubber on the pavement as he left.

I lowered my head to the ground, the pain too intense to hold it up any longer. Somewhere close by, I heard Scanlon's car screech to a halt. A moment later, he was at my side, stroking my hair.

"Oh, Jesus, Rebecca," he said. I tried to sit up. "Don't move, baby." I felt his hands pressing gently against my shoulders to keep me down. "The ambulance will be here soon. Just stay put…" Darryl's voice became quieter.

I closed my eyes.

FORTY-SIX

December 31st, 2012

I stood on the stone patio with my fingers clasped around a raspberry Smirnoff, gazing up at the sickle moon that peeked down at me through a brief parting of the clouds. Around the moon, a smattering of stars twinkled dully, unable to compete with its mesmerizing glow. Soon it would be hidden again, covered by the dark cumulus mass that quickly approached.

I chose to enjoy its beauty, knowing that my time with it was limited, knowing that my satellite would soon be taken from me.

I detected a scent in the air that told me snow was imminent. Then I heard an explosion off in the distance. I didn't need to check my watch to know it was midnight. Soon there were more pops, crackles, and booms and I saw some bright, colored lights bursting in the sky just below the clouds. Someone, not too far away, celebrated the New Year.

One week since my tumble, I was still on pain pills. I had suffered injuries the night I jumped from the SUV: my right radius was broken, necessitating a cast on my arm; and my right shoulder had been dislocated, so my cast was strapped to my torso. This was actually more annoying than it sounded. I was right handed and, I have to admit, not even the tiniest bit ambidextrous. In addition to my immobilized bits, I was covered with bruises, cuts, abrasions, and still stiff as hell.

The list made me feel like a real winner. But at least I was alive, and not being held hostage somewhere — two things I needed to be grateful for. I had more than that. Sue and Harry had relocated with me to a new hotel. They were the solid ground beneath my feet, the two people I could always count on, no matter how bad things got. I was also thankful for my friendship with Scanlon, although he'd made himself scarce since the incident, telling me he was very busy trying to find Tom.

My head filled with Tom, and my eyes must have filled with tears again, because the crescent in the sky became a blurry blob.

The police hadn't found him that night. I wondered where he was and what he was doing. One could travel a great distance in a week's time, so he could have been almost anywhere.

At this time thirteen years ago, and with the assistance of Roddy Jenks, Tom slit the throat of the Canadian club owner, Philippe Devereaux. But at that moment it seemed like I was the one dying, perhaps not physically, but my soul certainly was.

When given the chance, I had chosen not to leave with him. But, in spite of that, I felt as though I couldn't bear our separation. I longed to spend time with him in a way that was safe, as it was when he was in prison. I didn't want to live as a fugitive. It didn't matter how I felt. I was powerless.

I couldn't know if I'd ever see Tom again. But I knew I still loved him. At the same time, I hated him for marrying me, for ripping my heart out, and for leaving me broken, inconsolable and twisted.

I now realized an awful truth — once inside the Hunter's clutches, there was no escape.

ACKNOWLEDGEMENTS

Thank you to my family and friends for their support and encouragement.

My gratitude to Detective V.M. for his expertise about police procedures, to Vickie with the sheriff's office for being so helpful, and to Sherri, Evan, and John for their insights about the Washington State Penitentiary.

Thanks also go:

To my beta readers: Devrah, Holli, Janean, Renee, Eileen, Jennifer, Jessica H., Jessica P., Ann, Julie, and Michelle. I appreciate the valuable input from all of you;

To my wonderful editor April, for polishing my first book and making it shine;

And finally, to my muse for not abandoning me.

ABOUT THE AUTHOR

Amara grew up in Washington State, and resided in England for a while. She currently lives near Seattle with her children. *The Way Evil Does* is her first published novel.

You can get more information and contact her through her website: Amaradraska.com.

Amara is also on Facebook, and you can follow @amaradraska on Twitter.

If you enjoyed this book, please support the author and share it with your friends on Facebook and Twitter. Also, please rate this book or post a review online. Amara appreciates anyone who spreads the word.

Thank you!

Upcoming Books from Amara Draska

The second book in the Eisenbrey Trilogy, *The Darkest Need* is anticipated in 2015:

Novelist Rebecca Reis is still reeling from her last encounter with serial killer Thomas Eisenbrey. It's been several months since the release of the biography she wrote about him, and now, to her horror, more hunters have been found murdered in the Washington State wilderness.

Rebecca desperately wants to convince Tom to stop killing. The problem is she hasn't heard from him in almost a year. She has no idea how to locate the man that nearly destroyed her but, as she will soon find out, he is all too aware how to find her.

Rebecca must decide who to give her loyalty to: her obsession, a convicted psychopath; or the man that's trying to help her, Detective Darryl Scanlon.

Made in the USA
Charleston, SC
15 September 2014